THE SYNDICATE IS MADE

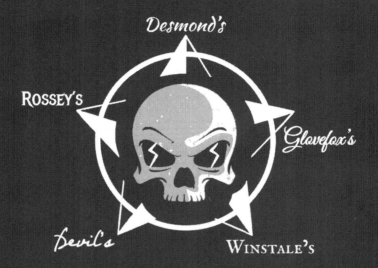

EACH REPRESENTING THEIR SPECIES, EACH HAVING AN ESSENTIAL & EQUAL JOB IN THE UNDERGROUND CRIMINAL ORGANIZATION. RUNNING THE SUPERNATURAL COMMUNITY WITH AN IRON FIST & A BLOODY TRAIL.

THIS IS THEIR STORY.

Stanley, Kira

Syndicate Mayhem

Editing: Melissa Smith with Homestead Book Services

Cover artist: Raven Ink Covers

TABLE OF CONTENTS

START PAGE

Trigger/Content Warning

Music List

Dedication

Chapter 1 – Rayla

Chapter 2 – Rayla

Chapter 3 – Avery

Chapter 4 – Ax

Chapter 5 – Falcon

Chapter 6 – Rayla

Chapter 7 – Cosmo

Chapter 8 – Lex

Chapter 9 – Rayla

Chapter 10 – Rayla

Chapter 11 – Rayla

Chapter 12 – Cosmo

Chapter 13 – Rayla

Chapter 14 – Rayla

Chapter 15 – Rayla

Chapter 16 – Ax

Chapter 17 – Rayla

Chapter 18 – Rayla

Chapter 19 – Falcon

Chapter 20 – Rayla

Chapter 21 – Avery

Chapter 22 – Rayla

Chapter 23 – Cosmo

Chapter 24 – Lex

Chapter 25 – Rayla

Chapter 26 – Falcon

Chapter 27 – Rayla

Chapter 28 – Rayla

Afterword

About Kira

Also by Kira Stanley

TRIGGER/CONTENT WARNING

Trigger Warning

This is a dark urban paranormal RH romance, which means the main female character doesn't have to choose a love interest. This book has dark themes, stalker vibes, adopted brother taboo, childhood trauma, death, gruesome, and bloody violent scenes.

This book has graphic sex scenes between consenting supernatural beings with magical bodies that are not able to get STD's or bacterial infections. Please do not think humans can make the same sexual choices without consequences.

Music Content Warning

There are scenes in this book that were heavily influenced by music, and as such you will see a music list on the next page. I have also added footnotes as to what scenes have been influenced by what song throughout the book. If this is something you find <u>distracting</u>, <u>don't like the music choice</u>, <u>isn't something you enjoy</u>, PLEASE ignore it and enjoy the story like you normally would. This feature is for those readers that really want to be fully immersed in the process of making this book and is ONLY HERE to enhance readers' experience. This DOES NOT MEAN that you must listen to these songs to understand what is going on.

Syndicate Princess Music List

1. Deal with It by Ashnikko (Chapter 2)

2. Falling by Trevor Daniel (Chapter 3)

3. Cant Get You out of my head by Ugg'A (Chapter 4)

4. Savage by Megan Thee Stallion (Chapter 6)

5. Dagger by Bryce Savage (Chapter 8)

6. Daisy by Ashnikko (Chapter 9)

7. Lovefool by twocolors (Chapter 13)

8. Boss Bitch by Doja Cat (Chapter 17)

9. Animals by Maroon 5 (Chapter 17)

10. Black Gang by SINDICVT (Chapter 18)

11. Devil in Her Eyes by Bryce Savage (Chapter 19)

12. Under the Influence by Chris Brown (Chapter 21)

13. OMG by Camila Cabello ft. Quavo (Chapter 22)

14. Like a Drug by Bryce Savage (Chapter 22)

15. Weak by AJR (Chapter 23)

16. All About Me by Syd (Chapter 25)

17. Twinbow by Marshmello & Slushii (Chapter 26)

18. Chantaje (feat. Maluma) by Shakira (Chapter 26)

19. Demons by Bryce Savage (Chapter 27)

20. Seven Nation Army by Gaullin & Julian Perretta (Chapter 28)

*CLICK HERE FOR LIST on YouTube Music

This book is dedicated to all you bad boy lovers. . .

The ones that don't mind someone sexy watching you though your window.

The ones that enjoy a little punishment with their pleasure.

The people who see a scowl or frown on a sexy man's face and says challenge accepted.

The ones that see a man in a suit and tattoo's and say come to mama.

The ones that are down for pretty much anything as long as your pleasure comes hot, fast, and first.

This book is for you.

CHAPTER 1

Today was the worst day. My daddy was upset, everyone was fussing over me, getting on me to keep my black dress clean, and my mommy . . . well, my mommy was dead in a box, and I couldn't stop staring at it.

The sweet smell of mixed flowers was in the air, failing to cover the heavy waves of sadness and pain. Sudden flashes of that day spread like wildfire in my mind, and the only thing I could think to say about it was it all happened so fast.

The last thing I remember was my mom kissing my head and telling me to make friends with the four other boys—the ones my daddy's friends brought with them. She said I needed to be nice, which was naturally hard for me. I remember her soft, cool fingers combing my hair back as she looked at me with her rose gold eyes, eyes that mirrored my own, while her blood-red lips smiled so big the tips of her fangs peeked out like they were playing hide-and-seek with me.

She played with the tips of my ashy-white hair that matched my daddy's and sighed out as she mumbled that I was always making a mess of myself. I knew she didn't mean it because she smiled. She cupped my face and rubbed her nose against mine in an Eskimo kiss. Her eyes sparkled so beautifully I secretly wished someday my eyes would sparkle like hers. That I could be as beautiful as she was with her long, dark red hair and rose gold eyes. Appearing like royalty, even in a t-shirt and jeans.

"Now, Ray, I want you to play nice with those boys. Your father and his friends are having a very important meeting and will not want to be disturbed because you bit or punched one of them," she tutted, and I winced at her tone.

Just yesterday, she had to pull me off some mage boy that thought it was okay to pull my hair and call me a blood sucker. I didn't know why he said it with such disgust, trying to make it seem like a bad thing, so I decided I would show him how gentle Mommy taught me to be and lunged for his neck. That, apparently, was not how to handle situations like that, but his blood did taste good. When I told that to my daddy, he laughed as my mommy frowned at him. Then daddy told me I wasn't supposed to do things like that, but when Mommy's back was turned, he gave me a thumbs-up and a wink.

"I promise. I'll be a good girl. No biting." I shook my head hard, making sure she knew I understood.

"No punching, either. I know your father is teaching you, and I support that with his . . . line of work . . . but we don't just go around punching people for no reason. You hear me, young lady?" She squinted her eyes and pursed her big lips.

I scowled down at my shoes as I called out, "No punching . . ." As she stood, I popped my head up, smiling wide. "But if they start it, then I can, right?"

She smiled down at me, glancing side to side before she whispered, "Absolutely."

That was the last time I got to talk to her. After that, I ran off to meet the four boys. I decided I would be the ringleader of the group and told them so. When the werewolf boy gave me some lip about it, I wailed on him, telling him it would only be worse for him later if he turned into a snitch and told his parents about it. I learned that from my daddy. Before he got to answer me, the ground violently shook and a boom came from the spa our moms were in.

I remembered the sound as the large stones slammed into the sand around the playground, the crackling of fire, and the building my mommy went into collapsing right before my eyes.

I didn't remember getting off the werewolf boy, I think his name was Ax, but I remembered all five of us standing side by side, watching on as the fire burned away, too stunned to do anything but be hypnotized on the scene in front of us. It was so silent and still, the only thing moving was the fire gobbling up the building like it was the last chocolate chip cookie on the shelf. All I kept thinking was my mommy went in there not too long ago, and I didn't know what that meant. We were vampires, so that meant she could get out of there, right?

Then our names were being called, and our fathers rushed to our sides. They snatched us up as if we were trying to get away, even though we stood in a daze.

My daddy called out to my mommy, the others' daddies did the same, you could feel the panic in every word. I called out to daddy, and he turned around to me as I pointed to the burning building.

He had turned in slow motion, staring at the fire before falling to his knees, and a soul-shattering wail broke from his lips as he gripped his hair and then roared to the sky. The sound vibrated in the air, choking me and everyone around him with his pain.

It was at that moment my daddy—a man I had thought could never be broken, never be taken down, never be left in pieces—became hollow right before my eyes. It was then I felt silent wet streams rolling down my cheeks, and a sob working its way up and out of my chest as I walked to him on shaky legs. I fell next to my daddy, grabbing at his hand, clawing at his closed fist to just hold my hand. I just wanted my daddy to hold my hand.

He whipped his head toward me and snarled. I cried out as I jerked back in fear. This was not the daddy I knew. My daddy would never look at me like that. My daddy loved me to the ends of the earth and back. My daddy thought I was the princess above all other princesses. This daddy was looking at me like everything was my fault. Like I was the source of his pain and anger. I was scared of this daddy, and I didn't like it.

As soon as his eyes collided with mine, his face changed, and he lunged for me. He whispered in my hair how sorry he was and that he loved me. Clutching so tightly it was hard to breathe, just saying those words over and over again. He clung to me like I did with my stuffy at bedtime. My stuffy, Mr. Bunny, that calmed me and made it easier to sleep at night, knowing he was there to protect me as my eyes were closed. I wonder if I did that for daddy now?

It was a whirlwind after that, full of ambulances, doctors, my daddy and his friends running around barking orders. Then I remembered being shoved into this death building in a black frilly dress I hated, one I knew my mommy wouldn't make me wear if I didn't want to, staring at a box that my daddy said Mommy was in. He said we were supposed to say our goodbyes to her in that box.

I didn't like the box. It was so shiny and reminded me of plastic. When I said that to one of my mommy's friends, she said it was a "high grade piano finish, and the finest mahogany wood money could buy." It still looked stupid. The only thing I thought my mommy would've liked was the complicated rose design carved in it so deep I wanted to touch it. It matched the rose pin my daddy put in my hair this morning, the one Mommy picked out for me when I was born, saying I was as pretty as a rose.

I saw the boys' mommies' boxes, and they were each so different. Some in stone, some in granite, and others with gold leafy accents. I liked that one the best, but I was told I wasn't allowed to say that.

My father was up front with his friends, with all the other boys' daddies, greeting everyone that came in for the funeral. Well, all the daddies except for the quiet demon boy's, Lex, I think his name was.

My daddy told me both his parents died in the explosion. I guess his daddy was having a conversation with his mommy outside of the sauna when it happened. I looked over at the quiet demon boy my age, black smoke wafting off his hands and neck as his head was down, not saying anything to anyone.

I looked at the other boys, too. The serious mage boy, Falcon—I remembered because it reminded me of a bird I saw at the zoo—nodded and acted like he was listening, but he had this blank expression on his face like he was feeling nothing. The chubby werewolf boy, Ax, was in the corner, facing away from people because he was sniffling, trying to stop the tears from leaking from his eyes and was embarrassed. He shouldn't be. I have been crying every night, but I don't want to cry in front of my daddy. I think it made him even more sad, and he was already sad enough. The gangly faerie boy, Avery, I heard his daddy call him, was the oddest one because he would talk and pay attention to everyone but then at small sudden moments, I would catch him touching his mommy's box, and then his eyes would turn into a kaleidoscope of colors before he breathed out. Then the next second, his eyes would be normal, and he would be talking to someone else. The demon boy, Lex, wasn't at his parent's boxes, instead there was a mean looking man that stood there, shaking hands with people. I think my daddy said that it was his uncle.

People would come up to my mommy's box and ask me how I was doing, or said that she was a good woman. It pissed me off, so I would then ask them who they were. They would gasp and walk off or shake their head, and someone would say it's because I'm "grieving," whatever that meant. This one guy tried to touch my shoulder, so I growled and kicked him in the shin. I didn't like being touched by strangers.

After a while of all of that, my daddy came over, scolded me for kicking that man, and told me to go into the other room to think about my actions. I said, "Fine," then stomped around the corner to the room he had me and the other boys wait in earlier when the boxes were being placed.

I threw open the door, mad at my daddy, mad at that man, mad at this stupid dress. As soon as I got into the room, I tore at the frilly shoulders and the poofy stuff around my legs that were so itchy. I was so into my tearing job, I didn't notice the demon boy, Lex, in the room.

"I don't think you're supposed to do that," he called from the dark shadowy corner he appeared from like a magician.

"It's itchy!" I whined as I scratched my legs. "Plus, I hate this dress, anyway. Good riddance." I stomped on it and stuck my tongue out at the tattered fabric so he knew how serious I was, how much I didn't care about the stupid thing and what people thought of it.

He said nothing as he nodded, not even watching me. His sorrowful eyes, hunched over body, and messy hair showed how I felt on the inside, and I didn't like it. I didn't like these feelings, being upset, like my heart would never beat again because of how gripping and unending my sadness was. I hated it. I hated it so much I wanted to carve my heart out, but I knew daddy would be mad at me if I tried that, so I took it out in other ways. I was being a brat about my dress, pissing off people, and making my daddy disappointed, all because I felt icky on the inside.

I was about to tell him to smile, to not let people know you're sad, all because I wanted him to stop reminding me of how I was feeling, when I noticed him holding his finger. There were black tendrils of inky smoke swirling around it, and I narrowed my eyes. A deep-red dot came out and it was like a switch flipped for me. In a rush, a sweet chocolatey scent filtered through the air, and I licked my lips. I made my way over to him, his blood pulling me to him. As soon as I was right in front of him, I lost all my marbles and wrapped my lips around his finger. The explosion of the sweet creamy flavors took over my senses, and I couldn't help the slurping sound I made. His blood was delicious.

I was about to pull him closer when I realized what I was doing and popped his finger out of my mouth with wide eyes. His eyes mirrored mine, and his mouth was gaping, his body was shaking, and he appeared too scared to say anything. I didn't want him to be scared of me . . . his blood's sweet scent was just calling to me . . . and I had a sweet tooth. "Oh . . . I . . . I . . . I'm so sorry! I . . ." I looked down at his finger and saw the cut was closed, probably from my saliva, and I dropped his hand.

Then I remembered he didn't lose only his mommy, like the rest of us, he lost his mommy and daddy. He must feel ten times worse than me, and I just sucked on his wound like an animal. *Stupid. Stupid, Rayla!* When he still hadn't said anything, just kept staring at me with those wide eyes, I wanted to crawl under a rock and die. This was so embarrassing. *But at least he didn't have that really sad expression anymore. That had to count for something, right?*

"Please, don't hate me," I pleaded with him. This boy would be a part of my life forever since his daddy was best friends and working partners with my daddy. My daddy even asked me if I would be okay with him living with us if he wanted to. I needed to make this right.

I kept my head down as I went to tell him he could suck my blood to make it all even when he whispered, "I don't hate you." My head snapped up. He didn't seem scared anymore. A red blush colored his cheeks, one that wasn't there before, and he kept glancing away from me as he wrung his hands together. He opened his mouth, then the door opened, and we turned to see who was coming.

The wolf boy, Ax, called out in a weepy voice as he opened the door with the mage and faerie boys at his back. "Our dads wanted us to check on you." All three sets of eyes were on me as they said it, but I knew I needed no one to look after me. I was almost seven, after all.

I pointed to myself, then to Lex because they had to be talking about him. "Him, right?"

This time, the faerie boy, Avery, stepped forward. "You, pretty girl . . . But, I guess, also you, Lex."

I tilted my head as I swung around to face them. "I'm not pretty. I'm fierce."

Avery's cheeks got red as he corrected himself. "All right, Fierce Girl." Then his face fell as he mumbled, "I just said it because that's what my dad always calls girls." I stuck out my tongue and made gagging sounds, and he smiled again. "Got it. No pretty girl for you."

"Nope." I smiled and gave him a thumbs-up.

Lex still hadn't said anything or looked at the others, which made me anxious. Was he going to tell the others what I did? Was he going to tattle on me to our daddies? I didn't want to get in trouble or tip off the others to what happened. In a desperate attempt to take our minds off everything, I had an idea.

"Come on." I grabbed Lex's smoky hand and went to the door that led outside to the cemetery.

"Wait for us!" Avery called as he rushed forward to catch up. I looked back, smirking at Ax until he rolled his eyes but reluctantly followed. Falcon seemed unsure as he glanced back at the door they came from before he ran forward to tag along.

I ran at normal speed since I was tugging Lex with me, searching for anywhere to go other than the building with our dead parents in boxes. A small stone building came into view in the back corner of the cemetery, and I went toward it. As soon as I stopped, huffing and puffing came from behind me, and I smirked. I wasn't even running at vampire speed. These boys had nothing on me.

I hid my smirk, trying not to laugh at them. Even I knew if I laughed at them, it would be too mean, and they would be self-conscious. That was the opposite of what I wanted to do for Lex and even these other boys that carried a dark cloud of sadness and pain with them. I quickly turned to Lex to make sure he was okay and was surprised he wasn't even breathing funny. He was just staring at our hands, my pale hand entwined with his tan one, and his smoke tendrils curled around our fingers and up our arms. When I squeezed his hand, he tilted his head up—eyes wide as he took a big gulp—then away and pulled at the bottom of his shirt with his other hand.

"Why did you bring us to a mausoleum?" Falcon asked, taking a few steps up and running his fingers over the beautiful door carving of a man and woman hugging.

I shrugged. "I don't know. I just wanted to get out of there, and it seemed like a lot of wide-open space. Plus, this looked like a good spot."

"It's a cemetery. Of course, there is wide-open space," Ax said, finding his voice as he scoffed at me like he was the smartest guy in the room.

I let go of Lex's hand and got in Ax's face. "No one said you needed to come." I put my hands on my hips and raised one eyebrow like my daddy taught me. It was my power stance. A flash of hurt entered his eyes before he covered it up and puffed out his chest.

"I was told to keep you safe. If you're out doing bad, stupid things, then I could get in trouble and . . . you're not worth it." Then he stuck his tongue out at me. I was holding myself back from socking him in the nose as I gritted my teeth together, trying to remind myself my mom didn't want me to punch this fool . . . but she was dead, so I could do it, right?

Falcon interrupted my thoughts. "Hey, guys, come check this out." Ax and I swiveled our heads in his direction and found he had the door to the mausoleum open and had walked right in.

"Cool," Avery said as he followed.

Lex glanced between Ax and me, and I grabbed his hand. "Come on, Lex, let's go check out the spooky, scary, death palace."

Lex followed me, muttering, "I don't think it's called a 'death palace.'"

I turned around and got right in his face. "Why not? It's housing the dead body of the person who had this built and constructed for him and his family. That sounds like a palace to me." Then I turned back toward Avery and Falcon checking out the room.

"Don't touch that! Someone is dead in there!" Avery yelled at Falcon, who ignored him and continued to stick his hand into the center stone coffin, the stone slab cover was slightly open to the left, leaving a small hole for a hand to get in.

Falcon was reaching around, his tongue out of his mouth as he felt around for something, and I couldn't stop watching him in amazement. What the heck was he doing? Then we all heard a click, and his open mouth turned into a wide smile. Falcon took his hand out of the coffin, and the whole thing rotated to the side to reveal a staircase that went down below.

We all turned to Falcon with huge eyes as I pointed to the stairs and squeaked. "How . . . How did you . . .?"

He smiled as he tapped onto his watch on his wrist. "Magic. This watch scans my surroundings and lets me know where all the rooms are. When I saw there was some room underneath this coffin, I knew there had to have been a switch somewhere." When we still stared at him like he was a three-headed monster, he sighed. "My father is very into technology."

Before anyone could say anything, I belted out, "That's so cool. I want one!" His face brightened as he smiled at me, his cheeks becoming flushed as he looked away, avoiding my eyes.

"I don't know if we should go down . . ." Avery said as he studied the dark staircase like it was covered in spiders.

"Let me go first. Vampire eyes and all." I tried to move between them to get to the stairs, but Ax beat me to it.

"Werewolf eyes are much better in the dark. I will go first." He puffed out his chest as I gave the after-you gesture while glaring at him. I didn't want to fight with him all day, so I had to pick my battles.

Before any of us stepped into the deep, dark place we most definitely should not be, our fathers panicked voices called our names.

"Rayla. Mina. Desmond. If you don't get back over here in five seconds, I'm going to . . . going to . . ." I could tell my daddy was thinking really hard about the punishment. Punishments were more Mommy's thing than his. "Make you eat a whole tub of ice cream until you puke!"

The guys turned around, laughter in their eyes for once. This time, it was my turn to be embarrassed as I groaned and smacked my hand over my face. "Why does he have to be so embarrassing!" The guys snickered, even Lex, and I'm sure they were glad that their daddies weren't making treats into punishments.

"I guess we got to go," I said as I eyed the secret stairway I wanted to go into so badly. The guys all did their own version of a disappointed sigh as they heard their daddies yelling for them.

"Maybe we can go see it next time?" Lex asked while shuffling from foot to foot.

It was the first time he talked to us as a group, and it made me smile. They all watched me for an answer. I knew it. I was the ringleader. I faced Lex, walked up to him, put my hand on his shoulder, and gave him my biggest vampire smile. "Oh, most definitely."

Their daddies barked out for them, demanding they show up now, and each boy headed out like their pants were on fire . . . all except for Lex.

There was a moment where it was just me and him, and we glanced around the mausoleum for another second before I nodded to the door. "We should probably go . . ." His face fell, and he nodded. It tore me up a little on the inside, and I made a quick decision. I pulled out my most-prized possession, my rose hair clip I'd had since I was a baby, and I handed it over to him.

"Whenever you feel lonely or sad, just hold onto this and think of me. Think of all the fun we will have next time we see each other and all the places we will explore, just like this super dark and scary death palace."

His smoky fingers curled around the rose pin, holding onto it like it was something precious, and I knew I did the right thing. Lex would be the only one out of all the guys to keep it safe and secure. To cherish it like I would.

He smiled up at me, eyes shining with tears, but it was okay because they didn't look like sad ones this time. "Thank you, Rayla."

I shrugged like it was no big deal, but on the inside, I was happy. We left and made our way back over to the building with the funerals, but my heart was a little lighter in the midst of all this sadness.

I didn't know this would be the last time I saw all those boys. That the bosses had all decided that to keep everyone safe and avoid another tragedy, they would split up into different states. Keeping the Syndicate of the five families going through messages, couriers, and video conferences. Making sure the underbelly of the world was ours but that our families were safer.

CHAPTER 2

22 Years later . . .

"HAVE YOU FOUND HIM?" I barked in my earpiece, waiting for Rick to respond.

"I don't have eyes on the target yet." He sings out his words, knowing it would piss me off.

I clenched my hands, fingernails biting into my palm as I ground out, "Find him." He said nothing because he knew he and Cosmo were the only beings alive that got away with pissing me off and living.

"Cos?" I called out to my adopted brother, knowing he was the most stable and reliable out of the three of us.

"Not yet, but he is supposed to come out any minute. Rick, get the guys ready." His cool, authoritative voice put my excitement in check. We would get him, and then I would make him pay.

I was standing on the edge of the top of one of the casinos we owned, scanning Sin City itself, Las Vegas—my city. The wind blew through my ashy-white hair, making it feel wild and free, just how I liked it, waiting for the words "*got him*" so I could get on my bike and meet them at the spot I picked out for my dearest ex-boyfriend.

That fucker thought he could get away with cheating on me. *On me!* He thought I didn't have eyes and ears all over the city? That he was untouchable just because he's the human mayor's son? He didn't think that people would squeal on him? Oh, they squealed good for me.

I lifted my hands and cracked my knuckles, remembering what Tonya said earlier. She wanted to pay her respects, wanted to get in good with me, and told me some very damning news about my dear now-ex Tre. She was scared I would find out later, punish her and her staff for the incident, but it wasn't their fault. They were only offering a service, a service the Syndicate gets a piece of, so that sounded counter productive. I thanked her for the information, threw some cash around to her and the staff, wanting them to know I was good to those that stayed loyal to me, loyal to the Desmonds. Then started my manhunt.

Cosmo took a breath before he called out, "Target acquired. Meet you at the spot."

As soon as he said "acquired," my blood pumped faster, and I licked my lips in anticipation. This would be fun. My dad always boasted about how bloodthirsty I was as a baby, always wanting more and more. I'm sure he didn't think his precious ray of sunshine would grow up to be bloodthirsty in the breaking-skin-and-bones way, too.

I let my foot dangle off the edge, foot steady as the wind blew around it while I took a big breath in and fell forward. I enjoyed the feeling of falling, the wind rushing in my ears, almost making it so I couldn't hear anything but the wind calling my name. Watching the ground surge forward to meet me at an incredible speed, my heart raced, my limbs flying in the wind, reminding me that, even though I was a vampire, I was still alive. I wasn't dead in a box like Mom.

As soon as I got to the tipping point of no return, I pulled and tucked my legs in, pushing them down while snapping my head up as hard as I could, making it so my feet were pointed downward. I pulled the lever in my hand. A mini parachute popped out, and the yank of the release caught underneath the small sail, and I stopped my descent before I pulled on the strings. I glided myself with ease on the way down to where my bike was parked.

Even though I loved the rush, the thrust of the fall, the calm peacefulness of the slow descent was always my favorite. I liked the duality of each feeling, one right after the other, and it always cleared my mind. Helped me focus on what I wanted to accomplish.

As soon as my boots hit the concrete, I let out the release and pulled on the opposite lever that automatically reeled my personal parachute into the backpack as I stepped up to my bike. Once it was all packed back up, I sat down on my bike, pulled out my fingerless gloves from my leather jacket, and slid the worn leather over my hands before I flexed them. Then I grabbed my all-black helmet that matched my all-black BMW S1000RR and slid it over my head before I booted up the kickstand and started my baby.

"Today we are going to kick some ass, baby," I called out
to the bike rumbling between my thighs.

"Are you talking to your damn bike again, RayRay?"
Rick's silly voice cracked in the earpiece.

"You don't understand the level of connection I have with
this bike." I scoffed. "How far away are you?"

"About twenty minutes. Why?"

I revved up the bike before I called out, "And I'll still beat
you with my baby." Then I took off. The city was flying
by at blurred speeds, but I didn't need to know much,
I had this city mapped out like the back of my hand. I
knew every turn, every twist. I mapped out the side streets
and the back alleyways I took to get to wherever I was
going. This city was my playground, and I knew all the
rules. Scratch that, I made the damn rules. That's what
came with being the heir to the Desmond crew. The head
family of the five families that made up the Syndicate.

I went down the windy 160 highway, getting farther and
farther away from the strip, heading to the mountain
springs. It's deep enough into the desert to not run into
people but close enough I wouldn't have to drive two or
more hours to get there. I didn't want to waste that kind
of time on this dirtbag.

I turned down a dirt path no one goes down and zoomed
my way to the base of the mountains, kicking up all kinds
of dust as I headed to Moonshine Spring. It was a nice
little spot that was far enough we would have privacy in
the dead of night.

It only took a few minutes until I got to the spot. I made sure Cosmo had instructed some men to prepare the space for us. As I rolled up, their heads lifted as my bike came to a stop. Removing my helmet, I shook my hair down as one of our men came up to me. "We just finished and have everything ready for you, Miss Rayla."

I took off my gloves. "Everything to the specs I gave you?" I flashed my eyes over to him, and he gulped at my tone, a tone that said if it was anything but perfect, I would hold him responsible.

"Yes, miss. Exactly." He never made eye contact, keeping his gaze down in respect.

"Perfect." I smiled. Before I could say anything else, I heard Cosmo's '69 Dodge Super Bee. That thing purred like a lion but was quick like a cheetah with a HEMI engine I gifted him a few Christmases ago inside it. I used to be jealous of his copper-colored beauty, but when he gave me my custom matte-black Dodge Hellcat for my twenty-first birthday, I didn't give a flying fuck about his oldie.

Rick popped open the passenger door and jogged over to me. The clan man I was talking to bowed his head and mumbled he and his guys would head out. I nodded, knowing I didn't need anything else from them. The less they all knew about it, the better.

"Oh my gawd, RayRay! I swear, you have the worst taste in men. Like, the worst!" When I rolled my eyes but didn't stab him, he took that as a license to continue. "Like, the whole drive, *the whole drive*, he was whining and crying. Asking us 'What did I do? Whatever it is, I can fix it, I swear! Do you know who my dad is?'" Rick laughed like a loon as he swung his arm around my neck. "I was so happy when Cosmo told me to shut him up, and I got to lay a big one on him." He mimed hitting him with his other hand. "Whoever said violence wasn't the answer got it all wrong. Sometimes, it's the only answer." He glanced back at the car then to my serious face as he leaned near my ear. "I swear, sweetheart, if I liked pussy, I would most definitely sweep you off your feet and save you from all these scumbags."

He gave me googly eyes, then I smacked his arm off me as I lifted one eyebrow in exasperation. "No, you wouldn't. You would criticize everything that I did, from the TV shows I watched down to the shampoo I used on my hair. Then I would kill you for being so annoying." I walked over to the hole my men dug, examined it, and found it to my liking. Lucky for Rick, because if they hadn't done it right, it would be his ass going down there and fixing it.

"You haven't killed me yet!" he sang out like it was the new Broadway tune.

I almost laughed, almost, as I called back to him, "Only my best friend and brother can be annoying and get away without bodily harm." He smiled widely at me as he knew the best friend status was given to him a long time ago.

Rick's father was the right-hand man to mine, and we grew up together. With his dark rich curls, strong swimmer's body and his sparkling hazel eyes, he was a looker. Our fathers had both had this idea that we would make a cute couple and when they noticed how close we were, they tried to actively get us together. It was very comical.

Rick panicked when we figured this out because he was exclusively into boys and only thought of me as a friend. I was fine with it, but as a teen not wanting to disappoint his father, he racked up years of worry over it. I told him I would play his stupid girlfriend if he wanted, but that he eventually needed to tell our fathers. Secrets were not good in the upper management of the Desmond clan.

I played along for most of our middle school years until my father said he better not catch us kissing, and Rick almost threw up in his mouth. That was a big red flag, and he told them everything. They were a little pissed we lied to them, but they didn't care about him being gay. I remembered my father gripping his chin, telling him, "I don't give a flying fuck who you love, fuck, or play around with, but if you fuck me or mine over, I won't hesitate to kill you."

I had to give Rick props. My dad was scary when he pulled out his gang-boss vibes, freaked out much bigger men than him, but he stood his ground and said he would rather kill himself than do that to us. Do that to me. My father nodded and told him he was to stick with me, watch and take care of me, and that's what he has done since then, been my left-hand man.

"I wouldn't count on her *not* killing you." Cosmo's matter-of-fact tone came out behind me. I turned to my tall, tattoo-covered, buzzed short, platinum-blond-haired, adopted brother grunting as he opened his door and yanked the dirtbag ex of mine over his shoulders and walked over to us.

At first, Cosmo didn't get along with Rick. In fact, he hated him when we were little. Cosmo came into my life when I was seven, my father claiming I needed a sibling to bond with to not feel alone. Since the day he moved in, he has been stuck to my side for everything, been my sidekick in life. Rick didn't start hanging around a lot until we were all eight, and that made Cosmo jealous. He thought Rick was trying to encroach on his brotherly territory, and he wasn't having it. Rick didn't let it faze him, he kept coming around, tagging along with us, and going along with the mischief I would force them into.

When we were about fifteen, Rick got shy around Cosmo and talked about how hot he was. I told him to keep that shit to himself. It pissed me off he would talk about my brother that way. I'd wished they would go back to hating each other until one day Rick said he was over him. That he wasn't all that and a bag of chips anymore, and he had his sights on men that were more obtainable. Whatever that meant. To this day, it was still one of the happiest days of my life when he gave up on Cosmo. Imagining my best friend and my brother fucking gave me the willies. From that day on, Cosmo and Rick got along just fine, working side by side for all my shenanigans.

As Cosmo got closer, I smelled the urine on Tre's pants, and my nose crinkled up, and a new layer of disgust for him filled my body. *What the fuck did I ever see in him? Oh, yeah, he had a big dick.* I looked down at my crotch as I scolded myself, *Damn it, Li'l Ray! You are not allowed to do the thinking for us anymore. Especially if you keep bringing around scum like him.*

"Awww, Cosy, you won't let her kill me, right?" Rick batted his eyes at him, holding his hands together in a silent prayer.

Cosmo eyed him up and down, then said in the most deadpan voice, "What Ray wants, Ray gets." Then he shoved my unconscious ex into the hole. I threw a mocking smile at Rick before I motioned with my hands for them to pick up the shovels, and they did.

Cosmo did it right away, catching on to what I wanted and shoveled the dirt back into the hole with my ex in it. Rick did the same but with a lot more attitude.

"Aww, come on, RayRay! This is *your* shitbag boyfrie—"

"Ex," I barked out.

"Yeah, yeah, yeah. Ex. Got it. Point is, don't *you* want to do the burying?" Rick asked as he huffed at having to do manual work.

"My part will be as soon as you finish. You know how I like a big reveal." They filled the hole a good two-thirds of the way as I took out one of my blood lollies from my pocket, savoring the sugary copper combination before they stopped to position him so we could keep his head on display once he was buried.

Cosmo got up, took off his shirt, putting all that beautiful ink covering his body on display, and I swear I almost swallowed my tongue. His tattoos covered every inch of him, from the top of his neck, where his first tattoo, the Syndicate five star with a circle around it and a skull with money signs in its eyes, was right beneath his left ear, all the way down his chest and arms. He was like a walking billboard of black ink and amazing artwork you wanted to get lost in.

It was only a few steps, but as he walked over to me, it was like one of those male model commercials going in slow-mo to get you all hot and bothered. The back of my neck singed my shirt, and my lolly slipped past my lips as my mouth opened slightly—lusting after a man I had no business lusting after, and my mind clicked back on. With my vampire reflexes, I caught the lolly before it fell to the ground.

As I straightened, Cosmo was right in front of me, smirking as he held out his shirt to me. "Can you hold this better than you did that lolly?"

I punched his gorgeous, sculpted chest, my eyes flicked to the grooves of his stomach, they called me to explore those ink-covered planes, to commit them to memory. I shook my head, reminding myself he was my brother, and he just wanted me to hold his shirt because he has always had a thing about dirt on his clothes.

"Fiiiinnne," I replied while I rolled my eyes. I just hoped he didn't catch my moment of bad judgment, ogling him as I snatched his shirt and put it over my handlebars.

His smile grew wider, like he was going to say something, before he shook his head, put his hand on top of my head, and messed up my hair. "Good little Ray." Then he turned around, and I had another moment of weakness and watched that sculpted ass as he walked away while playing with the plain silver thumb ring he gave me when I was eighteen.

Rick grunted, and I flicked my gaze over to him, looking like a fool as he straddled the hole, trying to lift an unconscious Tre up enough to have his chin at ground level, but he was having a hard time getting a good grip on him.

Cosmo barked at him, "Move. I will hold him as you fill the rest of the hole."

Rick dropped Tre, stood up, and jabbed his pointer finger at Cosmo's sexy bare chest. "Hey! This whole shirtless, serious, bad-boy thing does nothing for me, so you can't boss me around." He glanced back down at Cosmo's chest, eyeing it a little too long before he shook his head and sneered at him. "Okay, so maybe it does do something, but then I see it's attached to your face, and I'm like, yuckie!"

Cosmo laughed in Rick's face before he returned to being serious and growled, "Good. Now get to shoveling."

Rick cried out and looked at me for back up.

I licked around my lolly like I was thinking about it before I said, "Rick, you know the deal. Plus, Cos is doing the hard work of holding the shithead." I shrugged and motioned to the shovel for him to get on with it. Rick sighed then grumbled about being stuck between stupid psycho siblings but grabbed the shovel and finished the work.

As soon as they were done, I crunched on the rest of my lolly and chucked the stick out into the desert as they headed over to me. They waited by my bike as I got up, knowing it was my time to shine. I rubbed my hands together in excitement as I walked over to my ex, whose head was the only thing sticking out of the ground.

[1] I crouched down and knocked on his head like it was a wood door. "Knock, Knock, Trevy wevy!"

He wasn't waking up, so I decided he needed a shiner to match the one Rick gave him and clocked him hard. I hooked it a little, and a small crack rang out from the bridge of his nose. It was music to my ears. His eyes flew open, and he cried out in pain. It took him a second to gather his bearings and get over the pain, then shock took over when he realized he couldn't use his limbs, and he started to panic. "What?! What is going on!?"

I didn't give him a single moment to adjust as I grabbed onto his golden locks and yanked his head back. I watched the blood seeping out of his nose with rapt attention as he cried out. It was so tempting to run my finger across and get a lick of that liquid life I craved. He yelped, and it broke my blood trance as I shook my head.

His brown eyes widened as he saw me. "Ray?"

I let my mouth curve up as I gave him my best crazy eyes, making it more menacing than a true smile. "Hello, shit for brains!"

His eyes flicked around before his gaze landed back at me and anger flooded his face. "The fuck, Ray? If this is some stupid ass prank of yours, then I'm going to be pissed as fuck. I'll . . . I'll have to rethink you being my girlfriend."

Rick scoffed, and Cosmo clenched his fists, vampire hearing and all, but I wasn't fazed by his words, they meant

---

1. Song: Deal with It by Ashnikko

nothing to me. So I tilted my head back on a laugh and cackled out to the night sky.

I laughed for a good thirty seconds, slapping my knee to exaggerate how comical that sentence was before he growled out, which was strange, as he was a human. This was all my fault, really. I was testing it out, dating outside of supes for once, seeing if it was different on the other side. He was the mayor's son, and we occasionally ran in the same circles for city functions. Even though most supes and humans kept to their kind, having their own bars, restaurants, and night life, it wasn't illegal or anything to mingle, and some humans found the savage side of things to their liking, but I quickly found if a guy was a dirtbag, it didn't matter if they were human or supe.

"Oh, Tre." I sat down, leaning back on my elbows, lying like I was sunbathing. "Did you really think that you could cheat on me and get away with it? That there would be no repercussions for you?"

The pulse in his neck quickened, and my smile turned less smug and more savage. He still said nothing, so I continued as I ran my hand through his hair. "Did you think just because you were the mayor's son that you could fuck anyone you wanted?" I yanked his head back so hard some of the strands broke free of his scalp, and he cried out in pain.

I sat up, leaned into him, my lips at his ears, grazing my pointy teeth against the outer shell. "When I first bit you, I told you that you were not to let another taste you while we were having our fun, it was the rules. You knew that I would consider it an act of ultimate disrespect, and there would be no going back from it." He shivered, and his putrid fear came off him in waves.

"I'm sorry. She didn't mean anything. She was less than anything. You are my everything." His small, weak voice made me want to smash my fist in his face. I didn't do weak men; it was a major turn off. The trick was to get a strong man to like a strong chick, but I found that this was harder than it seemed.

I pulled away, continuing like I hadn't heard a single word he said, and got up. I dusted myself off as I told him, "So, this is me telling you that you're a worthless piece of shit, and that if you or your father try to do anything against the Desmond clan in retaliation for this punishment, we will respond with brutal force and"—his eyes flicked up at mine in panic as I tongued my pointy fangs in emphasis—"a savage, bloody retribution."

I turned to walk away, done with this piece of filth. He whined, "Wait. Wait! You're not going to leave me here, are you?"

I looked over my shoulder, flashing my fangs at him as I cruelly peered down at him. "I just broke up with you, sooooo." I shrugged, and then he cried out, sobbing like a little bitch. I rolled my eyes and said, "It's a well-hiked spot, so you'll be fine. It's a punishment, remember." I turned to leave but then lifted my finger as a final thought came to mind. "Oh, but I would watch out for scorpions. I hear this is a hot spot for them at night." I laughed as he screeched and pleaded with me to get him out, but I gave zero fucks as I waved my middle finger at him.

Cosmo and Rick were wearing matching grins as I swayed my way over to them, giving Tre one final look at my fine ass leaving him. Cosmo had his shirt on, and I pouted on the inside a little.

Before I could tell them I wanted to go out for drinks, my phone rang. I took it out of my jacket and saw it was my dad, which meant I had to take it. Last time I put him off, he had the whole clan searching all over Nevada for me.

"Hey, Dad," I said to let Cosmo and Rick know who I was talking to. They stood at attention like he was right there in front of him. It was so annoying.

"Hi, my sunshine! How are you doing? What are you up to? You know, give me the 520 . . . wait, that's not right . . . What is it you kids say?"

I sighed. "No, Dad. I think you mean 411, and even then . . . That's not what we say anymore. You're dating yourself." Rick snickered behind his hand as Cosmo tilted his head up and shook it at the sky.

"Well, you know what I mean. You still got it, so stop being a smart ass." I smiled because that was one of my top five favorite things to be. "Anyway. I have something to discuss with you, so I need you to come home now."

His voice had a weird edge to it, well . . . weirder than normal. "What's wrong? Is everything okay? Is something wrong with clan business?"

He gave a nervous chuckle. "No, Sunshine, everything is fine, promise. It's just that I would like to discuss with you some logistics about tomorrow."

I had no idea what he was talking about. "Tomorrow?"

His shaky laugh came out again as he dropped the bomb on me. "Oh, did I forget to tell you? Silly me. All three families are flying in late tomorrow for an in-person meeting. First one in a while . . . and we wanted to discuss the future of the Syndicate with all you youngsters."

My mouth fell open because, one, he hadn't told me, and he knew it, and two, I haven't seen anyone from the other families since the funerals almost twenty-two years ago. My week just got loads more interesting.

CHAPTER 3

"Why do I have to be here? I could be at the hotel right now drinking a margarita by the pool and having some hotties entertain me." I tore my sunglasses off as my father and I got out of the car, buttoning up my suit jacket out of habit as we walked across the pavement.

We landed around noon on our private jet then went to check into the Desmond clan casino and hotel. They gave us the five-star treatment. Prime villa, staff at our beck and call, and all-access VIP passes to anything on the strip. I thought I would be able to have some fun on this trip, living it up in Vegas, right? *Wrong.*

Instead, my father wanted to check out the local talent. Making sure they were all up to snuff for the Glovefox name. My father and three of his other friends might be co-owners of the Syndicate, but skins was Glovefox domain, and we controlled the trade.

Since it was mainly a faerie-ran industry, due to our illusion magic, we made sure everyone was doing exactly what they were supposed to do, and the clients were getting serviced like they should. Sure, we had a few werewolves, vamps, and mages in the mix, for the clients that wanted that specifically, but since the average faerie could magic themselves to look like your ultimate fantasy, it made it a faerie-dominated trade.

"You can do that at home. Why would we do that here?" my father said as we got to the doors to our first stop—the dream lounge.

"Because I thought I was tagging along for one or two meetings, and the rest of the time was vacation." I felt that was reasonable. I work long and hard hours back home in New York, in the city that never sleeps, which means I don't as well. There's always money to be made at all hours of the night.

My father gave me the side-eye before he puffed out a laugh. "It's much more than that, son." Then he opened the door and rushed in, leaving me hanging for the dramatics of it all. I swear, my father was one of the best showmen I knew.

I shook my head and went through the door of the place called Dream Magic. The first thing I noticed was lights blinding me as I entered the building. It was like they wanted to spotlight the customers just as much as the talent. It was a little jarring as the rest of the room was almost pitch black, other than the stage. That was a big mood killer. That would need to be changed. I worked my magic, cataloging everything that needed to be changed for the experience to be elevated. I would not put out half-assed work.

My father took one of the far booths in the back, gazing around the room and checking out the clientele. That was always his job, judging the clients and finding out what would work best, what kind of talent a crowd like this needed. It helped that he was a powerful high fae and could feel the emotions that the clients were putting off. He could tell when an act wasn't working, when an act needed tweaks, or when someone needed more of a spotlight. All of this to make more money, not only for our workers but for us. Money made the world go round.

Some barmaid came over to my father, flirted with him, and he let her. He touched her face and caressed her shoulder, but he never took it to the next level. Never.

One day, I asked him if it was because my mom was the love of his existence. He shook his head and told me the cold hard truth, that my mother and father got together because she wanted protection after the Awakening, when the supes came out to the humans. She was a fearful woman and did not trust humans would accept us. She made a bargain with my father: if he kept her safe, she would give him a child, one child he could raise however he saw fit.

It was strange when I was a teen, hating my mom while missing her. I was almost six when she was killed, but the few memories I have were good ones. Even if it was more of a deal between them, they were both obviously fine with it. No one was mad or upset the other didn't love them, they accepted their roles and went on with life. It was simple, but sometimes I saw my father as a lonely old man. I tried to get him to date, to take up some of the young women that threw themselves at him, but he always declined.

One night, he was drunk and fessed up that he had one love of his life, and when he tried to think of another, all he saw was her looking at him in disgust. He said that when he sees her again someday in the afterlife, he wanted to make sure she only regarded him with love and appreciation. It sounded depressing, and I was glad I didn't have that problem.

As soon as I sat down next to him in the booth, the seat squeaked, and I rolled my eyes. I pulled out my notebook and wrote down another thing wrong with this place. If one of the girls were on top of me dancing, it would ruin the mood if I heard a squeaking every time she moved.

"This one is good, but I think she needs less lights on her when she's on the pole but more when she's off and dancing to the song. She seemed to move her body easier when she was off the pole and on beat to the music." My father's calculated voice always made it seem like he was a doctor assessing people's insides versus watching naked women and men dancing. Always the perfectionist. I wrote it all down, like I always do. "Also, the bartender needs to go to a mixology school or something, this Old Fashioned tastes like shit." I nodded and added it to the list.

As soon as I finished, I slammed the drink that was placed in front of me and grimaced, underlining the mixology school. Just because she was hot, didn't mean her drinks didn't taste like shit. "You ready? I think we have a lot to go over with him, and I don't want him to think we want to demolish this place from the ground up."

"Now that you mention it . . ." he whispered as he glanced around, and I almost laughed, almost.

"You know that would be too much money to dump into this place, old man." I smiled at him, and he tipped his head and smiled back. While our hair was different colors, we had the same build, stature and style in clothing. Sometimes it was like I was looking at the future and it scared the shit out of me.

"After you." He waved his hand with a flourish before I snickered and moved out of the booth as we made our way into the back where the dressing rooms and office were.

"I'm going to let you handle this one, kid. I just want to be the clout if you need it." Everyone respected my father. Everyone. That's why with him at my back people did what they were told to do. Back in New York, everyone knew who the next skins' leader was, and they respected me for it. I worked hard to build up my cred, being a leader that not only knew the gang part of this life but also what the dancers went through. What worked for optimal results and what didn't. In these places we didn't visit regularly, they still needed to be reminded who ran the show, and it would always be the Glovefox clan.

As we went through the black curtains, a security guard came out. "Whoa, whoa, only employees allowed back here. Turn the fuck back, and keep your dick in your pants."

Well, that was uncalled for. I looked down just to make sure my dick was, in fact, in my pants before I slowly turned to him, letting him know I didn't fear his big ass. I hummed a tune, one of my own creation, and directed the sound for only his ears. His eyes glazed over, his face slack as I leaned over to him and whispered in his ear, "Taser yourself."

He pulled out a taser, gave it a few shocks, then plunged it onto his chest and seized up. Electricity flowed over his body until his eyes rolled back into his head, and he fell unconscious. My father peeked over my shoulder with a wide grin as he patted my back. "Well, that's one way to solve that problem."

Since my father and I were some of the last high fae in this world, we had a different kind of magic than the typical faerie. We had powerful magic that made people bend to our will, and while we don't like to use it too much, we do enjoy reminding people.

One girl backstage saw the whole thing, and I casually walked up to her. She backed up, eyes wide as she nodded at the security guard on the floor. "Is he dead?"

I smiled that swoon-worthy smile that had all the girls falling for me. Her eyes grew hooded as she flicked her gaze up and down my body, licking her lips as she liked what she saw. I put my hand under her chin and tilted it up, her lips parted as I ran my thumb over the bottom lip. "Oh, no, he's fine, pretty girl. He's just taking a nap."

She giggled and blushed as she mumbled, "Okay," and her eyes flicked up to mine before she looked away and blushed. I have always thought women were easy to deal with if you knew what you were doing.

I let go and asked where I could find Quinn, the troll who managed this establishment. Her eyes flashed with fear before she pointed behind her to a closed door and said she needed to get on stage. Well, that wasn't a good indicator of a worthy manager.

My father's feet shuffled forward, flicking his hand to tell me to keep going. I didn't know why he was so testy, it was him that taught me how to handle the talent.

We went deep into the back of the building. It was all blacked out—black-painted walls, black doors, black velvet curtains, and it gave off a sinister vibe, in my opinion. That was another red flag. As soon as my hand went to the doorknob, something thudded against the door, and a female cried out.

I looked back at my father, whose eyes darkened, violence spreading like wildfire in them, and I grinned because that meant I would be able to play today. It was always nice to flex my throat muscles.

I opened the door and a gruff voice barked out, "I'm fucking busy. Get the fuck out!"

My hand tightened on the doorknob, but I kept my cool and continued on through with a chipper voice. "Well, we don't mean to intrude, but this *is* our establishment."

Quinn's green meaty hand was wrapped around the neck of a pretty fae girl in a purple-sequined mini dress, who was already sporting a black eye. Quinn's large neck bunched as he turned his head and opened his large mouth. That was the thing with trolls, they were part of the faerie domain, but they were so grotesque, always jealous of the majority of the fae and our natural beauty. They always wanted to dominate the weak to make themselves feel good. We took in Quinn when he wasn't up to snuff for the Rossey clan for the fights, saying he was too slow, but now I saw he might be a bad fit for the Syndicate, period.

As soon as Quinn's eyes scanned me and my father, he released the young fae girl, who swiftly scrambled on the floor into the back corner of the room. Her teary eyes tracked the movement of all the men in the room, her distress going up tenfold, as I was sure she thought there were now more of us that would abuse her.

"Boss, I didn't know you were going to be coming here today. If I knew, I would've brought in some of my finest girls for you." Quinn's booming voice came out jovial, like we didn't just catch him abusing one of the talents, which we had explicitly told managers was a no-no. At least not in the form of simple punishments. If anyone betrayed us, sold information about us, or any of the other clan families that made up the Syndicate, then they were fair game and would be treated accordingly. I only protected those under my employment who were loyal to us.

I nodded as I smiled, and he let out a breath he was holding. "And what was going on here?" I asked, and my father closed the door behind us.

Quinn glared at the girl on the floor, and she tried to curl into herself even tighter. "This one has an attitude problem, and I was teaching her how she is to act in an establishment owned by the legendary Glovefoxes."

He sure was laying it on thick, wasn't he? I thought, shaking my head as I put my hands into my pants, making sure I appeared casual and not threatening. It was always the best way to catch your prey off guard.

I turned to the girl on the floor. "If that's true, sweetheart, you don't have to work here. We don't keep employees here as slaves. If this is not the life for you, then you can turn in your notice right now, no harm, no foul. If it's not for you, it's not for you."

The fae girl's eyes went wide. "No, sir. I knew what I was getting into when I started here. It's good money and . . . and . . ." Her eyes flicked to Quinn before she whispered, "I need it for my son. It's just me and him."

Quinn opened his mouth, but I held up my hand for him to wait. He seemed a little pissed about that and crossed his arms as he continued to glare at her. "Quinn, you have us here to unburden you with these petty squabbles. We are here to help you." I turned back to the girl. "Then what seems to be the problem, sweetie?"

She licked her lips, and I saw the war inside her eyes on whether she should tell us the truth. My father piped up, being the ladies man he was, "The truth is the best for us all, darling."

Her smile was one of relief pointed at my father. I'm sure he was putting on his charmer face that all the women—young and old—fell for as she nodded. "Quinn has been after me for sex since I started. He said it was a toll to be able to work here." She shuttered before she continued. "When I told him no, he said that he would let me work here on probation, and every day since, he has been after me."

My hands balled into fists in my pockets, rage surging into my veins at what was going on. This fucker thought he could abuse the employees because he was in a position of power? Did he not understand simple economics? If the employees didn't feel safe and appreciated, then their work morale would go down, if morale went down, then production was sloppy, and if production was sloppy, then clients would be unhappy, which meant money would be lost. Money owed to the Syndicate. *My money*. This fucker was messing with my money.

I glared up at Quinn, who gulped and then yelled, "Are you going to believe this fucking faerie trash?!"

"*Silence*," I sang out with my magic, and Quinn shut his mouth and stood still, eyes going wide.

My father went around me and put his hand out to the girl. "Come, pretty one, I think you deserve a couple of paid days off and some help with that shiner so your son doesn't see you like this. Then we can discuss what you want to do and what your interests are for your set, if you wish to still work here."

She put her hand in his, letting him lift her up. He was careful not to touch her unless she touched him first, giving her the respect and dignity of not treating her like a piece of meat he could manhandle. She nodded her head in agreement and went out the door with my father. He gave me a sinister look before he closed the door behind him. That meant the light was green to do what I do best.

I let my face morph into the cruel version I only allow the dead to see, and Quinn stepped back, crying out, but I barely heard it with his mouth still shut from my magic.

"I know your dumb, idiotic self didn't realize this, how could you? You're just a fucktard, ugly troll that doesn't have shit for brains." I let out an exaggerated sigh. "It's our fault, really. We let a piece of shit like you in, and we shouldn't have." I sat back down across from him.

I saw in Quinn's eyes he understood where this was going, and he tried to rush me, but I didn't have to move as I sang out, "*Sit.*" He quickly moved to sit in his chair, still unable to speak—just how I liked it.

"Now, I know you can understand that you were already going to be fired over how poorly you were keeping up the place. Now it seems like you hired only women you wanted to force yourself on, which is really pathetic. I mean . . . come on. Getting a woman is not very hard." I eyed him up and down and curled up my lip in disgust. "Well, for real men it's not. I'm a gentleman, a businessman, and I respect the merchandise because I understand that they make me my money."

I leaned forward and sang out, "*Grab a knife and slice open your cheek.*" He did exactly that, not saying a single thing as he tugged out his desk drawer and pulled out a large, thin blade. His eyes widened, his body shaking as he watched his hand with the knife inch closer and closer to his cheek. With wide eyes, he cut his own cheek, slicing it open slow and deep.

His muffled cries were exquisite, and I closed my eyes to enjoy them. When he whimpered, I knew we were ready again. I sang for him to do this to himself over and over again. He sliced his forearm, then tops of his thighs before slicing down his chest and cutting off his nipples, all the while, he could barely scream.

Soon, he was a bloody mess, tears falling down his cheeks, and I hadn't moved from my seat once. When I'd had enough, knowing my dad and I needed to stop at a few more places, I sang the last bit.

"Put the knife up to your throat and slice, slice, slice across. Let the blade drink every drop . . . slowly." He tried to scream, to yell one last time, but his arm moved at my command, and fear and acceptance filled his eyes as he placed the blade against his neck. Like a man carving up a turkey, he plunged the knife deep, going halfway through his neck at one side. I licked my lips at the sight as all hope left his body, and only fear and pain remained. He tugged on the knife to slide from one side to the other. At one point, he caught the knife on a tough part of muscle and went pale, but I called out to him to stay awake, and his eyes flew open in obedience. As soon as the knife finished the job, it was like his body had been held up by strings, and then someone cut them, causing him to slump in his seat.

Blood gushed down his front as his breathing stopped. I stood up, dusted myself off, and pulled out my cell. I pressed the number two, and it rang until Victor picked up. "Sir?"

"Hello, Victor, I need another manager at the club, Dream Magic, and I need them now." I thought about it for a second, then added, "Also make sure it's not a troll."

"Yes, sir. I will have someone over there in the next hour to take over and clean up." I smiled because he knows me so well.

"I left a list on the desk with all the things I want changed, added, or fixed for this establishment. Let this new person know I will be there in one week to check up on the place and make sure everything is done." I hung up and took a deep breath. A week should be long enough. Plus, I was just starting to enjoy myself . . . I might stay here a little longer and send my father back home. Who knows.

We made a stop over at another spot, the Lucky Palace, and it was much cleaner, the dancers seemed happier, the clients were already spending a lot of money, and it was just after lunchtime. We went to talk to the manager, Billy, and walked in on him getting a BJ. I was about to flip my lid when a man with bright-green hair and red eyes popped up and yelled at us for interrupting their husband-husband time.

I'll admit I was a little shocked at being yelled at, that isn't something I am used to, but when Billy recognized who we were, he quieted his husband and told him we were the Glovefoxes. That shocked the ever-loving shit out of him, and he apologized before telling us it was their anniversary, and he wanted to surprise him, spice it up a bit.

I was finding his partner's chatty mouth very amusing when Billy kindly told him to go get us drinks so we could talk. His husband scurried out, promising to bring us the best drinks we have ever had with an umbrella. Billy ran a hand through his long, dirty-blond locks, side-eyeing us with his deep-blue eyes before he waved for us to sit down and apologized. I laughed. Like, really laughed. After what happened at Dream Magic, I didn't give a fuck about the husbands getting it on at work.

I waved away his worry and told him we were in town and doing surprise pop-ups in some establishments. I told him with the massive overhaul that Dream Magic was, I was happy to see this was the opposite at Lucky Palace. That this place was run to our standards, and we wanted to congratulate him.

He surprised me when he said it was in part to his husband. He used to be a dancer in another state, and when they started dating, he came to this place and helped him. After a few years, they got married, and he helped out a lot more, wanting to build up this place's reputation. He attributed it to them working as a team. The dancers didn't feel threatened and listened to his husband while he kept the security guys and clients in line, then the money followed.

My father congratulated him on finding such a good partner in life and business. He was a sucker for a good love story, then we went on our merry way. Well, we tried, until we were stopped by Billy's husband running toward us with two glasses in his hand, wanting us to taste his signature drink, Nipple Magic. My father snatched the pink sugary martini and drank it in one gulp. I sipped mine, but was surprised when I found the sweetness coun- terbalanced with the savory taste and the hit of heat at the end.

My father shook his hand and complimented the drink. The husband blushed, telling us to come by again soon to see the new acts. We smiled and said we would if time allowed, then got back in the car for the last stop.

"I liked them." My father crossed his knees and looked out the window.

"Of course, you did." I was scrolling through my phone, overlooking emails from the accountant and some minor issues being handled in New York.

"When are you planning to settle down, Avery?" My father huffed, and I felt his eyes still on me through the reflection of the window, tracking my every move.

I let out an exaggerated breath. "Are you really bucking for grandkids so badly?" I threw my thumb over my shoulder. "I can go knock someone up right now?"

He turned and narrowed his eyes. "So vulgar." He scowled. "Why can't you just find some woman to settle down with and have a family. I would adore having a little one running around the house. Making this old man youthful again by just trying to catch the wicked thing." He chuckled before a pensive, far-off look creeped up on his face, a yearning for something he felt like he wasn't going to get. Then a small, wobbly smile showed up, and I knew he was playing out his grandpa fantasy.

"Let's just focus on this last stop." I didn't want to talk about it anymore. I didn't want to tell him being with a woman for a night seemed like the best time of my life, but being with one for an eternity felt like a prison sentence, and criminals don't do well with prison sentences.

We were soon in front of the last one, The Temptress, which was our biggest moneymaker because it was a mixture of a strip club and a dance club. I had high expectations out of the two-story building with cages and dance platforms in the air. Drinks that cost a shit ton of money because some had shaved gold flakes. This was where all the elite and moneymakers went to have a good time.

As soon as we pulled up, a man opened our door. "Good afternoon, Mr. Glovefox and Mr. Glovefox. Mistress Veshta is waiting for you."

I couldn't help the smile on my lips. That woman was the best at finding out secrets and being in the know before anyone else. I don't know if she had faerie powers of sight or what, but she always surprised me.

We walked up the red-carpet steps, a set of pure gold-flaked doors opened before we got to them, and a scurry little man showed us to the elevator that went to her private office. As we walked to the elevator, the dancers were practicing their acts. My father tsked. We were thinking the same thing. They were good, but they were missing some pizzazz. That spunk.

We got into the elevator, and my father played with the buttons on his jacket, so I thought I would razz him. "Are you excited to see your friend and lover?"

My father barked out a laugh. "Lover? Is that what you think, boy?"

When I shrugged, thinking what else could he possibly be nervous about, he shook his head, mumbling about my mind always being in the gutter. But I mean, come on, it was normal to always think about your dick, especially in my circles.

"No, Avery. I have only loved one woman in my life, and Veshta was not her." When I lifted my eyebrow for him to explain, he continued as he faced the elevator doors. "We are colleagues. Traveled and took care of each other before us supes came out to the world. We were more like brother and sister in the feelings department, but we are both vicious creatures and always enjoy keeping each other on our toes."

He didn't get to finish, as the doors wooshed open, and all of a sudden, a massive squid with sharp teeth came at us. My father shrieked, jumping back before he bellowed, "Veshta!" The giant squid transformed before our eyes, shimmering into the shape of a slight woman with dark-black hair pinned up into a bun and a blood-red dress with a slit very high for a woman of her age.

I mean, she was hot, and I might have been tempted to do something about it if my father didn't confess to her being like a sister to him in the old days. Now it was like my mind put a big red X over her whole body.

Her soft yet firm voice came out as she giggled like a schoolgirl. "Oh, Syris, stop being such a ninny, and get over your squid fear already."

"They are unnatural and vile creatures! No one should have that many legs!" my father yelled as he stomped over to her liquor cabinet and poured himself a drink like he has been here a million times. I guess that's what it was like when you had been friends for as long as they had been.

She walked up to me, her arms out as she kissed each of my cheeks. "Oh, Avery! It's so good to see you. Are you married yet?" My father snorted, and she gave me a pout and patted me on the head. "Don't worry. You will find someone . . . eventually." Then she turned, her wings on display as she went to her large, elaborate mahogany desk with gold-painted vines and sat down.

Not many of us faeries keep our wings on display. It was a weakness as well as a strength for the fae. Our wings were naturally clear, almost transparent, the only thing that caught your eye was our magic racing up and down the veins. When we found our mate, as soon as our eyes met, our wings underwent a transformation and turned an exquisite iridescent color. That was the only time faeries showed off their wings, so everyone knew they were taken. So, seeing hers on display so casually spoke to how bold and fierce this woman was.

"So, is my club to your liking?" She blinked a few times at me, knowing I wanted to correct her right away, but my father stepped in.

"Yes, it's quite exquisite." She blushed as she nodded, then he said, "But the talent could use some help." Her cheerful face went from sweet to vicious in one second.

"What do you mean?" The deadly tone in her voice made my father smile like a jackal, then I realized this was their little game and kept myself out.

"I mean, dear Veshta, I think your dancers need a tad bit more training. Just to really understand how to entice the customer." I don't know what my father was getting at, but I didn't like the sound of it. *How was he going to show them how to do that?*

Veshta stood up, slapping her hands onto her desk as she said between clenched teeth, "And who do you propose they learn this from?"

Without missing a beat, he said, "Why, Avery, of course."

My eyes flew wide for a second before they narrowed on my father's. *What the fuck was he up to?* My suspicions went up tenfold when Veshta settled down and turned to me, smiling widely as she clapped. "I think that's a great idea."

What the fuck?! How did this turn on me so fast?

Seconds later, I was ushered downstairs. We must have been in her office longer than I thought because the club was filling up. Veshta, she waved them off like it was nothing, saying they were the early crowd and nothing to worry about. She shooed the dancers off the main stage, and glaring bright lights illuminated around me as she announced me as a new dancer and the crowd would need to make noise to determine if I was good enough. Bodies came closer to the stage, excited to see a new act before others. Dancers on the sidelines waited for me to show them what they were missing.

I mean I knew how to dance. That was one thing I learned how to do when I was a young punk kid, then I turned it into my passion when I realized it was the only time I could truly be free. I let my body and soul take over and live carefree for those two to three minutes. My father caught me at some club one night and told me I had a real talent. Then he started asking me questions on what to do better, and the partnership between us grew stronger from that moment on. I rarely danced anymore, but I still knew how to do it.

[1] Suddenly, a song blared through the speakers, and I recognized the beat. It was a little slower than I liked, but I could work with it. It would give me a nice challenge, a way for me to stretch those dancing muscles and prove I knew what I was talking about.

As the lyrics started, I moved my arms one by one, like I was telling a story, as I was holding some pretend woman's ass, feeling on the curves, appreciating the view from the back. Then the beat hit, and I flexed my fingers around the fake hips before I grabbed the fake ass and slammed into it in time with the four beats.

The crowd screamed, and I smiled at them like they were in on a secret. I took my jacket off sleeve by sleeve, throwing it to one of the girls calling out the loudest, then dropped down and crawled on my hands and knees over to her. Right before the beat hit again, I got up on my knees, lifting one leg up as I thrust my pelvis in her face to the four beats. Her eyes rolled back into her head as she fanned herself, and I gave her a wink.

---

1. Song: Falling by Trevor Daniel

I was having fun, letting my body do the talking as I enticed and enchanted every lady up near the stage. It was fun to have all these women drool over me, over my body and what I can do with it.

I shifted into some harder moves, ones where I held myself up with one hand as I flipped and humped the stage floor. At that moment, I lifted my face to the crowd and was captured by a pair of rose gold eyes that sparkled in the sea of faces covered in darkness. They were so stunning, so vibrant, I missed one of the beats, and this woman's ruby lips curved up. Almost taunting me with her tantalizing eyes and pouty lips.

I shook it off and got up, hit one of the major beats by tearing my shirt off, popping all the buttons off at once, and those rosey eyes flashed with hunger as they trailed down my chest. My heart pounded harder, and my breath hitched. I couldn't even see this woman fully with the bright lights glaring down at me, but I would pick up on her shining eyes and kissable lips in any dark room. Her lips curved up, and she licked them as her eyes were fixed on me.

My focus zeroed in on her like she was the only person in the room, and I was doing a private dance for her. I performed all the tricks I knew, wanting to cause lust to flash in those orbs over and over, and she did not disappoint.

I wanted to show her more, wanted her to be so worked up she would crawl onto this stage and give herself to me. I wanted to fuck her in front of these people to show them how to worship a woman. I wanted to see what those rose gold eyes looked like when I plunged my cock into her wet, hot center.

Flicking open the button to my pants, the crowd went wild, but my eyes were only focused on her. I lifted my chin to her, signaling this was for her, and her eyes widened. She took one step closer to the stage, and my blood raced as my skin burned up. I told myself it was from all the lights on me, not because of a sudden fervor to have this woman.

I peeled the zipper down, showing the crowd I was shaved and commando, at which point they threw money at me, but in that moment, it was for the girl in the back with the sparkling eyes that called to the depths of my cold, empty heart.

I slowly pushed the waistband of my pants down, inch by tantalizing inch, when the song stopped, and Veshta came out on a microphone, asking the crowd if they liked the act, and they roared with applause and screams. It filled a part of my ego, but something inside of me pushed that all behind. Something pushed me to go and find that girl with the pinkish gold eyes and make her mine.

I didn't pick up my shirt or jacket, leaving them with the girls fighting over the expensive fabric as I zipped and buttoned my pants. Climbing down the stage, I pushed through the people congratulating me, asking me for my number or soliciting me for sex, but this thing inside me drove me to find her, and I pushed them all away. Every cell in my body told me to find the woman with the rose gold eyes.

When I finally got to the spot I last saw her, she was gone. Only a sweet floral scent was left in her wake, and I sucked it down like it was the last thing I would ever smell.

Before I could go on the hunt for her, my father came toward me, smiling like a loon as he counted bills in his hands. "Good job, boy, you have always been my lucky charm, and now Veshta knows we can entertain with the best of them." When I kept searching over his head, he grabbed my bicep, his face serious as he motioned for me to go back to Veshta's office. "I have some stuff to talk to you about tomorrow. Maybe it will clear up the whole settling-down issue you're having."

My eyes flew wide as my heart stopped, and I digested what he just said. *What the fuck was happening tomorrow?* I needed to follow my father and find out what he was cooking in that head of his, squash it, then go on a search for my rose gold-eyed maiden.

CHAPTER 4

I HAVE ALWAYS HATED planes. They're too constricting for me. Like I was trapped in a box. I hated that feeling. It reminded me of that day when I was a fat little boy staring at a single box in fear.

I readjusted myself for the fifth time, cursing these damn fucking seats that barely fit me. I don't know why we had to take a plane when we lived in Montana. We could've just driven to Vegas. I would've been much more comfortable in my Mercedes G-Wagon, it had ample room for my large frame. Also, with a car, if shit went south, I could just open the door or window or bash my way out and onto the ground. In this flying box, if I fell to the ground, that would be it. And I hated it. I hated feeling weak.

"Stop fidgeting," my father said from across from me. He was about the same size as me, but he looked at ease with his legs crossed and eyes scanning over spreadsheets. He flicked his eyes to me and frowned. "It's only a two-hour flight. We're almost there." Then he went back to his papers.

"You know I don't like flying," I growled out. My wolf was pacing back and forth inside of me, making me uneasy. "Remind me why I couldn't have just driven and met you?"

He smacked his papers down on his lap as he sighed. "This is no ordinary trip, and we need to be seen as a solid front. We first need to garner the respect the Rossey name deserves. We need to look at the local talent, make sure the fighting rings and gym are run correctly. Make sure our people know we were watching them. The second part is that we're meeting officially as the whole Syndicate. We need to show ourselves as a unified front in our stronghold, Las Vegas. We haven't had a meeting like this since . . ." His pause was poignant as he looked away and gulped.

Since all our moms died.

"I understand the recruitment and showing up to keep people accountable, but the second part I don't get. Why are we meeting now? Seems like everything has been going good with just the phone calls and video conferences you guys have been having." I shrugged. I mean, it's fun to get to come to Vegas, but I'm still pissed I couldn't just drive. It's only fifteen hours.

My father leaned forward, his suit stretching as he rested his elbows on his knees. "All four of us have agreed we need to figure out the future for the Syndicate. We need to bring the four of you in. We need to bring you all together to create a bond for the future."

My brows pinched, and confusion splashed across my face. The only thing I remembered about the other heirs was that the Glovefox boy was gangly and just wanted to have fun, the Winstale boy was cautious and tech savvy, and the Desmond girl. I thought back to those rose gold eyes that left an impression. She and I went a round on that playground when she was trying to exert dominance, and it was something I would never forget. Then there was the shy, quiet, and observant Devil boy from the demon clan. We hadn't heard from the demon clan since they disappeared after the funeral twenty-two years ago. We all thought they were dead.

He leaned back in a huff, and regret lined his eyes as he stared out the plane window. "We kept you all separate for your safety, to ensure the safety of our families, but in the end, I don't know if that was the smart move." He looked back at me, eyes clear and focused. "The whole reason we work as a complete organization is because those three men are like brothers to me. We respect each other and are each other's confidants. I trust those men completely, and them, me. It has made the Syndicate the powerhouse it is . . . but you kids haven't had that kind of experience. You barely even know each other. So, this trip is about rectifying that now that you are older and can each hold your own."

He paused, and a sparkle of deviousness entered his eyes. My wolf homed in on it, telling me to press him for more information.

I moved again in my seat, still not finding it comfortable as I rumbled out, "You have that look in your eye, Father, what is it?"

He chuckled at my tone, too excited about this next part. "It's just that Ternin had an idea for the four of you, and the closer we get, the more I'm thinking it's a good plan." Then he folded his hands in his lap, and I knew he was going to drop a bomb on me. "He would like to throw out a challenge to all you boys. The prize would be the hand of his daughter, Rayla Desmond."

My eyes bugged out of my head. "The vampire girl? Marriage? The fuck?"

My whole body seized up, not a muscle flinched in my sheer shock of what my father said. Marriage . . . that seemed a little . . . permanent. What the fuck was I going to do about marrying some fucking clan princess I'm sure didn't have a single manicured hand in the business. I'm sure that's why Boss Desmond wants to marry her off. My mind drifted to those few days when we were kids, her getting us into more trouble than not, and I knew she wouldn't have changed in all these years.

My father chuckled again, and my chest heaved, angry at him for making fun of the situation he and his buddies were putting me in. Well, I guess what they were putting all of us heirs in. It made me feel for the four of us and created a bond out of pity.

He stared at my narrowed eyes, giving me his don't-give-a-fuck-what-you-want face as he chided me like I was a kid again. "Yes. Marriage. You all are twenty-eight, old enough to start thinking about settling down. It would also make a statement to everyone that not only are we family by heart but by blood and contract, as well." He shrugged like he hadn't changed the course of my life in seconds.

When I opened my mouth to argue, he held up his hand. "I told you before we got there because I didn't want you to be caught off guard. I want you to hold your wolf tight to your chest while we are here. Keep your emotions out of all this so we can make the best choices for the future." My wolf howled in my head, arguing we did our best work when we banded together. *I know*, I told him, *but I will take my father's advice. He has never steered us wrong before.* He howled again before he curled up on the ground in defeat.

"Okay, Father. I understand, and I will do my best to represent the Rossey clan." At that moment, turbulence shook our plane, and a foreboding feeling hit me as I gripped onto both armrests. They creaked and snapped under the pressure of my strength.

I glanced up at my father with wide eyes and was met with his calm ones, ones that told me I was being ridiculous. Through the whole thing, he had his arms and legs crossed as he shook his head at my fear. I let go with a huff, put in my earbuds, and closed my eyes for the rest of the trip. *I fucking hate flying.*

We landed with no problems and took a car straight from the tarmac to one of our gyms. Our gyms were world renowned with the best-of-the-best trainers and the top-of-the-line equipment. Fighters from all over the world would come for a chance to train in one of our gyms, and Vegas had a large pool of international recruits.

Our role in the Syndicate was the organization and training of the muscle. The Glovefoxes' strip clubs' security were our guys, the Desmonds' casinos' security and
underground watchers were our guys, the defense and
security for the Winstales' weapons development facility
were our guys. To recruit the kind of muscle we were
looking for, we ran the gyms, fight clubs, and were the
main sponsors for some of the national fighting rings.

We had a lot happening in Vegas, and my father had to
meet up with the UFC owner to make sure the fight night
was going as planned, which left me to go check on the
gyms and scope out the talent.

I opened the door to one of our latest gyms we built and
was met with the smell of sweat and disinfectant in the
air. We had some of the highest standards for hygiene, as
gyms were cesspools for bacteria.

As I walked in, I saw fighters all over the place. Some were
working on their endurance with jump ropes and battle
ropes. I even saw one guy flipping a huge monster truck
tire from one side of the room to the other. Then there
were the guys on the other side of the gym using the
punching bags and dummies, a few were using the speed
bags, and some were using some of the wooden dummies
utilized for martial arts. Then in the center was the ring.
Fighters lined up all around it, watching two fighters have
it out while both coaches were yelling critiques at them.

The manager came out of his office, worry in his eyes
at seeing me unexpectedly. I always enjoyed the fear that
flooded a man's eye when they saw me. I knew my large
stature and muscular body was intimidating, but I really

enjoyed it when it was my name that made a man pee their pants in panic.

"S-s-sir. I didn't know you were coming. I would've—"

I lifted my hand at his skittish eyes and worried tone. "I'm just here on business and thought I would drop in and see how you're doing. How things are being run. Is that a problem?" I raised my eyebrow at him.

The whole room had gone quiet, all eyes on us as the trainers shushed the fighters, whispering my name and importance to those that didn't know.

"No problem, sir. We're always ready for any type of visit." He straightened his shoulders and puffed out his chest. "I can show you arou—"

Again, I lifted my hand. "No, it's fine. I just want to see how it all runs like normal." I turned to the rest of the room. "Please, keep going on like I'm not even here." Most trainers and fighters gave me a respectful nod and went back to it . . . all but one.

Out of a sea of fighters of all shapes, colors, humans, and supes, there was one staring me down like I meant nothing to him. Like he was the only one that wasn't scared of the man in a suit. I bet he thought I was nothing but some money man, some pampered gang-boss kid that didn't get dirty and came into the gym to feel like I knew what our hands were in. There was always one that thought that way, and I enjoyed eradicating that thought process from the root.

I stalked around the gym, watching the trainers and fighters, liking what I saw but never saying a word. That idiot's gaze drilled a hole into the back of my skull, but I kept going like I didn't even notice. I wanted to work up his anger so he provoked me, and there would be no going back. No one would leave today without understanding what it meant to be the Rossey boss.

I finally made my way around the whole room before I got to the ring in the center. This was where the defiant fighter was. Now that I was closer, I could tell he was a troll, and from the looks of it, a young one. They were always the ones that needed more violent lessons. Trolls were strong, considering they were part of the faerie realm, but they were no true match for me. Werewolves, by nature, were hunters, like vampires, but unlike the vamps, we didn't have their speed and precision. We were wild and rough, built like mack trucks, naturally the stronger of the species for all supes. It's why most of our guys were werewolves, but if you held your own in a fight, you could be a candidate, we didn't discriminate.

His anger at me vibrated off him; I didn't even have to look at him to know he was glaring at me. He needed only a little more of a push, and he would play right into my hand. I walked up to the ring on the opposite side of him and rested my arms on the ropes. I knew this was a no-no, but no one would call me out on it, well, except for the angry troll I was provoking.

He mumbled, "I'm a Rossey, and I get to do whatever I fucking want. Fucking prick."

I perked up as I rumbled out, "Got something to say, boy?"

That tipped him over, and he squared his shoulders as he clenched his fists. "Yeah!" he yelled, and everyone in the room stopped what they were doing, even the fighters in the ring, their heads going back and forth between us.

I leaned on the ropes further, all lazy like I didn't have a care in the world, and I motioned to him with my hand. "Then say your piece. There is no need to keep secrets in a place like this. Get it out, boy."

He glanced around, and several fighters were giving him a shake of their head, but he rolled his eyes and stood even taller, puffing out his chest as he bit out, "Everyone here is too scared to even piss around you. You're bothering our training. It's people like you that don't know how your presence affects our efforts and fighting."

A big wolfish smile settled on my face as I cooed out, "People like me?"

People gasped as he answered, "Yeah. Stuck-up, richy boys like you."

His defiance was like music to my ears as I got up off the ropes and walked my way around the ring toward him. I stepped right up into his face as I kept my tone light. "I bet I could wipe up the floor with you, poor boy."

That last part had him bristle as his face grew red and tight. He clenched his fists as he seethed out, "Get in the ring, then."

I leaned back as I unbuttoned my jacket. "Gladly." Then I turned around to go to the opposite side to start our fight. I took off my shirt as the manager rushed to my side.

"Sir, he didn't mean it. He's just some punk kid. I can get him to leave, and we never have to—"

"Never have to do what?" I barked in his face. "Fight?" I pursed my lips and tilted my head before I continued. "He needs to learn who he is dealing with. That's the only way boys like him learn to be men." Then I turned and smiled at my opponent climbing into the ring. "And I love being the one to smack them down." I handed the manager my shirt as I climbed into the ring.

He mumbled, "Let's hope he doesn't land in the hospital." I smirked at that because that was the current news running through the Rossey clan. The last guy I fought, I sent him to the hospital with a few broken ribs, his arm dislocated and chewed up, with one side of his face turned into roast beef. All for spilling red wine on my new suit. What they all didn't know was he did it on purpose to try and steal from my wallet, thinking I was an easy mark because I was a "rich kid." I puffed out a laugh. *Teaches that kid to fucking steal from a mark he didn't do his research on.*

As soon as I stepped in the ring, my wolf prowled, wanting to come out and play, to make a bloody mess of this idiot that dared to challenge us. I assessed the troll again and knew I would not need my wolf's help. Not with this punk. He might be strong, but he seemed like one of the dumb ones that needed his head bashed in to learn his lesson. I didn't want to kill him, and that's what my wolf would do. He was a bloody savage when fighting.

One of the trainers came between us, recited the rules we both knew as we stared each other down. As soon as he said fight, I leaned backward and let his right hook sail past me before I ducked and gave him an upper cut to the gut.

Making sure I was light on my feet, I moved to the side before he could recover and gave him a side kick right in the kidneys. He clenched his teeth as he fell to the floor but hoisted himself up, waving at me to keep it up. I smiled as I moved toward him.

He surprised me by falling backward, palms slapping onto the mat as he snapped out both his legs and kicked me square in the chest. It was a good shot, it took me by surprise, and I lost my breath for a second, but I was a werewolf, I was built like a brick house, and even his troll legs couldn't move me.

Before he could put his legs back down on the ground, I leaped on top of him. He gasped for air, not expecting me to take this fight to the ground. I trained with one of the best jujitsu fighters in the world, I knew how to ground fight just as well.

I pushed up, straddling him as I ground pounded him into the mat. He tried to put me into a triangle hold by lifting his two legs to wrap around my neck and pull me forward. The trick was to go with it, keep breathing as you bent forward like they wanted. I rained down small quick punches on his thighs and sides like I was softening meat. Just keep hammering into him until he unraveled his legs, and since I wasn't pulling my punches, they felt like anvils landing on his sides.

Soon, he let go, not using his brain and trying to get away. He tried to turn to roll away, which was the wrong move. My wolf tried to push forward, to shift and bite into the running prey, to rip him apart with only our teeth and paws, but I held him back. I only used my wolf when I needed to.

I snaked my arm around his neck and yanked him back. He tried to lift his legs to alleviate the strain on his neck, but I couldn't have that. Wrapping my legs around his to hold them in place, I pulled at his neck even harder, stretching his body in opposite directions as I was effectively choking him out.

The savage beast inside me wanted to come out, needed blood to spill and to be covered in it. I kept one arm wrapped around his neck, keeping my grip tight as I used my other hand to punch him in the face. His face was cracking underneath the fury of my hits, blood spraying all around me in puddles as I lifted my fist each time. The softer his face got, the more blood started to spill down around me. The drops hit my skin, and it was like a balm to my vicious soul.

I would hand it to him, he held out longer than I thought, but in the end, they tap out once I rear choke hold them. With my strength, there was no way to get out of it. It was a choice to either tap out or lose consciousness.

At least he wasn't a total shit for brains because he tapped on my arm lightly, and I unwound myself from his body as he slumped to the floor, holding his face and neck as he gasped for breath, choking on his blood. I stood up, glaring down at him. I needed to know if I made an enemy or a convert. This was the moment, right after a fight, when you got a glimpse into their true nature, true character. When they were broken and hurting, they couldn't hide their thoughts from you.

He peered up at me, one eye swollen shut and the other squinted in shame but also respect. I knew I would not need to watch my back, or inevitably have him killed. He learned his lesson, and he wouldn't underestimate another just because of outward appearances.

Finished with this lesson, I nodded to him and walked over to the edge to get my shirt and jacket. The whole gym was congratulating me, telling me how good I did, and how impressed they were and whatnot. I had to remind myself that because we weren't here often, they didn't know me that well. Didn't know what I was capable of like the big boys in Montana knew.

A few fighters and trainers started asking me questions, wanting my take on the training, and I let them know my thoughts. I was having such a good time, I invited them all to come see the fight tonight as my guests. They all whooped and hollered and left the gym, saying they needed to get ready.

My father was a little put out once I told him from the car that I was bringing about twenty-five guests with me to the fight tonight, but after I told him it was to put a good light on our name and to feel out some fighters to be recruited, he relented and made the tickets happen.

The fight was good. In the professional fighting world, they had fight nights where there was a fight card for human and supernaturals. They staggered each fight between the two so you had to watch it all, but the final fight was supernaturals and was usually the bloodiest. We liked to leave you on a fighting high when you left.

So, despite the fights being over, all the fighters were still pumped, looking for more action, and wanted to head out to some swanky nightclub. I told them I would think about it as they got into cabs, but the more I thought about it, the more I wanted to. It was Vegas, after all, and I wanted to have some fun, let loose, enjoy having some sweet honeys grinding their asses on me before I took them home and fucked them senseless.

I thought about what my father told me, how they wanted to marry one of us to the vampire heir, and I felt like the walls were closing in around me. There was a possibility she would pick me, and I was freaking out about it. Forever seemed like a fuck ton of time, especially being a supe, with our extended lives and shit.

Yes. I needed to find someone to get on top of, get this fear stripped from me before I went into that meeting tomorrow.

The club was hopping, massive amounts of people in line to get in. I heard the beat as soon as we turned into the parking lot, the vibrations of the notes pounded against my skin, calling me to move to it already. Dancing was one of my secret guilty pleasures. There was something invigorating about going out there and letting your body move to the beat, being controlled by something other than yourself. It was even better when you had a partner to do it with.

I called ahead and made sure they had the VIP booth ready for me. I didn't like being in with the whole crowd until I was ready. I liked to scope it out with a few drinks, shake hands with the higher-ups, and sit back as girls came to me in waves, and I would have my pick of the litter.

As soon as I got out of my car, I was greeted by the valet by name, then was brought up the stairs to the top portion of the club. The bottom portion was wall to wall with people. The DJ in a booth above them, looking like some lone puppet master controlling the crowd with the beat and melody of his craft. Lights were strobing, making it hard for me to not move my body along with the beat, but I controlled myself.

At the top of the second story was another security guard who immediately recognized me and opened it before my escort explained who I was. I nodded in his direction, and I noticed it was one of the guys I trained with in my younger days. "Malcom."

His eyes widened, my guess was because I remembered his name, as he lifted his fist and pounded his chest. "Sir."

I gave him a nod and followed my escort. The second story was different because it was darker, more secluded, less people around, and everyone was whispering. I was led to the back corner, hanging over the entrance, but with the best view of the club and the DJ. Nice and tucked away while also giving me the best seat in the house.

As soon as I sat in the booth, a bottle girl in a short skirt and crop top came over, swinging her hips and licking her lips, but she couldn't hide the greed in her eyes. Those were the bitches I didn't touch. They wanted to get their hooks into you and bleed every dime out of you. I preferred my women to be carefree and dumb. The less smart, the better. They tended to not talk a lot, and most took hard and rough fucks like a champ.

The girl bent over, tits practically spilling out of her top as she looked at me seductively. "This is on the house, Mr. Rossey. Do you see anything else you want?" She pushed out her tits so far I was surprised the nipple didn't pop out. I might not fuck around with the greedy types, but that didn't mean I didn't have eyeballs.

I glanced down at her tits and licked my lips before I flicked my eyes up to hers and smiled widely. "Naw, sweetheart. I'm good."

She shot straight up, glaring at me for a moment before she mumbled, "Let me know if you need anything else. I'll be around." She turned around to leave, but I couldn't help myself as I called out to her. I was a fucking prick like that.

"In fact, sweetheart, if you could send over some blondes with short pink dresses and, preferably, no brains, I would appreciate it." Her mouth fell open. "You can handle that, right?"

She shut her mouth and nodded, stomping off toward the bar. I picked up the bottle, and it was expensive-as-shit Russian vodka. Nice. I would get a good buzz.

Before I poured my second glass, I had three blondes that couldn't find their way out of a wet paper bag draped all over me, and I was feeling good. I didn't need to think about the stupid marriage thing, just the females sitting in my lap at the moment.

Blonde number one lifted my fourth glass to my lips, tilting it back as she whispered in my ear all the things she wanted to do to my dick while blonde number two was stroking me, and blonde number three was dancing to the music in front of me, giving me a show.

Blonde number two, being the sneaky minx she was, unzipped my pants. I was totally down until that fourth drink hit me, and I needed to relieve myself. I got up, and the girls all wanted to come with me, but I wasn't into piss play, so I declined and told them to wait for me.

I made my way over to the bathroom on the other end of the room in the opposite corner. *Why the fuck was the bathroom so far away from me.* I went in and made it quick, wanting to get this four-way started.

I washed my hands and walked out, feeling a little more clear headed but buzzed enough to make bad decisions. As soon as I stepped out the door, I saw a secluded booth to the left just like mine, but it was up close to the DJ, almost like you would have a front row seat of what he was doing.

[1] The DJ wasn't what caught my eye. It was the swaying hips of the sexiest woman I have ever seen, and I was only looking at her backside. Her hands were on the railing as she danced with the talent of a seasoned pole dancer but gave off a fuck-off attitude I found enticing. Her perfect hourglass shape was like my wet dream, partnered with white hair, and my buzzed mind told me she was the one. The one I needed to be on top of, or underneath, tonight.

---

1. Song: Cant Get You out of my head by Ugg'A

The one that could make me forget about my worries for the night.

She was wearing this black silk little number, backless and short, which had slits up either side that went up to her hips. My wolf came to the surface, taking over my eyes as they stayed glued to the moving ass I was eighty percent sure wasn't wearing any underwear. My wolf growled in a low tone, pushing me to grab this woman and take her home, but I pushed him back. *We are doing this my way.*

I walked up behind her, her fragrance of sugared jasmine partnered with a coppery tinge of blood permeated the air. *Vampire.* I almost rethought my approach as it made me think about tomorrow's mess of a day, but then she shook her hips from side to side, bent over to the floor, ass up, giving me a peek of that bare pink pussy before she rolled back up, my eyes zeroed in on that ass, and my dick kicked my head out, taking over my feet as I made my way over to her.

When she knew I was behind her, she missed a beat, but she must've decided she didn't care because she didn't stop her movements. I slipped my hands around her hips as I leaned close to her ear and whispered, "Your body was calling me like a siren. Is that what you are?"

She puffed out a laugh before the beat changed to something with more pop, and she pushed her ass further onto my half-hard dick to the beat. "No, but I could be your siren for the night."

My wolf begged me to soak her scent into his nostrils, clawing at my mind to get closer to her. To appease him, I trailed my nose along her neck, and she gasped at the touch. I smiled as I kissed her bare shoulder, savoring the taste of her dewy skin. Fuck, I already knew this was going to be good.

I played with the top of the slit in her dress, fingering that silky material as I envisioned tearing it off her body and fucking her right here and now. She kept swaying her hips, causing my dick to grow painful in my pants with each side-to-side motion. My fingers dug into her hips, my wolf's claws came out, gripping her so hard they punctured her skin. I waited for a beat to see if I went too far, but she just lay back onto me with a sigh, and I knew I could keep going. I let go of one side, trailing my hand up to cup her heavy breast, and she moaned.

Fuck, she was not wearing a bra, either. Not only was her body made for carnal desires, but her voice was like a burning whiskey that went down smooth but made you crave more to chase that high. I tugged on her pebbled nipple, and she panted harder for me.

Her hand snaked up behind her, her fingers sliding through my hair like she was made to do it. I purred against her neck, loving the feel of her. I tried to tug her around, to kiss her and see her face, but she was like stone and didn't budge.

Before I could say a word, she tilted her lips up and whispered against my chin, "I want you to fuck me, Mr. Stranger. I want you to lift the back of this dress and slide that fat cock into my wet and waiting pussy. I want you to fuck me in front of this sea of people like we own the joint." She chuckled, but she could be right. I didn't know if the Syndicate owned this place or not. "You game?"

It sounded like a dare, and buzzed Ax didn't fuck around. I pulled back and smacked her ass in response, and she bent over the rail and groaned. I lifted that flap she called the back of her dress and shoved two fingers into her, claws and all. She was right, she was already wet for me, but I wanted her to be dripping. I wanted her to soak my claws with her juices. Since we were going to do this stranger-style, I wanted her pussy to do the talking, wanted it to beg for my cock to pound into her, giving her exactly what she needed.

I curled my fingers, making sure the pad hit that spot inside of her while I unzipped my pants, and she cried out as soon as the DJ raised the beat high. With my booze-dazed mind, the beat thumping in my veins, and smells of sex and sweat taking over my senses, I ripped my fingers out of her, licked at her wetness combined with her blood on my claws before I lined myself up, thrusting into her deep and hard. Her body shook at the onslaught, but her scream of pleasure told me all I needed to know. This dirty little siren liked it. She liked the thought of people watching us, she liked knowing she got me hard quickly, and she liked the smells and the sounds of the club around us like it was cheering us on.

I grabbed onto her white hair and yanked her back as I whispered into her ear, "You like this, Siren? You like being my dirty, bloody, naughty girl? You like this cock pounding into your wet pussy like it was made for me?"

"Yes," she panted out. "I want more." She rolled the r, and I knew I needed to kick it up a notch. I let go of her hair and grabbed her ass, carved my way into her hip, and red trails followed my claws. I wanted to mark her, to own her, to make it so my hands, my dick, and my fucking presence were ingrained in her soul. My wolf lit up inside for a split second before I let one arm snake up between her breasts and grabbed her throat, squeezing as I pushed in hard and deep. Her choked gasps made the wolf in me want to explode out and rut her into the ground.

Her gasps of air were the only things my ears could focus on as her pussy clenched around my dick, gripping it so tightly I was barely able to pull out, so I shoved in deeper. My hand on her hip let go and went to her clit, giving it a couple quick rubs before I pinched it. Her raw and primal scream was fucking everything as she gushed around my cock.

I pistoned in and out of her as fast as I could, her hair flying around us due to my rapid, rough pace, but she panted, "Yes. Fuck. Fuck that cum right out of me. Fuck me through my orgasm."

As soon as she said her last syllable, I roared out my release, the music drowning out my howl as my cum shot into her, and I rested my forehead against her back. We were panting, trying to catch our breaths from this amazing fuck. She moved forward and then slammed her ass right back into me, essentially fucking herself with my cock as she moaned. Fuck, this woman was something special.

I kissed her neck before I grabbed onto a breast and pushed myself in nice and deep for one last thrust before I pulled out. My wolf and dick both pissed at me for leaving their new favorite place in this world. She smoothed down her dress as I envisioned my cum leaking out of her and down her thighs. I liked that thought, I liked it very much.

Before I could say anything, she used her vampire speed to circle around to my back, her lips grasping my ear, making my legs weak for a moment before she said, "Thanks for the good fuck, big guy." Then she licked the shell of my ear, grazing it with her teeth, which had my dick hardening and ready for round two. Then I felt the rush of air around me. I turned around and my little siren was gone. My wolf howled, missing her already. *Fucking damn it.* My new mission was to find that fucking woman.

I focused on my still-present claws, claws that still had her blood on them, and I licked them clean. Her blood was now in my system, and once I hunted for her, there would be no hiding from me.

CHAPTER 5

FALCON

It was a quiet plane ride from Texas to Las Vegas. My father and I were in a small private plane, tablets in our laps as we worked on our own projects. This was how we spent most of our time together, buried in projects, paperwork, reports, and analytics. It was how our minds worked.

At first, I always thought being the mages in the all-powerful Syndicate was a disadvantage, that it was why we needed to infuse technology with magic, just to keep up with our counterparts.

We were not as fast as vampires, we were not as strong as werewolves, and we were not as powerful as the fae. Well, as powerful in type of magic. While the fae and the mages both worked with magic sources, it was like we pulled it from different pools.

The fae's magic came from within. It would manifest from their core or their soul. It was why illusion magic and its various forms were at the heart of their power. The few that had abilities beyond simple illusions still had the core of it about themselves. What they liked to do, what they were gifted at. It was dependent on each individual. Mage magic was different as it came from the earth. All mages had elemental magic: earth, water, air, fire, and spirit. Some very gifted mages had a combination of two, like my father, but I was the only known mage with three affinities.

While most of my young life I felt like our counterparts were much more magical and mystical than us humans with elemental magic, I quickly learned this was not the case if you put your magic to good use.

For one, the fae only had that specific form of magic, where with elemental magic, we could make anything out of our magic. If a fire mage wanted to make a flaming needle or a fire elephant, they could. It was up to our imagination what we created with the magic we had.

My father was proficient in earth and spirit, which gave him the intuition to start developing weapons with our magic. With his spirit magic, he could see glimpses of the future and have intuition that was always correct. He saw a far future world that let the Syndicate know we would need elevated weapons that channeled our magic. That was the start of our weapon crafting, and it exploded from there.

It also helped that his son was gifted in air, water, and fire magic. Between the two of us, we were a powerhouse as far as mages went, and most fell into line behind us. We both had analytical and focused minds, both interested in furthering our reach in the world, and both liked to tinker with things, which made weapon crafting with technology come naturally to us, but it also made us awkward and not very social people.

We have tons of colleagues, coworkers, and acquaintances, but neither of us make much of a connection to people past that point. Past the point of them being useful. In the case of my father, I have to exclude the Syndicate leaders. My father has always told me they were like brothers to him, and whenever I heard him talk to them, he seemed more at ease and comfortable. When I saw him after one of their conversations, there was a softness in his eyes and a small quirk to his mouth. This was something I didn't understand. Especially when it came from the man who taught me to be as ruthless and cunning as himself.

I have always had a hard time finding value in friendship. It seemed like you had to risk a lot with a possible reward, and I didn't like those odds. I didn't play with maybes. I liked exact measurements, and if it was not seventy-five percent or more probability, I didn't even want to entertain the idea. It didn't seem logical or a good business sense.

My father called the stewardess, asking for a Jack and Coke, and I lifted my head, asking for the same. As soon as she left, we glanced at each other for a second. The unease in the air at our stagnant natures was growing until my father pointed at my tablet.

"How is the FNX45 model coming?" His hesitant tone almost made me laugh. Does talking with my father always have to be this weird? It's not like we don't know how the other acts. Sometimes I felt like Mom was the only one who made us connect. I shook my head from those thoughts because we were all we had, and I needed to make an effort like he was. For her.

I cleared my throat after I took a sip of my drink and set it down. "It's going fine. I have finally perfected the bullets and how much each substance needs to be in each. I just need to perfect the actual gun now, make modifications to it to trigger the specific bullets when required."

He nodded. "Yes. That would make it the optimum weapon. It would also be nice to have some sort of fingerprint safety on it."

I grabbed my tablet, jotting that down. "That's a good idea. It would make for less misfires, as well as make it hot and ready when you needed it to be."

We smiled at each other for a second before we shifted away from each other with unease. I reminded myself he was the first one to ask about my project, so I should talk to him in kind. We took a long hard drink at the same time before I asked, "And you? What about your security system?"

He straightened in his seat, excitement sparkled in his eyes as he picked up his tablet and pressed a few things before he handed it over to me. "If you look right here, we have finally found a way to be able to capture the speed of a vampire on video. That has been the hardest thing to catch from security, and with the optics and new upgraded motion sensors I tested, we had our first successful trial."

I clicked play on the surveillance video, watching a vampire move like they were walking. The only thing that tipped me off I was watching this at hyper speed was the background moving in slow motion. The leaves on the tree were moving at a glacial pace when a second ago they were blowing in the wind like normal.

"That is amazing, Father." His smile widened into something a little on the goofy side as I called out in awe. This was huge. No one has been able to capture vampire speed, let alone on camera. It was one of their biggest advantages, and even though the Desmond clan was one of the major vampire houses and head family of the Syndicate, there were still other vampire families, mainly in Europe, that were threats to our organization.

"Yes. This was one of the things I wanted to show the other heads. To show them where all their money has been going. It took a lot of cultivation of air magic, as well as the best lasers and lenses that are not even manufactured yet, created in our own labs, of course. Which means that I really wouldn't want to make it accessible to anyone else—"

"But the Syndicate houses, right?" I said as I handed him back his tablet.

"Exactly. It takes a lot out of the air mages to make one, and I only really want to do that for my brothers and their families." He tucked the tablet into his jacket, and I smiled.

"It will just make us that much more powerful. Having one-of-a-kind security and weapons." He nodded to my tablet, knowing weapons were more my passion. "It will make it so what happened to your mothers and the Devils won't happen again." He looked out the window, lost in thought like he always was when he talked about that day.

When my mother died, she took the flame of his life with her. He was depressed for a lot of my childhood. I think that was another reason we didn't know each other well. I was practically raised by reading and the maids.

I used to hear them talk about how worried they were that he wasn't eating, wasn't drinking. That his magic was getting weaker and weaker by the second. At a young age, I had been proficient in air and water, but once I hit thirteen, I manifested fire, like my mother. After my father heard of this, he started eating again and asked to see me. I remembered thinking he looked so weak and frail, but as his eyes met mine, he teared up. He apologized for being a bad father, for not doing what was best for my mother's son. He made more effort to get better and did more in the labs. He had a new renewed interest, to make sure this never happened again. To make sure his mistakes never happened again.

I was glad for my father to improve, for him to continue and make amazing and great things . . . but a secret part of me was angry about what he said that day. That he wanted to live for *her* son, not his son. It still wasn't about me, it was ensuring her legacy kept going. I know I should be happy my father loved my mother so much, but it made me angry. It made it so I never wanted to meet someone who made me feel that way.

I have never been a ladies' man, never been big into wining and dining them, even as they threw themselves at me for status and money. I wasn't a virgin or anything, but it was always a transaction for me. Always something logical like fulfilling a body's need, releasing energy, clearing my mind. It was never about who I was with, and it was definitely not about feelings. I didn't have a type because I didn't care enough. I viewed it as a two-person transaction, nothing else. That didn't mean I was bad at the deed.

I realized quickly the more I pleasured the women, the less likely they would be upset when I told them this was a one-time thing. Sure, there were some that wanted more, but when I gave them my face devoid of any emotions, they knew. They could tell themselves that at least they got theirs. That they used me for something, and I didn't mind that.

"I have to talk to you about something else," my father said, facing me, his hands folded and his face tight. This was the leader of the Winstale clan, the shrewd planner and beyond logical thinker of the leadership, always pulling up numbers and statistics for the best outcome.

I matched his stance, nodding for him to continue. Where my father uses his logical side as a mask, one he gladly adopts, I used it as my whole being. Always thinking in numbers and statistics. Weighing out the benefits and the losses. Logic was always what won out in the end anyway.

"There is another reason we are meeting with the others this time, one that has to do with the future of the Syndicate and is why we are all bringing our heirs to the meeting." Now I was intrigued. Usually, we were not allowed in their meetings, only the bosses could talk to each other about Syndicate business. They made decisions without outside forces around and then relayed it to us.

I stayed quiet, waiting for whatever he wanted to say to come out before I responded. "You know all of us have sons besides the head family, the Desmonds, who have a girl." I nodded slowly, remembering that wild and crass little girl with fire in her rose gold eyes and a savagery you could feel vibrating around her, but that meant nothing now. It has been twenty-two years, a lot had changed for all of us, and she could now just be another rich gangster princess in this world, not scared of anyone as she has the Syndicate behind her.

"Well, we went round and round about it, and her father had this idea to have one of you three marry her. This way, we could strengthen the Syndicate with not only money and friendship but blood and family." His eyes drilled into mine as he continued. "The idea was to have you all hang out, get to know one another. Create a bond that will solidify the four of you and then tie two clans together, making the four of you an unstoppable force."

I saw he was trying to assess me. Trying to glean what I thought about this plan, see if he could tell how I felt about it, but I felt nothing. I have never met any of them except at the funeral all those years ago. Meeting up with them and assessing their strengths and weaknesses would help me accept this plan. If they were acceptable partners, I saw no issues with this plan, I even saw the validity and how we could be just what the four of them had hoped for us to be—a strong, unbeatable group.

I leaned back, settling into my seat, not showing anything as I responded, "That sounds like a good plan. I look forward to meeting them all."

My father eyed me up and down. "And the girl? The marriage?"

I almost laughed because I was one hundred percent positive she would pick one of the others. Just like I had made a promise not to let a woman affect me like my mother did with my father, I was sure she didn't want some socially inept weapons nerd on her arm. In fact, the only thing I knew about the girl was that she had put in a special request with our lab for a small, compact, personal parachute that worked as she jumped off city buildings. I took on the project because it would be a challenge. Getting a thing like that to be ultra compact and precise and narrow enough to go between buildings and not hit the ground too hard was exciting. I enjoyed that project, but the woman who would want that, I was sure was not into being in a lab all day, going over statistics and numbers. No, she would pick one of the others, so I didn't need to worry about it.

"Well, that is up to her, right?" I replied. He tilted his head, not buying my calm demeanor, but what did he expect? For me to freak out? That would be ridiculous.

"And if she picks you?" His question caught me off guard because it would be ridiculous, but in the one percent chance that would happen . . . "If she does, then that means I would have the head family's backing to go forward with all of my ideas. I could see the positive in that." That answer seemed to appease him as he nodded.

We didn't talk again until the plane landed, which was almost midnight, but we had cars waiting for us. He still wanted to go check on the Vegas underground lab the Desmonds made for him as the headquarters for the Syndicate and where most of our stuff was produced. I told him I needed to test out some theories about the

FNX45. I would not sleep much anyway, thinking about the schematics and formulas until I got it right.

We said goodbye and agreed to meet at the villa the Desmonds set up for us by their casino at 2:00 a.m. as I was putting into my phone where the nearest, still-open gun range was. It was my luck that there was only one open. I put it into my GPS and drove there as fast as I could. If I hurried, I could get in a few rounds before they wanted to close for the night.

I caught the door before the guy closed, asking him for a few rounds before he shut down for the night. He reluctantly agreed, saying he already had one of his regulars shooting for a few rounds, why not add one more.

Slipping him a couple hundred dollars, he perked right up, asking if I needed anything or if he could be of assistance. I shifted my bag on my shoulder, telling him it was fine, and he told me I could pick any lane as long as it wasn't next to the other person at the end. Seemed like a weird request, but I wouldn't do that anyway.

I skipped putting on the earmuffs because I wanted to hear how the gun loaded and any kinks I should figure out, but all that went out the window when the pop, pop, pop, pop reverberated down from the person shooting at the end.

I peeked over, as it sounded like a glock with an extended mag, and lo and behold, it was. They pulled out a beautiful custom matte-black FN P90 with a rose gold inlay. I always wanted to play around with an SMG, submachine gun, but my father wanted me to focus on pistols and rifles. I appreciated the durability, ease, and magazine size of an SMG, which was why my eyes kept drifting toward the lane at the end.

The person faced their target and let the bullets fly, one after another, in such a rhythm it felt like it was its own deadly song. If I closed my eyes, I could feel the fire ignite as the pin pushed on the bullet, causing a small controlled explosion that propelled the bullet forward. It was like music to my ears. I loved the sounds weapons made. You could always count on a weapon, and if it sounded off, you could always figure out what was going on with it.

I shook my head, telling myself to focus on my own equipment like I came here to do. Loading and unloading my gun soothed my soul, the repetition and exacting motions were like second nature. I loaded them with dummy bullets that acted like the specialized ones I was making. I wanted the same effect without the magical aspect. Knowing how the magic worked, I needed to make sure the mechanics were as fine-tuned.

After a few shots, I could tell it was pulling to the left. I tried to adjust my stance, finger the trigger differently. Hell, I even tried it horizontal instead of vertical, but it came out the same. Slamming the whole damn thing down with a bang, I turned away from it, needing to think. I was too pissed the fucking tool wasn't working how I wanted it to. Its accuracy needed to be consistent or else the demonstration would be dismal.

I turned around, thinking I needed to try it all over again. Maybe I needed to clean it first? My whole body turned rigid as I saw it was taken apart, piece by piece, by this woman looking down the barrel.

"What the fuck?" I snapped, letting this person know with my tone I was not one to be fucked with. Her barely there silky black dress made her appear as if she had just walked out of the club and was in the wrong place, but she had leggings underneath, and I knew she had some sense of intelligence to think that far ahead. Everything above the waist was on display, her curves, her creamy pale arms, and her athletic build. Her breasts and hips were larger than normal for that type of body, but you couldn't miss the fact her arms and legs were sculpted like they were made out of marble. Her frosty hair was pulled up into a tight, serious ponytail. What made it really weird was that she had on tinted shooter glasses that concealed her eyes more than made it clear to see.

She responded in a low sultry voice, "I saw that you were pulling to the left and throwing a fit, so I thought I could help you out. I know a lot about guns."

"I know a lot about guns, too," I snapped back like I couldn't help myself. I wanted this person to know I was not an idiot and took care of my own guns, but it didn't faze her as she continued scanning each piece.

"You have to check the pieces for rust first." I mean, I knew that, but it was my gun, and I knew there wasn't any rust in it. My irritation rose by the second.

"Can you even put it back together?" It came out more like a sneer, which I didn't mean, but still, I didn't like being intruded on like this.

I almost swallowed all of my words when she put it back together in under ten seconds. Then she slammed it on the table and glared at me, I think, but I couldn't really tell with the dark shooting glasses over her eyes. "How many rounds has it run through?"

"Excuse me?" The shock on my face from her question had her cocking her hip out and tilting her head like she thought I was some invalid.

She repeated her sentence in a slow, exaggerated way that had my teeth grinding. "Hooowww mmaaanny rrooouunnnddds—"

"Four thousand. Give or take a hundred," I snapped before she finished insulting me.

She straightened up. "Oh. Well, that's why." The complete confidence in her statement had me hesitate, and I raised my eyebrow in response. She smiled, and her vampire fangs peeked out before she explained, "After three thousand rounds, the gun starts to have inconsistencies that even cleaning and good upkeep won't prevent. You can always get aftermarket parts, but I don't recommend that because then you can have a whole set of other issues."

Fucking damn it! I knew that. I did, but my brain was so focused on the bullets that I wasn't thinking about the longevity of the actual tool. I lifted my hand, calling forth my fire and instructing it to stay in a ball form. She tensed up for a second, switching her foot stance for a fight. I rolled my eyes and told the ball to go down to the end, stay for about ten seconds and then come back.

I watched as it sailed over her head and lit up her booth with ease. I was mildly shocked to see a whole arsenal of artillery. She had several handguns—different shapes, sizes, and attachments—lined up on the table behind her. She also had two rifles and the FN P90 I was eyeing earlier. This woman knew her guns.

As the fireball came and settled back into my hand, she let out a puff of awe before she closed her mouth and crossed her arms like she wasn't impressed. I pinched my lips before sliding the gun over to her. "What do you propose I do?" Since it seemed like she was an expert in this field, I wouldn't mind taking her advice.

"Well, what are you wanting to do with it?" She pointed to the gun, and I hesitated to tell her anything. This was a secret project, after all, but she seemed to know what she was talking about.

"Well . . . I am conducting experiments on the bullets, but I need the gun to be accurate before I do that." Her head moved up and down, and an uncomfortable frustration at not being able to see her eyes, to be able to judge her thoughts, built up inside of me. I was so vexed with communications with people, I found early on in life I read them better if I could see their eyes and body movements. I found key traits that told what the person was thinking without ever asking them, but the eyes were a big part of it, and it was like she was shielding herself from me. It made me want to dig in deeper.

"If that's the case, then I think you should start out with a new gun. Like I said, you don't want different parts, and if you are wanting accuracy, you should work with a gun that has less than a thousand rounds run through it. Any real gun owner knows there is normal wear and tear on a gun and can make the necessary judgments on how to aim better when that happens . . ." She left her sentence hanging, and I motioned for her to keep going. "If you are changing the bullets, then why does it have to fit this specific gun?"

I thought about it for a second before I answered, "Because I want to make further modifications to this piece." This time, she moved her hand for me to continue. I did, even though I made my sentence at a full stopping period. I inhaled. "Some modifications to the grip and maybe the sights."

She nodded like she thought so. "I think my question still applies. Gun owners are an odd breed and like their own brands for different reasons. If you pick about three of the major ones, you can make the modifications, and it still works for many different grips and styles of shooting. This way you won't have to worry so much about the specifics until you get to the implementing stage. You could show whoever you want to show with any of the three brands and still have good results while giving them the illusion of options and preference."

I kept my mouth shut and nodded, not making any firm stances, but what she said made a lot of sense. I'm sure not everyone in the Syndicate used the same handgun, but if I got a few different styles, it was more likely I could run tests with different groups down the road and get a lot better data for improvements.

She turned to leave, and I found that a small piece of me didn't want her to. I found her information valuable, and she didn't bother me with unnecessary questions or chitchat. The whole conversation was very factual, something I enjoyed. Before she took a step, my curiosity got the best of me, and I asked her, "Why do you shoot with tinted glasses?"

She chuckled before she slowly turned around. "Why? So I can practice being impaired. When I find that I need to up my game or have a challenge, I like to intentionally impair myself to see how I do, then make adjustments slowly to increase my accuracy. Today was visual impairment day."

I was starting to find this woman more and more fascinating by the second. Done with the question, she turned and walked back to her area, picked up a pistol, and began shooting. I studied her form, and it was damn near impeccable.

After a few minutes, the shop owner came in and scurried toward her, waited behind her like a dog while she was shooting, then tapped the table when she was done. She switched her gaze over her shoulder to him, and he said something quietly to her before she nodded, replied, and he scurried out.

I wondered what that was about until she walked up to my side, doing the same as him and waited for me to finish before tapping the table. I looked at her in question, and she said, "The owner had to leave, but he knows me and trusts me to lock up. Let me know when you're done." I was mid-nod until I saw the FN P90 in her hands, and I stared.

She must've noticed the drool nearly coming out because she chuckled and lifted it in my direction. "Want to try it?"

I hesitated, not used to people letting me use their toys, especially not a gun enthusiast. I went to grab it, my fingers twitched in anticipation, but she quickly pulled it back, and my heated gaze snapped up to hers, pissed she would play a trick like that on me.

She wagged her fingers. "Not like that. She's not just some bargain-dollar hooker. This is a prime piece of artwork, handcrafted and put together by the weapons god himself." I rolled my eyes as she moved over into my box. "Here is where you—"

"I know how to work a gun," I threw out, irritation getting the better of me, again. It was a weird experience for me to keep bouncing between excitement and vexation with another being.

She stopped what she was doing and turned to face me. "Look, buddy. I was trying to be nice, show you something I'm very proud of, and thought that as another tools enthusiast, you would enjoy basking in the glory that is this gem." She trailed her finger down the barrel lightly before snapping out. "But if you start getting snippy with me, then I can just take my happy ass back over to my booth and be done with it." The bite to her words reminded me she had something I wanted, and that meant that she was in control. I took a deep breath and calmed myself as I opened my eyes back up.

"Show me," was all I said, and I waited patiently for her to tell me what she wanted.

Her lips curved up before she turned back to her gun. "You see this here? Just make sure when you fire, you don't let your hand be loose here because it can blow back and hit this button, which would be a no-no. Got it?"

I nodded and waited patiently for her to hand it over. As soon as she did, I lifted it, but she hovered around like a mother hen. Before I shot one bullet off, she came up and slid her hand up my shoulder as she positioned the butt of the gun at a specific spot on my shoulder. I was about to tell her to get her hands off me when her silky voice vibrated my ear. "That's the best spot for you. Less of a recoil." As quickly as she came, she let me go and was leaning against the back wall. The scent of Mogra wafted in the air, causing my senses to overload.

I took a deep breath, still feeling the traces of her fingers up the side of my arm as it tingled where she'd touched. Never before had I felt something like that. I shoved it away and refocused on the task at hand. I pulled the trigger and let the bullets fly in rapid succession until the magazine was empty.

It was a rush, feeling all those bullets leave in rapid succession. Knowing if anyone was in front of you, they would be dead faster than you could count to five. It's the only thing that gave me any true emotions, holding a weapon and knowing I had a person's life in my hands. Knowing at any moment, I got to choose what happened to them and how it happened. It was the ultimate control that filled my veins with joy. Made me feel like a god.

My chest rose and fell, the come down from all the excitement had me in a daze until a clapping sound came from behind me. I looked over at the smiling vampire girl, even with her eyes covered, I could tell she enjoyed the show.

She stood up next to me and pointed at my target. "Look! All in the second ring and a few in the first, and it was your first time with it." She looked down at the gun and sighed. "She's amazing, isn't she."

I nodded, just watching her stare at the gun lovingly pulled me to this woman. She knew weapons, she didn't waste time with idle chatter, she seemed comfortable in her own skin, and wasn't afraid to speak her mind. I was impressed by her and a little jealous of her at the same time. Of how she could talk to someone she never met before and find some common ground.

She tilted her head up at me, and I quickly glanced away as I shoved the gun into her hands. Trying to cover up my embarrassment as I walked over to my gun. I took it apart to put it in its case. "Thank you. I think I'm done for the night."

"Oh." She sounded a little disappointed but turned around and walked over to her booth down the way. I knew I could've just left, bolted out the door to leave her to lock up, but I didn't know this part of the city well, and I didn't want to see her body mangled up in the paper the next morning. Knowing if I had just gotten over myself for a second, she would've still been alive. So, I waited for her at the door.

She had a lot to pack up. I almost went over to ask if I needed to carry the huge bag that was about her size, but then she hoisted it up over her shoulder like it was nothing and walked my way. I held the door open, and she mumbled her thanks. She went to the store counter as I closed the range room door. She swiped some keys and nodded to the front door.

We walked out in silence, unease and tension was now there when it wasn't before. This was why I didn't do people. I hated this. I mean, sure, I liked it when I was telling someone what to do or intimidating someone, but when I was just minutes ago enjoying her company for it to change to this was a little torturous.

She turned to lock the door, and, like an idiot, I set my bag down to see if she needed help with hers while she got the door. Like a flash before my eyes, someone swooped up my bag and took off.

Before I could say a word, the vampire girl dropped everything she had with a loud clunk and took off after the little vampire thief. I was about to run after them when I heard a dragging sound, and when I raised my hand with a ball of fire to light up the dark street, she was hauling an unconscious body behind her.

As she stepped closer into my light, she set the body on its knees, grabbed his head, and yanked it to the side as she reared her head up before she bit into him like a savage, spilling blood everywhere as the vampire thief's eyes shot open. Once he saw me in front of him, glaring, he pissed his pants.

She released him, kicked him into the ground as she pulled out a handgun from fuck knows where and put it to the back of his head. "Now, tell me you're not stupid enough to steal from the Syndicate, are you?"

The vampire on the ground froze, his whole body shook in fear as he whispered out, "I . . . I . . . I didn't know. I s-s-swe-ear. I would never."

It took me a second, but I immediately grabbed my gun and pointed it at her. I still couldn't see her eyes, but I could tell she was annoyed as she exhaled and stuck out her hip. I barked out, "I never told you anything about me being with the Syndicate." Suspicion clouded my judgment as I berated myself for falling for her wiles. I bet she planned this, maybe scoped me out at the airport and heard where I was going.

"Hey, dipshit," she responded as I glared at her, fire lining my hands as I kept my gun pointed at her. She lowered her gun, stomped on the vampire thief and told him to stay down as she took a few steps up to me. She slowly wrapped her fingers around my hand with the gun. The hand that was on fire, and I almost yelled at her to let go, to not touch it because she would get hurt, but she kept going.

Once her whole hand covered mine, she rested the gun to her forehead, not even flinching at my fire. "You think I would betray the Syndicate? You can shoot me now if that's what you think, but I would advise you in the future to not have *our* symbol on your bag if you didn't want people to know. People around here know to fear that symbol. Right, thief?" She threw that last part out over her shoulder to the quaking body still face down in the street.

"Yes! The bag was turned around, and I didn't see the skull with the star and money signs. I swear. I swear. P-p-pl-l-lea-ase, don't kill m-e-e-e-e. Please, sir." He was making a sobbing mess on the ground with his pathetic spit dripping out. Fuck, this thief was pathetic. I should just shoot him now for being annoying, but this vampire girl was taking up all my attention.

I slowly lowered my gun, knowing that what she said was true. She saw the symbols, knew we were not the ones to be fucked with. It made sense. What didn't make sense was that when I looked at her hand, it wasn't a charred mess. It was perfectly fine. My fire did nothing to her, and that was . . . impossible.

A ringing sounded, and she cussed as she pulled out her phone from her pocket and mumbled about needing to go. Before I could open my mouth to tell her to stop, I had more questions for her, she used her vampire speed to zoom to the shop, lock the door, pick up her bag of guns, and zoom over to her bike.

"Wait. What is—" The revving of her bike covered my voice, and she was gone in a flash. "What was your name?" I said to the wind, knowing I wouldn't get an answer.

"That was Rayla, sir." I sharply turned around to face the vampire thief still on the ground.

"What did you say?" I stalked over to him, looming over him like the grim reaper himself. I wasn't paying attention to him earlier, but I was now.

He held out his hands like he could prevent me from hurting him as he cried out, "Rayla. That was Rayla Desmond. The heir to the Desmond clan. There is not a single being inside of the city that doesn't know who she is."

I took a deep breath. Rayla Desmond. Well, isn't that interesting. Interesting that the girl meant to pick one of us for a marriage alliance, one I was not even remotely interested in, was the very girl that made me curious about her.

I stared down at the cowering vampire and knew what I would have to do. I lifted my hand and a shot rang out, consuming the vampire in flames. He cried out, wailing, and I knew I couldn't have that, so I flicked my fingers and called on my water magic. I watched as it filled his throat, staying concentrated there so he wouldn't be able to scream, choking to death as my fire consumed his body. He only twitched for a few minutes before the flames did their job and reduced him to ashes. Best part about fire magic was no cleanup. It was very efficient.

I picked up my weapons case and turned toward my car, hesitating for a second as I looked down the road Miss Desmond disappeared down. Tomorrow would be interesting indeed.

CHAPTER 6

WHOEVER TOLD YOU THAT vampires slept like the dead were fucking lying and should be burned in hellfire and pulled apart by minotaurs.

With the sunset streaming through the slit in my curtains, I snarled and cursed at it as I woke up a little cranky and ready to fuck some shit up after the couple of days I'd had.

It was a myth that vampires couldn't handle sunlight, that it would burn us up from the inside out, and we would crumble to dust. Sure, we preferred the cool darkness of night, our night vision was way better. It had something to do with our regenerative properties working slower during the day, making us slightly weaker, and vampires didn't do weak.

It was the same misunderstanding that werewolves only change with the full moon. They recharged under the moon's rays and had a few holidays surrounding the moon, but that was it. They could shift whenever they wanted.

Mages were not devil worshippers in disguise. In fact, they were in tune with nature, so in tune that nature gifted them and their lineage with the power over the elements and knowledge about casting they kept tight-lipped.

And the fae didn't have pointy ears . . . and it was my understanding they stopped snatching up humans for their amusement and life force, even before the Awakening. They now siphon little sips of life force when they work in the clubs or major entertainment. I know of a few that have found their mates and didn't even need the sips of life force anymore. They sustained cycling through the mate bond.

Oh, and not all demons had horns, only the higher-leveled ones, and even then they rarely had them on display. Most demons now weren't even born in hell, only the really old ones knew about hell and its landscape after the Awakening, sustaining their life down there while most other demons needed humans for either their blood, lust vapors, or their soul. The demon type determines what they need. Some made deals for souls, some worked in the sex trade, and some did assassin work for the blood. Souls, sex, and blood fueled demon's powers.

I slipped out of my soft Egyptian cotton bed, upset it didn't give me the restful sleep it usually did, and went to put on long johns and a baggy shirt before I went down to the kitchen. It wasn't like I wore a nighty or anything to bed, but when I went down in my matching black silk booty shorts and cami, Cosmo threw a fit. I tried to prove him wrong a while back, and that backfired when a couple of the clan members walking around eyed me up and down. One even ran into a wall. Before Cosmo could reprimand him, I laid into them. I let the whole house know if they ever looked at me sideways again, I would fucking decimate them before I had my first bloody sip of the day. No one made that mistake again after that.

I walked down the stairs, thinking about yesterday. When my dad called me home in the wee hours, interrupting my fun with my idiot ex, he sat me down and told me all of the Syndicate was coming to town for a meeting. I blew up at him, of course, for not plugging me into this any sooner, but he waved me off with a smile. Telling me I had nothing to worry about, and he had taken care of everything.

When I calmed down, I asked him why they were having an in-person meeting in the first place. He said something about wanting to strengthen the bonds, see old friends, and get a real pulse on what each family was doing. Also to have all their kids meet so we were not all strangers when it was time for us to take over. It all seemed above board, but I got this feeling I wasn't getting the whole story.

Before I could grill him on it, he told me to go to bed, and as soon as I woke up, he would have Cosmo take me to my appointments. When I asked him what fucking appointments, he giggled and said he set me up for the works. I was going to a spa for any and all the treatments I wanted, then I would get my hair and nails done, then, afterward, Rick would take me shopping. I yelled at my dad, telling him I didn't need to get all dolled up for these fuckos. He smiled and nodded through my rant and told me he just wanted me to relax, not worry about anything, because the hard work would happen after we all met. He said that he expected me to take the boys out and show them how we run things. I quickly calmed down because he was right that a calm and relaxed me would make a better host. So, I went to bed and did all my appointments the next day without a fuss.

Cosmo didn't complain once as he took me everywhere. I told him I could take myself, but he insisted on being there, especially now that the other Syndicate leaders were coming into town. He said trouble followed me, or I made trouble, and he wanted to do damage control as soon as it happened. I rolled my eyes and let him come. It was no sweat off my back. Then, when Rick joined us, he had a field day. Rick enjoyed shopping more than I did and went around the store, picked out everything I should try on, and shoved me into a dressing room for a fashion show.

They both sat down in front of the three-way mirror as I came out. Cosmo always said nothing, but he didn't have to. I could tell by the expressions he gave what I should and shouldn't get. If he looked like he was pleased, it was a no-go, if he looked like he was pissed, then it was a yes, and if he glared around to make sure there was not another man in the store, then it was a hell yes.

The boys helped me carry my bags into the car as Rick and I convinced Cosmo to stop for ice cream. At the ice cream shop, which served both supes and humans, I couldn't decide between the vampire bunny tracks ice cream, where the "tracks" were filled with caramel and blood, or the regular mint chocolate chip. They were both good, but I was craving that caramel blood flavor. I picked the bunny tracks, even as I looked at the mint chocolate chip with a forlorn look. I felt better when I heard Cosmo order the mint, I knew I could con him out of a few bites. Win win!

After we got back to the house, I unloaded all my clothes, and my dad asked me if he could borrow the boys for a project. I told him, "Sure," and they went with my dad. I quickly got bored without my sidekicks. I fingered all my new clothes and decided I would go out, break an outfit in. Cosmo would be pissed I went out without either him or Rick to watch my back, but I was a big girl. My brother could just suck it. I picked out the sluttiest dress Rick got me while Cosmo wasn't aware and went out to Veshta's spot, The Temptress, first, then maybe I'd make an appearance at one of the casino's clubs to end the night.

I sat in my dark booth at The Temptress and was surprised I would get a show tonight. Usually the dance shows were at the beginning of the week, since it was slower. Maybe I would see one of the regular dancers and take one into the back and see if we could play a little game I liked to call Hide The Penis.

My jaw almost dropped when I saw this stunning fae man with bubblegum-pink hair and piercing jade eyes come out on stage. Did Veshta get a new dancer? Did I dream this man into existence because my heart was pounding the second I saw him. He danced, and my eyes were glued to him. Even with his clothes on, I was almost out of my seat, gripping the cushions to keep myself in check. The way his hips rolled, his cocksure smile, and the bulge in his pants that kept catching my eye whenever he would move a certain way had me all kinds of hot and bothered. I was a weak woman for a big dick. It was my kryptonite.

Then our eyes met, and the world turned on its axis. No shit, I almost fell face-first into the table in front of me. His eyes were like shots of pure magic, luring me into them, telling me it was okay to fall in and stay there for the rest of my life. The way his skin glowed as he took off his shirt and how his poised, graceful body moved like a pro. I knew I wanted to fuck that fae man in the worst of ways.

As he began unzipping his pants, getting to the good part, my anticipation skyrocketed, and the music stopped, signaling the set was done. He took a single breath with our eyes still locked, then turned to make his way down the stairs. As soon as he turned, the spell he had me under was gone, and I remembered my promise to myself about not falling for big dicks anymore. My vagina was not the boss of me, and I had told myself no men for at least a week due to Tre's betrayal. *Ha!* My vagina was laughing at me.

I panicked when I realized if I met that man, I would definitely jump his bones right here and now because of how much he turned me on. My thighs were already rubbing together at the thought of us together.

I needed to calm down, or better yet, find some idiot with a small dick to fuck, to get the edge off, because I knew if I slept with that man tonight, I would be under his bewitchment for the rest of my life. I was not mentally prepared to take on a perfect specimen of man like that. Especially not after a breakup. So I ran.

I ran at vampire speed out of there and found myself out in front of one of the clubs off the strip and thought that dancing would take my mind off him. Who knew I would find some dark and growly stranger to bang me out on the railing, good and dirty like, giving me an even bigger high. I knew what I was doing when the strangers hands circled my waist, raising up the hem of the barely there dress. I knew what would happen even before it started, and I wanted it to. I got off on fucking right there in the club, with anyone able to watch me. Since we were supes, we didn't need to worry about anything like STD's like humans do, and I never missed my monthly shot to protect against pregnancy, so I was good to go.

Fucking a stranger was a new excitement for me. If I had to guess, I would say he was a werewolf, with his growly voice and clawed hands that made me bleed in the most pleasurable way possible. I even felt the ghost of his claw digging into my hips when I thought about it. I convinced myself if I couldn't see him, then I couldn't fall for him. Making sure I kept idiot boys at arm's length. I just buried my last boyfriend, I didn't want to mess up and make the boys dig another hole. They would be so pissed at me. Even without seeing a damn thing, I felt the passion-filled connection with this rough stranger. Like we were drawn to each other before we even knew what the other was, just two horny savages that knew we had found our forever fuck buddy.

After his big dick filled me up, making me cum so hard I saw stars, I didn't want to ruin the magic of what we did by seeing each other. With my luck, he would be a super dick and would make me have to kill him, so I left. Using my vampire speed once again, and I was gone.

It was late, but my skin was still crawling, like I was restless. I needed to do something I was good at, something that was violent and vicious. If I couldn't fuck this feeling out of me, then I needed to beat it out. I thought about the fighting rings, but they would be wrapping up by now. Then I had an idea. I ran back to my bike, which was still at Veshta's, and as soon as I sat down, Rick called. He was wondering what I was up to, so I avoided the question as I told him I needed him to grab my gun bag and a pair of leggings. Then to meet me over at old Larry's for some good old-fashioned gun-range therapy.

He groaned, of course, his perpetual state of moaning and groaning like a child, but he always did what I said. I met him outside the range and thanked him for bringing me my stuff as he hauled out my big black bag. He told me he could buy me a couple hours before Cosmo lost his shit trying to find me. I thanked him again and promised I would be back in my bed in a couple of hours, no fuss, no muss from good old Cosy.

I popped into Larry's range, got the last stall like I always did, and let it rip. I started to shoot and didn't stop until all my guns were empty. I shot out my frustration and aggression with a haze of bullets flying at my target. After my first round, the target was left in tatters on the ground, and I needed another one just to keep going. As I started to refill my clips, I saw another person at the opposite end.

I watched this posh, straightlaced-looking man out of the corner of my eye and smirked. I could tell from here he was a rigid and logical man. He had his gun laid out just so, even moving it a smidge to have it in the right spot. He lined up the bullets before he loaded the clip. It was all so regimented, and the evil kid in me wanted to swipe the table of all his organization and see what he did. Would he flip out and rage? Would he look at me calmly and threaten me? Would he try to punish me for my act?

I used my vampire speed and zoomed up next to him, taking apart his gun to find the problem. Once he noticed, he freaked out that I was all up in his business, but I knew a lot about weapons, growing up the way I did, and I knew I could find the solution to the issue. Once we were on the same page, we talked about the gun, well, I talked, and he was snippy, but I didn't mind. I kinda figured that would be the case with a guy like this, and I liked it.

We parted, when I was no longer needed, and carried on. That was until Larry scurried over, telling me his kid got into a spot of trouble with the police over a bar fight. I told him to tell the police he was one of my guys, and he would be set free within an hour. He thanked me, telling me he would never forget my kindness, and I told him he better not. He smiled at me before he scampered off to get his kid. This was the third time I was getting this kid out of trouble, and I thought maybe I should scare him straight to give Larry a break.

To try and soften the guy up, I offered to let him play with my SMG he was peeping at with a lustful expression earlier, and his eyes sparkled like a kid at Christmas. He had the butt of the gun in the wrong place, and I immediately went into fix-it mode. As soon as my hand touched his shoulder, I felt a jolt. Like electricity had coursed through my whole body.

I shook it off as I stepped back to let him shoot, and I saw his gun case had the Syndicate symbol on it. I put two and two together and realized he was one of the weapons lab workers we hired, probably trying to figure out some problem with a cool new toy he was making for us, and I was getting a sneak peak!

When he finally said that he was done for the day, I was a little bummed, surprised I enjoyed myself so much, but nodded as we packed up in silence. As we were leaving, some stupid motherfucker thought it was smart to try and steal from us. I caught him, wanting to see what he would do with a thief when he pulled his gun up at me. I wasn't scared of the mage, he would have to catch me if he wanted to kill me.

Then Cosmo started to blow up my phone, calling and texting at the same time. *How the fuck did he do that?* I sped off, getting onto my bike before we finished talking, hoping he took care of the thief himself since he thought he could raise a gun in my face.

Cosmo was already waiting outside of my room, giving me an earful as soon as my hand hit the door. Then he saw my outfit with my leggings underneath. You would've thought I had gone out naked and begged every man I saw to fuck me. When I said just that, he got mad at me and stormed out. I was so beat, I only had enough energy to get changed and then crashed for the night.

Fast forward to now, and I'm in the kitchen, grumpy and hungry, as all these men were bustling around the house to get ready for the other members of the Syndicate. I already knew we would meet them at a different location for the first meeting, but we all knew my dad would invite them over. He loved to play the host. *Fucking psycho.* Who enjoys having people over? A crazy person, that's who.

Lisa, our house manager, came over to me and clucked her tongue. "Now, Miss Rayla, you need to get a big breakfast in you for the big day. Go into the dining room with the others, and I will bring it all out." I whined out as she pushed me toward the double doors. I hated eating in the dining room, it made me feel hoity toity, and that wasn't me. I was a sit-on-the-kitchen-counter kind of girl.

As she shoved me through the doors, my dad popped up out of his seat to greet me. "Oh, my lovely little sunshine! Come, come. Sit with us for breakfast. Like a real family." I looked down the long table and only saw Cosmo on my dad's left and then a seat for me on his right.

I stumbled over to them and plopped down in my seat. Lisa set down a plate of eggs, toast, and blood jam. Then she slid over my favorite drink, hot blood chocolate with red foam on top. I quickly slurped it up, needing the sugary goodness to wake up.

Once I was finished, I looked up to my dad grinning ear to ear. "What?" I asked, wanting to get that freaky smile off his face.

"Well, my dear daughter, I'm just excited to bring you with me to this meeting today." He popped one of the grapes on his plate in his mouth, smiling at me still, but he clenched his jaw for a second. I narrowed my eyes at him, knowing he wasn't telling me something.

"What's going on?" I glanced over at Cosmo, who also had his eyes narrowed at my dad. Well, at least he wasn't involved.

"Eat, my little Ray. Eat up, get dressed, something nice preferably, then meet me at the door, and I will tell you all about it." He popped out of his seat and used his vampire speed to flee.

I yelled, "Coward!" but he was already gone, laughing as he left. I flicked my eyes over to Cosmo and pointed my butter knife at him. "What do you know?" It was a family rule that I wasn't allowed to have any knife sharper than a butter knife at the table. I was apparently a little too "willy nilly" with throwing them at people when I was eating.

He rolled his eyes as he set his toast down, annoyed at my glaring gaze. "I know as much as you."

I didn't know if I believed him, so I pressed. "Then what were you doing for him yesterday?"

He folded his arms and leaned back in his chair. "You know him. He was in one of his weird moods and wanted to do some father-son bonding"—I puffed out a chuckle as his fingers clenched his bicep—"which was just me, him, and Rick searching in the desert for some cufflinks he dropped when he buried somebody out there. Talking about every little thing that came to his mind." At the end of his rant, he grumbled under his breath, "I wish he would just let me do the damn job he hired me to do."

I set my knife down and scowled at him. "Job? You are his son—"

"Adopted."

I didn't think, only reacted to my rising anger, as I picked up the butter knife and chucked it at him. It made me so pissed he always saw himself as separate from this family.

How he always considered himself lower on the totem pole, more of a hired brother. I know him and my dad had some kind of talk, agreement, when he adopted him, but my father craved having another child and treated Cosmo like he was his own blood. He would try to connect with Cosmo on a deeper level, but Cosmo always kept him at arm's length. Only ever letting me get closer to that smooshy center I knew he had.

He caught the knife and set it down like it was our normal routine. "Keep that up, and you will get no knife privileges soon."

"Then don't be a snitch," I replied tartly, and he smiled.

"Oh, I don't plan on snitching. That is beneath the Desmond name . . . but maybe punishing you for every infraction would be more productive." He was trying to be menacing, trying to threaten me, but my mind flipped those words around in my head, and I was envisioning those punishments in my bedroom, me strapped to the bed, and him smacking my ass as I moaned.

My face must've shown something because his eyes widened, and he got up, reminding me I shouldn't be thinking like that about him. I quickly shoveled food into my mouth, giving myself something else to focus on.

"You should just . . . just get ready and find out what he wants. It's always best to give him what he wants." I nodded at his words, still eating as he went to the door.

"But, Ray"—I looked up, his back to me as he was stopped at the door—"I will always be with you, by your side to weather whatever shit he's going to throw at you." Then he took a deep breath and turned his head toward me, grinning with a devious twinkle in his eye. "Your big bro has your back."

That got my blood pumping for a whole different reason as I grabbed my mug, shot up, and chucked it at him. He dodged it with a chuckle and went out the door as I yelled, "We are the same age, dipshit! Big bro my ass!" He was lucky I had finished my damn drink before I threw it.

I sat back down when Lisa came in, saw where my mug was on the floor, and frowned. It was all their fault. What was with the men in this family! It was like their favorite form of amusement was ways to torture and bug me. I needed to teach these two a lesson in why they shouldn't mess with me anymore. My mind went over all the ways I could make them go crazy as I settled down to eat the rest of my food, catching Lisa side-eyeing me.

I needed to get ready for the damn leaders meeting, and I shoveled the rest of the food down my throat as fast as I could. Then told Lisa I was sorry about the mess and thanked her for all the food before I ran upstairs to get ready.

I walked down the stairs and felt like a boss bitch in my black, silk, off-the-shoulder blouse, perfectly framing my breasts, partnered with a blood red, waist-high, pencil skirt and strappy rose gold heels. I knew I looked like a million bucks.

My father, Cosmo, and Rick were at the door talking, and when they heard me coming, they all faced me. My dad's smile slowly grew as Rick's mouth dropped, and Cosmo's eyes widened enough to know it affected him, and that was the goal.

My dad walked up to the end of the staircase and put out his arm for me to take. "You look fierce and stunning, my sunshine. Just like your mother." I beamed at him. He knew I loved when he thought I was like her. She was so much better than me, kind and sweet, fierce and strong, while also being strategic and cold. She was everything I wasn't. Whether it was a curse or a blessing, I took after my dad, but every once in a while, I did something like her, and I liked being reminded I was her daughter, too.

The boys opened the doors for us, and I took the opportunity, now that he was pleased with me, to bug him about the thing he wasn't telling me. "So, Dad, are you going to fess up to what you have been hiding?" I side-eyed him as we walked to the garage with all the cars lined up.

He looked over his shoulder at Cosmo and Rick. "Can you guys go to the warehouse ahead of us and get everything ready for our guests? I need to talk to Rayla alone." They nodded and jogged ahead in their black suits. It was at that moment I realized Ben, my father's right-hand man, wasn't with us. Before I asked, my dad spoke.

"So, Rayla, you know I have always valued you. I never once thought of you as just an heir but as my daughter, who I love to the ends of the earth and back." I nodded, holding my tongue to hear what he was trying to tell me. "So, you know I want only the best for you and your future?" I nodded again, and he gripped my arm to pull me to a stop. I turned to face him as he took a large breath. "And, well, let's face it, you are shit at finding yourself someone of your caliber. Someone worthy of you to be your partner in life."

My back stiffened, my spidey senses tingled as I cooly responded, "I don't need a partner in life when the whole clan will be *my* responsibility."

My dad gave me a sad and lonely smile as he whispered out, "But I want better for you. I want for you what your mother and I had. Someone to balance you. Someone to take care of you when you have the whole world on your shoulders." I shrugged, thinking to myself I had Cosmo and Rick to lean on.

Then my dad tilted my face up as he quickly said, "This first meeting I put in place is to bring all the heirs together and to find you a husband." My eyes widened, and I was about to tell him I would not go with him when his eyes flicked behind me. A silk cloth covered my mouth as I was prepared to yell at my dad, and I inhaled a heavy amount of chloroform.

My dad swooped me up as he cooed, "This is for the best, my sunshine. You are so pig-headed and strong-willed. There was no way I would've gotten you to this meeting any other way. I love you . . . And think about this . . . the next time you open your eyes, one of the men in that room will eventually be your husband." My eyes started to droop, and the last thing I thought was *not if I could help it.*

As I was coming to, I heard my dad's excited voice. "Oh, see, here she is. Here is my Rayla." My head lulled to the side as the feeling went back into my limbs. I made out a large circular table that had seven figures around it. It was a long walk from where I was, but I was gaining feeling and use of my extremities quickly. Two sets of hands carried me across the warehouse toward the table. I burned with embarrassment at being dragged around like this, like a useless girl. I looked up at the men carrying me, preparing myself to not seem betrayed if it was Cosmo and Rick because they had to have known what my dad would do. Right?

I was so relieved I let out a big breath when I saw two of my dad's henchmen, the twins. I never tried to learn their names and always called them the tweedles. As we stepped closer, I started to feel like my normal self, wiggling my fingers to make sure I got use of my limbs, but now I was in cranky-bitch mode.

The tweedles didn't expect me to kick off the ground and fly around, effectively twisting out of their grip. [1] I used my vampire speed to grab their guns in their holsters, and as soon as I landed, I shot them both in the kneecaps. "That's what you get for helping him," I called out while they cried and clutched their legs as they crashed into the concrete.

---

1. Song: Savage by Megan Thee Stallion

Then I used my speed to run up to where my dad was sitting and placed one of the guns to his head and whispered my rage into his ear, "That was a dirty, nasty trick, old man."

He laughed his head off, howling at the ceiling. "My little sunshine, it was all in good fun. Now, please,"—he patted the chair next to him—"we have guests, and Daddy doesn't have time to play with you just now." He looked me in the face, past the gun, and lifted one eyebrow, daring me to take this deadly game further. His fangs peeked out from his smile, and I gave him a low growl before I lifted the gun away from him.

"For now," I warned, and he solemnly nodded in agreement.

"For now." Then he turned back to the room, playing the jolly happy host as he clapped his hands, and I sat down in my seat, keeping the guns in my hands and at the ready. I was a little twitchy after being kidnapped by my own father, sue me.

"Now that we have my beautiful and amazingly wonderful daughter." I rolled my hand for him to continue, I didn't need him to butter me up. I was in the damn seat, wasn't I? "I can now introduce you all to her."

That unfocused my brain, and I realized I didn't even get a good look at the other leaders and heirs in the room. I sat up straight as he pointed to the man to his left. "This is Syris Glovefox and his heir, Avery." Syris appeared younger than I expected, soft features, royal-blue hair, and eyes that sparkled with half truths. Then again, he was a faerie, so he could change his appearance. He smiled at me sweetly, waving his hand as he said, "It's so nice to finally see you in person, my lady. Your father speaks very highly of you." I nodded to him and thanked him, which made him smile wider, and I felt my cheeks blush. I quickly looked away from this foxy old man to his heir and almost swallowed my tongue. Right there in front of me was that cotton candy pink-haired, carved-to-perfection faerie dancer I'd seen the night before.

His neon-green eyes widened, looking as shocked as I felt. As soon as our eyes met, that sizzling current that drew me to him in the first place snapped out, and he jerked forward in his seat a little. I clenched my hands together, not wanting to do anything stupid. I had nothing to say as I stared at him, and my dad coughed as he continued.

"Next is Manic Rossey and his heir, Ax." I shook my head, clearing the faerie daze he had me in, and took in the next man. He was a large man, definitely gave off werewolf vibes with his physique, but with him tucked into his expensive Armani attire and wild red-brown hair, he seemed like a poised and proper ruffian. It was kinda hot, and I gave him a small smile as he said, "Is that how you always greet your father?" His judgmental tone made me smirk, so I gave him an honest answer.

"When he drugs me to comply, then yes, yes, that is how I greet my dad. He was asking for it, and he knows it. Disrespect is not handled lightly in the Desmond household, even with leaders." I looked back at my dad, expecting him to scowl at my insolence, but he beamed at me like a proud parent seeing their kid stick up for themselves. It was weird, even for him.

"Right she is, and I'm most definitely not looking forward to what her retaliation will be, but que será será." He lifted his hands in a what-do-you-do motion, and I rolled my eyes.

The next thing I knew a deep voice purred out, "Well, hello, Siren." My head snapped over to the Rossey heir, and he eyed me up and down with his striking honey eyes like I was the perfect snack for him. I scanned him in his white button-down with the sleeve rolled up, ink spread out all over his neck and arms, looking like he was about to bust out of his shirt at any moment with the muscles on top of muscles this man had on him. My eyes snagged on his large hands folded in front of him, remembering how those claws felt digging into my skin as he fucked me against the rail. I almost licked my lips until he growled out, and the memory was broken.

"Hello, stranger," I cooed. He wasn't the only one who could play this game.

His father's gaze flicked between us before he asked, "Do you two know each other?" The hopeful curiosity in his voice was sickening as I remembered why my father wanted me here in the first place.

"Just in passing," I replied, but I saw the anger swirling in Ax's eyes at being dismissed too easily. I doubled down my efforts by focusing on the next set of men.

"And these are the Winstales, I presume?" I asked my dad. He played along, always willing to stir the pot to see what happened.

"Why, yes, my darling. This is Easton Winstale and his son, Falcon." Again, I was surprised because both men looked so similar with their fair hair and sharp angular features, but that wasn't what surprised me the most. It was the fact that Falcon was the guy I met at the shooting range last night. The mage I kinda hit it off with when we talked about weapons. Well, at least until he accused me of betraying the Syndicate. That still left a sour taste in my mouth, even if it was because of a miscommunication.

The older Winstale tipped his head down at me. "It is a pleasure to see you again, Rayla. It seems that the spitfire that convinced our boys to go trouncing around a cemetery has flourished into a raging inferno of a woman." I smiled at him because that was one hell of a compliment. It mentioned nothing about my beauty and made me feel powerful. I already liked him.

He peered at his son, Falcon, who was the only one out of the heirs that didn't seem surprised at who I was. He nodded and pulled out his phone, reading something. His father whispered for him to "put the damn phone away," and it made me giggle. Yep, this was not going to happen.

My chair scratched the concrete as I stood up, the sound echoing in the large empty warehouse. "Well, it was nice to meet all of you, and I look forward to working with you in the future." My dad's face was pinched as he tried to keep his smile going for the group. "But I am *not* going to marry anyone in this room. In fact, I'm sure that this group has much better things to discuss than *my* marriage." I took a big breath as I picked up the guns I took from the tweedles, and everyone moved back an inch. "I am Rayla Desmond. I have been born in this Syndicate, molded by it, and I need *no one's* help to hold it. I am just as bloodthirsty and savage as the rest of you in this room, and I will not hesitate to cut down anyone in the name of the Syndicate. I'm loyal, trained, and can take on any challenger that comes my way." I glared into the eyes of each man in the room before I declared, "And I will not be told who or when I will marry. That is final." I turned around, the only sound you heard was the click-clacking of my heels as I walked toward the exit.

"She is just kidding. She would make a great wife." My dad tried to schmooze.

"No, I won't! I don't do shit if it's not bloody," I threw over my shoulder.

"She doesn't mean that." His wobbly laugh reminded me I was definitely making the right choice.

"Yes, I do!" I yelled again as I continued to walk away.

"She's just a very passionate and strong woman." He tried to rationalize.

"That's code word for 'she's an uncompromising bitch!'" He scoffed, and I knew I had won that tête-à-tête.

A couple of the clan members came toward me, and I raised my guns, ready to shoot them if they tried anything funny. My dad called out to them to leave me be, and I walked out of the warehouse unscathed.

I realized I would need some wheels to get out of here, and I saw two cars that were ours and had a naughty and devious idea. *My dad should've never messed with me.*

PIOLA

CHAPTER 7

I WAS STANDING ON the sideline, in the shadows, the whole time, like Ternin told me. It has always been weird calling him Father, but he insisted, telling me it would be weird for Ray if I didn't, but in my mind, he was always Ternin Desmond. It was also weird thinking of him as a father because that meant I was obsessively lusting after my sister, and even I knew that was wrong, but I couldn't help it. I fell in love with her on the first day I saw her all those years ago.

I remembered that day like it was yesterday. Ternin and I rolled up in the car to a large house, larger than anything I could've dreamed of. He ushered me out of the car as he called out to a small girl with white pigtails, arms crossed as she appeared at the front door, telling her she needed to greet her new brother. She barreled down the steps in her vampire speed, stopping right in my face as she stared me up and down with a sour look. "What is the meaning of this?"

Those were the first words she said as she motioned to me, and I immediately felt this pull toward her. Her ashy-white hair bounced with loose curls, her stance and tone were strong, but it was her eyes that captured my soul. Those sparkling rose gold gems made you want to get closer just to make sure they were real. She reminded me of an angel, her beauty ethereal and striking, something not meant for this world. Not meant for some nobody like me.

It took a few weeks of following her around like a puppy for her to get used to me, but when I let her stab me over a blueberry muffin, not letting out a cry or telling on her to Ternin, she huffed as she munched on the muffin, telling me she might like having a brother around to play with. It was the first time I remembered smiling, first time I felt truly happy.

Being in a supe orphanage was vicious for a child, and that was the only life I knew for six years. You had all of these little monsters running around with different deadly abilities and no one older to teach you how to handle your nature, so you used them on each other or started to hang out with the wrong crowd and got used for your gifts by someone you looked up to. I learned at an early age never to let anyone take advantage of me, especially someone older. That's why I was surprised Ternin adopted me right away. He said he saw a cool, calm fire in me, one that rivaled his daughter's, but where she was all red and flamy, mine was blue and steady, ready for anything.

I enjoyed Ray's red fire, her spark. While it made her unpredictable and a little stabby or shooty, it made her fiercely loyal and deadly dedicated. Which was why I enjoyed the show my firecracker gave as she told these men what was what, and I couldn't have been prouder.

When Ternin brought her unconscious body to the car, I was flipping out on the inside. My muscles shook, and my brain kept going in a loop, asking myself if she was okay, if she was breathing, then reminding myself Ternin wouldn't truly hurt his own daughter.

It was my duty to keep her safe, and I failed. Then Ternin looked at me, shrugged his shoulders, and said, "It was the only way to get her to come." Then I knew this was all planned; Ternin planned everything from the moment he called us in to tell us about this meeting. All her appointments, keeping me away, his cheery mood, it was all a ruse to get us to this moment.

Even if my duty and loyalty was to Ray, I still had to obey Ternin. I watched him place her in the car as I rolled out of the garage. Rick's body froze, his eyes widened as he quickly looked at me, but I shook my head, telling him not to get worked up. We needed to keep a level head if we were going to help Ray in the end, and to our surprise, she didn't need our help. Not one bit. She defied her dad, told the leaders and their heirs off, and peaced out like the boss she was. No one would tie Ray down, *and that's how I wanted it.*

The whole time Ternin was introducing her to the leaders, I was thinking of all the ways I could kill the heirs. It would be easy. I could wait until they felt safe, felt at home in the Desmond compound, and then I could sneak into their villas at night and take them out one by one. No one would take Ray from me. I knew I couldn't have her how I wanted, but there was no way in hell I would watch some other guy have my Ray.

Sure, she has had boyfriends and lovers, but I knew it was just sex. She never brought them home or had them meet her father. Her dream was to stand on the top alone, running the Syndicate like a savage queen, and I would be her right hand, always helping her until the end of time. The perfect knight to her royalty.

My thoughts were broken as a panicked-looking vampire from the clan came rushing forward, standing behind Ternin with fear in his eyes. Ternin barked out, "What is it?"

"Um . . . boss . . . it's . . . it's Miss Rayla." He turned to face the vampire, and I thought the messenger was going to faint, but he kept it together.

"What about her?" Ternin asked in a fake chipper voice.

"Well, sir . . . well . . ." The vampire wrung his hands together behind his back, and I smiled. *What did my little Ray do?* He blurted as he bowed to him, "She lit your car on fire." He flinched, waiting to be reprimanded as everyone in the room fell quiet, all attention on Ternin.

It took him a second, his jaw clenched, and then he barked out laughing for a full minute. He pretended to wipe his eyes like he had tears, but we all knew Ternin didn't shed a single tear ever again after Ray's mom was killed.

"Oh, man. My little sunshine is in a blaze of glory today." He slapped his knee, and some of the leaders looked at him like he was crazy. Well, mainly the Rossey leader. I have a feeling he has been strict with his wild side and has a hard

time seeing others being what he deems out of control.
The Glovefox leader was smiling like a loon, almost like he
was even more impressed with her. The Winstale leader's
face was pinched, confused, like he didn't know how he
should react.

After Ternin was done laughing, the messenger was visi-
bly at ease until he told the room, "That's why I brought
the back up."

The vampire gulped, his face paling even more than his
natural state. "S-s-s-ir . . ." Ternin went stiff as he motioned for him to continue. "Miss Rayla took the backup,
sir."

It took everything inside of me to stay still and unrespon-
sive when all I wanted to do was laugh at the turn of events.
Ternin always was a good planner, always anticipating
people's reactions and moods correctly, but Ray was his
weakness. Whenever he seemed to get one step ahead, she
always forced him two steps back.

He gave a small, annoyed chuckle under his breath, mumbling about her being like her mother, before he called out,
"Cosmo, come here."

I stiffened at his request, not expecting to get called out
for this meeting. *Maybe he wanted me to go after Ray.* It was
only a second before I walked up to his side, waiting for
his command with my hands behind my straight back.

He lifted his hand toward me to the group of men in
front of him. "This is my son, Cosmo." I made myself very
still, wondering what he was scheming as we both knew
what my real function was as his "son," and it was most

definitely not to have anything to do with the Syndicate leaders.

Boss Rossey was the first to speak. "This is your *adopted* son, correct?" His tone was aimed to put me in my place, to let me know I was not an heir, little did he know I didn't want to be, so it didn't bother me. I knew my role in this family, but apparently Ternin had an issue with it because his growl caught me off guard.

"He may be adopted, as you put it, but he would be the only one I would put in charge of the Desmond clan if something happened to Rayla and me." His hands balled into fists on the table. "He is my son in every way but DNA." His eyes flicked to mine, then back to the bosses as he followed with, "He has been loyal and true to the Syndicate from day one. He is Rayla's right hand and has been a true brother to her since the day I brought him home." I held back a wince as he said that last part, all my thoughts earlier about how I wanted to devour Ray when she came down the stairs looking so stunning had me feeling guilty at his praise. If he knew how I felt, he would kill me.

"Apologies, I meant nothing by it," Boss Rossey said in my direction. I nodded but said nothing more. I felt like more was less with this group.

Ternin smiled a toothy grin before he clapped his hands to get everyone's attention. "So, I know that my daughter is a little . . . extra, but she has been raised in the Syndicate by bloodthirsty mobsters"—he shrugged—"to expect anything less than the stunning creature she is would say more about you than her."

In Ray's words, my spidey senses were going off, and I was bracing myself for one of Ternin's shocking ideas that I, nine times out of ten, hated and required work I would actively like to avoid, but I was a good soldier, and I kept my mouth shut and waited for the bomb to blow.

"I'm sure all of your fathers have told you by now that I would like one of you to marry my daughter." The heirs all nodded slowly, realizing they all knew about this before Rayla did, and that made my stomach burn for her.

The fae one, Avery, tried to keep it cool, but I saw the curiousness in his gaze. The werewolf, Ax, looked excited, licking his lips as his eyes went to the door she was last seen walking through. My hand twitched at my side to grab my gun and shoot him dead in the heart with a silver bullet, but I knew that would sign my death warrant, and I was not willing to leave Ray's side for this piece of shit. The interesting one was the mage, Falcon. The whole time, he seemed disinterested, and yet, his eyes were focused now.

"Despite what you might think, she not only has been raised in the Syndicate, but she has been helping me run it for the past five years. She is the head of our fund's acquisitions team, overseeing the worst cases herself. She is in charge of all the money coming into the organization and has a firm grasp on the major players in the skins, muscle, and weapons sectors here. She has also acquired new accounts and has kept up a lot of the peace on the strip."

"Ternin, what would you say that you do?" Boss Glovefox chuckled underneath his hand.

Ternin kept going like he said nothing, but he winked at him. "She is tough as bricks and a little bit on the savage side of things. Despite what you might have seen today, she is fiercely loyal and dedicated to the Syndicate. She would be a great asset to you as well as a devoted partner in this particular life we live."

"Why do you want one of us and not someone else you could control?" Falcon asked. Ternin looked at him, giddy someone had asked.

"The Syndicate has been running as four separate entities that co-run the group as a whole. I would like to see us be even closer than just me and your fathers being friends. If I had two more daughters, it would just be a matter of which one liked which of you, but as it stands, I only have the bandwidth for one." He chuckled at his own joke before continuing. "We are also hoping that once this business is settled, you all will 'hang out.'" He turned to me and whispered loudly, "That is what the kids call it nowadays, right?"

"Yes," I responded, and he nodded, pleased with himself.

"We want you all to start to get to know each other better. These three men are my closest friends and confidants. They know everything about me, and I, them. It has been what makes us strong and able to work afar from each other for so long," Boss Glovefox said.

"We might have done you all a disservice raising you up separately, and we would like to rectify that," Boss Rossey called out.

Then Boss Winstale finished, "We are getting old and tired. Wanting to pass on the torch, but we can't do that without seeing you all work together as one unit."

There was silence after that, everyone thinking about what was said until Ternin announced, "And that all starts with winning my daughter's hand."

Avery was the first to speak up. "And how do you propose we do that when it seems like marriage is the last thing on her mind?"

I had to remind myself to keep calm, to not show my hand. *How can I turn this situation around? How can I help Ray out of this?* My brain continued to work as they all talked.

"Well, my boy, that's going to be part of the fun. I love my daughter, I really do, but she can be a little . . . passionate at times." Without meaning to, I puffed out a small laugh. *Passionate.* By passionate, did he mean when she found out that this werewolf she was seeing was skimming off the tables in our casino, she skinned his toes and fingers one by one for the betrayal? Was that what he meant?

They all turned to me, Ternin a little perturbed by my interjection, but I nodded for him to continue. He rolled his eyes as he focused back onto the room. "Which means that her future happiness has been placed into my hands. The deal is this, boys, whoever can capture her and keep her for—" He looked at his watch, then raised his eyes up to the ceiling and mouthed numbers like he was counting. "One hour, gets the girl. Clean and simple."

"An hour?" Ax howled out a laugh. "Don't you want to make this a challenge?"

Ternin's gaze turned sharp, his fangs on display as a cruel smile rose on his lips. "Oh, trust me. One hour with her will test your character and how well you might be able to get along with her." Then he shook off the smile and lifted his finger, his face getting serious. "Don't forget that she is highly trained in all types of fighting styles as well as stealth practices. She is one of my deadliest assets. I wouldn't underestimate her."

They all appeared to take that into consideration, even the cocky wolf boy seemed to think it over as he folded his hands on the table, staring at the floor like he was thinking really hard. "Now, I am not just leaving you in the dark. I know my daughter is a minefield, which is why I am allowing one neutral party." I closed my eyes for a second, wishing, praying he would not do what I was thinking he would. "Cosmo knows Rayla better than anyone in this world, I would even say better than me." I opened my eyes as he lifted his hand to gesture to me, and my stomach turned rancid. "He will be the only person that you can ask questions about her or get advice from about my daughter." He flicked his hand up at me as he said, "He will be a neutral party for both sides but is instructed to not actively help her against you all."

Fucking shit! I didn't want to do this.

Falcon opened his mouth, but Ternin beat him to it. "Please save all questions until after the rules have been set. Thank you."

"So." He continued on. "This means that if she gets away from you on her own, that is fine, but Cosmo can't be the getaway car or wingman in getting her out, but he can give her warnings. We have to keep it even. Information versus information." He looked up at me, narrowing his eyes as if he was laying down the law. "Understood?"

I hesitated, and he picked up on it. I didn't want to do this. Rayla would feel like it was a betrayal. Then I glanced at the other men and a thought came. *I could help her against them, I could be the shield that she needed.* Ternin cleared his throat as he glared at me, and I choked out, "Understood."

He nodded and smiled at the bosses and heirs. "Now I will take questions."

They were all quiet, the bosses all smiling as they watched their sons in thought. They were all enjoying this while I felt like I was swallowing nails with each gulp.

Falcon was the first to speak. "Am I allowed to use tools?"

Then Avery perked up. "What about magic?"

Ternin's grin widened, showing off all his teeth as a twinkle of savagery flashed in his eyes, his voice went from jolly to sadistic. "All is fair in love and war, boys, and trust me, you *are* going to war."

They nodded, their faces lined with intrigue, excited for the hunt, while a red-hot rage brewed deep inside my soul. These men were not worthy of Ray. Avery with his stupid pretty-boy looks, Ax with his cocky attitude, and Falcon with his quiet smarts. Nope, not one of them held a candle to my Ray.

"Cosmo, just for shits and giggles, let's not tell my little sunshine about this game until tomorrow. Let's give the boys a fighting chance, eh?" He giggled as he folded his hands together like a Bond villain. The worst thing Ray did was instill movie night every Wednesday with him. Now everything that Ternin did was something from a movie, and he thought it was hilarious.

I nodded, not trusting myself to not tell them all to get fucked, and if they ever touched my Ray, I would suck them dry in the most painful way possible. That would break the stupid rules. I needed to get out of here before I did something stupid. "Is that all you need, Father?"

I got my desired effect as his eyes lit up. He always liked when I used that term instead of Ternin. "Yes, my boy, that is all." I turned on my heel, ready to get out of there as fast as my feet could take me when he followed with, "Oh, and make sure Ray isn't terrorizing the strip. You know how she gets when her temper is high." I gave him a curt nod and walked to the door.

The rest of the bosses whispered to their sons before they each got up and left as well. Looks like they all were going to take advantage of her being in the dark. *Dicks.*

Rick caught up to me as soon as I got to the car, panting like he wasn't a vampire that could run and not break a sweat. "What are we going to do?"

I opened the door and leaned on it before answering, "What we always do. Help Ray as best we can." I slid into my seat, waiting for him to get in.

I hoped whatever support we could give her would help. *It had to.*

CHAPTER 8

TENDRILS OF SMOKE WAFTED off my hands and neck as I glared at the glass ball in front of me. My fingers slid around the smooth sphere as I gripped it hard. A swirling storm of rage slowly worked its way to being an all-consuming tornado inside of me about to burst. A familiar headache worked its way from the back of my head up to my temples, and my horns pierced their way out.

I let go of the crystal orb, not wanting to ruin it in my fit of anger, it was the only way I could see my little rose. My rose, the one those men were competing for. My hands clenched as I envisioned punching them right through their chests, taking their hearts and crushing them in my hands as they crumbled before me for daring to take what was mine.

So, they thought they could have a meeting like this without me? That they could compete for my rose's hand and not give me my due? That was unacceptable. Unforgivable. I might be the Syndicate heir they thought they got rid of, the one they buried under a rug when I was too young to be of use, but the fact of the matter was, I had Devil blood in my veins, and that meant I was a rightful heir. I was a part of the Syndicate, whether they wanted me or not. I would be fucking damned if I would let any of the heirs have her. Rayla Desmond was mine.

Stomping over to the abstract painting of a black heart on my far wall, I tugged on the frame, revealing my hidden safe. I huffed as the smoke and shadows skated across my arms and escaped from my fingers, my power leaking with my emotions running rampant as I took out my key and placed it in the lock. My left hand pressed on the pad next to the lever for the hand recognition software. As soon as it beeped, giving me the green light, I yanked it open and pushed aside the things I would need for a quick getaway until I found my most-prized possession.

I grabbed the rose hairpin carefully—like it would break at the slightest touch—and placed it in my palm, and the ruby petals sparkled, and the gold stem and leaves shined, making it the beacon of light at the center of my smoke-wielding hands.

I'm sure she never knew what a lifeline she gave to the shy, sad demon boy who was orphaned and alone. How it felt to hold her porcelain-white hand in my inky one as she dragged me around, making sure I wasn't excluded, even then she had so much heart for us. All of us.

Back then, I had a lot less control of my power. I'm sure it was weird for her to see this boy with bronzed skin who had dark swirls of smoke traveling along his skin like a moving tattoo. I have much better control these days, only showing my smoke and horns when my emotions run high.

How euphoric it felt when she wrapped her lips around my finger, sucking the blood leaking from the cut I got from one of the roses on my parents' caskets. At first I was stunned, not having been around vampires much, but when she pulled on that red liquid, my body lit up, and I couldn't take my eyes off the deadly beauty. I had pulled away, embarrassed by the rush of feeling and heat I was undergoing. In a few seconds, she made me forget about my depressing and lonely existence without my parents and had me focused on her, a positive thing. I vividly remember thinking I would never let her go. Then the others came barging in.

I remembered that day like it was yesterday, when the five kids who had lost their mothers were looking for something to do, some other state of being than the sadness they all felt. Then Rayla, my rose, took my hand and called out to the others, giving us the adventure we'd all craved to escape our reality. Even now that adventure was the best memory I had to date.

That was until my uncle overheard the other bosses saying they wanted to have me killed and wanted to absorb the Devils' portion of the Syndicate. That night, he rushed into my room, scaring me with his urgency and anger. I remembered his bruising grip on my arm as he yanked me to his car. He didn't even pack any of my stuff or buckle me into the car in his haste to get away in the middle of the night. That's how I knew it was bad. My uncle saved my young life from the cruel fate the Syndicate wanted to hand to the newly orphaned boy. That night, we left everything behind. We let everything crumble so I lived. My uncle promised me we would get our revenge one day. That he would teach me everything I needed to know about being a demon in this world.

Once I got to a certain age, passing all of his tests of strength and power, we started to gather demon followers again. It was very underground, no one could talk about it or speak the name Devil without having death handed to them. We had a few mages we worked with, who supported our cause in trying to take the Syndicate down, to rebuild it with better leadership. They created induction spells that if you even tried to say the name Devil you would drop dead, your insides splitting into pieces until your heart became stone and cracked down the center.

The goal was to take over the Syndicate, and when we heard they were going to be together for the first time in twenty-two years, my uncle felt like this was our chance. The thing my uncle didn't know was that even though I planned to take down the Syndicate, my rose was to be excluded from the carnage. She was to be the ruthless queen by my side, ruling the underground together. This was something I would not compromise on, so I kept it close to my chest. I had never told my uncle about her or how I felt, knowing his blood lust for the Syndicate would overtake any reason I would try to lay at his feet.

After we ran, my uncle took me to an underground bunker, a safe house he had just in case. We lived there for a while, and he never let me go outside, for fear of them finding me. I became depressed in hiding, having no one besides my uncle for company. It didn't take him long to notice and take pity on me. He got me the crystal orb, telling me it was for training purposes.

Crystal orbs were expensive and hard to use due to the one caveat: the only way you could watch someone was to have something that belonged to that person, something they cherished. My uncle wanted me to start small. To steal things from targets of small jobs we started to do for money. I would steal an item and then use the orb to stalk these people, report to him their daily activities, and he would finish the job.

I got good at watching people, picking up on body language and social cues. I knew my uncle thought this work was beneath him and wanted to give me something to do, but I found I enjoyed it.

Then one day, I stuck my hand under my pillow, rubbing the pin Rayla gave me, and I had an idea. What if I could watch Rayla?

That night, I desperately held onto the hairpin as I ran my finger over the orb, praying I saw a glimpse of the rose gold eyes and white blonde hair I spent most nights dreaming about. Then it happened. I saw Rayla clear as day as a young vampire boy our age with short white blonde hair was introduced to her as her new brother. I would've been mad that day, seeing another boy take my place beside her, but I was just so happy I found a way to see her. Connect with her.

The next time I tried it, I saw glimpses of Ternin in his office before it would switch back over to a clearer vision of Rayla. I asked a mage once why I would see someone clearly and another person inconsistently and very fuzzy, and they said this can happen when the item had two owners who cared deeply for it. They explained that the strength of the connection depended on the strength of the bond between the person and the item. I knew her father gave it to her, which was probably why I also saw him on occasion.

From then on, after I gave detailed notes to my uncle on targets, I would tune in to see Rayla. I would watch her train, create mischief with Rick and Cosmo, and sometimes, if I got lucky, I would watch her feed. That was one of my favorite times to observe her. At first, I was fascinated with it because of the blood, the viciousness of the act, until I noticed when she got older she was more careful with her prey or with the prey she cared for. It was addicting to see all the sides of my rose growing up, almost like I was beside her the whole time.

I was enraptured by her, so I started to take notes on her. What she liked, what she didn't, who she gravitated to, and what her preferences were. I wanted to suck up every scrap of information I could about her. She quickly became my paramour, my dark secret, my sinful obsession. My everything.

When I turned sixteen, I went through a short stint of trying to hate her. Trying to convince myself I could ruin her when the time was right. She was the enemy's daughter, after all, and she got to be recognized and revered in the Syndicate. She got to have her rightful place and grow and flourish, and a piece of me wanted that. Wanted that same opportunity so I could be at her same level. I quickly got over that jealous phase after I saw her crying over her first boyfriend and his betrayal.

[1] I witnessed my beautiful, vibrant rose weep for the pathetic thing; he was selling information about her and the Syndicate to a lower-level thug trying to make a name for himself.

With rapt attention, I watched as her tears dried up and her hands clenched so hard they turned iridescent against her already-pale skin. I feasted my eyes on her as her back straightened and her eyes filled with a rage that rivaled my own. I felt this tug in my chest, not of pity or sadness, but of kinship, of understanding. I realized we were so alike, she and I.

My face leaned closer to the orb, drawing me to her like she had a direct tether to my angry heart. She rose and grabbed some pliers before she snuck out of her house, went across town, and snuck into his bedroom. I clutched her hairpin so hard it pierced my palm, but I didn't dare take my eyes away. Her beautiful face was set in determination, and her rosy eyes grew sharp and cutting as she carefully straddled him while he slept. Using her vampire speed, she lifted both his arms and cuffed them to the bed. At first, the idiot thought she was getting kinky with him and smiled up at her. That's when my dark rose chose to strike with her spiky thorns.

She stuck the pliers into his mouth, securing his left fang between the metal clamps, smiling down at him as she whispered, "This is what happens when you betray the Syndicate."

She yanked the tooth out, causing him to scream in pain. Blood splattered onto her face as she smiled down at him in

---

1. Song: Dagger by Bryce Savage

glee. "And this." She used his pain to her advantage as she opened the pliers, dropping the bleeding fang, and secured them around the right one. "This is for me."

Opposite to how she handled the other fang, she twisted it slowly, drawing out the pain. He tried to fight, tried to buck her off, but my rose's thorns went deep, and she squeezed her thighs, knees digging into his kidneys to give him a different kind of pain. As soon as he'd given up, his cries turned into sobs, which were the sweetest notes I'd ever heard.

Even though I was watching through an orb, I heard her smooth and soft voice over his cries. "Betrayal is the highest form of disrespect, and disrespect will *never* be tolerated." Then she yanked out his fang, covering her in even more blood, and it excited me.

I was glued to the scene in front of me as she closed her eyes and tilted her head back and sighed, his painful screams in the background only highlighting her beauty. I held my breath as my eyes roamed the curves of her sensual body. Her chest rose and fell as she took in deep breaths, calming herself. My breathing turned rapid, wishing I was with her, by her side to witness it all live. My dick grew harder with each of her breaths.

I would never forget how she looked down at him, cocking her head to the side as his loud cries echoed in the room. She lifted her hand and smacked him across the face hard before shooshing him like one would a crying child. His loud cries turned into soft whimpers as she cooed in his face. "If you ever do anything against the Syndicate again, I will cut you open and splay you out on the street like roadkill, draining the last bit of blood in your heart until it crumbles into ash. Do you understand me?"

His eyes darted away from her as he whispered his blood-soaked promises to never again talk about the Syndicate, repeating over and over again that he understood. Once she was satisfied, she hopped off him—in her gory, bloody state—and walked out the door like what she just did was as normal as breathing.

I couldn't take it anymore, and I let go of the orb, the image of her opening the door fading into nothing as I lay down in bed and envisioned her on top of me in her blood-soaked clothes and splattered face, riding me into the next world. I came so hard that night I had to clean my jizz from my wall. That night solidified my obsession with her. My hunger and need for only her, no one else would do. No one could compete. It was to be her and only her for me. I wouldn't settle for anything else.

That night, I became her stalker, her phantom, her shadow, but I wanted more.

I wanted to be by her side, ruling the world together, but I knew I needed to bring something to the table, too. From that night on, I worked harder to be the man a woman like her deserved. I kept watching her as much as I could, but I also had to dedicate my time and energy into building back up the Devils' empire.

Back in the day, the Devils handled any assassin jobs for the Syndicate. It would occasionally land into the torture realm, too, but it was my understanding, from my uncle, that all the bosses enjoyed that type of play, so it wasn't common for us to always get that kind of a job. We were world renowned at what we did. So good, so clean, that people didn't know who or what killed them, and they made us out to be boogeymen. They would tell their men if they betrayed them, the Devil would know and would punish them. We were the Syndicate's ghost weapon.

It took my uncle and I a while, waiting until I was about eighteen, to really start to recruit, to build everything back up, but also keep it hidden. It was slow at first. Well-known individuals from back in the day didn't believe any Devil family members were alive, and we had to prove ourselves a lot. That's why we didn't do this until I was ready. Until I knew I could take on all the most vicious and cold-hearted killers of this world. Once I proved myself over and over again, we gained their trust, their allegiance. Then we started to build our network.

When we came up with the plans for how we would take them all down, it started with attacking them separately in their home turf since they all have been bunkered down. The plan was to kill the leaders, like they wanted to do me, but I wanted to give the heirs an option. An option I was never given as a child. I wanted to give them the choice to die or to help run things under the Devil name. My uncle continued to fight me on this, as we were co-running the Devil clan, but I didn't want to budge on this. If we do to them what they tried to do to me, then aren't we just the new them? The little boy inside remembered playing in a mausoleum with them, laughing at the ridiculous things they said, sharing that same lonely bond . . . I knew I didn't want to outright kill them. I felt like this option was acceptable. Fair.

With the meeting I just witnessed, I tried with all my power to stay after Rayla left. I focused on her father and only him as the scene played out, flickering in and out as I tried to hold it. I heard a majority of it, but what bugged me the most was the heirs' faces. I saw their desire and lust plain as day. Even Falcon, who I thought would be disinterested in this setup, was curious, only asking questions to gauge what he could do to capture her. They didn't crave her heart and soul like I did. They didn't obsess over her or make sure they were the kind of man she would want. They did none of the back work, had no piles of notes about her . . . and yet, they got to be first choice for a life mate?!

I closed my fist around the pin. *Fuck them.* Fuck them all, and if capturing her for one hour was all it took, then I guess I would be a dark horse in this little race for my rose's heart. I had time. I could play their little game, ensure I would be the winner after watching all their failures, and they would fail. A crooked smile took over my face as I thought about how my rose would surprise them all.

There was no doubt in my mind she would be the victor in this game . . . but that didn't mean I couldn't win, too.

@Tpiola_

CHAPTER 9

I SQUEEZED THE WHEEL of my dad's backup car as [1] I blasted music as loud as I could. *How could he do this?* How could he think it would be okay to just hand me over to these . . . these . . . strangers! I mean, they were sexy strangers, strangers that were part of the Syndicate and knew how the life was, but still. This wasn't the fucking Dark Ages where he could just hand me off to the suitor of his choice! I was my own damn woman. I was a fucking boss, and I needed no man! *Argh!*

I slammed my foot on the peddle, racing down the highway in record speed, trying to clear my mind of this whole cluster fuck he put me in. Also, what the hell was that chloroform nonsense? It was a dick move, even for my crazy dad.

---

1. Song: Daisy by Ashnikko

I mean, he knew I wouldn't go if he had told me the idea from the beginning, so, I mean, I kinda get it—*No! No. No. No. It was still a dick move, Rayla.* I had this sudden urge to do more, to fuck up more shit on purpose, just to piss the old man off like he did me, but I knew better. I needed to calm down, center myself, and then find a way out of this mess because I knew my dad, and he wouldn't give up just because I told him no. Especially if he thought he was doing this for my own good.

The worst part was I was actually interested in the heirs. Avery, with his magnetism that called to me, tempted me, which made me want to give in to him without a thought. I felt his eyes on me the entire meeting, singing to me without words. Then there was Ax, who had this raw, animalistic sense, this passion that knew no bounds, and the knowledge to know how to use it. Even though the marks and wounds from our fuck had healed the second I left, I still felt the ghost of his touch, but that smug look on his face made me want to rebel, to ignore it. Then there was Falcon, the thinker of the group, with his vast knowledge of weaponry I could appreciate and his control issues that made me want to push his boundaries, to see what would happen when they were messed up. I also felt a kinship to him, an ease in conversing with him. I had this sense about being on equal ground with him that I never had with another man. It was always a pull for power, but I didn't get that from him, I felt relaxed.

It was strange to try and connect those guys with the boys from the funeral. I felt like I stayed the same old me, but, man, did they grow up in the best way possible. I had to put that all behind me on fucking principle alone, and I was a little pissed off at it.

My plan, after yesterday and meeting all of them separately, was to seek them all out for maybe a date, have a good time, weed out the one that fit me the best, and maybe start something. I had never dated three guys at once, and I thought if I was honest with them from the start, then that would be okay, right?

After today's little bum-rush meeting, knowing they were the heirs, I had to scrap that plan and come up with something new. I tried to think of a way I didn't have to take a loss on anything . . . maybe we can be fuck buddies? I mean, we can't really be together, they all run their operations in different states, and I don't do long distance.

I replayed the meeting in my head and realized none of them looked surprised by the news, which means . . . those fuckers knew about it before the meeting, it was just me that was left out. My anger boiled over, getting the best of me again as I punched the steering wheel. *Fuckers! All of them. Bosses and heirs!* All of them can eat shit as I stick their dicks in an ant-infested hole!

Through the haze of picturing them all crying out over their ant-covered dicks, another thought hit me. Why would the heirs be so okay with marrying me? If rumors were true, Avery was a ladies' man that always lavished women with gifts and expensive dates, but it lasted only twenty-four hours before he was on to the next one. Ax was said to be a fuckboy, plowing through anything with half a brain or less. Not a lot was said about Falcon, he kept to himself, but that doesn't mean he isn't in this for another reason.

My brain was going around and around until I figured out something. The Desmond clan was the head family, and the only family with a girl as an heir . . .what if the bosses all agreed to the Desmond clan to being the head family because I eventually had to marry someone? Maybe they always knew they would do this because I was a woman? Then the other heirs would find it an advantage to marry me and essentially have two families be the head families. Those fuckers want to step on my turf and try to take over.

A snarl ripped from me, the vampire in me taking over, telling me to hunt them down and gut them for trying to take what was mine. I would be the only one at the top of the Syndicate. I decided this long ago when my dad explained everything about the family business and our role. I have done everything, made sacrifices to be what the head of this family, this organization, needed. The last thing I wanted was to let some leader wannabes take what was always mine.

But first, I needed to calm my ass down, and I had the perfect place to do it.

I got off the freeway and hooked a right, turning around to go to the place that always let me rage, let me take control while also losing control. Plus, the manager had a little crush on me and let me have a run of the place whenever I wanted. He also had a nice butt, which made for a great view every once in a while.

I parked in front of a small brick building. The sharp sides have been worn down with time, and there were pieces of brick missing in certain sections. It looked like it was five seconds from crumbling, and I smiled. Guy's Gym was the place I went whenever I was pissed as a kid, which happened a lot. It's also where my dad had me train a lot, the man who owned it was extremely loyal to my dad. Something about saving his wife or something like that. My dad was always a sucker for a love story.

The gym started as a Syndicate-only place, but when the Rosseys expanded, this place became more of an old-timer gym, the place you came to if you were in the know. Guy originally owned it, but when he wanted to retire, I bought it, working into the deal that his son, Sam, could run it. He would get a hefty paycheck with the understanding I got to use it however I pleased whenever I needed to. It was a solid deal for Sam, and his father got to vacation all the time with the money I gave him.

I opened my car door, grabbed my keys, and walked up to the door. The lights were on, so I strolled in.

I didn't see anyone at first glance, so I went left into the women's locker room to locker number one with a set of black leggings and sports bra in it. I changed in the middle of the room since no one else was around, stuffed my skirt and blouse into the locker, and as I left, I called out into the quiet space. "Sam? You here?"

All of a sudden, I heard a crash, then Sam was swearing before he hopped out of the bathroom with blue paint all over him. His blushing cheeks had me smiling wide. I chuckled a little behind my hand, it was hard not to.

"Hey, Rayla." His paint-covered hand went to his neck, rubbing the back and making a big streak of blue appear. "Just redoing the bathrooms like we talked."

I walked up to him, nodding as I smiled. "Yeah, I see that." I lifted a finger and touched his neck where he got paint. His eyes widened as he opened his mouth. "Wha—" I lifted my finger away and showed him the blue that was on his neck. His cheeks flushed further as he backed up.

"Looks like you got it all covered, more than covered." I giggled, and he smiled, his face redder than a lobster.

"Yeah," he replied. "What brings you in?" His tone wasn't accusatory or authoritative, so I answered him easily.

"I needed to blow off some steam without all the thugs at my house hovering over me." Then I had an idea and slid closer to Sam, getting a close view of his gorgeous and kind cerulean eyes. "But I could use a partner to spar with. Someone who knows what they're doing." I let the tip of my finger run down his arm lightly, and his eyes shuttered, and he took a breath before he opened his mouth to respond.

Before he could respond, a loud gruff voice sounded out. "I wouldn't take this siren up on her offer, mate. She's a wily one and is more likely to sucker punch you than kiss you."

I knew that stupid voice. I rolled my eyes as Sam stiffened, glaring behind me at our intruder. Sam spat out, "Who the fuck—" I lifted my hand, and he stopped, his eyes flicking to mine as I gave him a little shake of my head. I would take care of this.

I turned around slowly. "How do you know?" I glared at Ax leaning against the doorframe, smirking at me. I resisted licking my lips as my eyes trailed up his massive muscular body. It really was a work of bulky perfection. He had the kind of body that made you feel like he could smash a head open between two fingers. It was annoyingly attractive but had me raising my guard and cocking an eyebrow in that I-don't-care attitude sort of way.

He opened his cocky mouth, but I knew it would just be some line or something equally as stupid, so I cut him off. "What do you want, Ax?" Then I glared at him, remembering his smug face back at the warehouse. "What the fuck are you assholes scheming?" I thought for a second and followed with, "Tell me, and I might give you a reward?"

His eyes lit up at that thought before he quickly shut it down. He kicked off the wall and walked over to me with a cocky swagger. "I don't know what you are talking about, Siren, but if you are in need of an adequate partner to spar with"—he walked right up to my face, his breath caressing my cheek as he finished with a smile that showed off all of his pearly whites—"then we both know I would be the most qualified for the job."

I felt Sam behind me, ready to fight on my behalf, but I didn't need that. I lifted my hand to keep him quiet, not wanting to start a war just because he disrespected the Rossey heir. "I didn't mean to interrupt your work, Sam. Luckily, Ax Rossey here came to visit and has offered his services to give me the challenge I need. Thank you, Sam, for all your help."

Sam inhaled sharply at the mention of Ax's name, trying to hint to him Ax's position in the Syndicate, but he still continued. "Rayla, I can always—"

I swirled around to face Sam as I barked out, "You think I can't beat him? That because he's a Rossey that automatically means he's stronger than a Desmond?" While Sam started to sputter out his words, Ax's little sly comment didn't go unnoticed.

"Uh, yeah. That's exactly what that dipshit means."

I whirled around and punched Ax in his middle by surprise. As soon as my fist connected with his hard-as-fuck abs, he flew in the air and crashed into the old brick wall. My gut reaction was to yell, to scream at him, but I kept myself in check as the throb in my hand dissipated. That was what he wanted, to get under my skin, and I couldn't let that happen. Instead, I took a breath and whispered in a deep, arctic voice, "Get in the ring, Rossey." Then I turned away from the idiot dislodging himself from the wall, broken bricks and dust wafting off him as he walked over with a smile and entered the ring.

"You got one hell of a punch, Desmond. But it still won't be enough." He climbed into the ring in one jump, making a show of unbuttoning his shirt slowly before draping it along the ropes. His chest and arms were covered in yummy tattoos, and I attempted to roll my eyes at him, to show him he didn't faze me, even as I wanted to run my finger along his inked-up body and see the work of art. I didn't even get a chance to really see them before he threw out a punch, and I had to dodge it. "You're quick, too." Then he kicked at my legs, and I hopped back before they landed.

"Or you're just slow. I can't decide." My taunt made Ax smirk.

"You got a mouth on you, Siren." He made another move to take me down as he tried to tackle me, but I leaped up over him and landed on the other side.

"You're right, and it has only gotten worse with time. *Very bad* wife material." I prodded, hoping he took me seriously.

He turned around and made another lunge for me, but, this time, it was for my legs, and when I jumped, I didn't pull them up high enough. He snagged my foot and yanked me down onto the mat with a thud.

He quickly scrambled on top of me, getting right into my face as he heaved out, "I like that mouth of yours."

"Oh, come on," I breathed out before rolling to the side with all my strength, effectively switching places.

With my hands around his neck, I cut off his breathing. He wheezed out, "I like this, too." It was true, too. I felt him rapidly growing harder between my legs as my hands tightened around his throat. His hands cupping and caressing my ass.

I growled in his face out of frustration before I leaped off him. I didn't want this fucker hard, I wanted him bleeding and crying to go home. "Get up, Rossey. Stop playing and fight me like you want to win."

That got his attention, and he stopped looking at me with humor in his eyes, replacing it with the fire of competition. That's what I wanted. I got into my favorite fighting position, ready to finally start when I heard a crash to my left.

I turned toward the sound and saw Sam fumbling with some gym equipment. His eyes widened, and I knew I made the wrong decision. As soon as I turned my head, two arms circled me, trapping my arms at my sides, my face crushed to his chest, and he was just . . . holding me there.

"What the fu—" I gasped before his body vibrated, and his muscles puffed up, almost making him thirty percent bigger, which only meant one thing, he tapped into his wolf, and now he had impossible strength even I couldn't break out of.

I tried to find some wiggle room to escape, but his grip made it impossible. Then I tried to kick him in various spots: thighs, knees, shins, but nothing seemed to hurt him or make him vulnerable. His huge python arms responded by squeezing tighter and tighter the more I struggled.

After a few minutes of my struggling, he whispered to himself, "I'll be the winner. No one else but me." Then he bent backward, lifted me, keeping me locked in his arms as he maneuvered us out of the ring.

"What the hell, you fucker? You're not going to fight me? You don't think I can take you?" I had my forehead resting on his stupidly sculpted pecs, trying to keep some room between us so I could breathe.

"No, Little Siren. I'm just playing a different game. One I intend to win. So, be a good little girl and just stay like this for an hour." He chuckled at his own words, words I didn't understand.

Sam called out, "Hey! Where are you taking her!?" He trailed after us, determination set on his face, but even I could tell Sam was no match for Ax, especially if he was wolfed out.

"Keep out of this," Ax growled as he kept going.

When I noticed he was taking me to the front door, I yelled out, "Sam! Call Cosmo and tell him what is going on."

Ax laughed as he opened the door. "Yeah. Call Cosmo. Tell him I'm going to need a witness for my win."

I stiffened at his words. *Did Cosmo have something to do with this?* I didn't want to believe he would betray me like that, but if my dad ordered him to, then he didn't have a choice, but that still kinda hurt my heart.

I let go of my hurt feelings, needing to focus on what was happening because I didn't know about this *game* he mentioned, but I knew I needed to find out. I relaxed, waited for my moment as he got me over to his car.

He shoved my back up against a large black SUV, his nose diving for the nape of my neck as he took a long whiff and breathed, "That's right, Little Siren. Relax and give in to the inevitable."

All of my carefully crafted plans of putting him at ease smashed to pieces as my rage surged. The bad bitch in me rose to that "inevitable" comment. "Inevitable? You think you have won something that has to do with me?"

I barked out a laugh before I flipped my crazy switch and glared at him, promising as loudly as I could. "Just relax for one second, and you will see how fast I'll reach down your throat, grab onto your intestines, and rip them through your mouth so you can taste your own shit!"

At first, he looked at me in shock, his eyes not computing what was happening in front of him. I bet all the girls fell over their feet for his growly voice and annoyingly cocky attitude on the daily, but not this little lady. You challenge me like that, and I would ensure you didn't win. I would break my own neck to make it so.

His eyes sparkled, showing me just how insane he was, as he grinned down at me with his rugged, handsome looks. "No one has ever talked to me like that . . ." He clutched me harder as he ran the tip of his nose along my cheek. "I think I like it." He pressed his hips up into me so I felt exactly what he meant as his hard dick ran against my thigh. "Keep spitting your venom at me, Siren. I want it all, and when my head is finally between your thighs, and you change your tune to praise, I will relish in your ruin." He crowded in even closer as his breathing turned rapid, and his dick throbbed, telling me he was *really* into it. *Fuck!* That was not what I wanted.

"Sir?" We turned our heads at the same time, pissed off at whoever had interrupted our little game of push and pull.

"Sir, did you need my help getting Miss Desmond into the car?" He didn't look at me, which was wise, but I was in a pissy mood.

"If you fucking touch me, I will make sure you are split open, holes put into your shoulders as I hang you on a pole like a flag and watch your insides flap in the wind." The guy gave Ax a pleading look, wanting to be out of this situation faster than having his pants on fire.

Ax grunted at me. "On this, I agree with you." He faced his thug and threw his chin at the driver's seat. "Go into the front, wait for me to get her in the car myself, and then drive us to the villa. You understand?"

"Yes, sir," he said as he scurried to his new post.

"That son of a bitch was fast," I mumbled.

"You don't have to worry about that with me, Siren. I can last for hours, but with you"—I felt his eyes roam my body, lust clouding them—"I could last for days and nights worshiping this body."

I rolled my eyes at him. "Oh, come on. Does this shit really work on girls? Or do you only fuck the dumb ones?" He bristled at that, and I felt like I had hit a nerve, so I kept going. "Now that I think about it, that makes sense." Then I placed my lips along his Adam's apple as I whispered, "A guy like you couldn't keep a queen, only dealing with the easy prey."

That was apparently the right button to push because he loosened his arm to yank open the car door, and I saw my opening. I reared up my head and slammed my teeth into his chest, making sure not to pull any blood but cause the most amount of pain. He jerked back as he groaned out, and I quickly ripped my teeth out of his skin and used my vampire speed to run as fast as I could away from this would-be kidnapper.

All I heard in my blur was a roar, not of pain like I wanted but of frustration. Of longing. After a few seconds, the wind around me carried the sound of a howl, a howl that signified a wolf on the hunt, and I knew I needed to get away as fast as possible.

@Tpiola_

CHAPTER 10

I RAN A GOOD distance from the gym, not knowing if Ax would wolf out and come after me or not—better safe than sorry. Once I got to a main road, I slowed down. I didn't think he would make a big scene in public, but I didn't know the man, and that was half the problem. I didn't know these heirs, which meant I didn't know what they were capable of. Sure, I could go by the rumors going around, but that always seemed drastically inaccurate. You could always make people think one way about you when, really, you were the opposite of that. It's all in how you present yourself and maintain that reputation. I bet they knew that very well.

I wondered about some things Ax said. He was playing a different game and implied Cosmo wouldn't help me. I won't lie, that hit me the hardest.

Cosmo has always been there for me, whether I wanted him to or not. He never gave me a choice. At first, I hated it. It made me feel like everyone thought I couldn't protect myself, that I would need a man to always be with me to take care of me, and I wanted to prove them all wrong. I would put myself in horrible situations to prove I needed no one.

When I turned eighteen, I thought I was hot shit. I wanted to prove to my dad, to the clan, that I was worthy of being a lone leader. I went to take on this midlevel thug that owed us lots of money alone, with no backup, not telling Cosmo or Rick what I was doing.

Refusing to use my dad's name to get it, and I let him think I was an average Desmond clan member. He didn't have the money, and he didn't know I was the Desmond, so he had twelve of his guys beat me up, keeping me in a mage confinement trap to prevent me from escaping. They dumped me behind one of our casino alleys, half-conscious and bleeding. It was one of the most shame-filled moments of my life.

Somehow, Cosmo found me. He had been searching the strip for me and stumbled upon me in the alleyway before anyone else did. I remembered him telling me he was sorry for breaking my one rule as he coerced me to release my fangs. He placed my head to his neck, my teeth brushed his skin as he whispered against my ear, begging and pleading with me to drink from him.

Being in so much need, feeling the beat of his pulse against my teeth, I sunk in and pulled at his life-sustaining elixir. I remembered the taste of his blood, the overwhelming taste of sweet bourbon-covered cherries rushed down my throat and burned as it filled my veins. I remembered clutching at him, pulling harder and harder, trying to grab every single drop of his intoxicating blood. A moan sounded in the background, I think, but I was so focused, so consumed with his blood that the rush in my ears, and his taste on my tongue took over all my senses.

I don't remember releasing him, but when I cracked my eyes open and saw the blood on his neck, I apologized. He smiled down at me, and relief flooded his eyes, as well as a twinkle of some other emotion I couldn't put my finger on. He hushed me, telling me everything was okay. When I tried to get up and wobbled, he caught me, telling me I needed to rest, and he would take me home. Humiliation and regret overtook my body, and for the first time since my mother died, my eyes watered, beseeching him to not tell my dad, to not take me home. I couldn't face him. I didn't want to feel even worse from his rage and disappointment.

The sight of me pained Cosmo as his eyes trailed over my bruised and bleeding face and body, the healing barely starting with his blood in my veins, and he reluctantly agreed. He covered me with his jacket and got us a room at the casino. Cosmo called my dad and said I was too drunk and wanted to stay the night here to sleep it off. He was a little miffed at him for letting me get that drunk, but he agreed and said he wanted to talk in the morning. We stayed in the room the whole night. I lay on his chest and went into a deep-healing sleep, and in the morning, I was refreshed and had a silver ring on my thumb. He told me to always wear it to remind myself he was always there for me. It was both the worst and best night of my life.

From that day forward, even though I had never drank from him again, I still tasted his essence on my tongue when I looked at him. That delicious combination of a fruit sugar and oak tasting burn, making the perfect combination. I felt him lingering inside my veins, and it brought me peace. Something clicked that night, and I was never again able to see him as my annoying brother. Instead, I saw the man. He was someone I wanted with the depths of my soul, but the one person I could never have, shouldn't have. It's why I was so vigilant at not drinking from someone unless they were mine. I couldn't go through something like that again.

Even with the boyfriends I've had, drinking from them never felt like that. It was never some soul-deep connection, a taste I couldn't get rid of. It was a function of my body, a way to fuel me from a source that was mine, but I still didn't divert from that rule. It was why when I bit Ax, I didn't pull at the blood available and wiped my mouth, only using my teeth as a weapon. Even then I got the littlest bit of a drop, and the flavor was explosive. Wild and earthy. I knew I made the right choice not drinking from him.

Which was why it was so shattering to think Cosmo was a part of this, that he would either go against me or, worse, not help me when I needed him, but I couldn't make myself remove the ring from my thumb. It had become bigger than a reminder of that night.

The pavement was hard against my feet, the repetitive pounding causing me to lose myself in my own thoughts, not paying attention when I heard a car coming up behind me. That was until I felt a strong current lift me up off the ground and propel me into the sky. I turned my head to look down and saw Falcon in a black Porsche Boxster convertible with one hand on the wheel and the other controlling his air magic currently suspending me in the air.

Since I didn't get a lot of exposure to mages, I always found their power so interesting, which was why instead of being fearful and yelling about being up in the air like most supes would be, I was fascinated. I watched the currents flow up, hoisting me in the air and moving around my body gently, almost cradling me before it lowered me.

I was lowered into the seat next to Falcon, the air pulling the strap next to me and buckling me in. The whole time, I was staring at Falcon in shock, thinking all of this magic was so cool and handy as he kept his face pulled tight and focused on the road in front of him. He tapped something on his watch, something that looked vaguely like a timer, and then spoke with an even tone. "You can turn the car stereo on if that makes you feel better."

When I continued to stare at him, not moving or making a sound, he flicked his gaze at me briefly, seeing my obvious change of clothes, then back to the road. "Did you need to get your clothes?"

I straightened my spine as I cooly replied, "What? Are leggings and a bra too risqué for the Winstales? Not proper enough?"

His hands tightened on the wheel as he mumbled, "No. I just didn't know why you kept looking at me."

I leaned back into the seat as my hair flew every which way. I kept having to pull it out of my mouth as I talked.

"Oh, well, it couldn't have anything to do with the fact that you scooped me up off the road like I was some paper on the sidewalk and then put me in the car and buckled me like I'm a five-year-old child." His whole body went rigid, glowering at me from the corner of his eye at my sarcasm.

"It was faster and safer this way."

I slumped in my seat, occasionally spitting out my hair as it kept getting into my face. You would think with medium-length hair, I wouldn't need to worry about that, but no such luck. After my third attempt to get the strands out, the air changed around me. Almost like they were pushing away from me instead of into my face, and my hair settled. I had a feeling I knew who took care of that, but Falcon kept his eyes on the road. The only indication it was his doing was on his right hand, his pointer finger was up, I assumed controlling the air.

"Thank you." I tried to match his tone from earlier. It was this perfect blend of "it's not important," "why am I here?," and "I guess" attitude I seemed to not be able to master. If I did, I think my dad would be very happy with me. "Is there any way you could take me home? I don't have my phone, and my car . . . was wrecked." Yeah, that was plausible. I wrecked it, and that's why I was walking on the side of the road.

I didn't want to admit that Ax was trying to kidnap me; that just made me sound weak and helpless, and I didn't want that to affect our new relationship of being heirs to the Syndicate. Plus, I would deal with him later.

"It seems like a lot was sprung on you at the meeting." His matter-of-fact tone calmed my nerves immediately.

"You could say that again. My own dad drugged me and brought me to that meeting because he knew I wouldn't come if he told me ahead of time." I thought about it as a leader for a second, putting myself in his position. "I mean, it was probably his only move, so I understand it, but still. I don't like being drugged. It sucks."

He glanced at his watch and then turned off the highway, staying silent for a few minutes as he drove the backroads of the strip. I pointed to the next left. "You can make a left here."

When he didn't turn where I said, I frowned at him. "It's okay. You can make a left over—"

"How do you know so much about weapons?" His sudden deflection got my attention, causing the hair on my arm to stand up. How did he know where I was? Why was he there and ready to scoop me up? Why would he want to keep me in his car? Those questions paled in comparison to the questions I wanted to know right now.

"Falcon, why are you not taking me home?" He flinched at the question, still not looking at me, but I felt his gaze on me nonetheless. *How did he do that?*

"I thought that—" He glanced at his watch.

"And why do you keep looking at your watch? What are you planning? Tell me the truth, or, so help me God, I will . . ." I had to think of something horrible because I had a hunch that normal things like bodily harm didn't matter to him. "I . . . I will go to the labs here and smash everything I see." I drilled my glare into his head, wanting him to feel the intensity of my gaze and understand I was not messing around. There was no doubt I would do what I said, even if it was just to get even with him.

He sighed, sounding more annoyed than anything, but I got a hint of fear, too. I think he didn't like that I found that weakness of his so soon. "Listen, this wasn't my idea. In fact,"—he twisted to the side and faced me as we were at a stop light—"It was your father's idea." I crossed my arms and motioned for him to continue. Knowing my dad, it would be a doozy.

The light turned green, and he faced forward again, but his eyes kept sliding to the side to view me. "He set up this . . . challenge to us heirs." My back bristled at the thought he would go behind my back yet again about *my* future. Something I told him not to do because I knew what I was doing. It was just another way I felt like he didn't trust me.

"He said that if any of the three of us 'caught' you and kept you for one hour, we would win your hand in marriage." He checked his watch again, and I flipped out. I used my vampire speed and strength to rip the watch off his arm and throw it onto the side of the road.

"Hey! That wa—" I unbuckled myself and got right in his face as I flashed my fangs.

"Take me home now!"

His face turned cold, his voice menacing as he said, "No." The only indication he felt something was that his hands glowed red, melting the steering wheel.

I motioned to his hands. "Look, you don't even want to do this. You don't know me. I doubt you would even like me, let alone love me."

Before I went on a longer tirade, he quipped, "What does love have to do with this?" he asked like he was genuinely confused, and that stunned me.

"What do you mean? Don't you want to spend the rest of your life with someone that you love? Someone you care so deeply for that you can barely stand being away from them for too long? Don't you want to find your . . . what do you mages call it? Your . . . neutralizer? Your mate?"

His pulse quickened, and his breath grew heavier as he spoke. "You know nothing about that. I would suggest you don't talk about something you have no idea about."

So, I guess I got under the ice king's skin. I guess I should do more of it, maybe he would make a bad move, and I could counter it to get out of this mess. "So, what? Are you trying to say that you don't want to find your neutralizer?" I put my finger to my chin and pretended to think. "I guess you are right. I wouldn't want another person's presence to suddenly change my world and the way I wanted to live it." I shrugged like it wasn't a big deal, but from the tic in his jaw and the way he was grinding his teeth, it was.

He jerked the car to a stop, and I flew forward so fast, if I didn't have vampire reflexes, I would have smashed my head on the dashboard. He turned his body to face me, vibrating with the power he was keeping inside as he grabbed my chin and jerked it up. "You know nothing about a mage's neutralizer. It's the one person in the world

182182

182182KIRA STANLEY

that cannot be hurt by the mage's magic. The one person they can't control or coerce into doing what they want."

He let go of my chin like I was on fire, staring at his fingers that just touched me. When I rubbed at my chin, he faced forward as he continued in a soft tone, trying to get me to understand. "It was the person that was supposed to feed our soul and make our magic stronger by making us stronger, healthier beings. Reminding us of our humility and anchoring us to this world to make sure our power didn't overcome us. Our neutralizer is to be revered, not made fun of just so you can get your way." He spat out that last part, and I felt a little bad about it until I remembered he wasn't taking me home, and then I threw all those emotions out the door. He was hiding something from me, and I knew it.

"What's going on, Falcon?" I made sure my tone gave no room for any more excuses.

He took one big breath as he closed his eyes, and then he opened them again, and all emotion was removed as he faced me again. "I will be entertaining you for an hour at the villa. You can do whatever you want as long as you stay inside of my villa."

I tilted my head forward, narrowing my eyes on him like a viper ready to strike. "I am going to give you one last time, Falcon. What is going on?"

He put his car into drive as he mumbled, "Fuck, I didn't want to have to do this." Before I could do anything, he pushed a button on his dash and out came some smoke from the air vents. He lifted his right hand and used his air magic to make a sphere around my head, circling the smoky substance around my face.

I started to get sleepy as I fumbled over my words, realizing what he had done. "And they say only women use drugs."

He huffed out a laugh, but my vision was hazy, and I only saw his outline as he caught my drooping head with one hand and laid me down gently. "It's not poison or anything, it should just give me enough time to win. I promise nothing will happen to you."

I tried to laugh but it came out a snort. "I'm going to fucking kill you."

Right before my eyes closed, and everything went dark, he whispered, "I know and I'm sorry."

I woke up all groggy, turned to the side to dry heave, but nothing came out. *What the fuck did that dickhole give me?*

I felt around my body, all of my clothes were on and in the arrangement they were in before I went night night, but he could be meticulous, so you never know.

My gaze flitted around the room, wincing at the light in the corner shining brightly. I could tell this was one of our villas that we gave each family for their stay. Seems he was telling the truth when he wanted me to go to his villa.

I slowly got up, moving my muscles around to get the stiffness out. My shoulder felt weird, and I turned around, glaring at the couch that made my body all achy. As soon as I got out of here, I would have to replace this piece of shit from all our villas. It sucked ass.

Mumbled voices caught my attention, and I paused, trying to listen in on the conversation. It sounded like some chatter from two guards walking around, complaining about the bosses not letting them guard them and wanting to go to the casino if they were not needed. I waited until they passed the door to this room.

I needed to get out of here, and now. Especially since Falcon left me unguarded, that meant the odds were in my favor. Slipping out of the room, I quickly recognized I was in the room to the back of the villa, opposite of the front doors, but that didn't matter. I knew these villas like the back of my hand, and there was a back door for catering in the kitchen to my right.

I tiptoed my way over to the kitchen, making sure to not make a sound, but it was oddly quiet here. Over at my house, if I wasn't yelling, fighting, or playing around with my dad, Cosmo, or Rick, there were always clans members walking around, checking on things, and keeping us updated on everything happening. Here was like a ghost town.

I opened the door to the kitchen, excited about only being steps away from freedom, the grogginess dissipating with each step, and there stood Falcon at the island, staring into a coffee mug with a gun beside it. His head lifted, and our eyes met, his eyes widened as I paused. For a second, I thought I saw a little admiration twinkle in his eye, but I could just be projecting. It was only a second of a pause, but I knew I shouldn't have, I shouldn't have waited because that was all it took before his gaze hardened, and he raised a gun only inches from my face.

"You should have been out for another twenty minutes."

I smiled and shrugged. "Vampire's process toxins and foreign substances quicker than any other species." He nodded, opening his mouth to say something, like he knew that, but I continued. "Also, I had a dad that wanted me to process them even faster than others knew, so we would practice on each other. It's probably why he thought it was okay to drug me to get me to that stupid meeting, since we used to do that to each other all the time, building up a tolerance so our bodies knew what to do quicker than usual. Also, what's going to happen in twenty minutes?" I stepped closer, and he took one back, eyeing me like a tiger out of its cage. He wasn't wrong.

"You don't think I will shoot you?" His tone told me he would most definitely shoot me, but I also smelled why.

"Oh, I know you'll shoot me. Especially since your gun is full of more of that substance that took me out earlier." I tapped at my nose when he looked at me in disbelief. "I was encased in a magical air sphere of that crap. I can now distinctly pick out those smells."

Then, with vampire speed, I grabbed the barrel of the gun with my left hand and tilted my head to the left. Before he even got a shot off, I slammed my right palm into his wrists, twisting the gun out of his grasp and turning it around on him in less than a second.

I smiled as he raised his hands. "I think you knew there was a chance of me waking up, it's why you had this ready"—I waved the gun around—"but you got a little lazy or cocky, you can pick which, since you know yourself better than I do." I stepped back toward the exit, and his eyes flicked to the door, then to the watch on his arm.

"Are you going to tell me what is going on?" I kept the gun pointed at him, and he smiled.

"You are either going to have to stay around for the next fifteen minutes for me to explain, or you're going to need to escape. You can't have both, wild girl." He smirked at me, already knowing I hated those choices. I wanted both, but I also knew if I waited around for the answer, it would be too late, and he would win. I couldn't have that.

"For being the quiet one, you're kinda a dick." His grin widened into a full smile, and I pulled the trigger. A small pellet-sized ball hit his cheek, breaking on impact, and the substance went up his nose. I turned and ran for the door, flicked the lock, and swung the door open.

"Thanks for the toy," I threw over my shoulder as his eyes drooped, and I ran off the property as fast as I could.

CHAPTER 11

I RACED OUT OF the villa and went toward my home. I was getting ready to march up to my dad and demand to know what he started until I remembered who my dad was. He was the type who would think it would be funny to keep that information from me, having this be some kind of test, then commenting for months about how I failed the simple test. I was not going through that again.

I stopped running and thought about all the little pieces I had gathered from everyone. It seemed like there was a game he instructed, with Cosmo playing some part where he couldn't help me, and with the heirs capturing me for an hour. At this point, I escaped two out of the three of the heirs, which meant for the last one I should take the fight to him. Maybe I could learn the rest of this idiotic plan my dad has concocted and then blow it up in his face. I rubbed my hands together, grinning at the picture in my mind of my dad being shocked I didn't get captured in the time limit.

That's right, old man. You thought you could trip me up, but you trained me too well. I can take these boys on. I'm not afraid.

I thought about Avery and what I've heard about him. They say he's a playboy, always on the prowl for his next twenty-four-hour woman, but he was meticulous with his clubs and didn't like management messing with the talent. I'll also admit he was easy on the eyes. His delectable body with his sharp, smooth features, and his devil-may-care smile to match his cotton-candy-pink hair. A man like him would want to do work and pick up a lady, not wasting his time doing it separately. I changed my trajectory and headed in the direction of Veshta's place.

Even if he wasn't there yet, I knew he would eventually be there, and I could wait for my prey.

I was right, he wasn't here yet, it was still a little early for the clubbing scene as the music was more radio stuff, and the performers were getting ready. I grabbed the most-secluded booth not in the VIP seating area because I needed to watch the door. As I was sitting there stewing over everything that had happened, I wondered why Avery wasn't gunning for me? It seemed like this had a time limit, and the other two were right on point. So good in fact that after this ridiculousness, I would need to ask Ax and Falcon how they found me so quickly.

I had been caught off guard by both of them, and I was determined not to have Avery do the same. Since I didn't have my phone to ask the normally reliable resources to help when doing my research, I had to rely on the facts I already knew.

I knew he was fae, which meant he had wings but didn't take them out unless they needed to for survival. He was also an heir for the skins side of the business, which meant he didn't mind getting his hands dirty. He would probably be experienced at disarming people. Then there was power. I didn't realize Ax was stronger than other wolves and didn't have that much experience with mages to know how Falcon's magic worked. With Avery, I had to keep his magic at the front of my mind.

Most fae had various types of illusion magic. So, I needed to keep my wits about me. He could change himself or the area around us. I know if I had that power, then I would pretend to fight someone, only to back them up into a cage they didn't know they were in. I wanted to make sure this didn't happen, and so I started to feel out the room, get as many smells and textures of the place down so if he messed up those small details, I could pick it up. My dad used to say illusions were only as good as you let them be. I was also a vampire, so their magic only affected us for so long.

Vampires by nature took blood from others, consumed it, then their DNA changed it into vampire blood that gave us longer lives and stronger and faster bodies. My dad explained that because of our nature to adjust at a faster rate, causing our bodies to change in a quick time frame, made it so fae magic only stayed in our system in shorter increments. This differed from mage magic since it happened outside of our bodies.

Since the Desmonds have a direct line to the source vampire, we had a much stronger stock than normal vampires. Same could be said about all of the heirs. They all have bloodlines that were tied to either the first or royalty of their species. It's what made most supes fall in line, but we didn't shy away from proving our strength to those that thought to challenge us. Once all four of these families came together as one unit, this made it so most of the supernatural world knew their place among us. So, really, I didn't know how fast I could burn through his magic, but I guess I would find out today.

A sweet-looking little pixie of a girl sauntered over to my booth with pep in her step, and her bright-pink underwear peeked out of her short, pleated skirt with each sway of her hips. Her top wasn't even clothing, it was some kind of iridescent tape that lifted her boobs, which I was slightly fascinated with. Wasn't that uncomfortable? She scanned me with hungry eyes, like she wanted to lick the inside of my mouth. She was coming on a little strong for my taste, but I bet it worked for all the macho men and their wallets.

She pressed her hip into the table as she leaned over, but since her tits were taped, they didn't move and give her the cleavage she was going for. I leaned back, putting my arms out around the booth as I smirked at her approach.

Before she even got a word out, I asked, "Is that comfortable?"

She blinked at me a couple times in surprise, stunned I wasn't drooling over her before she shook her head as she stumbled over her words. "Um . . . I . . . I mean, it's . . . fine, baby."

I shrugged. "I wasn't trying to trip you up or anything, I was just curious. I would be nervous about the tape part around the nipple area."

She looked down, stunned, before she puffed out a laugh. "Yeah." She dropped the sultry attitude and gave me a bashful smile. "I mean, it's not super fun to take off after work but . . ." Her eyes traveled around before she leaned in. "If you're into pleasure-pain play in the bedroom, then they could be a useful tool on those sensitive parts."

I gave her a lewd smile as I clasped my hands together and rested my chin in my hand. "Well, thank you for the tip, sweetheart. I'll need to try that out." She giggled and shook her head like I was the bad one.

"I'm Kiki, by the way. So, what will you have, girl?" She gave me one last look of wonder, trying to figure out which way I swung.

"How about a big dick that isn't attached to an even bigger dick?" She laughed at my joke, both of us smiling now.

"Oh, girl, I don't even know if they exist." She sighed.

I pursed my lips like I was really bummed. "I'd hoped you wouldn't say that." Then I shrugged again, knowing it was a lost cause. "At least there's enough gin and tonic in the world to drown my sorrows in."

She nodded. "So that means you want two?" She winked at me, giggling. It was cute, I bet she would get higher tips with the cute girl angle than the sultry one.

I went to reach for my wallet but remembered I had fuck-all with me than the clothes on my back and the gun that made people go to sleep. "Just tell them to put it on the Desmond tab."

Her mouth dropped as she asked, "Are you Rayla? Rayla Desmond?"

My smile widened as I gave her a wink. "Are you new to the strip?"

She blinked a few times before answering, "Yes, but I was told as soon as I got here how it all worked and who was in charge." She put her hands together, trying for the prim-and-proper vibe, but I waved my hand at her.

"Hey, honey, you just act normal. Trust me. As long as you don't talk about us, or anyone on the Syndicate, you won't be in trouble." I tilted my head, narrowed my eyes, and made sure they were void of all emotion as I cooed, "Take this as a warning, though, we have ears and eyes all over. You won't get away with it if you break the rules. It's better if you come to me before making any side deals with the lower thugs." I didn't break eye contact with her, drilling my eyes into hers until she nodded her head in fear.

I flipped the switch, smiling like I wasn't threatening her as I sat back, and she looked for a quick retreat. The beat to the music kicked up a notch, and I swayed a little as I said, "I have a small favor to ask." She paused her escape and turned to me, waiting.

"Do you know Avery Glovefox?" She quickly shook her head, and I sighed.

"I wasn't in yesterday, but some of the others were here and saw him." Her hesitation made me laugh. It was like she expected me to ask her to kill him for me. Most people here know I liked to do that part all on my own.

"Perfect. When he comes in tonight, can you just whistle." She gave me a puzzled expression, and I found it adorable with her short baby-blue pixie cut. I pointed to my ears. "I'm a vampire. I will hear your whistle from the bar. I will look at you, and all you need to do is point out what VIP booth he is in. That's all."

She appeared unsettled, and I rolled my eyes. "We are both a part of the Syndicate, and I wanted to play a . . . prank on him. That's all." I held up my hands like I wasn't threatening, but fear flickered in her eyes as she nodded. I wasn't fooling her.

"I'm going to get your drinks." She backed away, and I kept smiling like a loon. I didn't want to freak out the poor girl, but first-timers needed to know the severity of their situation.

Soon, she slid two gin and tonics to me, and I smiled my thanks as I waited.

It was a while. I counted my drinks on the table. One, two . . . five drinks later, and I was second-guessing my place of choice. Did he go to the club I met Ax in? Maybe one of the strip clubs on the strip?

As I contemplated leaving, I heard a high-pitched whistle and looked at the bar. My blue-haired faerie caught my eyes and nodded to the left. There stood Avery, dressed to the nines in a light-gray suit with pink socks that matched his hair, and he walked up the stairs to the VIP section. I waved my fingers at my waitress and went to the back corner, knowing about a spot the posts were where I could climb up to the second floor without being noticed.

I was stealthy and swift, and I hoisted myself up and made it over the railing, timing it for when the bouncer wasn't looking.

He shook hands with the security, waved at a couple of the waitresses, and winked at some of the other VIPs before he claimed a booth in the back next to the bar. I would admit I was a little green with jealousy at the moment. He has been here less than two full days and the whole section already knew him and liked him. It was obvious he was the social-butterfly type with his ease at commanding a crowd.

I was the opposite. I liked to sit down and have them come to me. Make them have the balls to approach me, then I didn't mind entertaining the person, but Avery was a man of the people. Which was why I was slightly surprised he sat in the booth I always had reserved for myself. It was off to the side and behind the bar, covered in shadows and darkness next to one of the service doors. I liked to keep tabs on the workers but also have a place where it would be easy for them to talk to me without a whole lot of prying eyes.

That's why him sitting at my table was a benefit to me. I went with vampire speed to the service-closet door on the opposite side of where he was. It was a single half-circle closet with two entrances, so if either bartender had to come back here to get something, they could. Also, some waitresses and performers used it as a place to take a moment away from the customers, to get a break from the pawing hands and ridiculous comments. It's why I always respected the staff, they endured all of that and didn't punch or stab a customer in the face. I was not that strong.

I snuck into the closet, grabbed a steak knife, and made my way to the other side. I waited for one of the bartenders to come in so they had the discretion of going out the door, and I could sneak out behind him. If I went out on my own, the door opening would catch his attention, and I didn't want that. This whole plan hitched on being stealthy.

It wasn't long before a tall blonde-bombshell bartender came in. She was surprised, at first, a little scared, but when I gave her the same excuse I gave Kiki, she did what I asked. She went out first, deliberately caught his eye and kept his attention as I crawled out and got behind him.

I didn't waste any time as I grabbed his hair, yanked his head back, and sawed the knife lightly over his throat before I cooed into his ear. "Hello, Avery."

At first, he tightened, the aura around him changed as what felt like an electrical current came out and surrounded us. My guess was he was pulling on his magic, but as soon as he heard my voice, he let it go and chuckled. That was not the response I wanted.

"Hello, Fierce Girl. I was wondering when you would come out to play." He kept his legs crossed and his arms up on the lip of the booth, acting like I wasn't about to saw his throat open.

I pushed it in further, ensuring I was making him bleed with the teeth of the steak knife, letting him know I was okay with hurting him. "Well, isn't that lovely, because I was here for some answers." I gave his head a firm tug, and he hissed out his displeasure.

"I will give you any answers you want, Fierce Girl, but, first, can you let go of my hair? I do a lot of work to keep it this soft and luscious, I don't want to lose some because you are being rash and stupid." Yep, that did it. I officially had enough of these heirs fucking with me. Having met my limit for the day, I raised my arm with lightning speed and stabbed him in his shoulder.

I had to give him props, he didn't scream like I thought he would, he gave a closed-lip groan, one easily covered by the pounding music and the performance going on down below, so no one paid us any attention.

"The fuck, Rayla!" he growled out as I walked out from the back of the booth and slid into the right side.

"I have had it with you fucking heirs today, that's what. So just be glad that you're not fucking lying in a pool of your own blood on the floor for calling me stupid." I bit that last part out because it was mean and unnecessary.

He had the decency to huff out an angry laugh as he grabbed the knife and pulled it out. He set it on the table and gawked at the new hole in his suit. "Awe, man. This was new."

"Sorry about it." I was not at all sorry and would do it again in a heartbeat.

He glared at me before he said, "I don't think you're sorry in the least." I shrugged, not giving away anything, with my lips in a thin line and staring at him like my whole day was his fault. He huffed before he rolled his shoulder back. "Look, you're right, I shouldn't have used that word." I nodded at his apology, just wanting to get to them kidnapping me on my dad's okay that I seemed to have missed out on.

"And this game you all are playing? What is that all about? Why are you not playing?"

His eyes flicked to mine before going back to the entertainment, pretending to watch them when I could tell his whole attention was on me. Probably watching out for another knife.

"Listen, I'm not into the whole kidnapping-a-woman-who-doesn't-want-me thing. It's a little too much effort for someone like me." I took a breath at knowing at least one of them had a brain attached to their head. At least that was what I thought until he continued. "Plus, I'm playing the long game." I growled at him, pissed with his workaround for my question. He put his hands up. "Hey, hey, hey. I wasn't the one that put this all together, that's on your pops."

I clenched my fists under the table, feeling the bite from my nails cutting, but I would not explain to him that going to my dad would be useless. I let out a sigh, tired of all the bullshit games, just wanting answers. "Just tell me." My body sagged against the booth, and I realized I needed a nap after all of this.

His jade eyes searched mine for a second, something akin to consideration flickered in them. "Your father wants the three of us to compete for your hand in marriage. He said that there was an advantage for only the first twenty-four hours in that you wouldn't know about the game. The winner of the game would've had to have kept you in their possession for one hour before declaring themselves the winner for your hand."

My body woke up as rage filled my veins, but I knew I wasn't done with my questions yet. I barked out, "And Cosmo's part?"

His eyes pinched, tilting his head as he tried to figure out why I asked the question. "I thought this was a weird request when your father suggested it, but he is supposed to be our neutral party. We could ask questions about you and get answers. He was also ordered not to help you right away."

That was what that fucker Ax meant when he tried to goad me into calling Cosmo. Something inside of me felt hollow, alone, after Avery confirmed that. He always promised to be there for me, but, in the end, he couldn't. He was bound by his oath to the Desmond clan, and, essentially, my father ranked higher than me. He couldn't help me. "So, I only have to live through twenty-four hours of this shit." I let out a sigh of relief as I snagged his drink and gulped it in one swoop.

He opened his mouth but decided against it when I slid the empty glass back over to him and signaled the bartender that he needed another. He smirked at me as he put the empty glass onto the edge of the table.

"Yeah, I don't think it's only twenty-four hours, Fierce Girl." When I leaned toward him, my eyes turned cold, and my lips thinned. He winced but continued. "My father said we wouldn't leave until one of us had your hand in marriage." My mouth dropped open because what the fuck?! All of the bosses were in on this now!

The bartender set down his drink, and he took a stiff sip. "Also, I got the feeling that this whole twenty-four-hour thing was more about you than us."

I focused on the table, lost in my racing thoughts when I asked, "Why?"

He shrugged. "It's just a feeling I got from your father. It was like he was almost pushing us to go after you, which, why would he do that unless he thought you would win?"

He had a point, but still, it was all a lot of what-ifs and maybes. As I was thinking everything through, trying not to let my emotions run wild. He scooted a little closer. I raised an eyebrow at the space between us. "And what's your game? Your angle in all this?"

He lifted his hand and gasped in pain. A twinge of guilt hit me about his shoulder, especially since he was so forth-coming with information, but I could already tell it was on the mend. That was why I always liked to play around with supes, they were less fragile. "I'm a little offended!" I looked at him expectantly, and a smile broke across his lips.

"Let's just say that I want to get to know you, and I figured the surefire way to get you all pissy and awkward around me was to try and kidnap you for an hour." He shrugged. "You're an heir, we're going to have to work together sooner than later, I would rather be on better terms with you in the long run."

I nodded because it all made sense, it was the smarter move for longevity, but I had this feeling it was more than that. I turned toward the entertainment on the stage. It was two of the best dancers Veshta had, who were an actual couple, and they were so good at dancing together, feeding off each other's sexual energy, that it made you crave a partner like that.

I turned to ask Avery for his keys when I found his face an inch from mine. He was crowding, taking up all my breathing room as he stared into my eyes like they were a looking glass. "Plus, I wanted to know more about the woman who entranced me with these rose gold eyes that sparkled even in the pitch black of the crowd. These eyes." He lifted his hand and lightly touched the corner, running the pad of his finger down my face and the column of my neck. "I want to know what they look like when they are set free."

I was being pulled into his atmosphere of lust and passion. Of something electric and explosive. I wanted to feel it, I craved to take the plunge and see what we could make with our bodies when we had the luxury of time and space. His aura called me in like an old lover, caressing me to fall into him. My eyes flicked down to his luscious lips, and I couldn't help but wonder if they would be soft or firm? What would he taste like? Just one taste couldn't hurt.

I blinked for a second and remembered my situation, jerking back right before I took this past the point of no return. He sighed as I collected myself, grabbed the knife that still had his blood on it, and scrambled out of the booth. I almost ran out of there, but I felt like that made me seem weak, and I refused to be weak in front of the other heirs. They were my equals, not better than me just because they had a dick between their legs.

I slowly turned, putting on my boss-bitch mask as I tilted my head and gave him a cruel smile. "See you later, Avery. This has been most educational."

He stiffened at my change, and I could tell it bothered him, but he didn't let that crack his knowing smile as he bowed his head at me. "Until we meet again, my fierce girl."

I then walked slowly through the club until I got to the main door and down the outside steps, then I ran home like my life depended on it.

CHAPTER 12

I WAS WORRIED, PISSED off, and down right at the end of my tether. My stomach was in knots, and my jaw hurt from all the clenching I had been doing. Rick and I had split up to try and find Rayla all day. We searched all over the strips, starting with her hangouts. I was getting more and more pissed at her for not answering my calls. *Why was she not picking up for me?* We always picked up for each other, even if we were mad, it was like a fucking rule.

We blew through all the local places quickly with no luck and then looked around the outskirts and some of the businesses she had bought up over the years. I was heading over to Guy's Gym right when Sam called me in a panic, telling me he watched Ax Rossey pick her up and was trying to shove her into his car. I slammed my foot on the gas and tried to get there as fast as I could. My heart thundering in my chest, racing with each mile I tore up, thrilled I fucking found her. I didn't know what I could do, but Ray fucking needed me, and I never once let her down when she needed me. Oaths be fucking damned.

When I screeched into the parking lot, Sam ran up to my car biting his nails with tears in his eyes, telling me she had taken off. She successfully fought off the Rossey heir and ran toward the main streets. He gave me a description of her clothes and told me she left her phone and other clothes in her locker. I went in and grabbed her stuff, pissed when I saw the millions of texts and calls that went to her unanswered. Well, at least that explains the no pick ups. I gripped my steering wheel, crushing it in my hands before shaking my head and reversing out of the parking lot, heading in the direction Sam said she went.

I again went as fast as my car could take me, squealed around corners and weaving in and out of traffic, but I found her nowhere. It was like she had disappeared into thin air. My hand ran through my hair, tugging on the short ends hard enough to hurt me because it made me feel better. I should hurt, I should be in pain. I failed Rayla. I started to sink into that space in my mind, the place that told me I was a worthless orphan that didn't deserve the Desmond name, wasn't worthy of being her protector. My body grew heavy as desperation sunk into my psyche.

It brought me back to that day when I felt this way before, the day she disappeared, and I couldn't find her. Hopelessness consumed me that day, making me scared to tell Ternin I lost her. I was so pissed off at her. I cursed her name, calling her a myriad of things, damning that stubborn brat side of her, but I was determined. Giving up was not an option. I kept searching the streets three, even four times, as it was pouring down rain. Then, by some miracle, I found her in the alley in the back of our casino. When I saw her lifeless form covered in blood and dirt, all those thoughts disappeared in a second, and all I thought was she better not die, she couldn't die. She was my everything, and I would not fail her again.

I snapped myself out of my memories from ten years ago, when I almost said fuck it and confessed my feelings to her. I reminded myself I was in this position before, and, like then, I needed to stay focused and determined. I didn't fail her then, and I won't fail her now.

What I needed to do was think like Ray. If she ran, then I would assume she was trying to run home. She drank a lot of blood this morning, so she should be juiced up enough to speed run the entire length from here. I flipped a bitch, called Rick, and told him I would go to the house but that he should stay out on the streets looking.

Once I got home, I took the stairs two at a time, ran down her hallway, and crashed into her room, which was depressingly empty. I called for her around the house until one of the clan members said she wasn't home. I went back to her room and sat on her bed. Having her scent overwhelm my senses calmed my heart, even though I was feeling lost. I ran today's events through my head. Did either Avery or Falcon get her after Ax? Were they holding her in their villa?

I decided to go check on each of them. I knew every crook, cranny, and secret entrance in our villas. I knew how to spy on them without them knowing. When Ternin had secret tunnels put into each villa, I asked him once why. In a deciduous voice, he said, "Whenever we house a rival, we can always be one step ahead of them."

I knew he meant it for non-Syndicate members, but I would use that to my advantage. It's not breaking the rules, after all.

I went down to the cellar and used the tunnel that led to the first villa. Once I was on the other side, I snuck around, using my vampire speed to avoid the few members each family brought with them. I caught Avery in the shower singing to himself dreadfully off-key, but no Ray. I wasted no time going back into the cellar and hitting the next villa.

It was weird because this villa had very few clan members, and even weirder, I found Falcon on the kitchen floor passed out. There was a cold, untouched coffee on the counter, which I found odd as well. I wasted no time as I searched the whole place, and Rayla wasn't there, either. I was growing frustrated as I went back down into the tunnels and to the last villa. I easily found the Rossey heir cleaning up what looked like a wound caused by vampire fangs. Smiling, I thought, *That's my girl,* as he growled, cleaning it. What I didn't like was after the pain subsided, he got a far-off look and a dreamy smile. Like he was reminiscing. Nope. I didn't like that, but Ray wasn't here, either, which meant this was all a bust.

I left the Rossey villa, at a loss for what I would do, when Rick called, telling me he had searched each casino, store, coffee shop, and alleyway, and she wasn't there. I was really starting to get worried again. I did another whole sweep of her hangouts myself before I went back home to confront the source.

If I had more than just me and Rick searching, we would have a better chance at finding her. Plus, this was all

Ternin's fault, he needed to be the one to put the manpower behind it.

As soon as I got back home, I barged my way into his office. He quickly assessed who it was and smiled widely with his arms out at me. "My son! What can I do for you?"

I growled before I tore up the distance between us and slammed my hands onto his desk. "This is your fault. Ray is missing because of this whole stupid thing."

He didn't seem fazed in the least. He sighed as he plopped down into his seat, rubbing at his temples, mumbling about how he should've put a lojack on her a long time ago.

I stood straight and glared down at him with my hands clasped behind my back. "I need at least six men to come with me, and we will find her—"

Ternin rolled his eyes as he blew me off. "Oh, Cosmo, sometimes you take your job too seriously. My little sunshine is fine. She always finds her way back home."

I clenched my teeth so hard I felt like they would start to bleed from the root. "Ternin, this is serious. You have three thugs going after her, and she has no idea as to why. She might just trust them because they are Syndicate. It's not like we really know these men and what kind of morals they have. It's not fair to Rayla and the Desmond name to put her life in danger like this!" I yelled that last part because while I was talking, he swiveled around in his chair, finding a squeaky spot.

"Do you hear that?" He bent down and moved the chair again until it squeaked. He mumbled to himself as he reached down to fiddle with his chair. "Well, this won't do."

I took a deep breath, ready to explode on Ternin, consequences be damned, when the door to the cellar behind his desk opened and in came all the other bosses.

"I would've taken offense to that slight on my son if you weren't just trying to defend your sister," Boss Glovefox said as he pointed at me but gave me a wink as he sauntered in with a bottle of cognac in hand. I put my hands behind my back, keeping it straight, my gaze forward, being the good soldier I knew they wanted to see but not acknowledging what he said because I wasn't sorry.

Boss Rossey rumbled out, "I mean, he kinda has a point with *your* son." Since his frame was so large, he had to turn sideways to get out of the doorway, and he was also carrying a bottle, it looked like red wine.

Boss Glovefox sat down on the couch behind me as he called out, "Riiiigggghht. My son, who has had practice and patience with many different types of ladies, is the threat." I pictured him rolling his eyes before he growled, "Your son is the one with the *beastly* behavior." He threw it out there as a direct jab at Boss Rossey, and, of course, he took the bait.

"My son! My son might be a little rough around the edges, but he can control himself." Then he slid his eyes toward Ternin accusingly. "But, I mean, come on, Ternin's girl is much more beastly than my son." He let that hang out there, and I felt everyone's attention switch over to Ternin, who was sitting at his desk, hands folded as he glared at Rossey.

Then, in very typical Ternin fashion, he stood, smacked his hands onto his desk, and let out a huge laugh.

"Yeah. My little sunshine has the power of the fucking sun in her veins, what else did you expect?" He crossed his arms, proud of himself until the Winstale Boss waltzed across the room with a bottle of whiskey.

"And she was raised by your crazy ass. I'm surprised you even raised such a strong, smart, and independent woman. The fact that she's only a little unhinged seems to be because of how strong her mother's genes are." He picked a single lounge chair in the corner near the bookcase, grabbing a book and opening it up like he didn't just drop the bomb of an insult onto Ternin while praising Rayla.

With Ternin glaring at Winstale flipping pages in the book, Boss Glovefox broke up the silence as he was the first to burst out laughing. "Gods, I missed this."

Ternin rolled his eyes and sat back down before he sighed and addressed me. "Cosmo, I didn't think I would need to explain this all to you, but I did not just think this up on a whim. I had talked to all the bosses about this beforehand, learned from them who their sons were and if Rayla could handle herself. I trained her to be able to handle any man on her own, but you are right that I didn't really know these men."

He looked over at one of the bosses and nodded toward me. I heard an exasperated breath as I turned toward the other bosses expectantly. Boss Glovefox was the first to speak, it seems this was his role in the group. "Look, even if Avery is a little bit of—"

Ternin cupped his hand and whispered, "A manwhore."

"*Experienced*," Glovefox grumbled. "I don't think he would go for Rayla with the obvious smash-and-grab way. It's not his style." He shrugged. "And even if he used his magic, Ternin told me that he has been training you and Rayla on how to minimize the effects of normal fae magic on your psyche. She won't be in harm's way due to *my son*." He lifted his hand and rested it on his chest with flair, then gave Boss Rossey the side-eye, effectively throwing shade toward him.

With Rossey's arms still crossed, he clutched at his biceps as he ground his teeth. "My son won't hurt the girl . . . much." He winced at his words and suddenly backtracked. "At least not anything the firecracker couldn't take. The little vixen seems like she had more than enough fire and spunk to put my son in his place, which is why I encouraged him to go for her." Then he looked over at Winstale and pointed. "His boy is the dark horse in this crowd."

Winstale clucked his tongue, still not looking away from what he was reading as he poured himself a drink, took a sip, then gave his rebuttal. "My son is hardly the one to worry about. He isn't even interested in much outside of his projects and machinery. If he was interested in her, I don't think he would even know what to do with her, let alone harm her." He left that out there as he turned the next page.

"Seeeee," Ternin said like I was crazy and putting on all the demands of him. "We thought everything through." He walked over to Boss Glovefox, who had a drink waiting for him. He lifted it to me in salute and then took a sip before he said, "This beginning bit was more about testing her reaction to them than thinking that any of them would actually win." He laughed it off, but all the other bosses glared at him. So Ternin didn't clue them in to all of his plans, good to know. At least he was being consistent.

"Fine. But still. Ray is missing, and she's not with any of the heirs. I'm getting worr—"

The front door banged open as Ray yelled so loud it echoed through the house. "Fuck you, Dad! You know what you've done, and I'm pissed more than a den of angry vipers scraping for food. I don't want to see you until tomorrow. I mean it!"

Ternin's smile turned from pleasant into a jackal in two seconds before he flipped his hand out. "See. She's fine."

I glared before I zoomed with my vampire speed to the door but had to stop myself short when Ternin called out, "And, Cosmo."

Stopping right outside his office, I turned only my face toward him as he said, "You should start to have a little more faith in your sister."

I clenched my hands into fists at my sides, digging my short nails into my palms, angry that he even thought that. "It's not that I don't have faith in her. It's that I don't have faith in anyone else."

Having had enough, I sped out, catching the sound of his voice down the hallway as he yelled from his office, "That was a low blow, Cosmo! I know that was a dig at me! And don't take it out on me if your sister is a little pissed off!"

I ignored him as I caught up to Rayla going up the right side of the wing steps. I sped over to her and grabbed her arm to stop her. "Ray, where have you been?" My voice was desperate as I begged her for an answer. Just so relieved to have her back home and safe.

She stiffened before she yanked her arm out of my grip. I pulled back, stung by her reaction to my touch, but I waited, still wanting an answer. She slowly turned around, and being a step above me, she looked down at me like a queen to her subject. One she was mad at. Her anger I could take, I have been taking it for the past twenty-two years, it was the slice of pain and betrayal that cut me to ribbons where I stood.

"What do you need, Cosmo?"

I paused, trying to figure out what made her so mad at me. Was it because I failed to get to her? Was she in trouble and needed my help? I needed to know; my mind was going crazy with possibilities.

I opened my mouth to speak, but she continued in the emotionless tone she used when talking to strangers. "You know what, why don't you ask your new *friends*? I bet they would love more *neutral* information."

She knew. One of those fucking bastards told her before I got to tell her myself what was going on and must've made me seem some sort of conspirator with them. *Fuck!*

I went to grab her hand again, but she pulled away before I could. "You know what, never mind. Don't worry about me, *brother*. I can take care of myself." She turned and zipped over to her room, slammed her door, but not before her eyes started to water. I heard all the locks switch on, and I knew I would not get to talk to her tonight. To explain myself and the situation her father put me in.

I stood on the stairs, just staring at the space she left. I would not ever be able to erase those eyes from my memory. Her golden-pink eyes usually looked at me with appreciation, respect, and confidence, and now they were marred with poisonous questions and disbelief. My chest felt like it was caving in on my heart as my blood started to run cold. She was always the reason I felt warmth, but now I acutely felt the loss of her presence, and I wanted it back.

A hand landed on my shoulder, giving me a pat. "Just let her cool down, man. You know her. She won't be mad forever." Rick took his hand away as I turned to look up at him, lost with what to do with myself if I wasn't with Ray, thinking about Ray, protecting Ray. "Fuck, man. Don't look like that. It kinda scares me when you are not the stone-cold-faced one. It's the only way we work." He pointed to himself as he smiled. "I'm the lovable funny one, and you are the cold and scary one. It's our own version of good cop, bad cop."

I didn't smile at him, just stared off into space again until he grabbed my shoulders and shook me. "Come on, man. I know it's more than that, but we have bigger fish at the moment. We need to figure out the heirs' game plan so Ray wins in the end. Remember, this is only the beginning of the game."

That caused me to think outside of my pain and focus on something I could do. Rick was right. I have lost the battle, but it was more important to win the war. I slowly nodded as he tugged on my sleeve. "Come on. Let's head into the kitchen, get ourselves some fuel, and then start our planning while Ray is pouting her night away."

I nodded as I followed while Rick kept talking about something I wasn't listening to. At least this was something I could work toward, some way I could prove to Ray I was on her side, I would always be on her side. I glanced back at Ray's door, wishing she would just whisper my name, and I would be at that door in one second, but it never came.

CHAPTER 13

THE SOLES OF MY bare feet sliding along the carpet were the only thing I could focus on as I was pacing back and forth in front of my bed. Every time I felt a heaviness in my muscles, my eyes snagged on my comfy, fluffy bed in longing, but my mind was in overdrive and refused to calm down. Thoughts kept circling around in my head like a rotary; my interactions with the other heirs, what they said, my dad's deal with them, and their fathers going with it. Then I would recall they all talked behind my back about *my fucking life,* and my whole body seized up, my nails digging into my palms as my fury rose. The pain in my hand reminded me it was all real and not just some horrid nightmare.

I turned away from my bed, faced the door as I crossed my arms, and my thoughts drifted to Cosmo. The second those thoughts hit me, I had this overwhelming ache in my heart. It was so strong it sliced through my thoughts, and those pesky feelings took over. *Fucking Cosmo.*

Exhausted with myself and my mind, I slammed my back onto the bed with an exaggerated sigh. I knew, somewhere deep down, I was being unreasonable about him and his involvement. That he was just following what my dad told him to do, but was it unreasonable for me to expect him to disobey my dad for me? That after everything, he would pick me over him? I mean, what was the worst thing my dad would do to his own son? I'm sure whatever the punishment, it wouldn't be that bad. If the situation were reversed, I would've taken any punishment for him . . . And I guess that was the problem. With him following my dad over me, it felt like the bond we had created was strained.

Since we were young, it was always him and me against my dad. Covering for each other, doing things to capture his attention off the other one, making sure we had each other's back. He has always been there for me, but when it was for something life-altering, something like marriage to someone I didn't even know, he was nowhere to be found. In fact, he was told to help the opposition. My heart clenched and felt empty.

I rubbed my hand over my chest, trying to massage those annoying feelings out. I hated feeling this way. Lost. Confused. Lonely. These feelings brought me back to a time before Cosmo, a time after my mom died.

I remembered I was so alone. My dad had to work, needing to build the Syndicate's name back up as the other families dealt with their grief. While they had time to hide, to figure out life without their wives, my dad was out there being the savage face of the Syndicate. Reminding everyone who they were fucking with. It was necessary, I know that now, but at the time, I missed having someone around. I knew I needed to be strong, like my dad, and I forced myself to turn my sadness into anger.

The house always had clan members around, doing whatever I asked, but when the loneliness set in, I kept to my room. The second anyone would try to coax me out, I would threaten them. I was this little angry ball of fire that burned anyone in my path with no remorse or care.

When I started to be unreasonable, getting violent, my dad brought in Cosmo. At first, I was a total terror to him. I treated him like a servant, telling him to do stupid things, and, for the most part, he did them without question. He wore me down day by day, doing everything with that stoic face until I yelled at him and called him horrible names for doing all those things I said. He would stare into my eyes like he could read my pain and sadness I tried desperately to hide, to feel something else. He would just respond with, "Well, if me doing these stupid things makes you smile, even if it was at my expense, it's worth it." Then he just stood there like he was waiting for my next stupid request.

After that, I invited him to do real things. Train with me. Sit with me at school. Talk about things that mattered to us. After he professed his devotion to the Syndicate, he told me he was committed to being by my side after I took over. I was impressed by his dedication, by his steadfast loyalty and unwavering inner strength. That was when I started to bring him into the fold, telling him my thoughts on the future and the dreams I kept hidden in my heart. It took years as I eased him in, tested him over and over again until I knew I could count on him explicitly. This was why, even as my mind said he hadn't betrayed me, he was just following orders, my heart screamed that he did, and it was fucking everything up for me right now.

I tried to convince myself to stay logical, to keep my emotions at bay like my dad always told me I needed to conquer. I took a deep breath, let the air fill my lungs, then imagined all my feelings leaving as I blew out that breath. Doing that a few times, my heart rate lowered, and my body started to cool.

It took me a few minutes, but when I was finally in the right headspace, I imagined being in my dad's shoes. I tried to think about things from his position, things that had nothing to do with me as a person and more as a cog in the Syndicate machine.

The Syndicate, as it stands, was divided by each family, and even if we had the same overall goals, it was still only good as long as we benefited each other. The only thing keeping it solid as a rock was the brotherly bond our dads had with each other, something us heirs didn't have. I saw my dad's point that marrying one of them would speed up that process, would ensure a stronger bond with one of them, a bond not easily broken, even with emotions and turmoil. If it stood as it was and any of us heirs got too mad at the other, they could sever the ties with little care.

In a weird way, I saw how a quick and simple marriage could be a Band-Aid for the problem, but it had some downfalls, too. What if none of them liked me? What if I didn't like any of them? Sure, we could still get married, but that bond would be half-assed, which would not do us any favors in the long run. Then what if more than one wanted me? Fighting and animosity would trickle down in generations to come.

I tapped my finger against my chin as I gazed at my ceiling, trying to follow the lines in the web my dad had created. He was no idiot, even if he acted silly sometimes, he could see these holes in this plan, which further brings me to the question of why? Why still push for it? Why make it a game? A game . . . A test?

A test. Now that was more like my dad, to use these rules and parameters to test us, but what would he gain from a test like this?

My head was hurting with all the possibilities and theories going around, trying to guess my dad's motives and moves to plan my response because he knew I would not take this lying down. It just wasn't in me.

I wasn't able to focus on a thought for too long. My fingers grew tingly, then a smile slid across my face. I knew the beginning symptoms of having low blood sugar, and that meant it was snack time.

Lifting my legs to rock me forward, I stood from the bed. I placed my hand on the knob, ready to zoom out, but then I remembered Cosmo trying to coax me out of my room to talk a bit ago, and I stopped, trying to hear if his controlled breathing was on the other side. I didn't have the energy to argue with him right now. When I didn't hear anyone, I slowly turned the knob, pulled the door open inch by inch until it was wide enough for me to fit through. I didn't see anyone in the hallway, so I blurred my way down the hallway and stairs. My mind now focused on that icy-cold, sugary treat calling my name.

Reaching the door of the kitchen, I paused and listened again. When I didn't hear anyone, I beelined straight to the refrigerator. It was weird I hadn't bumped into anyone. My dad didn't like any guards to be on our second floor where our bedrooms and his office were to give us all some privacy, but downstairs, we usually had a couple standing around, just in case. I opened the freezer and saw the two tubs of ice cream from my favorite shop, mint chocolate chip and the blood-filled bunny tracks.

The handle on the freezer door cracked as I clenched it. My heart was pounding as I knew who got me my two favorite treats. It was the person who knew these were my comfort flavors and that I would want both after everything. The person who made me feel what I didn't want to feel. It was little stuff like this that made me want to crack, that had me wanting to march upstairs, bang on his door, and when he opened it, I wanted to wrap my arms around his neck and kiss the ever-loving shit out of him . . . but I couldn't.

I repeated what I had been telling myself since that night he rescued me eight years ago. *He's your brother. You're not allowed to feel these things for him. These little gestures were not declarations of love, it's just kindness to his sister in need. He told you so eight years ago.*

I grabbed both tubs and kicked the door closed. Tonight, I would be double fisting my problems away. I cracked up at my joke as I opened the drawer at the island and pulled out a large spoon. Didn't need a bowl when it would just add an extra step. Plus, they're both for me anyway. My dad liked double chocolate, and Cosmo secretly liked strawberry. My mouth lifted at the time I caught him asking for a sample, and as soon as his stern lips wrapped around that mini spoon, his eyes closed for a second, and he sighed. I looked down at my two tubs, guilt and appreciation gnawing at me as I rolled my eyes and groaned. *I'm going to need to get strawberry ice cream later.* That way we were even, and no one was making any declarations, just brotherly and sisterly love . . . right?

With my mission complete, I ran out of the kitchen toward my room, then I stopped on the stairs at the cackling of male laughter coming from my dad's wing. I haven't heard my dad laugh like that in, like . . . ever. It was the sound of comradery and ease in his voice that caught my ears, that signaled it as strange. When I heard others laughing with him, it was like they were calling me to spy on them, to figure out what could have my silly, calculating dad be so at ease. Maybe that's why there weren't any guards around, he didn't want them to witness this.

I set the ice cream down on the top step toward my wing before I tiptoed my way over to the noise coming from my dad's office. Since I was dealing with supernatural bosses, I walked slowly and inched my way against the wall. Even if they heard a sound, they might think because of the placement and speed it was a mouse or something. Going this way was annoyingly slow but effective in not getting caught by supes. As I got closer to the closed door, I heard my dad with the three other bosses talking about us heirs.

A deep bark of a laugh rang out. "East, how do you feel about your boy being found knocked out cold by his own device?" I didn't hear anything other than the groan of a leather chair being gripped tightly.

"It's better than having a kidnapper for a son. I mean, come on, is that how he gets all of his ladies. How beastly of him, Manic." While the Rossey boss had a deep rumble of a voice, this was flippant and controlled, which meant it had to be Easton Winstale.

Manic replied in a strained voice, "That was the point of the game! Right, Ternin?"

A splashing of some liquid hit the bottom of a glass as my dad casually said, "I mean, that's one way to go about it." Neither confirming nor denying his claim.

I heard a puff of air before Manic barked, "At least he did better than Sy's boy. He didn't even try for the advantage."

Someone took a sip of something before a smooth and cultured voice called out in ease, "That's because *my* boy is the smart one. He's playing the long game to ensure his win. Unlike some mongrel trying to catch a beautiful butterfly out of his league." *Wait, was I supposed to be the butterfly?* I was a tiger or a dragon, not a fucking butterfly.

"Mongrel?!" I heard feet stomping before my dad called out.

"I think you all are forgetting one major piece of information . . . that it was *my* girl that beat them all in the first twenty-four hours. Pay up, boys." I could tell by his voice he was wearing a smug face, probably leaning against a wall or his desk with a drink in his hand for the extra fuck-you effect. He liked to make a show of his smarts.

Everyone was quiet for a second before I heard the smooth voice I knew was Syris's. "Well, she didn't technically beat my son, he didn't use his power, so we don't know yet how that outcome will be, but I will say that your little girl is a hellion. You've trained her well, Tern." I wanted to beam at the compliment but realized they didn't know I was there, and, therefore, it was more of a compliment for my dad than me.

The others mumbled their agreement, even Manic, though he sounded more reluctant than the rest, but still acknowledged my triumph. I practically felt my dad's joy beaming through the door. My body shook as I held back the sudden urge to march in there and give them all a piece of my mind. How could they toy with us like this? How could they pit them all against me? Was it because I was a woman, so they thought I would buckle easily?

I tongued the points of my fangs as I smiled at an idea forming in my mind. If that was how they wanted to play this, then I could figure out how to flip the board on them, making them a part of *my* game. Yes. I clenched up, trying not to move so they wouldn't hear me, but I was giddy with the ideas forming in my mind. They would be in for a rude awakening if they thought I was some weak female that needed a man. My goal was never to be a Mafia princess, I would be the ruler, the fucking kingpin at the top of this pyramid. Fucking watch me.

I put my hand on the cool metal of the door handle, about to bust in and tell them all that when feet shuffled toward the door.

"I'm going to have an early morning tomorrow, heading out to Smashers before the competition. I want to make sure everything is up to snuff. You know how they all get when one of us is hovering over them," Manic said as someone cracked their knuckles.

"Yes, I need to get into the lab, too. My project needs to go into beta testing, and I don't trust them to do it correctly without me there." That was Easton, and he wasn't wrong. I have been to the lab, and those guys can get messy. They were great at execution but not so much with the inventing part.

"I will talk to Veshta about the new *issue* we talked about earlier. See if she can put out some feelers in the right markets." Syris sighed. "Plus, she has *graciously* offered her office as my workstation while I'm here, and you know her, if I tell her no, she will take it as if I had spit in her face."

"I don't know why you put up with that woman," Easton called out in disbelief.

Syris chuckled. "Look, I know she's difficult, a strong-willed fae woman, but the partnership is better than a rival. She's the best at what she does, but she has no ability or manpower to expand like we do. Her only requirement for me is to not be looked at as an employee but as a co-owner of that one club. Plus . . . she helped me before the Awakening and after Reina died. She's more like an annoying sister than anything."

I didn't know that Veshta and Syris knew each other before the Awakening—when all the supes came out to the humans and established a new world order. That was when these men in this room banded together. They were friendly rivals before the Awakening but partners and best friends after. Enemy of my enemy and all that. From what my dad said, the few years that were the Awakening were the most bloody and vicious on both sides until

supe leaders came to a set of agreements with the human
leaders.

Nowadays, we had supernatural representatives and businesses, but we all still abided by the human laws established
before the Awakening. It was also agreed upon they needed
a supernatural force that took care of the unsavory supes,
the ones that didn't like to abide by laws, which was why
the Syndicate was created. Each race represented, taking
on the criminal underground, but also controlling it, and
the supes, with an iron fist. That was the agreement, and
how these four men were in the position of power they
were in. Why it was important that it continued even after
them.

"She is very talented and brings in a lot of money for us.
Plus, are any of us less eccentric?" My dad's voice volleyed
toward the others, provoking them to prove him wrong.

"I'm not eccentric like you guys." Manic tried to whisper,
but with his rumble of a voice, it came out more like a
revving engine.

I heard a big dramatic exhale that made me think of
Syris. "You are the *worst* of us all. The three of us have,
at least, embraced our weirdness, you're the one that likes
to pretend he's always in control of it. You need to let your
beast out every once in a while, my friend." He had more
of a concerned tone to him, which was why I think Manic
didn't yell at him.

The room was quiet until Manic asked, "Plan is to meet
in twenty-four hours, right?" That question woke me up,
and I realized they would start coming out the door soon.
I tiptoed back the way I came, not hearing the ending of

their little boys meeting but not having the time to stay until the end, but I didn't need to. Now I knew this was truly all a game for the four of them.

As soon as I was at the staircase, the door clicked open, and I rushed to grab the tubs of melting ice cream and got to my door before any of them saw me. [1] I maneuvered the tubs around and put my hand on my doorknob when someone cleared their throat behind me.

I closed my eyes, wishing it wasn't who I thought but knew my life never worked out that clean. I slowly turned around to see Cosmo a few doors down, leaning against his door frame as he assessed me. He took in the ice cream in my arms, and a ghost of a smile crossed his lips. It was so fucking attractive, I subconsciously bit my lip. I loved it when he smiled. It was always a rare occasion but something I held onto in the depths of my heart.

Then all those feelings from before came rushing in, and I glared at him. He picked up on the change in my mood, and his lips thinned. "Don't think that this"—I pointed to the ice cream—"makes everything good with us because it doesn't."

He blurred for a second, and then he was in front of me, closing in on my bubble so much I smelled the spearmint toothpaste he used before bed. "I didn't—"

I lifted my hand, letting go of one of the tubs, and he caught it. *Fucking damn it.* I snatched it back and tucked it under my arm for safe keeping. "Look, I'm not ready. I thought you would have my back over anything, anyone,

---

1. Song: Lovefoolby twocolors

and now I know different." His eyes filled with so much pain and regret it hurt to look at him, so I opened my door and went through.

I turned my face to the side as my back was facing him. "Don't follow me tomorrow. I have things to do that don't concern you or Rick. Something that I need to accomplish myself." Then I shut the door in his face.

I closed my eyes for a second as he cursed under his breath and thought he walked back to his room. When I expected to hear his door shut, he whispered against my door. "Ray, I will never fail you again. You're everything, and I'll make sure you understand that." Then a second went by, and his door closed, and I let out a whiny groan.

Why can't he be a normal fucking guy and let me be mad at him?! I already wanted to forgive him, and it hasn't even been twelve hours since I put him in the bad box. *Ugh!*

I stomped to my bed, crashed down on the edge to devour my make-me-feel-good snack and forget about the man down the hallway, to focus on my idea for tomorrow. It could go either very right or very wrong, but I was willing to take that risk. I was the Princess of Vegas, after all, lady luck was always on my side.

@Tpiola_

CHAPTER 14

I WOKE UP EARLY the next morning, needing to get a jump on the first stop in my plans for the day. I snapped on my best set of leggings and sports bra and slipped on my tennies as I prepared to go over to the new gym Manic said he would be at. I figured if I wasn't going to be able to convince my dad to quit this marriage nonsense, then I would need to convince the other bosses. If I got them on my side, it didn't matter what my dad had planned. He always told me the Syndicate was run by them all equally, so that meant if I got the three of them on my side, they could outweigh my dad's decision. It was a long shot, but my only shot.

I jogged down the stairs thinking about how I would go about hitting my first target when I heard the fast click of familiar footsteps, and Cosmo called out to me at the top of the stairs. "Where are you going?"

I knew him so well that even as he was trying to feign indifference, it came out like a psycho boyfriend trying to keep tabs on you. Normally, I thought that attitude was adorable and would banter with him about it, but I was still mad at him and wasn't in the mood. Plus, if he knew what I was about to do, I was sure he would try to talk me out of it or demand he came with me, and I couldn't have that . . . but I had to give him something.

"Don't worry about it. I'm going to see if I can fix this mess." I turned away as his spearmint and clean laundry scent wafted down the stairs and up my nose. I took a deep breath of it, his scent always calmed my nerves and reset my focus, as I closed my eyes. As soon as I opened them, I zeroed my gaze on the door, and I said with a bite, "Don't follow me, and don't wait up."

I didn't stay to see his face or how shocked he must've been to hear me say those words. It was rare I ever said something like that to him, let alone meant it. I raced down the stairs and out the door, knowing if I stayed any longer, I would give in to his familiar strength. It had been a long time since I was a lone, strong girl and didn't want him to watch my back, but I just couldn't deal with him as I was going to take on the three main bosses of the Syndicate. I didn't want to deal with his practicality, I needed to dig down and find that endless bravery and lack of self-preservation I was so good at.

My tennies hit the pavement as I stared up at this large two-story building of the new fight gym, Smashers. This gym was brand new and was meant to be used as one of the legit businesses we ran money through. It opened a week ago, and I hadn't been inside yet. While I loved Guy's Gym and the hometown ambiance it had, coming to the Rossey gym was like seeing your ex and being jealous of whoever got to ride that dick now. It was nauseating and gorgeous at the same time. I took in a big breath before I planned to take on the Rossey boss. *Let's go show the big bad wolf who not to mess with.*

The large lobby doors whooshed open to this wide gym that sparkled with its newness. The ripping of tape and pounding of the bags to the left of me caught my attention first.

Lined up against the edge were several punching bags hanging, each taken by men and women fighters. The repetitive punches and kicks made its own rhythm, grunting with all of their effort between. Faces furrowed with their focus and determination to improve and meet their reps. The rhythmic sounds mesmerized me by the precision of their strikes.

The clanging of weights being dropped had me swiveling my head to the right. It was a woman at the dead lift station with the biggest weights I'd ever seen. I noticed she had six hundred-pound weights on each side. That told me she was a supe, but it didn't stop others from watching her lift twelve hundred pounds.

"Keep going, Ren, and watch those upper cuts!" A bulky bald man was yelling at a fighter in the cage in the center of the room. A few people were gathered around, watching as they went at it, but the bald man just kept yelling at both fighters, which made me think he was someone who knew where I would find Manic Rossey.

I sauntered up as he spewed out his next words. "You drop that right shoulder now, Hamish, or, so help me God, I am going to knock it right out of you." Well, if that wasn't a pep talk, I didn't know what was. My hand covered my mouth to muffle my snicker because this guy almost sounded like my dad when he had been training me.

I tapped him on his muscular shoulder, and he flicked his eyes to me and sniffed before moving his eyes back to the fighters. "What do you want, vamp?"

I turned my attention to the fighters, mimicking his stance before responding. "You must be new here, wolf." He took a sharp breath as he was about to tell me off, and I cut him to the chase. "I'm Rayla Desmond."

That gave him pause for a second before he slowly turned to me as I continued to watch the fighters. I pointed to the one he called Ren. "That one is going to need his left knee to be iced. I can hear the clicking when he puts his foot back and see the blood circulating around his knee."

He studied me before he opened his mouth. "What can I help you with?" There was a slight hesitation in his voice, and I smiled before I turned my head his way.

"Oh, no vamp this time?" I cocked an eyebrow as I smirked, and his lips thinned. He knew his mistake, but he didn't want to admit it. I didn't have time to train this newb, so I took advantage of him tripping over his words. "I need to know where the boss is."

His eyes shifted around for a second before he leaned closer. "I'm not supposed to tell anyone, but since you are in the inner circle . . . he's in the office to the right." I tilted my head as I glared at him and tongued one of my fangs as I tried to figure out if he was lying.

"Are you sure he isn't in the back?" I tilted my head back.

He didn't take a step back in the way I liked when I intimidated people, but he straightened up and looked me in the eye as he said, "There is an office in the back, but it's mine. He appointed me to be in charge of this gym, so he took the one on the right side to be more hidden." I watched his eyes and listened to his pulse to detect a lie but didn't find one. I liked this guy. He wasn't a pushover by any means, laying out that this was his gym, but he still gave me the respect by giving me the information I wanted. Most men couldn't pull that off so smoothly.

I gave him a wide smile and nodded. "Thanks. I'll be headed that way. Make sure we're not disturbed." I wanted him to know that even if he ran this place, the Syndicate owned it, and I was the Syndicate.

He gave me a sharp nod and eyed the back of the room to the right. I took the hint and made my way over. It was a dark hallway, not lit up as nicely as the rest of the gym, but I guess Manic would try to deter people from coming to see him.

The hallway was eerie, just a simple solid door at the end of it, but that made me hesitate. It was the worst possible situation to surprise him in, and that was the plan. With each boss, I needed to show them I was a threat, a contender, someone they needed to at least hear out. Not because of my dad or because I was a part of the Syndicate, but because I was a badass in my own right. I would need to play it differently with each of them. With Manic, it would need to be about strength. I needed to show the boss of the muscle I could hang with the best of them, and I was not someone to be thought of as weak. I couldn't outdo him head-on, which meant I needed to sneak up on him.

I eyed the smooth gray walls and the white marble floor. Little traction could be made with floors and walls like this. I threw my head back as I sighed, trying to figure out what I would do when I noticed there was a chip in the ceiling tile. Tile . . . regular, office ceiling tile made of fiberglass, wool, and clay. I lifted my finger and counted the tiles it took to get to his office, and I came up with an idea.

I walked over to a corner, making sure my steps were light and untraceable as I found my way around his hallways. I put my leg up, instantly glad I had tennies and leggings on because this would have been difficult in a pencil skirt and heels. Pushing off the wall, I moved upward, forcing the tile away as I grabbed the solid wall edge. Once I hung on, I lifted the tile with my other hand and set it aside before I heaved myself up.

As soon as I was in the ceiling, I replaced the tile and looked around, finding the ceiling tiles that made it look like a walkable floor, but I knew better. I kept an eye on the wooden beams that could hold my weight as I made my way over to Manic's office. I didn't use my vampire speed, knowing his wolf ears could hear a whooshing of the air around me if I had, so I moved slowly and carefully.

Moving at a glacial speed but knowing that the end result would be worth it.

Once I made it to the edge of his office, I kneeled and put my ear to the tile. I could hear the clicking of the keyboard and was able to pinpoint him to the other side of the room. I tiptoed to his side, bent down, and slowly lifted a tile to get a vantage point before I struck.

He was right beneath me and suddenly paused his typing, tilting his head toward the door. I held my breath, hoping he didn't hear me. He only paused for a second before he resumed, and I sighed internally. I put the tile back down and moved back one so I could get him right where I wanted.

I bent down, feeling the back of my shoe and popped off the rubber heel. I worked my finger around and slid out the silver knife I inserted this morning. As a kid, I was a little obsessed with weapons and finding places to hide them in myself. Clothes, hairpins, lined jackets, discrete torso holsters, I tried them all. Once my dad found out about it, he started to make a game out of trying to find all the spots. It was a fun father-daughter bonding activity while I was at my most rebellious.

It wasn't until I was older, and my clothes got tighter, that I had a harder time finding a consistent hiding spot that gave nothing away. Shoes were still the best spot for small blades and compact weapons, so whenever I ordered shoes, I sent them down to Robin, the head mage for the lab here in Vegas, to craft hiding places in all of my shoes. He always enjoyed my shoe projects because they broke up his repetitive days of weapons and surveillance. It was always wise to get in good with a mage.

With my knife at the ready, I lifted myself up, took a second to listen and make sure he was still typing in the same spot, and a shiver of excitement ran up my spine as adrenaline pumped through my veins. Cosmo always said I was too much of a thrill seeker for my station in life, but what was the point of life if you didn't feel alive some of the time. I cracked a smile before I jumped feet first into the ceiling tile, crashing down swiftly.

He kicked his chair out of the way and turned toward me. I knew I had little time, so I used my vampire speed to wrap my arms around his neck and my legs around his torso, locking them in with the knife poised right at his Adam's apple. He growled low and deep in warning, and the vibrations of the growl skittered up my arms. A small part of me wanted to let go to ensure my survival, but, instead, I tightened my grip on his thick, corded neck.

He took a deep breath before he called out, "What are you doing, little vampire?" His tone was even and calm, but his body was coiled tight. I don't think he's had someone come at him like this in a while, and those few seconds of hubris was all I needed.

I'll admit it was an awkward position, me wrapped around his back, knife in hand, like a psycho koala, but I had little choice when he was so much bigger and taller than me.

I kept my voice low as I chuckled. "You all thought it was going to be that easy to make us do what you want? The boys may fall in line, admittedly half-heartedly, but I'm not the one to mess with, and I will not let you all control my life." I let the knife bite into his skin to emphasize my seriousness. The smell of his blood filled my nostrils. It had a woodsy scent of pine, minerals, and fresh rain. It was pleasant but didn't make my mouth water like his son's.

He didn't even flinch as I cut him, in fact, he chuckled as he gave a slight nod. "Then what is your proposal, little vampire?" When I hesitated, he turned his neck into the knife further to bark out in disbelief. "Surely, you thought of something to bargain with to get my support?"

"Um . . ." I bit my lip and tried to think of something smart or intelligent to say, but, instead, I blurted out the truth. "Not really. I heard you admired guts and strength, so I was hoping you would be impressed with the stones I had to come after you myself."

He laughed. The big bad Manic Rossey, the control captain, the leader of all the muscle, laughed a big belly laugh like he hadn't done so in years. It caught me off guard, which was why I didn't see his right hand snake behind me, yanking me off him by the waistband of my pants and lifting me like I was a naughty child before seeing my stunned face and laughing at me again.

I grew frustrated at the switch of my situation, I swiped at the arm holding me up, and he immediately dropped me as he hissed at my silver blade. He changed his tone real quick when he glared at me as I stood up and brushed myself off.

"Oh, don't be a baby. It barely broke the skin." We both looked down at his arm knotting itself back together, but I saw a flash of white, which meant I got down to the bone. I gave him a small smile and shrugged before sitting in the chair across from his desk. I bent down to slip my knife back into my shoe, to show I was no longer trying to threaten him now that my grand entrance was already behind us. His chair scraped against the floor as he pulled it back to the center of his desk before it creaked at him taking a seat. I was surprised at how small the desk looked compared to this mountain of a man. It made sense why others had told me being in his presence was intimidating. As he set his elbows on the desk, hand clasped, he took up three-fourths of the desk.

"Look, girl," I raised my eyebrows at his tone and choice of words, and he rolled his eyes and huffed. "Fine. Rayla. Don't you see how this arrangement is for the betterment of the Syndicate? If one of them marries you, it will create a bond that cannot be broken."

I shook my head before I leaned forward, placing my elbows on my knees, my eyes imploring him to listen. "That's where you're all wrong. Just because I marry someone doesn't mean the bond will be any stronger than what me and the other heirs have now. In fact, what we have now is so fragile you run the risk of causing jealousy or contempt. That's the opposite of what you want."

He sat back in thought before he countered. "Pitting quality fighters against each other makes them strive for the better."

It was my turn to roll my eyes and sit back as I tapped my chin in thought like I was giving his words serious consideration. "Sure. But that doesn't make them bond." He narrowed his eyes at me as I smiled, letting him know I won that round.

He looked away for a second, his jaw clenched and hands twitched, probably wanting to fist them in frustration, but he didn't want me to know I got to him even a little bit. In that moment, I was preening, proud of myself at schooling a boss, my elder, but I should've known better when he glanced at his watch and turned back with a vicious grin.

"I'm interested. You say that you want to impress me enough to take the Rossey clan out of this marriage deal, but you're going to have to do more than catch me off guard . . ." He left it out there just enough for my desperate ass to grab ahold and pull the thread.

"Name it. Name your price, and I will pay it." I hated the desperation in my tone, but it couldn't be helped, I *was* desperate.

I knew as soon as the words left my mouth I just got caught up in his game. He brought his hands to his mouth with a twinkle in his eyes. "Have you ever heard of the werewolf ritual of Othaman?"

I shook my head, digging my fingertips into the soft leather, trying desperately to not start picking my nail against the hide. It was a nervous tick I needed to get rid of. I wanted to give away little in my interactions with the bosses.

Instead of answering me, he grabbed a pen and wrote on a scratch piece of paper. He quickly ripped it off and slid it across the desk. "It's a silly little ritual that the locals wanted to enact, and since we are the strongest pack, we must attend and host."

I picked up the paper but didn't glance at it yet. Examining it meant I was going to do it, and I didn't want him to have that satisfaction this early in the game. "What kind of ritual?"

He let out a puff, and irritation creeped into his eyes. "That's not your concern, but what is your concern is how you win." It was normal that supe species held rituals and kept weaknesses a secret among their own, especially the wolves. They liked their traditions to be pure. I furrowed my brows but motioned for him to continue.

"All you need to do is win a fight against seven other girls. If you win, then I will gladly take Ax out of the running. A woman who could do that would be too wild for my son anyway. He needs a soft nice girl to round him out."

My insides were screaming for me to kick over his desk and demand he take it all back, that I was perfect for his wild son, but my logic told me this was what I wanted and to not fuck it up. I didn't want Ax to chase me for marriage . . . but the thought of some sweet young thing taming my wolf . . . I mean, Ax, was hitting a nerve.

Manic stuck out his hand as he sharply said, "Do we have a deal?"

I shoved all those feelings deep down before I let logic take over, and I shook his hand. "Yes. We have a deal." Plus, how hard could it be taking down seven other girls.

I got up to leave, now that my goal was set, and I walked to the door. I went to grasp the handle when I noticed the paper in my hand. I forgot about it while my mind kept spinning of the description of Ax's perfect girl. I opened it and saw 9:00 p.m. with some longitude and latitude coordinates.

His grinning face shined down at me as he barked, "Don't be late." Then went back to typing on his computer, effectively dismissing me.

I opened the door and called out, "See you soon."

Before I closed the door behind me, he called out, "Oh, and. Rayla, a piece of advice . . ." I cracked the door open some more. "Don't try a stunt like this with the other bosses you are visiting today." I opened my mouth to argue he was wrong, but he lifted his hand to stop me. "They won't take very kindly to ruining their property. Especially Winstale."

I felt my cheeks redden, and I nodded, closing the door. That was easy. Well easy-ish.

As I walked down the hallways, my footsteps echoing off the sterile white walls, I hoped the next one would go smoothly, too. I'd heard Easton Winstale was unpredictable . . . and most geniuses were . . . but he'd never made a deal with me before.

@Tpiola_

CHAPTER 15

It was still early, and I needed a complete change of clothes if I was going to head down into the labs next. I would take Rossey's advice and just waltz in there for a little chat, but I needed to look the part to not warn him ahead of time. I didn't want him to have the upper hand.

I dragged my feet up the stairs. All my stamina and gung ho-ness left when I entered the house. Mornings and days were not my thing.

As soon as I hit the top step, I felt a whoosh of air in front of me and sighed out loud. Did I have to deal with this now? "What, Cosmo? What do you want?" I crossed my arms over my chest to show him I was not done with my anger yet.

His calculating eyes roamed my body, assessing every inch of me like it would give away what I was doing. He took a small pain-filled drag of breath before he crooked up an eyebrow and said in disbelief, "You went to the gym?"

I rolled my eyes and shoved past him toward my room. I didn't have time for his emotions or thoughts about me going to a gym without him. We have a state-of-the-art home gym and fight room he and I used together, always. We have never worked out without each other since he came into my life, and I was sure he was a little butthurt about it. I huffed out, irritated by the situation because it wasn't like that, but I didn't need to tell him that. "Yeah, but I obviously didn't work out." I motioned to my sweatless body and perfectly kept hair as he trailed behind me like a hound catching his scent.

"Then what were you doing?"

I got to my door and twirled around to confront him in a snotty voice. "I am not at liberty to say." His eyes narrowed on me as his teeth clenched.

"Ray, what the fuck is going on—" I had about enough of his questions and was getting to a boiling point.

"Look! I'm going to be real with you. I am still pissed at you."

He slammed his hands against the rim of my door as he growled, "When are you going to forgive me?!"

I crossed my arms over my chest as he gave me his puppy-dog eyes full of pain, but I was not giving in. "When I fix all of this marriage shit, then I will be on the okay train, but right now, I need to focus on getting this fixed"—he opened his mouth, but I finished—"on my own."

He stared at me, trying to figure out how movable I was on this, so I made my eyes cold and unwavering. He let go of the door frame with a tsk, grumbling about how unreasonable I was being. "At least take Rick with you. For backup."

I wanted to give in to his plea. He rarely asked for anything, and his light minty smell was making my mouth water, but, on this subject, I would not change my mind. No matter what my body was craving. "No." I left it at that and ran into my room, shutting the door in his face.

A bang sounded on the door—it sounded more like a head than his fists—as he called out, "Okay, Ray, but can you promise me that you will come home tonight unscathed? Please."

I placed the palm of my hand where I thought his head would be, trying to ease his worry. "Okay," I whispered just loud enough for him to hear me. After a few seconds, I heard his sure and steady steps walk away from my room, and I let out the breath I had been holding.

I turned around, my mind focused on my mission as I went to my walk-in closet. I needed to put on some conservative clothes and pack some clubbing clothes because I would not come back here to change for when I met Glovefox. I would change in the car before I had to deal with this all over again.

The lab that we had here in Vegas was the second largest, the largest in Texas, where Falcon and his father lived, but ours was the most stocked. The tricky thing with the labs was that they needed to be hidden. The weapons and items we used were custom-made for us and our groups, tailored to what each clan needed, and we didn't want any rising rivals to know about them.

I rode my bike up to a large self-storage facility. This was one plot of land my dad purchased under a shell company that has no ties to the Syndicate. He leased out the land to a national self-storage company at a low rate with a thousand-year lease with the contingency that we own a block of units. All these steps make this location as safe and hidden as possible.

I pulled up to the roll-up gate, number 1562, which was one of the ten-by-twenty units. Just large enough for a car to fit. I got to the lock and pretended to put a key in but, really, there was a set of buttons on the back that you had to hit at different intervals to unlock. As soon as the lock popped open, I pulled up the door.

There were a few boxes of stuff in the back, scattered between the two corners, and I rolled my bike in. As soon as I closed the door, it locked from underneath, and I stood in the center where a large circular slab was and waited. It only took a few seconds for the gears to turn, lowering me underground.

The whole lab was underneath and had several storage units all over this facility that worked like this. Each rented under different names with fake stuff inside to make sure it all looked legit. It always made me feel like a fancy super villain going into my lair whenever I came here.

As the platform lowered, a bright-white light blinded me for a second before my eyes adjusted, and I could see the whole lab. It was one large area that was split up into several sections of ten-feet walls. There was the testing section to the left side. It had a large open range to shoot weapons, a shop and welding section to make adjustments, and a smaller enclosed area to test toxins.

To the right was a set of offices and conference rooms. It was made into a minimalist and collaborative space, which was why the office walls were thick, bulletproof glass. You could see some had mini labs or components in the office along with their desk and computer, depending on what field they focused on. People wrote with markers on their glass walls, staring at equations to make sure it worked.

On staff here, we always had two manufacturing engineers, two biochemists, two weapons experts, two stuntman testers, and two project managers. It's a well-oiled machine that pumped out what we wanted whenever we wanted.

I did a quick glance around for either Winstale with their trademark-blond hair, impeccable posture, and stoic faces. A few people glanced up at me, then put their head back down, focusing on what they were working on. I didn't see the younger one, Falcon, but the older one had his head down, furiously writing something on his desk. Perfect. As soon as the platform jerked to a stop, I hopped off and made my way over to the office he holed himself in.

I unzipped my black leather jacket, revealing the white, tucked-in blouse with my skinny legged pants as I clicked my way down the concrete hallway. Normally, I would wear a pencil skirt or a wide-legged pant when I was trying to look professional, but neither of those would work for the bike. Everyone looked up from their desks as I strode to the back office, but when my eyes roamed over them, they tucked back behind their computers, not wanting to meet my gaze.

I hooked a left, ready to march into the room I last saw him in when I glanced through the glass and saw it was empty. *What the fuck?* I slowed my stomping, turned to my left and right to see if he took a step out for a second, but couldn't see anyone. Well, that took the wind out of my sails. I had a whole power entrance and everything. Rolling my eyes to the ceiling, I decided I would just wait in the office for him to return. I was not leaving until we talked.

I yanked open the glass door and made myself at home in the seat across from his desk. I went over the plan in my head of what I would talk to him about. First, I would commend him on his special project, the one with the lightning speed surveillance system. I wanted to butter him up before I took a bite out of him. Then I would appeal to him about his son and I being a horrible match, how I was much too into partying and having lots of sex to be a viable candidate for his wicked-smart and capable son. If he still didn't budge, then I would go for the threat of "I will make your son's life a living hell" and see where that got me.

It was hard trying to think of things to offer the man that could have or make anything he ever wanted, but that didn't stop me. If I couldn't drown them in honey, then I would take him out with the stinger.

Something shiny caught my eye in the corner of the room. I recognized that piece of machinery and slowly rose from my chair to see if I was correct. In the back corner of the room on a small clear podium was a diamond-encrusted watch with a solid onyx screen. It was stunning to look at, with all the sparkles and glam that oozed off it, but as long as my eyes weren't deceiving me, I remembered seeing something like this before. Not this exact one but similar. A long time ago in a mausoleum.

I picked up the watch, about to hit the buttons to figure out how to use it, when a hurried voice called out, "Don't touch that. It's a gift for your father."

The watch clanked onto the podium as I dropped the piece and swirled around to Easton Winstale hastening into the room, moving around his desk, and sitting down without looking up from the tablet in his hands. He rushed out, "So you want to get out of the whole marriage deal, right?" Before I could say anything, he kept going. "Why don't you just ask or battle it out with your father? He's the one that started this all in the first place."

I was quite irked by his tone that spoke volumes of how capable he thought I was, which sounded dismal. I swiftly moved over to the chair across from his desk, hoping he would look at me and take me seriously, but he didn't. He kept scribbling on his tablet, waiting for me to answer him. I took a deep breath and reminded myself I needed to get this man on my side.

"You know my dad. He won't let up once his mind is stuck on something, or I prove to outfox him and his scheming ways. This seemed like a better option for all involved." I shrugged, but it wasn't like the man had seen it, he still hadn't looked up from his damn tablet. It was annoying as shit, and it made me feel like he wasn't taking me seriously. I would have to change that real soon.

"Hmm," was his only response as he was reading something, still acting like I was a pest. That was it. I picked up my legs and slammed them onto his desk, kicking some desk ornament off in the process, and it landed with a loud thud. Opps. Sorry, not sorry. My bitch mode was going to have to come out sooner rather than later. I always liked using the stinger approach better anyway.

His head snapped up, his eyes assessing me with a flash of irritation and anger before he narrowed them at my intrusive shoes. Good. At least he was fucking looking at me now.

"What the hell . . ." he seethed, but I was done playing nice and was now going to take over this meeting. He had his time, and he used it unwisely.

"What I'm trying to tell you is that it would be a much better outcome if you stopped supporting my dad on this silly little game of his and started to back up your son." His eyes flared at me, getting his full attention now that I made a splash.

He set down his tablet and crossed his arms as he leaned back in his chair, finally taking me seriously. "What benefit does it do for me to make an enemy of your father?"

This time, it was my turn to narrow my eyes at him. "Really? That's the card you want to play here? We both know that the Syndicate leaders are made up of men who are the best of friends. It's not like you guys have not disagreed on anything before. You wouldn't be making an enemy of him, and you know it."

His eyes took on a calculating edge before he said, "True, but that's because, between the four of us, its majority rules."

The corners of my mouth tipped up as I lowered my feet to the floor. "That's exactly my reason for being here."

His lips thinned as he perked up. "Then what are you offering? It's not like I'm going to give you something just because you're part of the Syndicate. You're the daughter of my best friend, and I do know some things about you, but, let's be honest, I just met you, and I'm not going to take much on face value or the words of a doting father."

Was it weird that I already liked him? This was some of the no-nonsense type of attitude I always wanted my dad to have. My fangs peeked out from my smile. "I understand, which is why I can tell you truthfully that I'm not for your son." His eyebrow rose, and I kept going as I flicked my hand out.

"Look, I am more of a wild card. I have my brother and my best friend at my side all the time, not to protect me, but to protect others from me. They are like my gatekeepers." He folded his hands and waited, so I kept going. "Also, I'm not the type to enjoy sitting in a lab all day or do a deep dive into research."

"Yes, but isn't it good for you two to be different? Be able to bring in the other side to balance each other out? I know that this was one of the main reasons I fell so deeply in love with his mother." He was trying to reason with me, and I understood it, I really did, but that was not the case here.

"I am happy that it worked out for you and his mother, but tell me this, did you both spend time with each other before you got married?" I tilted my head, already knowing his answer.

"Of course," he woefully said as his eyes glazed over, and he stared off into the distance. I'm sure reminiscing about his wife, but I needed to bring him back to the here and now.

"Then that won't be us." That woke him out of his trance as he snapped his intellectual gaze back to me in question. "You all are not giving us opportunities to get to know one another. At this point, I think the three of them can barely stand me because I'm just trying to survive, but they are doing this to make all of you happy. So, I ask again, is that really what you want for your son? For the rest of his life?" I could tell the wheels were turning in his brain, and I needed to find something, just a small something, to tip him over the edge.

"What about this . . . what if we have a friendly wager?" I proposed, hoping he saw I was trying to be logical about this.

He tilted his head, making him look slightly more human before his face pinched in disgust, "Just like you're doing with Rossey?" I smiled, making sure I kept my laugh in as I learned they were talking to each other like a little gossipy girl group.

"Yes and no. The terms would be the same, if I win, the Winstale clan will support me in going against my dad's wishes for this shotgun marriage—"

"And if I win?" He interjected, and I smiled, knowing he would want it all laid out now. With Rossey, I had to make it a challenge, and I knew he would take the bait, but, with Winstale, I would need it to be thoughtful in my phrasing.

"Well, we should figure out the game first, right?" I was trying to give myself time to come up with a win for him that I would be okay with.

His lips quivered for a second in humor before he straightened them, continuing like this was a regular business deal. "You are the one to propose this *arrangement*, you should come up with the *game* to at least give you a fighting chance." A furious chill ran up my spine as I clenched my fist at his assumption that I could not beat him.

The anger started to boil underneath my skin as I blurted out, "Why don't I go up against your best, Falcon, at something recreational that he excels at." I didn't know why I threw that out there. I didn't want to fight against Falcon. Even after being around him for such a short amount of time, I could tell he was a perfectionist, and I was sure the list of things he did for recreational purposes was a short one I was sure he'd mastered.

Winstale lifted his folded fist up to his chin, resting on it as he thought about it, then he flicked open his phone, punched in a few numbers, turned on the speaker, and waited until someone picked up.

"Yes, Father." The voice was short and clipped. No non-sense, no pleasantries.

"Hello, son. What do you excel at recreationally?" Winstale looked up at me and winked. It was the first time that he gave me a solid shot of personality, and I was taken back a little by it. *Did the Winstale's have secret charm?*

"Excuse me?" Falcon's voice wavered like he was not used to this kind of interaction, and I had to cover my hand over my mouth from giggling.

"Recreational. Do you need me to get you a dictionary?" Winstale said in a slightly livelier voice. It was fascinating hearing them talk to each other. You thought the older Winstale had much less personality when you first met them, but hearing him talk to Falcon, it was apparent which one was more expressive.

"No need. Um . . . Cars?" He spoke in a softer tone, like he didn't want anyone to hear him say it.

"Is that a question, Falcon, or an answer?" Winstale lifted his head toward me and rolled his eyes up to the ceiling. It was at that moment I realized everyone had parent issues. They were just different kinds.

"That's the answer. What is this abo—" Winstale hung up the phone and turned back to me like he wasn't just on the phone asking his own son about his hobbies.

"Well, you heard my son. How about a car race?" I nod-ded, still reeling about the information I gathered from their one conversation.

"We will, of course, need time in order to get a car ready for a race of this caliber." His smile looked weird on his face, like he was stretching it in a way his skin wasn't used to.

I nodded as I grabbed a pen and a small unused pad of paper and wrote down the location and time before he tried to pick that, too, then slid it to him. He picked it up immediately and nodded before putting it in his pocket.

"Do you know where that is?" I pointed to the paper, expecting him to ask me for more details. It's not like he lived here, and that vague location was only known by the local drag racers.

"It won't be hard to figure out. Now what is it that you are willing to do if I win?" His eyes zeroed in on me, the look reminded me of a cobra circling his prey, hypnotizing you with his stare. This was his boss mode, and I now understood how this intellectual science man fit in with my dad. While they have the same look, my dad would be the one to boast about how smart he was to your face, while this man would only have to give you a look, and you would know you were fucked.

So, what did I do? I blurted out the first thing I could think of that a man like him would enjoy. "If you win, then I will beg Falcon to marry me on my hands and knees in front of all the Syndicate leaders. Then tell them all how the Winstales are the only family smart enough to outfox me." As soon as my brain caught up with my reckless words, I had to bite the inside of my mouth to stop from freaking out.

What the fuck, Rayla! That was a risky-as-fuck wager! My pride could never handle a hit like that.

I knew I hit the right button when his eyes widened, sparkling like they were salivating at the picture I painted. I guess Papa Winstale was really into humiliation and winning in front of his friends.

"Deal." He sat back, arms crossed, satisfied with this wager and what I offered in return. I was still feeling uneasy about the whole thing, but I kept my straight face and put my hand out for the shake. There was no deal without a shake with this man. He seemed like he was a stickler for the rules.

He looked me up and down slowly, uncrossed his arms, and grabbed my hand in a firm grip. I smiled, "See you on the track."

He chuckled. "Oh no. It will only be Falcon. I don't like going into areas with a lot of people I don't know." He squeezed my hand harder as he continued. "But I will be watching all the way up to the finish line. Be sure of that, Rayla Desmond." He said my name like he was committing it to memory, like it was a threat and a reward in one. Then he let go of my hand and went back to his tablet, tapping away at something, effectively dismissing me.

I took the hint, got up, and walked to the door. Not wanting to be there longer than necessary and risking my mouth running even worse than it already had.

My hand was on the door handle, my escape almost made, when I heard, "Thank you, Rayla. You have made this trip so much more exciting than I thought it would be."

I smirked over my shoulder and saluted him as he watched me carefully. "Always ready to serve the Syndicate and its needs." He puffed out a half laugh as he went back to what he was doing, and I got out of there as fast as I could manage to save face.

As soon as I was back outside of the storage unit, I opened my phone and called Rick. "Oh, my God, RayRay! I have been waiting for your call for a while. Why are you being such a—"

"Rick." I interrupted his bitch fit before it got too deep. "I need you to bring my car, Talula, to the track at eleven p.m."

"Done. But what about—"

"No. I'm still a little pissed at you and Cosmo, so I don't want to talk. Just get the car there, and I will think about forgiving you." We both knew my anger wouldn't last forever, but I was going to make him and Cosmo feel as shitty as I did when I found out everything. It was an eye for an eye, right?

He took a big breath, ready to chew me out. I had my finger hovering over the end button, ready to shut him down quickly when he surprised me. "Okay, Ray. I will see you at eleven."

"Thanks, Rick." I hung up the phone before I let him get another word in because when Rick gave up, that always made me a little sad and more likely to give in. I liked my little firecracker of a best friend.

I looked at my watch, realizing I had enough time to go get something to eat before I needed to change back into the gym clothes and meet Rossey at 9:00 p.m. at the coordinates he gave me. Then after I won that, I would need to race down to the tracks to get ready to win the car race with Falcon, then turn around and try to get over to Veshta's before midnight to talk to the last boss for one more bet.

My life was about to get real interesting.

CHAPTER 16

"ARE YOU SURE YOU can handle me, stranger?" She cooed in my ear with her sultry voice, and shivers ran down my spine.

I grabbed her pale hand, moving it toward my dick tented in my slacks, ready to get the party started. "I think the better question to ask is"—I leaned backward, grabbed her chin, and pulled her face to mine, our lips a hair's breadth from each other—"are you going to be able to handle me, Siren?"

She melted into me, ready to let me take over, to ruin her body and then put it back together in the most delicious of ways. I gripped her shoulders, ready to lay her down and feast on the first course, when I heard an annoying sound in my ear.

Ring. Ring. Ring. Ring.

"Are you going to get that?" she asked from beneath me.

I jolted up, and, with my eyes closed, I grabbed the phone and turned it off before I settled back into my bed. I was dreaming. I looked down at my rock-hard dick and winced. Could I have dreamed of something a little less tortuous?

I checked the caller ID and reluctantly picked it up. "Yes?"

My father's bark cleared through the receiver, making me jump. "Are you still in bed?! Moping around because you got beat by a girl?"

I rolled my neck, trying to work my frustration down instead of up. "No. I just had a long night."

"Ugh. With more idiot bimbos? When are you going to get out of this phase?" he huffed, disdain for the way I liked to live a carefree life, but, for once, he was wrong.

"No, I didn't go out." I moved to sit up, maybe wake myself up a bit. "I was going over the new fighters list for the next couple of big fights here. It would be nice to scope them out and see their progress before fight night. Then I scrolled through social media to find some new potential talent."

"Hmmm. I know you were moping about yesterday, after the little vampire got the drop on you, but I'm glad that you got some practical work done." I gripped my phone, holding my tongue about the little vampire remark. I don't know why it irked me, but it did.

"Was there a reason for this wake-up call?" I would rather get to the root of this call sooner than later, then maybe fall back asleep to finish that dream.

"Yes. I need you to be at the clearing at 9:00 p.m. for the Othaman."

I grimaced before responding, "Do I really need to go to that? We both know I'm not going to pick any of them."

"Doesn't matter. This is tradition. It is said that the strongest females out of all the local packs are to fight for their right to choose to approach the strongest male and ask for a mating session. Since you are the strongest unmated male, you are obligated to go." When I didn't say anything, he blew out a long breath. I could envision him slumped on his desk in frustration with me.

"You are not obligated to accept, but you are obligated to go and watch. It's your duty. When you eventually take over for me, there are going to be a lot of things you won't want to do but still need to. Plus . . ." He hesitated while I was half listening as I reluctantly slipped out of bed and went toward the bathroom. I guess I have to wake up now.

"This time, I have a side bet that I don't think you'll want to miss." His teasing voice intrigued me.

"Yeah? What's that?" I grabbed the shower handle to turn it on, then leaned against the counter and waited for the light dew of steam to creep over the top of the shower curtain to let me know it was time to get in.

"If I told you, then there wouldn't be anything left to entice you to go. Oh, and be on time." I huffed out and smirked. He wasn't wrong.

"Fine. I'll be there. But this better be worth it. If I don't see blood and gore within the first ten minutes, I'm out." Then I mumbled, "They could at least make the event entertaining."

My father laughed, which was a rarity, since he liked to have complete control over his emotions. "Yes. I think *she* will perform. See you later, son." Then he hung up while my mind was still caught up on the *she* part of his sentence.

Who the fuck was she, and why was she making deals with my father?

My father was not one to dabble around with women. While my father still stayed loyal to my dead mother, I was the opposite, making sure I never got tied down to one pussy. I didn't want any woman to have control over me, asking me questions about what I do, giving me problems if they couldn't handle the reality of what I do. Naw. It was just fine for me to sink my dick in some groupie pussy and forget them the next day. *Except for her*, my brain cooed, and it wasn't wrong.

The steam had covered the mirror in the bathroom, so I knew it was time to get into the shower. I climbed into boiling hot water that hit me right in the face and sighed into it, enjoying the pain of the searing heat on my skin.

I ran my hands over my face as I thought about how my brain wasn't wrong. I couldn't stop thinking about my little siren. Not only was her pussy the most euphoric feeling in the world, she had a sharp attitude that went with it. It drove me to want to do my two favorite things: fight or fuck it out of her.

When I saw her at the meeting, I was completely surprised. My eyes glued to her, watching with rapt attention as she shot her own men in the knees and then put the gun to her father's head. It was a ballsy move. I mean, I didn't blame her, her father basically kidnapped her, but she showed she could hold her own, even against her father. She proved quickly she was more than the Syndicate princess I had her pegged for.

A memory of her wailing on me when we first met in that playground, trying to establish dominance, made me smile. When she first came onto the playground, I thought she was an angel with her white hair and sparkling pink eyes, which just hid the devil inside of her as she walked up to me and punched me in the face before I got to say hello. It seemed that girl couldn't stop leaving me gutted, one way or another.

I put my body underneath the spray and melted into the raging-hot water. Scolding rivulets flowed down my body, but as soon as those water lines skated down my arms and over the place she sank her teeth into, my dick hardened. I looked down at how swollen it already was, throbbing to be in its new favorite home, and was taken back to that moment she marked me in the parking lot.

I was no stranger to a vampire bite, both in a fight and in pleasure, but this was something else. She didn't even take any blood, using her fangs like a weapon instead of a way to feed. As soon as those teeth pierced my skin, an all-consuming, blissed-out sensation took over every follicle of my body. I had moaned from it and loosened my arms, knowing she would get away, but I couldn't help it. I was thrown off guard and off kilter. I still felt a ghost of euphoria when anything touched that spot.

It's distracting and all-consuming, this feeling she had marked me with. I didn't even want to go out and find someone to wet my dick because all I could think about was when I would see her again. It was like my dick only

wanted to work for her. The worst part, my wolf agreed.
I could hear him in the back of my mind, whining and
whimpering to be near her. Wanting to find her and sink
our claws into her hips as we rutted into her. Then, once
she was screaming around my cock in pleasure, he wanted
to rip into her throat and mark her as his with his teeth as
his mate.

I wouldn't lie, the thought of her mouth dripping with
my blood, the ruby-red liquid spilling down her gorgeous
body, making her look like a heathen drenched in carnage,
was a very appetizing scene. I could see my wolf's appeal
to it . . . but to mate with her? Didn't he know that
was forever? Mating her would be more final than even
marriage.

Wolves not only mate for a lifetime but rarely outside of
our species. Hell, most supernaturals stuck to their own
when it came to mates, but sometimes you had that special
circumstance. Our wolves were the decider of our mates,
being a part of our DNA and knowing each individual
to its core, it would immediately recognize its match in
this world and would pull you toward it. Our wolves were
our guide, picking only one mate in our entire lifetime,
pushing us toward the person they thought would complement us the most, but like everything in life, you still
had a choice. If you wanted to reject it, you could. You
would give up the right to ever find another, since our
wolves only did it once, but if you were strong enough in
your convictions, you could refuse.

With the way my wolf was acting, I got the feeling he
wanted Rayla Desmond as our mate, but did I? Did I want
to refuse?

The water started to cool, and I pushed away the thoughts of mates and how her bite made me feel, focusing on the part I wanted, that my body craved. I would need to fuck her again to make sure this all-consuming need wasn't a fluke.

I stepped out of the shower, wondering where she was, and picked up my phone, ready to start asking around for what she was doing today when I remembered I promised my father I would go to the Othaman tonight. *Fuck.*

It was sometimes annoying to be a powerful pack. We always had to visit other packs, especially since I was an unmated male, just in case my wolf would find its mate. I hated having all those she-wolves grabbing at me. It was one of the only times I truly felt like a piece of meat. I could see all the single women's eyes salivate at the chance to create pups with me. Like I was some prize to be won, a ticket out of the situation they were in or something to put on a shelf for the rest of their friends to see.

Not a single one has ever tried to get to know me. Never asked me what I liked to do or what my plans were for the future. It was always questions like: how many pups do you want? How much do you make in a year? What were my expectations of body upkeep and status? How would they be taken care of? Then blabbing on about how they would do the Rossey name proud.

Yeah, fuck that. That meant shit to me, and, surprisingly, Rayla wasn't like that.

She was the opposite of that. Always trying to escape or run away from me instead of toward me. Of course, the one woman I would enjoy entertaining would need to be chased down. A growl from deep in my chest rumbled out my mouth, my wolf letting me know he enjoyed the thought of chasing her.

I set down my phone, knowing if I started to search for her, I wouldn't stop. I wouldn't give a rat's ass if I was late to the damn Othaman if I was closing in on her scent. My wolf bristled, wanting to go find her, tugging me to follow our instinct, but I reined him back. *We need to make good on the promise to our father.* When he whined in my head, I cooed to him, trying to get him to calm down. *We needed to appease the old man in order to run free. Once we finished, I promise we'll start the hunt for her.*

I felt him settle down, accepting the deal I offered. I knew my father was all about controlling the wolf inside with an iron fist, that he thought I was letting my wolf run wild by making deals with him, soothing him, letting him run free occasionally, but I found that it worked for us. We rarely argued, and he almost never took over my mind unless it was a fight-or-flight type of situation. He was able to go into survival mode, where I kept going until there was nothing left. He was the reason I made it out of some tricky situations in my youthful years, not heeding his warnings when he gave them to me. I learned my lesson a long time ago. It's better to work with him than fight with him.

I decided I would go to the gym, get in a good hour, then make some calls on some things happening in other Rossey hubs across the United States. Handle anything that needed to be handled and then get ready for the Othaman. I smirked to myself, the sooner I got that out of the way, the sooner I could go find my little siren and show her what a wolf bite was like, and how tasty I thought she was.

My hands tightened on the wheel as I turned onto Highway 159 toward Red Rock Canyon. It was only a thirty-minute drive from the strip but then was a treacherous hour trek on foot to the wolf clearing.

Soon, I parked my car and took a deep breath, reminding myself I just needed to act like I was mildly interested in this whole event. I needed to stay until the winner was announced, let the winner know I was not interested in them, and then off I went.

I stepped out of my car, and a cool breeze raced across my face, and I closed my eyes, tilted my face to the sky, and let the moon's rays hit my skin. There was magic in those rays, magic that called to any wolf. Magic that could tame us or rile us up on its whim. It was a full moon tonight, and my wolf was itching to run free, but I kept a lid on it. Father would most definitely not approve if I showed up naked, clothes shredded from the change.

I hiked up the forest-covered trail, following the scent of fur and wildness. I reminded myself these events were not the worst. Sometimes they could be entertaining, especially when the women got vicious.

Othaman was the night that gave the she-wolves all the power. They got to fight over the males they wanted, and the winner was treated like a queen until the next

Othaman. Us wolves valued strength in all its forms. While my father valued inner strength, I enjoyed bodily strength. I wanted to see a brutal and bloody fight. It got my blood pumping and the adrenaline in my veins racing. Male or female, it didn't matter. The only thing that mattered was that the strongest opponent won.

Sometimes it was the one with the best strategy, and sometimes it was the one that got the win from the sheer will to win. No matter which you enjoyed, us wolves knew how to put on a good show and keep you entertained.

I was about halfway up when a blur of a vampire raced past me and up the mountain. *What the hell? What was a vampire doing here? Were they here to cause trouble?* Then they would learn today that wolves were not the ones to mess with.

A familiar sweet scent was left in its wake, filling up my nostrils, and gave me pause. Was that . . .? I picked up my pace, practically running, because I wanted to confirm if my nose was smelling the real deal and not just making it up because I wanted it to be her.

I heard a few howls, my wolf panting to respond, but my mind was consumed with finding the truth about who that vampire was. I wanted to see her with my own eyes, but why would she be here? This wasn't Syndicate business; it was strictly wolf tradition.

As soon as I broke through the clearing, all I saw was a large group of wolves and people standing around. It was a large turnout with several local packs, which meant it was about seventy to eighty werewolves in attendance.

I was immediately recognized and greeted by every wolf that could get their hands on me. Alphas wanting to shake my hand, letting me know who they were and what they could provide for the Rossey clan. Betas backing up their alphas, in the circle but not talking to me. A few omegas were around, sticking to their alphas like glue, never looking me in the eye.

Some men liked that. The thought of an omega; something kind and sweet, someone to bring their pack peace and harmony. I was not one of those men. I found them a burden, an annoyance. Someone that got in the way. It was because of the life we lived in the Syndicate, and having an omega was like having a beacon of weakness, and that was not acceptable. Not worth the time.

I nodded and smiled. A few of the she-wolves competing today came up to me, telling me they were fighting for me. It was always bold when they did that. If they won, then it was a show of strength and determination, but if they lost, then the boasting was shameful and disappointing.

A large auburn-colored wolf shoved its way between all the others surrounding me, using its body to push all the others aside. A few growled until they saw the wolf and glared at her back. As soon as the red wolf was in front of me, she shifted. The fur reseeded, and her skin took shape. Once she was done shifting into her human body, she flipped her golden-red hair up and smirked at me with seafoam-colored eyes.

"Hello, Ax. I'm Laura Grothmen. I'm the strongest female wolf in these parts, and I'm planning to be your mate." She ran her hands over her round naked hips and up her tight stomach before she cupped her heavy breasts. "I know I can satisfy you in all the ways that you need." She moved a few steps closer, running her hand up my chest as she pressed into me with her body. "I can make you into a—"

A familiar sultry laugh on the other side of the clearing took my attention away from the bombshell in front of me. My eyes snagged on my white-haired, rose gold-eyed vampire, and I was captivated. She stood next to my father, who looked like he was the one approving her presence, but that wasn't what caught my attention. No. It was that she was talking, *laughing*, with some large, lone alpha who looked like he didn't have a pack with him. Which meant he was single and on the prowl. *Oh, fuck that!*

I shoved the she-wolf off me. "Please, excuse me. I need to speak with my father." She gasped behind me, but I didn't care. I was on a mission, and it was to tear that alpha's head off. *How dare he make her laugh!*

I stalked forward, my eyes snagging on my father for a second, and I paused. He was regarding me with a large smile across his face, almost showing teeth. My father didn't smile. He grinned or smirked, he gave scary horror-filled smiles that were feral and mean, but this smile was more triumphant.

My steps slowed as my father's gaze reminded me this was my territory, and that alpha would know it soon enough. I didn't need to show him how much he bothered me. I stalked up to my father and nodded.

"Well, you made it on time," my father said, announcing my presence. Both of us turned toward Rayla, expecting her to say something, but, no, she didn't even acknowledge my existence. She kept her eyes on the other alpha as he laughed this time.

"I mean, I'm definitely excited to fight. I have been itching to practice with other supes, but I only had my brother and best friend to fight with consistently." She smiled up at him, and my blood boiled. *Would she stop doing that?! Why did she have to keep smiling at him?*

"Yes. I think it's important to test your skills on other supes. We all have such different fighting capabilities." He puffed out his chest before he continued. "You know, if you ever need—"

That was it. I was done with their conversation. "Rayla. What are you doing here?" I didn't mean for my voice to be loud and accusing. My father even turned and raised an eyebrow but didn't say anything. I kept my attention on Rayla as she turned toward me like she didn't even know I was here, which was a lie . . . I hoped.

"Oh, Ax, I didn't see you there." Her light and airy voice gave off an indifference that had me gritting my teeth. This woman knew how to push my buttons. Then she giggled and put her hand on the alpha's arm to get his attention. "You know, when we were kids, he was just as argumentative. As soon as I—"

"I will ask again, why are you here?" My eyes flicked to where her hand connected to his forearm, and I fought desperately not to rip him away from her. I had this deep need to force him to bare his throat to me, to show her who the real alpha here was. Even my wolf was growling in my head, pissed off that this other wolf was getting between him and his mate.

Her lips pinched into a thin line as she replied in a deadpan tone, "I'm here because of a bet." Then she turned away from me and focused back onto the alpha, going back to ignoring me.

I opened my mouth to yell at her, to just bring her rosey gaze back over to me and off that alpha, when my father clasped my shoulder. "The event is about to start. Let's go sit in our section." Then he turned to Rayla. "You should head over to the start line." She gazed up at him, respect clear in her eyes as she nodded, then thanked the alpha for the chat.

As my father was pulling me away, the dopey-ass alpha watched her with hunger in his eyes, tracking her movements like she was his to keep an eye on. Oh, I was going to kill this fucker just to make myself feel better.

"He means nothing." My father's voice brought me back from my daydreams of gutting him with only my claws. "He's low on the totem pole. If you think she's interested in him, you are incorrect." His assurance of her preferences had me narrowing my eyes on him. *When the fuck did they get chummy? Which reminded me . . .*

"What bet is she talking about?" My voice was low, but I couldn't keep the growl inside that came after.

"Oh, it's nothing you need to worry about. She just wants support, and I told her I would give it to her, if she wins." His flippant voice made me skeptical.

"What does she need support for?" I didn't know what angle my father was working, but I wanted to know anything that involved my siren and my father. Also, if she needed Rossey support, why didn't she come to me? I would've given her anything she asked for.

He didn't answer right away, scanning the crowd and nodding to some of the other older alphas before we went to the section of the clearing that had seats. We were directed to the center front row while the rest of the packs filled in around us, based on pack size.

My father leaned over and whispered, "She came into my office this morning." He chuckled to himself like it was a secret. "I hate to admit, she surprised me when she fell through the ceiling."

I snapped my head toward him, eyes and mouth wide. "Keep your face forward," he growled out, and I turned away from him as I clamped my mouth shut. "It's all about perception, son. We can't let anyone know we don't know everything that is happening at all times."

I nodded absently, hearing this for the millionth time. "Continue."

He chuckled under his breath. "Well, she came crashing through, held a silver knife at my neck, and told me she wanted me to break off the Rossey support for the whole marriage deal." He smiled as he watched her get in line, then be pushed by some she-wolf, to which she responded to by smacking her across the face, telling her if she fucked with her again, she would slit her throat. *God, she was hot when she was threatening people.*

"And you then made a deal . . .?" I was still trying to understand what happened, and he was stalling, which was so unlike him.

"She impressed me, but it's not like I could give her something for nothing, so I came up with a deal." He sat up, put his hands in his lap as he continued. "If she won the Othaman, then I would pull the Rossey clan from the marriage agreement."

I sat back in the foldout chair too small for my large frame, conflicted. While on the one hand, I knew this marriage deal was not something she wanted. She made that very clear from the beginning, and I couldn't blame her for finding her own way out of it. At the same time, I was a little disappointed. I didn't know why. I mean, I didn't want to get married, either, but it was kinda fun to spar with her. To chase her.

She threatened another she-wolf, and I smiled. The sheer determination and power she was giving off was blinding. I enjoyed basking in her predatory glow.

I wanted her to win because I wanted to see the smile that would light up her face, the smile of victory. I also wanted her to lose because I was not ready to give up on her yet. I wanted to see what two beings like us could do, what kind of a wild mess we could make.

Then a thought hit me. If she won, that didn't mean I couldn't go after her anymore. All it meant was that neither of us were being *forced* into marriage. I could still pursue her on my own terms, in my own way. Either way this played, I could manage the outcome, and I realized there was no downside to the bet for me, so I relaxed and decided to enjoy the show.

Fight with all your might, Little Siren. Give us a good show.

CHAPTER 17

I FELT HIS EYES on me, roaming my body, watching my every move as I stood with the lady wolves for this crazy Othaman tradition.

When I first showed up, I was assaulted by the overwhelming musk wolves gave off. It wasn't technically a bad smell, it was just so powerful my nose twitched. Manic came up to me right away and steered me over to the side of the clearing. He told me this was usually a very hush-hush kind of tradition, and that by him inviting me, it would make some elders mad, but he didn't care. He wanted to show them he was the true leader of the group, and this bet gave him the opportunity to flex that muscle. Even so, he wanted to keep me with him until it was time to get ready.

I told him I understood but needed him to explain what this all was. He smiled down at me and nodded. "This is an old tradition of ours to give the women of the pack the opportunity to find a mate."

"How do wolves mate?" It was something I never had to think about before, but I found it interesting all the same.

"This is one of the times that our wolves are more in charge than our human side, and our wolves are particular." He looked off in the distance like he was remembering something before he continued. "Each wolf within us knows us completely. Our weaknesses and our strengths, and they try to find someone that will complement us in every way. Some wolves see the potential in many, and it takes time for them to make a decision, some wolves can just see someone and know that it's the right person, zeroing in on them and only them."

He took a frustrated breath. "Some wolves take their sweet ass time . . ."

I giggled, knowing he was complaining about Ax, and he glanced at me sheepishly, almost like he regretted saying that out loud.

"We all just want our kids to be happy, Rayla. I know that's why your father put this all into motion. It's also why the three of us agreed to it." His face softened for a second. "This life, being a boss, takes a toll on a person. You make decisions that you wish you didn't, hard truths that you need to face, and situations that make your heart hurt, but you need to endure. Enduring is hard on a being if they don't have someone to shoulder the burden, even if it's only a second. Even if it's just reminding you that you are not all mighty and powerful. Family and love keep you grounded, even as it makes you weak."

"Forcing that on us is not going to achieve the results you all want." I didn't want to argue because I knew there was some truth to what he said, but I guaranteed he had never told his son this the way he just told me. I knew my dad hadn't. Maybe it was because I wasn't his kid that he could rationalize it better.

"You try raising little brats like you four then come back and tell me what you will or won't do." His voice had a bite to it before he cracked his neck and relaxed his shoulders.

I lifted my hand behind him, he tensed up, waiting for some hit he could block, but I just slowly lowered it to his back and patted him. "It's okay. If there's one thing I have learned, it's that you all raised strong kids. It's both a blessing and a curse."

He relaxed again, grumbling, "Don't I know it."

Suddenly, I felt *his* arrival. I felt a change in the air like the woods grew more musky, and the breeze was electrified. I knew the second that Ax was on the other side of the clearing. I thought I recognized a familiar smell when I zoomed up this mountain, but I just told myself it was Manic.

A part of me was still a little pissed about what happened at Guy's Gym, but the irrational part of me was thinking about the club and how intoxicating his rough hands were. To top that all off, he was the epitome of cocky, rugged manliness that called to me. My wildness matched his, coaxing it to come out and play with us.

I almost stepped in his direction but caught Manic watching me from the corner of his eyes like he was hoping

I would go to him. Which made me want to do the opposite, so I looked around and saw a big, tall blond walking by in a Blood Ravens fan shirt and called out, "I don't know if you should be wearing that, man, they're having a rough season." It was easiest to talk to random people about things like music and sports.

The big lug stopped in his tracks, opened his mouth to yell something at me until he saw me, then his eyes lit up with interest. He smiled with all his pearly whites on display as he made his way over to me. He noticed I was with Manic and nodded to him in respect, I had to give some points to the lug for that. Manic nodded back, not paying him much attention as he was keeping track of his son.

"Aww, come on. It hasn't been that bad?" He tilted his head as he took me in, and I smiled back, flashing my fangs. "Wait! Are you competing?" The shock on his face was hilarious, and I couldn't help but laugh.

"Yeah, but not to find some mate." I waved him off. "Just the opposite, actually."

With his face pinched, he said, "So, to dissuade someone from mating?"

His guess wasn't far off, so I nodded. He laughed and came a few steps closer. "Well, that's new for the Othaman."

"That's me, always doing things backward." I shrugged as I kept my tone light and approachable.

"I'm Alex, by the way." His sweet smile and expecting tone made it comfortable for me to introduce.

I lifted my hand to my chest, wanting to be cordial since this was not my normal scene. "I'm Rayla." I looked around before I asked, "So, do you have a wolf in this race?"

He gave me a perplexed look before he chuckled. "My sister, Laura. She is the favorite to win today." He rolled his eyes and pointed to the auburn-haired girl who was naked in front of Ax, talking to him about herself. Well, that made me want to scratch my eyeballs out while I yanked that bitch's hair out and made a rug from it.

"So, she is a good fighter?" I unclenched my teeth, hoping he gave some good dish on the competition.

He nodded. "She's a very good fighter, but her real edge is that her wolf is larger than other she-wolves, which means her jaw is larger." Then he leaned toward my ear. "Plus, she sharpens her teeth to make the bites that much worse."

I tilted my head to his ear, cupping my hand and whispered, "So, is the bulk of this fighting in wolf form?"

His eyes flicked to Manic, who was distracted, talking on his phone in a clipped manner, so he leaned in closer. "Were you not told that?"

I shook my head. "Nope. This was a spur-of-the-moment situation. What else should I know?"

He smiled again, this time, his interest in me was evident. "Okay. So, the start line is there." He pointed to a red line that was about fifty yards away. "As soon as they say go, all the women will shift and run into the woods looking for their cub." I did a double take as my body froze and my eyes widened. *A cub? What the fuck did I get myself into?*

He chuckled at my expression. "It's a stuffed wolf. None of the women with actual cubs wanted a bunch of single vicious ladies to fight over their cub. It can get pretty brutal and bloody." He looked toward his sister in a grimace. "Then whoever makes it back to the red line with the cub 'intact' wins."

I flicked my eyes in that direction as Ax stepped around Alex's sister, his eyes laser focused on us as he made his way over. We were not buddies, so I decided I would give him some harsh medicine and do something he would hate—ignore him.

"I mean, I'm definitely excited to fight. I have been itching to practice with other supes, but I only had my brother and best friend to fight with consistently." I smiled, wanting to show Ax what it was like when you got on my good side.

"Yes." He nodded vehemently. "I think it's important to test your skills on other supes. We all have such different fighting capabilities." He puffed out his chest as he continued. "You know, if you ever need—"

"Rayla. What are you doing here?" Ax's tone made it known I was not welcomed here, and I gritted my teeth. *Fucking arrogant wolfboy.* Manic, who got off the phone when he saw his son coming over, raised his eyebrow to him in question, surprised by his tone as well.

I took the bitch road and purposely kept my voice easy, laughing under my breath. "Oh, Ax, I didn't see you there." I took it up a notch by giggling like a schoolgirl, grabbing onto Alex's forearm to take the conversation away from Ax. I was already tired of looking at his gorgeous face with his red-gold hair that shined as the moon beams hit it. *I knew what would get me to not feel hot and bothered by him.*

"You know, when we were kids, he was just as argumentative. As soon as I—"

Apparently, talking about the one time we were kids together was too much because he barked, "I will ask again, why are you here?" His eyes were concentrated on where I was touching Alex, and I realized why he was being such a turd. Well, too bad, I liked talking to someone that wasn't always trying to fight me.

Even so, I didn't like, nor would I tolerate, being talked to like that, so I replied in a deadpan tone, "I'm here because of a bet." Then sharply twisted back to Alex, wanting to let Ax know he did not affect me.

Manic clapped Ax's shoulder, Ax's mouth opened to say something else stupid when his dad beat him to the punch. "The event is about to start. Let's go sit in our section." He pointed to the other side of the clearing, then he turned to me. "You should head over to the start line." I gave Manic a nod of respect. I was just glad he gave me this opportunity.

I waved at Alex. "Bye! It was nice to meet you. Thanks for the history lesson." I swiveled on my heels and made my way over to the red line, trying to forget the eyes drilling into my back as I did.

The line already had a few women there, clothed and waiting, as a mage was putting a talisman on their wrist like a tattoo. One of the she-wolves shoved me out of the way, and I immediately turned around, swinging with my hand open. I smacked her across the face and bent toward her ear as I said loud and clear, "If you try to fuck me with again, I will slice your throat open, stick a straw down it, and drink you up like a fucking slurpy." She backed off immediately.

The mage moved over to one of the timid-looking women, and I peeked over at what they were doing. "So, what are those for?"

The mage's eyes flicked up to mine in cold detachment. "These are your broadcasting anchors. As soon as the event starts, I will be broadcasting to the group each individual's perspectives. This makes it so there is less cheating and informs the medics on standby if someone needs their attention."

I nodded, realizing she was a spirit witch. When she said broadcasting, what she meant was she would be expending a lot of energy to make psychic screens for each contestant so the viewers could see everything in real time.

I was paying attention to what the spirit witch was doing, fascinated with their magic, when someone shoulder checked me, forcing me to stumble back. "This place isn't for you, bitch. Stay away from Ax and my brother." I looked up at the naked auburn beauty who was trying to talk to Ax earlier and fought off my initial desire to growl at her. I would not take the high road, that was for suckers. I was going to take the better-than-you road.

I eyed her up and down, and as soon as I got to her face, I gave her a bored kind of look, one that told her just how threatened I really felt, which was not at all. Her left eye twitched, and I wanted to smile. "Don't worry, sweetie."

She growled, and I held in a laugh. If she was really as badass as she portrayed, that little dig wouldn't have made her so mad. "I'm not here to find a mate. The opposite, in fact." The other contestants that had circled us gasped.

I leaned in closer to Big Bad Red and whispered like we were best buds, "Word of advice. Stop trying so hard to be someone's beta and join me on the alpha side. It's much more fun."

Apparently, that was the wrong thing to say, so she took a swipe at me, which I dodged and readied myself to tear into her side when I heard, "Desmond!" I stopped my attack and spun to her back, catching Manic glaring at me over her shoulder. I took a big gulp of breath as I shut my mouth and bit my bottom lip, my face flushed as I lifted my hands and shrugged. *What did he want me to do? Take one for the team? Fuck that.*

He frowned, pointed at the red line, and told me to behave with his piercing eyes. I rolled my eyes and made a move to turn when my gaze snagged on Ax. He had his arms folded, back hunched, and his teeth grinding in my direction, but those milk-chocolate-molten eyes spoke another story. They bored into me like he wanted to come after me, wanted to tackle me and rip off my clothes to sate his growing hunger.

I gave him a cocky smirk, letting him know I saw it, before turning back and sauntering over to the red line like a good little vampire. I didn't want Manic to get all pissy and try to call the deal off. I didn't care about these wolfy politics. I wanted to collect my win.

Naked-wolf Barbie shoved her way around me, standing on the line as she glared at me in her tanned perfection. If she thought that would intimidate me, she had another thing coming. I ignored her, facing forward, trying to scope out the trajectory of my starting run.

It didn't take long for a man who seemed like he was in his sixties to step in front of all of us. Reciting the rules.

[1] "Remember that anything goes but the final death blow. This tradition is about finding the strongest female but also the most cunning." He lifted his hand with an old-fashioned revolver. "On your mark . . . get set . . . Go!"

As soon as the last word hit, I shot off. Trees were blurred in my side view as I was running faster than the wolves. The cracking of bones shifting, paws hitting the ground, and howls in the air were behind me, and I pushed harder.

I came to a stop and sniffed around. All I could smell was the sap from the pine trees and the minerals from the dirt, so I thought about where this little stuffy could hide. I heard the faint sound of growls and yips, alerting me that fighting between wolves had started, and I needed to figure this out fast before they caught up to me.

Alex said they used to use real cubs, so they would want you to think that they hid them down below in the ground or up high in the trees . . . but that's also what they wanted you to think. Where else would they hide it if not up above or down below?

---

1. Song: Boss Bitch by Doja Cat

As I was thinking, I could hear and smell some heavy breathing, and I jumped to the side as a gray wolf flew over the spot I just left, crashing to the ground. "I smelt your bad breath before your paws left the ground. Might want to chew on some mint leaves." The wolf growled at me before it bared its teeth at me, trying to threaten me, but I'd dealt with worse than wolves.

I shrugged. "Fine, then. Have it your way."

The wolf lowered to its haunches, getting ready to jump and strike at me, but, this time, my back was turned. I lifted one arm, making a come-at-me motion with my fingers. The wolf launched at me, and I smiled and waited for it to be mid jump before I leaped at it, wrapped my arms around its neck, and pulled it down to the ground. Once we landed, I tightened my arms, cutting off its air supply while incapacitating its most dangerous tool, its jaws. While the wolf's jaws were ineffective, it sure made use of its claws, drawing blood, but I didn't give up. I kept my arms tight until the wolf stopped fighting back.

I let go and pushed its heavy body off me. As soon as the body hit the ground, it shifted back into its human form. The sound of the pumping of blood in the heart of this brown-haired girl told me she was still alive. I lifted my thumb, sure someone in the clearing was watching and would come get the girl as I went back to my mission.

I walked around to my left, still thinking of where I would find this stuffy when I heard the faint babble of a brook. If a cub made it out here, I'm sure it would want water. I quickly ran toward the noise and found myself in front of not only a creek, but a creek that led to a singular stone cave. *Jackpot!*

I ran into the cave in a flash, searching until I saw a little wolf stuffy in the back corner, covered in dirt and leaves, tucked under a rock. *Yes!*

As soon as I touched the stuffy, wolf Barbie growled, "Drop the cub. Now, vampire." I gripped onto it, and the soft fur bunched between my fingers as I lifted it with me and turned to face her.

First thing I saw was it wasn't just her standing there, four other she-wolves surrounded the entrance in wolf form as she stepped forward in all her naked glory like the queen bee in a bad teen move. I rolled my eyes, I couldn't help it, it was just too basic for me. Give me a badass that would fight me woman to woman, or one that tricked me into giving her the stuffy, maybe even waited until right before I crossed the line and snatched it out of my hands. Something that showed she was the smart one or the badass, but no, she went the bitch route. It would be a lesson to her today that I could out bitch any bitch.

I tucked the stuffy between my breasts and through my sports bra, knowing it was secure and it opened my hands for this fight. I patted its head. "Just wait for mama to get rid of the big bad wolf, and then we will go home."

"Are you fucking talking to it, you idiot?" The more I heard her voice, the more it made my blood boil, and that wasn't good. I didn't want to kill her, that would be bad for Manic, and the whole purpose of this was to get him on my side.

"Ummm . . . yeah. What's it to you?"

She narrowed her eyes on me, getting into a fighting stance, and she had the gaul to put out her hand. "Just give it here, and we'll let you leave."

I laughed to the sky for a full three seconds before I turned it off and looked at her deadly serious as I responded, "Back the fuck up, or I'm going to carve up that pretty face of yours. Your choice."

She growled before she shifted and lunged for me. I knew she would, so instead of going straight for her, I ran up the sides of the cave, using my speed to defy gravity as I circled the cave like a Hot Wheels track. She crashed into the stone wall and crumbled to the floor all on her own. *See, basic.*

I landed in front of one of her bitch wolf gang members and wasted no time in punching her square in the nose. It crunched under my stone fists, and the wolf went down immediately. The remaining three tried to circle me, swiping at the cub in my chest, but I kept my reflexes sharp and dodged, bended, and twirled out of their grip.

When the cat-and-mouse game didn't work, they left formation and went at me on their own. That was my time to strike. The first one, white wolf, lunged for my feet, but that was the wrong move. She thought she was doing something smart, but all she did was bring her face closer to my foot. I used my vampire speed to swing my leg back and kick her jaw open. The other two jumped out of the way of her limp human body flying through the air.

I turned to the next one that thought they could sneak up on me from behind, and I jumped up, did a backflip, and switched up the game with me behind her. I straightened my fingers, making my hand into a blade, as I swiped down her back as she howled out in pain. She limped away in wolf form to lick her wounds as I laughed.

I turned to the last one, ready to take this one out, and she was retreating into the woods. Well, that made sense. She only had balls when she had her friends beside her.

I wasted no time as I readjusted the little guy from the fight, tucked him back between my boobs, and ran toward the finish line.

I was about a mile from the finish when a flash of auburn hit my peripherals, and my instincts told me to stop. As soon as I did, a golden-red wolf leaped in front of me, growling something fierce. Well, it looked like wolf Barbie didn't hit herself as hard as I would've liked.

"You want a fight, then let's go." Instead of going straight for me, she leaped to the side, her paws landing on the tree trunk as she pushed off and came at me from the side. It was a good move, I'll admit, a move that would take out a mage or even another wolf since they didn't think about tactics like that, but not a vampire. Or more like, not a Desmond vampire.

I jumped up and grabbed onto a tree branch, climbing until the branches grew too dense to see through from the ground. I pushed some leaves out of the way to see her circling, sniffing, and searching for me. Now, let's show her what they meant by cunning.

I bounced to another branch on another tree, then another, then another. Drawing her attention to wherever

I bounced. I picked up speed until most of the branches were still moving by the time I dropped down behind her.

She craned her neck up, still trying to find me, when I grabbed her tail and swung her into one of the tree trunks. She fell to the ground in her human form, a large bruise already taking over her torso as she grunted out in pain.

I walked over to her, patting the stuffed cub's head like I was comforting the little guy as I bent down toward her head. "You got lucky. If this was in the outside world and not under the rules of your tradition, you would not only be dead, but carved up, heart drained dry, and guts spilled out around you. Know your lane."

Then I got up and ran the rest of the way toward the finish line.

As soon as I crossed the tree line, I found Manic and Ax at the finish line eyeing me with different expressions. One grinned like a mad man, and the other clenched his teeth. I never thought I would ever see a smile that big on Manic's face, but I guess small miracles were a thing. I didn't know what was up Ax's butt, but I didn't give a flying fuck. The Rossey support had been won, and that was all that mattered.

I had prepared myself to be a little hated by the wolves, beating them at their own tradition, but I had a lot of people come up and congratulate me. Telling me how strong I was, or how smart my tree move was. I didn't realize the cub was still in my bra until the person who shot the gun came up and asked me for it back.

I snagged the little guy out of my bra and gave him a kiss before handing it over. That little guy just won me one out of the three votes I needed, he was now precious to me.

Alex came over, and I straightened my shoulders, expecting him to be pissed about how I handled his sister. Instead, he gave me a hug. For a second, I stood there, unmoving, not expecting this and not knowing what to do with my hands. Do I pat him? Do I hug him back? No, that's weird.

"You took her down a notch. Let's hope she learns her lesson in fucking with the Rayla Desmond."

I stiffened, not remembering I gave him my name before I was yanked out of his grasp with a growl. "My father needs to talk to you."

I yanked my arm out of his grasp, knowing Ax's growly voice anywhere. I turned back to Alex, whose fist tightened as he glared at Ax. He opened his mouth, but I didn't have time for wolf drama.

"Thanks for the history lesson, Alex, it helped me more than you know, but I need to talk to Manic before I leave." I waved before turning around. When I noticed Ax wasn't following me, I pulled his arm, pushing him around forcefully.

"I hope to see you around, Rayla," Alex called out at my back, and I lifted my hand in acknowledgment. I didn't want to lead him on when there was nothing there.

Rage vibrated from Ax as we walked toward his father. "What crawled up your ass?"

He didn't say anything, just faced forward and kept walking to his father. Well, I tried. Whatever. I would not let him ruin my win.

"There is the little vicious psycho!" Manic grinned, pulling me closer to him with one arm around my shoulders. He bent down and whispered in my ear, "You made me a lot of money tonight, so thank you. And you have my support."

I tried to keep myself neutral, but I couldn't keep the happiness from my win out of my eyes. He winked at me, taking a cigar out and lighting it up with joy. Then I realized what he said and muttered under my breath, "You bet against yourself?"

He turned me to face him. "I knew you would win. Ternin raised you. There was no way that you wouldn't be brutal and cunning . . . I just needed someone else to see it." He mumbled that last part, but I heard it just the same and frowned.

He patted me on my cheek before he made a move to check his watch. "I think you have somewhere you will need to be soon, right?"

I nodded and turned away while mumbling, "You all are a bunch of gossiping nillies."

"Yes. Yes, we are." He laughed. "I'm sure I will see you soon, Rayla. Thanks for the entertaining night." I waved without looking at him, expecting to see Ax, but the space was empty where he had been. I was going to say bye to him, keep it cordial, but I had somewhere to be, and I wasn't going to track him down. Plus, I was sure I would see him sometime later.

Using my vampire speed, I ran through the clearing and down the side of the mountain, knowing I had a way to go before I hit my car.

As I was running, a sharp crisp air sliced through my hair, the smell of fresh clean pine raced up my nose, and at the velocity I was going, it felt like I was flying. This was what I enjoyed. A combination of the solitude and unruliness that set my soul free, made me feel alive. I closed my eyes for a second and let myself fall, letting the wind take me where it wanted. At least until I heard a howl right next to me.

My eyes flew open, and I twisted to the side to skid to a stop before turning toward what was racing beside me. There was a low rumble nearby as I slowly stood up and turned around, ready to fight whatever that was.

My gaze collided with a huge red-furred wolf with golden-tipped ears. I flicked my eyes up and down, and it had paws as big as my head and a wolfish smile full of razor-sharp teeth, ready to slice into its next meal. Like it knew what I was thinking, its long-wet tongue circled its lips like it just saw a tasty snack. I better put a stop to that.

"I have no problems with wolves, find your next victim elsewhere . . . or you might regret it." I cracked my knuckles in emphasis. There was something familiar about the vibe this wolf was giving, but before I could figure it out, it launched itself at me.

I narrowly avoided being swiped by his claws. He might be a big one, but he was also quicker than most, which would make for a drawn-out, hand-to-hand combat. I made a snap decision and ran.

I knew this would only spur the wolf on, excited for the hunt, but I was hoping to catch it by surprise. A loud howl sounded from behind me as its paws hit the ground swiftly. I pumped my arms as I weaved through the woods, leaving a trail of my scent for it to follow. Once I hit a creek and stopped, knowing that the wolf was just a few miles behind me and coming in fast, I jumped over the creek and then jumped back. I wanted the wolf to think I had gone over the creek so I could sneak up behind it.

I picked one of the thicker trees and hid behind when I heard panting. It hit the creek and sniffed around. I peeked out from around the tree, and the wolf sniffed at the air, backed up a few steps, and made the jump. That was my cue.

I ran up and made the jump again, ready to sneak up a couple of steps and circle its neck when the wolf turned on its hind legs and lunged for me. I tried to backtrack, but at the angle I was in, my back hit a tree and the wolf's front paws hit the bark, boxing me in.

Before the damn thing could bite my face off, I shoved my hands up and gripped its thick neck, squeezing it with one hand and pushing its jaw up with the other to prevent any face eating. I was seconds away from tearing its head off when it started to shift into naked human form. Refusing to let go, I kept a grip on its neck and jaw, but as its body got smaller, it crowded me more than the damn wolf did.

[2] "I just wanted a little chase, Siren." I rolled my eyes. Only Ax could sound cocky and sly while having his Adam's apple seconds away from being ripped from his body. And what a body it was. His chest was lined with muscles and tattoos that went along his arms up to his wrists, his muscles bulged, the grooves between them deep valleys that spoke of a lot of training and working out to get to that perfection.

This time, I was close enough to him to see that both arms were forest scenes that lined his arms and shoulders. One of his pecs was a moon and the other was a savage wolf looking like it was about to tear up its next victim. It was stunning imagery, but the one that caught my eye was the Syndicate tattoo on the inside of his left forearm.

I pushed up harder on his jaw, warning him of his smart mouth, but his smile widened. "I thought you were out and about pouting about me winning. All that work for nothing now, eh?" I tried to keep the smug happiness out of my voice, but, judging from his growl, I didn't do it effectively.

He yanked his head back, escaping from the hand pushing his jaw away, and circled his face back to me as he tightened the space between us. We were out in a forest, but with his arms caging me between him and the tree, it was getting a little hot in here.

"You think that I need a fucking competition to come for you?" The vibrations skittered down my hand still holding his throat as he laughed. His face lowered right in front of mine, our foreheads meeting as he cooed, "Those were

---

2. Song: Animals by Maroon 5

just shackles keeping me in line, now that I have been freed of them, I don't have any rules . . . and I will make you mine my way."

With my brows furrowed, my hand around his neck loosened, and he took advantage of that by pressing his body against mine. "But I thought . . ." Ax was already trailing his nose up the nape of my neck, sniffing his way up and down like he was committing my scent to long-term memory.

He moved back to face me, our lips only centimeters apart as he whispered, "You didn't think I would let you go so easily, did you? I only got a small taste of you that night in the club . . . and I'm craving more."

While my mind was still trying to catch up with his words, my body was responding, pushing my cheek into his, my breath turning into sultry pants of need and want. My body remembered what it felt like to have his rough hands on me, to have his claws dig into my flesh, how good it felt when he pushed himself inside of me and fucked me like he couldn't get enough.

He must've seen or felt the change in me because his hands moved from caging me in to holding me at the hips, gripping them as he rubbed his growing cock into my thigh. "It was hot seeing you put those wolves in their place. Showing them who the real alpha was." He dove back into my neck again, and my hands betrayed me by trying to bring him closer. When my hands landed on some very naked abs, I almost let out a groan. I let my eyes wander from his hungry eyes to his moist lips, down his broad inky shoulders and the swirls of art on his massive arms to his perfectly sculpted chest and stomach, down to his fully erect cock. It was almost like it was straining to say hi.

"Like what you see?" He chuckled, and I nodded as I licked my lips like he was a juicy steak.

"Now that I got a good look at your front, I can say that it matches how it feels." I couldn't help biting the inside of my lip, the little bit of pain making me quake. My body was trembling, wanting a round two as much as he obviously did. I lifted my hand to touch him, to see if it was a fluke or not, but then my mind reminded me of what we just got out of. What we fought for, and I pulled back.

"What am I doing? I just got the Rossey clan to side with me to get out of that stupid marriage deal," I murmured as I put my palm on his chest and pushed him back. He went back by an inch before he met my hand with resistance.

"So, you want to push me away, but you're more than willing to grab onto that other fucker?" The end came out in a growl, and fury radiated off his body, enveloping me.

The heat was like this delicious blanket I wanted to snuggle into, to warm up these cold bones. It made my limbs limp and my head fuzzy. I blurted, "He meant nothing, and you know it."

His body froze, the heat changing from sweltering anger to red-hot desire. He crowded me again, pushing back my hand with his chest. "That's right, he means nothing because you and I mean everything."

I opened my mouth to rebut, but he kept going. "You know that we're electric together. The smell of you." He lifted one hand and trailed a finger from my collarbone down the center of my body. "The feel of your body against mine." His trailing hand cupped my pussy, rubbing his thumb against my fabric-covered clit. I let out a small gasp, and he surged forward and captured my lips with his.

His tongue slid in masterfully, swiping at the right spots that made me open to him and purr. His hot mouth started off with taking, all pressure and pulling. His need bled into that initial kiss, and I couldn't help but to respond to the call. He may call me a siren, but I was fighting off his summon. It was an invitation to play, to let go, to let us be like what he said, electric and wild together.

The palm on his chest expanded, my fingers digging into his pec like I was going to hold on for the ride. He pulled back enough for me to snake my other arm down his front and grasp his cock.

He hissed out as I squeezed before he bit down on my lip so hard blood came out. It was my turn to moan. My nails dug into his pec, wanting blood for blood.

As soon as my nose picked up his tantalizing blood scent of adventure and wilderness, my teeth slid out, pulling me to just take a taste. His bruising kiss paused as he used his tongue to lick each fang, and I almost came right there.

"Are you excited, Little Siren? Are you wanting a taste?" he whispered against my collarbone as he yanked my leggings down to my ankles, took two handfuls of my ass, and squeezed as he lifted me against the tree so rough the bark scraped my back. His hands dug so far into me, and his pinky and ring finger teased me against my channel as his pointer finger teased my puckered hole. It was forward as fuck, but the bad girl inside of me liked it. I wanted this untamable man, the one that fucked me against a railing in front of everyone because he had to have me.

I grabbed a handful of his wild golden-red hair and yanked his head back. I would give it back to him, but my rough treatment didn't even faze him, and his fingers kept up with their exploration. Placing my lips just above his, I said, "I want to taste a lot of things, but, for now, I just want that fat dick to fill me up. I want you to fuck me like we only have now." You never know, we might only have now, but also, I just wanted to let go. To let go for a second with my plans and my future. My roles and responsibilities. I wanted to be a bad girl, fucked by an equally bad and wild wolf.

He chuckled against my lips before he shoved both sets of fingers into my holes so roughly I arched my back, face to the sky, as I moaned. "I see what you need, my naughty siren. I can taste it in the air. You need a man who can take you just how you want. You want someone to match your badass, take-charge energy and fuck you like they own this tight body. You came to the right man." He ripped my leggings, and they fell to the ground, leaving my bottom half exposed to the forest.

A rush of air flowing through my hair was the only warning I got when my back slammed to the ground. The smell of dirt and leaves wafted around me as he smiled down at me like he would carve me up. I smirked as I widened my legs, letting him know that was exactly what I wanted. "Make it good, wolf."

Something snapped inside of him, and his arm snaked out, grabbing my throat to pin me to the ground. The tips of his nails dug in, and I knew his claws had come out to play, his wolf so close to the surface. My eyes flared with excitement at his snarling face, half-crazed as he and his wolf battled for dominance.

I wasn't very patient when it came to this kind of stuff, so I wrapped my legs around his back, pushed my heels into his ass, and pushed him inside of me in one fell swoop. I was already so wet from the teasing that he slipped right in. He paused at my cry of pleasure, his dick fully inside of me, my hips still moving, effectively fucking myself against him. He squeezed my neck and lifted me to snarl in my face.

"So impatient, Siren. Bad girls need to be punished." Then he slammed my head back into the ground, pulled out of my pussy, and shoved his dick into my ass. I screamed at the entry, and he pumped in and out, rubbing my clit in time with his thrusts until my screams turned into pants. Soon, I was panting for more as the pain and pleasure melded.

"Yes, punish this bad, bad girl. Fucking break me." My voice was hoarse from how hard he gripped my throat, but it was also exciting. How far could we go with each other? How much more wild could we get?

I licked my lips at the sight of the blood dripping down his chest from the cuts that my nails dug, and I decided it was my turn. I gripped the hand on my throat, used my vampire strength to push it up. His eyes widened, and he hesitated for a second, but a second was all I needed. I moved my leg and kicked him off me. He flew up for a second and huffed out when he landed on his back.

I used my speed again to climb on top of him, this time holding his neck to the ground as I whispered in his ear, "My turn."

I sheathed myself onto him, taking him deep into my channel that was wet and ready for his fat cock. He cried, "Oh, fuck!"

I laughed as I moved up and down his cock, fucking him into the ground as hard as he had done to me.

"Holy hell, Rayla. Your pussy gripping my cock is the perfect heaven or the sweetest hell. I don't know which." His cries turned short as I closed his windpipes with my hand, his gasping shallow breaths music to my ears.

"Are you going to cum for me, my wolf? Are you going to spill your seed in me? Fill me up so full that I burst?" I leaned down to his ear, grabbed it between my teeth, letting my fangs play with his lobe before I said something I didn't mean to. "Are you mine?"

Since I had a firm hold on his throat, all I got were muffled noises between pants, followed by whimpered yeses. Pleased with the answer, I let go and put both palms on his chest as I fucked myself wild on his dick, pushing my tits in his face, almost smothering him. The swirling heat of my orgasm was working its way out when he took one of his clawed fingers and stuck it up my ass, hooking it just the right way that my channel immediately clenched around him, and I exploded.

I screamed out my orgasm, scratched down his chest, drawing rivulets of blood as he pushed up into me, fucking me through my orgasm until he cried out, and his warmth shot into me, filling me up just how I'd asked. I fell to the side of him, panting, because that was just how I had envisioned sex with Ax—hot, wild, and bloody.

Before either of us could say something to ruin the moment, I got up and kissed his cheek. "Thanks for that. I needed it . . ." I looked at my bare legs and the ruined leggings. "Also, you owe me a new pair of leggings."

He quickly scrambled up. "Ray—"

I was already needing to be somewhere, so I blew him a kiss and ran as fast as I could to my car. As soon as I opened the door, I felt soul-piercing eyes on me, watching me. Devouring my body with its eyes as a pulsing vibrant need surrounded me, almost choking me. It was like nothing I had felt before, and I glanced around, trying to find who it was, but there was no one within a mile radius. I shook off the feeling as I got into my car and started the engine. I could've sworn I heard a wolf howl in the distance as I took off.

CHAPTER 18

I RACED DOWN THE freeway, cars blurred blips as I zigzagged through the throngs of people. I was still half-naked, but I wouldn't be for long.

What was I thinking, doing that with Ax?! *You were thinking about some good dick.* I mean, yeah, I was. And it was some good dick. I still felt the aftershocks in my pussy and ass, and the ache was delicious. It was how you felt the next day after you had some amazing sex, but the damper was trying to think of any scenarios that this choice would fuck me. I just got out of the damn marriage deal with the Rosseys, I didn't want to invite them back in for a good time.

Maybe I was overthinking it. Maybe all it meant to him was a good fuck, too. Right? Plus, a guy like him, rumored to be a player among players, wasn't trying to settle down. No, he just wanted a good time, and I had to hand it to him, we always had a good time.

A little twinge of jealousy hit me when I remembered how Laura was all over him with her naked perfection. I wanted to rip her face off, tell her to back the fuck off him, but I came to my senses and calmed myself down. No use fighting over a man who wants to be free. It was also why I didn't taste his blood even though he offered it.

I was not a good sharer. I knew if I tasted even a drop of his blood, any woman that looked at him in a seductive manner would cause me to rip their earrings off and shove them down their throat, then rip them from the inside. I was very territorial with those I bit. Not only was it a source of sustenance, but, also, there was a connection when you exchanged blood. Getting to know someone at a cellular level. It's why I had my one and only rule while dating me. No exceptions.

Plus, he was an heir. It's not like he didn't have women aplenty trying to be with him, throwing themselves at him. I needed to play this cool. To be calm and act like I didn't care, even if he was the wild beast I never wanted to tame. To let him go wild on me and see where we could take each other, but we shouldn't. That would give our dads the wrong idea, and I didn't want that.

As I got closer to the track, I pulled off to the side and grabbed my bag from behind me for some clothes. I imagined opening the door as I was, half-naked, and seeing Falcon's eyes explode. I smiled to myself at that. It would almost be worth it, but this was my hometown, and I was always representing the Syndicate, so that was a no-go.

I liked having my legs free when I drove, so I put on my black, stretchy mini-skirt with a slit up the side and a black, off-the-shoulder, ribbed crop top. I have a set of rose gold strappy heels for later, but when I drove, I liked to have boots on. There was nothing sexier and more practical than some thigh-high boots.

I cleaned myself with some wet wipes I always kept on hand from the mess Ax and I made. Cum and blood can get messy, and you needed these bad boys for any clean up. I got back in the car, revved up the engine, and took off to ensure I made it on time. I knew that the Winstales would be there right on time, maybe even earlier, and I didn't want to disrespect them.

The coordinates I gave him were on the outskirts of Vegas in the desert. Once upon a time, some rich guy thought he would build a massive exclusive casino out here, trying to make it a mecca for celebrities to feel normal and secluded from the world.

Surprise, surprise, most celebrities didn't want to be that secluded, and he only got the bones of the hotel made before he scrapped the whole thing and filed the project for bankruptcy, finding a new focus on going into outer space.

His loss was the drag-race world's gain because it had layers of floors that interconnected and sturdy ramps put in place to the floors that didn't. There were a few ways to get up to the top with their own challenges that tested a driver's stamina and ballsiness. It was also a place where if people crashed into things, it wasn't a big deal since it was all concrete and solid stabilizers.

I turned off a dark dirt road you wouldn't know was there unless you had been there a few times. The racing community was tight-knit, and the only way you could get in was if someone brought you here. By giving him the coordinates, I was testing him by a) seeing if they would be able to find it, and b) seeing if they could get past the guards to get in. I was half expecting to see Falcon on the side of the road fuming about not being let in without another racer present.

I was surprised when I saw the iron-rod gates that circled the massive estate entrance in the distance and didn't see Falcon or his dad. *Were they late?* I couldn't imagine that either would do that with how rigid they both were. *Did that mean they made it in?* I guess I'll see.

I rolled up to the gate with five guards with automatic rifles, a shot gun, and a rocket launcher at the ready. Deesil, the trackmaster, was always so cautious and liked to keep all of us criminals in line. That's what I liked about him. It's one reason I financially backed him in purchasing the bankrupted land for the drag-race games.

The games used to be in a custom-made dirt field that Deesil's uncle owned, but everyone complained about the grime on their cars, how the dust would make it hard to see the winner, and the girls didn't like having the layer of dirt stick to their over lotioned arms and legs. One day, I asked him if he wanted to level up his game, make more money, and draw in a bigger crowd with higher stakes. He salivated at the mouth when I brought it up but quickly reminded me he didn't want to mess with the Syndicate if he didn't have to. I convinced him he would only deal with me personally, but he was correct that the Syndicate would need to take a small cut. He waffled until I named the price I was willing to give, and he didn't hesitate to sign a personal contract with me. I never did anything by a handshake, that was for idiots who trusted too easily.

When my dad confronted me about the money I was spending from my account, I smiled and said it was a business decision, another revenue stream for us to build on. He was a little miffed for a couple weeks, but once he saw the cash flow, he praised me for my business sense and left the whole thing to me. For me, it was an easy investment because I knew Deesil would run a tight ship. That, and he was the ultimate entertainer, which kept the customers excited and the money rolling in.

As soon as the guards saw my matte-black Koenigsegg Agera roll up, they whistled and opened the gates. As I slowed my vehicle, I asked the head guard, Lenny, "Where's Sil?"

He tried to keep a straight face, like he always did, but I caught the way his eyes traced my body. His vampire fang peeked between his lips as he nodded. "Miss Rayla. He's in the VIP suite getting ready."

I nodded, that boy took longer to get ready than a damn showgirl. I bit my lip, letting him see it as I flicked my eyes up to him in a seductive manner. "Oh, and, Lenny, did a rando show up today? Mage. Tall with blond hair? A little stuck-up?"

He wasn't a part of the Desmond clan, but all vampires in this city knew who to obey when it came down to it.

He leaned in. "Yes. He started to spout off about being a Winstale, and I told him to keep his mouth shut about that. That the Syndicate was more of an underbelly here than the main show. He said he was sent here by you, so I let him in."

I smiled. "Thank you, Lenny. You're always so helpful."

There was a red tint to his cheeks as he stood up. "Anything for the Desmonds." I winked at him before pushing my foot on the gas, wheels squealing as I pulled in.

The place was already in full swing. There were cars lined up everywhere, hoods popped, and crews either talking or working on the cars as I rolled past. Music was blasting from every corner, girls all walking around half-dressed.

I usually had Rick as my mechanic and Cosmo as my backup to watch the car as I browsed what the others had invented. Half the cars here were still being worked on, trying to create buzz about some new thing they created or trying to show off some piece of machinery they purchased from overseas. The other half were like me, just in it for a thrill, and found that in racing.

A few smaller gangs came, though, trying to act all bad and tough, trying to get some Vegas girls, but they knew this was a neutral zone and didn't start anything with me. Plus, they knew they couldn't take on the Syndicate. They could try, but it was their death sentence.

I slid into my usual spot, new people gawked at my car, while the regulars either glared with jealousy or shined with appreciation. I got out, and everyone within a hundred feet watched me as I locked my car with a *beep beep* and gave a warning over my shoulder. "Touch it, and I will make sure you die a slow and painful death."

People shrunk back, knowing I would follow through on that promise, and everyone gave my car a wide berth. I made my way up the stairs to where the hotel's lobby would've been, and in the corner was a rolling rack with clothes and a large vanity with Deesil sitting in front of it complaining about the amount of makeup his stylist had put on him.

"Yes, I wanted you to hide any imperfections, but I didn't want to look like a newly made vampire. Look how pale you made me!" The end was left in more of a whine, so I thought I would help his stylist out.

"But I think you look completely edible as a new vampire," I called out like I was offended.

He turned around in his chair and smiled at me. "Oh, my Ray-as-a-day!" He uncrossed his legs and got up, shooing his stylist that said hi to me and nodded in my direction before escaping out the back.

Deesil waltzed over to me in his all-white suit, with a bright orange v-neck underneath that matched the hue of his hair. He lifted his arms for a hug, and I complied. He was tall and a little lean for my taste, but he was still drop-dead gorgeous with his aristocratic looks.

He sniffed my hair before he pushed me away by my shoulders. "What a pair we make." He pulled me next to him, and, in the mirror, I could see what he meant. With my white hair and pale skin, matched with my all-black outfit, I appeared dark and dangerous, paired with his all-white suit, pop-of-color neon-orange shirt and hair, he seemed fun and bubbly. The perfect opposites.

"That's why we're friends," I commented as he eyed my body like a snack. Deesil was fae, which meant he was gorgeous, and he knew it. He liked to surround himself with equally gorgeous people. It helped that he was bi and really had no preference as to men or women, always saying, "A hot body is a hot body." It's also why I knew I would never take that fae for a spin. I was a possessive lady, and that free love wouldn't work for me.

"With the way he's looking at you, I would've guessed you were lovers." A crisp, familiar voice sounded behind me, and I pulled my lips in to prevent myself from smiling at the hint of jealousy I detected.

"I'm sure to you it would," I snapped, crossing my arms over my chest as I turned around to Falcon, with his strong lines and sharp angles, glaring at me. Is he still pissed about that smoking-gun incident? That was ages ago.

I continued. "I have a feeling you don't have many friends and can't tell the difference." I eyed him up and down, appreciating his attire for the night. He had on a black button-down with rolled-up sleeves, showing off those strong mechanic forearms, paired with black fitted slacks and some brown toe boots. His short blond hair and crystal-blue penetrating eyes that could mesmerize any-one in only a second. It was the perfect match to my light-and-dark combo. *Fuck, he looked good.*

Deesil whistled out and laughed nervously, eyes shifting between the two of us in question. "Ray and I are the best of friends. So good, in fact, that she won't let me sleep with her. She's mean like that." I chuckled under my breath at his polite dig. Always the mediator.

Deesil stuck his hand out toward Falcon. "I'm Deesil, the trackmaster here." Falcon didn't take his eyes off mine as he grabbed his hand roughly and shook it.

"Falcon Winstale. But you already knew that, didn't you"—he switched his piercing gaze to Deesil—"or else you wouldn't have let me in when the security called you."

Deesil's smile grew into a devious grin as they let go. You could tell there was some macho-man show happening with the sizzle in the air, but I didn't care about all that. I slid my arm into Deesil's as I cooed, "We better get the races started. You know how the crowd can get when you run late, pumpkin." He smiled down at me, enjoying the game I was playing. Deesil was always down for games.

"Plus . . ." Deesil and I walked slowly past Falcon, and I ran the tip of my finger down Falcon's naked forearm. "Our race is the last of the night, so the faster we get through the rest, the better." His lips parted at my touch, the only indication I affected him, but it was enough for me to look at him through my lashes and bite my bottom lip before facing forward and walking with Deesil out of the building. This would be an interesting night.

I heard Falcon's clipped shoes as he followed us all the way to the starting point around the side of the building. Deesil had a whole outdoor cabana booth setup for those of us in the VIP section that overlooked the finish and start lines. Deesil walked me over to my table and sat me down, kissing my hand before he walked off to the announcer booth to start the show.

Falcon quickly sat on the other side of me as the first set of cars went off in the background. His focused gaze never left my face as I scanned around and nodded to others in their booths. Some were human and some were supes, but all of us in the VIP section had loads of money, but I was the only one that put my money where my mouth was and raced occasionally.

"Thanks for setting me up back there," Falcon ground out, and I turned toward him. His forehead was all bunched as he spoke, and I felt like I needed to do something about it. Us Syndicate heirs should always look our best. I scooted over to his side of the booth, his eyes tracking me like I was a snake in the grass, but I didn't intend to bite him . . . not yet.

Once we were inches from each other, his lemongrass and orange scent made my mouth water, I lifted my hand slowly and placed it on the center of his forehead, smoothing out the lines. "Don't do that. You will cause wrinkles with all that, and no one wants that." He grabbed my wrist, and I was surprised his grip wasn't bruising or brutish, it was more like a firm caress, and I liked it far too much.

"I don't enjoy being played with." His nostrils flared before he put my hand down, and I rolled my eyes.

"I didn't play with you." He snorted and rolled his eyes in disbelief as he glanced around the VIP room. I sat back, still close to him but less in his face. "Okay, maybe it was a little bit of a play, but I had to get you back for that smoking-gun stunt."

"You already did, don't you remember?" He stared daggers at me. "You got me back so good I woke up on the floor with a few of my men standing over me, dumbfounded."

I lifted my hand, giggling behind it as I remembered his face when I gave him a dose of his own medicine. "Sure, but when a Desmond is involved, we don't get even, we get revenge." He, again, snorted under his breath, half frustration, half understanding, and I appreciated it. Deesil spoke in the background, getting the races started before the gun went off, and the sound of screeching tires followed.

I released a sigh. "Look, I had to see what you would do. It's an exclusive track, and I wanted to know how you would handle yourself in that kind of situation." He turned toward me with one eyebrow raised, so I explained. "If you were the type to crack under pressure, you might have come in guns blazing. If you were the giving-up type or the spoiled type, you would've been waiting for me at the gate. If you were the resourceful type—" I smiled sweetly at him. "You would make it in with no bloodshed or issues blown back onto me."

"So, are you satisfied?" His question surprised me as he watched me like he was memorizing everything about this conversation.

I stared off in the distance, not used to his penetrating gaze. "Yes. Immensely."

I risked looking back at him and saw a small uptick in the corner of his mouth as his fists tightened on the table. I was about to change the subject when all hell broke loose, and everyone in the VIP section stood with their guns in the air. I peeked my head out of the booth and noticed a small drone heading down toward where Falcon and I were sitting.

Falcon didn't seem fazed, even relaxing his muscles as he leaned back into the booth, watching the drone with a bored expression. The drone swiveled around and spoke out, "This is Easton Winstale, and I'm only watching in the interest of the bet between myself and Rayla Desmond."

Everyone glared at me, and I resisted the urge to face-plant onto the table because, of course, Falcon's dad would want to watch the race. Manic did, too, I just expected it to be in damn person.

I tapped Falcon to move out of the booth as we were more on his side than mine. He relented and moved out of my way. Once I had scooted out, I lifted my hands to all the others in reassurance. "You can all put your guns away. What he's saying is correct, and all he wants to do is witness the last race."

Everyone calmed down, mumbling about the damn Syndicate and their weird shit, but I didn't let it faze me because it was weird. I should've counted on Easton Winstale to do something like this. My bad.

As the drone kept on its descent to my table, I whispered under my breath to Falcon, "I guess we are even now."

This was as embarrassing as the whole gate thing I put him through.

I was suddenly enveloped with his citrusy scent as his lips grazed my ear. "We are not even close . . . but I'm starting to get some ideas." His breath danced along the back of my neck, making it hard to think about what was going on in front of me. I couldn't help the shudder that worked its way down my spine. I was surprised because he wasn't the type that would normally do that. He was the smart one, the calm and patient guy. The one that thought of all the angles and executed it in all its mathematical perfection, the exact opposite of me, but each time we were around each other, I felt this smooth, sharp darkness. He was like a fine katana sword, built to perfection and precision, something you only take out when you want that goal met swiftly but just as bloody and deadly as anything else.

He made my skin shiver in excitement. Something inside of me wanted to push him to the edge, see what he looked like when he lost all that carefully crafted control. I bet it was glorious. Hopefully a little bloody.

I took a breath before I tore myself away from him, trying to cool my body down now that I knew we had an audience with his dad. Almost as if right on time, the drone landed on the table as we settled back into our seats.

"You didn't think I would miss this, did you, Miss Rayla?" Easton's voice crackled through the speaker from the damn machine. I saw the lens turn, changing focus to clearly read my reaction.

I flicked my gaze at the plate-sized electric bug, acting like none of it amazed me, but, really, I thought that was a cool entrance. "I'm not fazed in the least, and I expected nothing less."

"So, when is your race going to happen? I have a project in the lab I am waiting to cure, but the timing needs to be precise." Easton's voice sounded distracted, like he was looking at something else completely.

I flicked my eyes to Falcon, who shrugged and folded his arms with a huff. I couldn't help the small smile that formed on my lips. I had the same look on my face when my dad did something I thought was extra or outrageous. I guess we had that in common. Both our dads were extra in their own ways.

I nodded to Falcon. "Behind you on the side of the track is a set of red flags in the ground, tell me how many are up?" He turned around slowly, cheers sounded in the distance before he turned back.

"Five. They just put the fifth one up." I nodded and turned back to the drone.

"We are next up. We should probably get ready." I made a move to scoot out of the booth but then remembered something and turned to the drone as I stood. "Are you going to follow us airborne?"

Its silent propellers started up as it rose level with my face. "Yes, but I'll make sure to keep my distance. The lenses are military grade that I have upgraded with night and see-through vision. I don't want to miss a single move but also don't want to get in the way. As soon as the race is done, I will have Kemp drive the drone back, as I have stuff to do."

I tilted my head as I smirked. "Always efficient doing business with you."

I could almost hear the smile in Easton's voice as he replied, "That's what us Winstales are for, efficiency. Good luck to the both of you." Then the drone took off into the night sky.

Falcon was standing near me, head moving side to side like a lost puppy, so I scooped his arm into mine. His steps faltered for a second before he shook his head and walked in time with me. I led us down the steps into the throngs of people still gawking at cars. I spotted the setters heading our way, and I put my hand out to him. "Do you have your keys?"

He nodded, pulling them out but not handing them over, waiting for an explanation. I guess I shouldn't expect him to trust me. I pointed to the two men making their way over to us. "The setters are going to pull up the cars to the line for us. I set up this race to be only between you and me. Since we're VIP guests, we get some level of different treatment."

His brows pinched, and his nose crinkled. "I've never heard—"

"It's a Deesil thing." I flicked my hand out, sure that explained everything, but when he didn't take his eyes off me, I elaborated. "It's Vegas. VIPs are expected to be treated very differently here and get the king's treatment for the money."

"So, you pay for a membership?" He pried, interest lining his voice, but was interrupted by my cackling laugh.

"Ms. Desmond." The setters had arrived, and I fished my keys from between my breasts. Falcon and both setters stared at my chest as I did.

I cleared my throat. "Eyes up here, boys." The setters snapped their heads up, but Falcon's gaze lingered a few beats more, which made my neck hot. "You know the car." My setter nodded and ran off.

Falcon reluctantly handed over his keys. "It's the McLaren Senna in all white." His lips thinned as he watched the setter like a hawk. I tugged him by the arm toward the other side where the start line was.

"To answer your question, no. I don't have a membership." He looked back down at me, still walking but keeping his attention laser focused on me . . . and I liked it. "I funded Deesil's aspirations to make this underground track the best in the country. Attracting all the deep pockets with money to burn and searching for a thrill."

He glanced around with a critical eye before saying, "So, the Syndicate owns it." He made it a statement, and I felt I needed to clarify.

"Yes and no. Think of it more as a business partnership with Deesil. He runs it completely. Collects the cash, keeps up the track, contacts the high rollers, has it broadcasted to those special few that want to bet but are not able to show in person. He also deals with the fall outs or mishaps that happen occasionally. I just offered to financially back him in exchange for a twenty percent cut. Simple and clean."

"He seems to run a tight house. The guards were adequate, and the VIPs appeared excited. It seems like it was a good investment on your end." His compliment caught me off guard.

I was so stunned that I let it slip. "Well, I'm an adrenaline junkie, and I needed to have a place where I could let my kink run free."

His eyes drilled into mine before he moved a few strands of hair behind my ear. "It's still a good move. Whether your motives are selfish or not." He paused for a second as his eyes flicked up at something. "Our time is up. Just remember to not take it out on me when I beat you, wild thing."

My eyes followed him as he walked up to his car that just rolled up to the start line. I was turned on and piping-hot mad as I watched him. I saw red as my body heated with rage. It was the right kind of mixed feelings I needed to spank his ass in the race. He thought he had an edge with that suped up car of his, but he just gave me my rage, the edge I needed to make risky choices. I would not lose this race.

I watched my car slide up to the start line and strutted over to it. People were cheering for me, bets were being taken, and the roar of our engines bloomed excitement inside of me.

The smell of fumes hit me as I walked to my door and checked Falcon out over my hood. He was fiddling with something, and I scoffed. If he thought whatever that was would help him on this track, then he was delusional.

The setter got out and ran off into the crowd as I took my seat. Sliding across the butter-soft leather as I got into a comfortable position. My hands gripped the steering wheel, and I took a deep breath. I felt his eyes on me, looked in his direction, and saw his window was down, and his mouth opened as he tried saying something, but I was done with that. I turned up my stereo to blast some music to hype me up.

Deesil frowned down at us before scanning the crowd and charming them through the microphone. "For the last race of the night, we have something special . . . A personal bet between two prestigious families in the Syndicate!" He lifted his hands, and people cheered, clogging up the sides to get a better view.

"While the reasons might be hush-hush—" Deesil put his finger to his lips with a coy smile. "The stakes are very real, so real, in fact, that the heirs of the Winstale clan and Desmond clan are going head-to-head! With, of course, the clan bosses watching." He pointed to the drone hovering high above us.

"Don't miss this once-in-a-lifetime battle of smarts against guts!" I resented that statement a little bit, knowing I was representing the "guts" side, but I knew Deesil was just hyping up the crowd, and, in the end, making us more money.

As he continued pitting us against each other, coaxing the crowd to pick a side to root for. I tuned the rest out and focused on the road ahead of me. My heart started pumping faster by the second, my breathing coming out short and quick as the anticipation and excitement overtook me.

[1] I glanced one more time at Falcon, his profile calm and serene until he turned, and our gazes collided. Even his stone-cold face couldn't contain the emotions boiling out of his eyes. They screamed white-hot determination, flashed a spec of amusement, and settled on excitement as he winked at me and turned his attention back to the road.

He surprised me with how incredibly sexy that look was on him, how it made my excitement go up tenfold and my insides knot.

I shook off his look and turned to focus on the road, tightening my hands on the wheel just before the gunshot that signaled us to go.

I stepped on the gas, and the jerk of my three-second car propelled me forward as my seat rumbled beneath my thighs. The vibrations from the engine went up my legs and settled in my core, giving me a jolt of pleasure as I took off. All my beginning nerves dissipated as my vision tunneled, and I focused on the here and now.

We were neck and neck, which I found annoying because I wanted him to overdo it on the first leg and spin out on the first turn. The beginning of the track was to go around the building, then you entered the open-walled building from the other side to wind your way up ten floors to finish at the top. The trick was to not fall off any of the floors, which was hard when the other car or cars were trying to push you off.

---

1. Song: Black Gang by SINDICVT

As soon as we hit the first turn, I sped up and pulled on the handbrake to throw off the back tires and drift into the turn. You did this to keep the momentum high while racing, but it took a lot of practice to master.

I checked my rearview mirror, expecting to see him eating my dust when I saw nothing but dirt road. I swiveled my head to the side, and he was right next to me, smirking. *Okay. I didn't expect him to know how to drive like that.* That was street driving, not the kind of driving that someone of his smarts would've been taught. I ran my tongue over my teeth as I faced forward and reminded myself I had more tricks up my sleeve.

The opening came into view, and I knew I needed to be on the right side to get the edge of being the inner car. Being the inner car made it that much harder to run off the side of the building.

I pushed open a button on my wheel that automatically lifted the passenger seat cushion and showed a plethora of colorful vials. These were how supes played with cars and bets. Everything goes, even magical items.

I pulled out a glowing baby-blue vial cold to the touch. I needed a distraction so I could pull ahead for a second and get into the right position when we entered the building. Knowing he had an affinity for fire magic, I knew he could handle this without dying, but it would take his attention off me.

I threw the blue vial over my hood, and it smashed onto his. As soon as the blue liquid was free, it made a mini blizzard on top of his car that froze his hood and locked up his tires with ice.

His eyes widened before he called on his fire with precision to take off the ice and quell the blizzard in flames. It only took him a few seconds, but it was the seconds I needed to get ahead and turn into the building on the right side.

His car revved behind me as he picked up speed at a fast clip. I smiled to myself. Looked like someone used his NOS a little too soon.

As soon as those thoughts left, my tires began to wobble, and I peered out my window to see a thick amount of water beneath my tires fucking with the tread and speed. I looked in the mirror behind me and saw his determined smirk. *Fucker!*

I hissed as I grabbed a small bag of magicked sand, opened the bag, and said, "Tires," then poured it out onto the ground. Sand worked into the grooves of my tires, giving me some traction before the first turn going up to the second floor.

I was still in the lead, but he was coming up on my right side fast. He pointed his finger at my tires and threw white-hot fire at them, trying to melt them, but his puzzled face when it didn't work was like getting a Christmas present. I had the whole damn car magicked to withstand any heat, even the magical kind. It was a pretty penny, but so worth it at this moment.

In his haste to get around me, his car lost traction on the concrete and leaned over the ledge. This was why it was important to stick to the inside. He bit his lip and used his air magic to keep the car from falling off the edge and regain control. I was prepared to step in and save him if he needed it but was impressed with how easy it was for him to correct it. I pictured having to explain to my dad what had happened if he fell over, and a shiver went down my spine. That would not have been pretty.

He crept back up behind me, this time, looking around to get his bearings on the area, not worrying about advancing just yet. Smart. We still had a few floors to go.

We rounded the corner in unison, sailing past the third, four, and fifth floors. Suddenly, I heard a rumble, and the elevator doors opened to the side. So, because this building was half built, they put in the elevator shaft and floor doors but not an actual elevator box, so when the doors opened, it was a direct shot to the other side of the floor. If you positioned your car just right, you could go through and gain a lead on the competition.

As I turned my wheel to head to the door, I felt resistance. My wheels wouldn't turn. I looked up, and Falcon pointed at my wheels, using his air magic to lock them up, and he passed me and raced through the elevator doors. As soon as his eyes left my wheels, the air let go, and I slammed on my accelerator to follow him through.

My nails dug into my steering wheel, glaring at his car in front of me, and I lost it a little bit. As soon as we hit the seventh floor, I slammed into the back of his car to throw him off.

He yelled out his window, "This is a nine hundred thousand dollar car!"

To which I responded, "That's a pretty pricey coffin!"

He didn't like that and surprised me by slamming on his breaks, causing me to swerve to the outside next to him, right where I didn't want to be. He glared at me and pressed something. A side part popped off his car, and a twirling razor blade made its way to chew up my tires and take me out of the race for good.

As he turned up the eighth floor, he moved closer to my tires, pushing me to ride the edge of the floor to escape the carnage his blades would cause. It was my turn to glare at him.

"If you call it quits, I won't run you off the floor." His face gave off no emotions, just facts as he pretended to look over the edge. "It looks like a long way down."

That was it. I looked at my passenger seat and found the molten-red vial, so hot it burned the tips of my fingers to hold it, but the pain was worth it when I popped off the lid and splattered the liquid onto the blade. It immediately ate at the metal, disintegrating it at an alarming rate. I had a mage bottle up the power of a volcano's magma into that vial just for an occasion like this.

He frowned at me, and I felt like it was a win. I got him to show some facial emotion, even if it was a negative one. I chuckled as I took the moment of triumph and slammed into the side of his car. He swerved as we rounded the ninth floor.

The pressure went up as we realized we were getting closer to the finish line. In a last-ditch effort, he threw fire at my window. The hot flames licked against my cheek for barely a second before I slammed on my brakes to escape the inferno coming straight for me. I didn't want to come out of this looking like a fourth-degree burn victim.

I was about to bellow in frustration, pissed I would lose, upset that my self-preservation hindered my potential to win when a familiar rumble happened. I looked to my side right as he blew past me, and a set of elevator doors opened. Those doors glowed like my last salvation, and I gunned it for the opening. I just needed to make this jump, and then I would be in the lead.

Turning my car that way took some effort and time, time I didn't have as I heard the ding of the doors closing. I pressed down on the gas pedal as hard as I could, committing to this path whether it worked or not.

For a second, my car flew in the air, the adrenaline of not knowing if I was going to make it surged through my veins, and I almost let out a pleasure-filled sigh. This was the feeling that I chased, this was what I wanted when I raced someone. I needed to thank that stone-faced asshole for providing me with the excitement that I was looking for.

I barely made it through the first set of elevator doors, closing my eyes halfway through with a prayer I would make it out on the other side. I gasped, my eyes flying open when I heard a loud scraping sound. I looked in my review mirror to see the last set of doors scraping against the back of my car before I bounced up out of my seat at the impact of my front bumper and tires hitting the concrete.

I made it! I fucking made it.

It took me a split second to turn and see Falcon's shocked face on the right side, as the back of my car crashed on top of his front. I pushed on the gas as the smell of burning rubber filled my nose, and smoke rose from my back tires grinding on his hood. Like a bullet, I shot off in front of him.

I rounded the corner to the tenth and final floor as Falcon tried to catch up, but I swerved back and forth in a serpentine pattern, ensuring he couldn't get in front of me as I turned the corner and crossed the finish line on the roof. There was a large crowd waiting to see who the winner would be.

As soon as I skidded to a stop, Deesil bellowed over the loudspeaker, "And the winner is Rayla Desmond!"

I closed my eyes and laid my head back for a second, reveling in my win as a car screeched to a stop next to me. I cracked my eyes open to see Falcon staring at me.

He opened his mouth but was interrupted as a little drone appeared between us. The lens turned toward me as the speakers gave way to Easton's distracted voice. "You have won the Winstale's support, Rayla Desmond. Congratulations." Then it took off into the sky, heading back the way it came.

Adrenaline was still pumping through my veins, making me giddy as I was laughing in my seat. My hands shook in my lap, the excitement getting to me and needing an outlet to calm down, and my eyes landed on Falcon. Those gorgeous glaring eyes caused my thighs to shake, that chiseled chin and angular jaw made him appear dangerous and intelligent, turning me on faster than a faucet. Then my mind whispered a very bad idea in my head.

With my blood pumping around my body too fast, causing me to react instead of think or reason with myself, I called out to him, "Come on."

His brow lifted in question, and I swear that one annoyed glare made my pussy damp. With my body making all the decisions at the moment, I knew I needed him to calm myself down before I met with the last boss tonight.

Hopefully he was up for a little fun.

Chapter 19

FALCON

I SHOULD BE PISSED. I don't lose. Ever. I have made it my life's mission to excel at anything I put my mind to, and this was the second time I had lost to this wild woman. It didn't make any sense.

All my life, I have been the smartest person in the room. I never felt the need to boast about it, letting my success speak for itself. I was ahead of my class by three grades all my life, graduating from college with a masters in biomechanics and physical science at the same time by the time I was twenty-one. I have always been number one in school. Leader in all labs. Head scientist, underneath my father, for the Syndicate research teams.

When my father started to pressure me to find a mate, I dated a slew of women. Had background checks, family trees, and intelligence tests run before I even entered a date. I consulted sex experts to make sure I knew what I was doing and when to do it.

Coincidentally, I only took it to that level with a handful, but the feedback was more than favorable. A few even tried to persuade me into a situationship just for their carnal desires, but I saw no benefit in that for me, so I declined—gracefully, and with a nice stipend for their time. It made it so rumors were always favorable and few.

I was not used to feeling this way. To have to face my own failure but also face this stunningly wild creature while dealing with these newfound feelings.

I was so sure I would win with my superior machinery and magical affinities. Even going as far as making a deal with myself that I wouldn't use my magic, only my enhanced machinery, unless it was a dire situation. I broke that within the first few seconds. I didn't expect her to have magic ready to counter mine.

Even with the magic and superior machine, in the end, it was all about risk. She saw an opening and went for it headfirst, even though it was the most risky of scenarios. A scenario that wouldn't ensure her the win, but she still took it anyway for the chance.

As I was trailing behind her on the roof, I gripped my wheel so hard I almost bent it as I went over all of my missteps in my head. I should've made different moves in the beginning. I should've used more magic. I should not have let her smile and her perfectly crafted body distract me from the start.

I was not used to feeling so many feelings. Anger, desire, irritation, want; these were feelings I was able to live without, or at least in such small doses it never befuddled my mind . . . until I met her. Right from the beginning, when I didn't know who she was, she had me intrigued and vexed all at once.

I rolled up next to her, planning to glare at her, planning to be pissed at her, but as soon as my eyes landed on her silky white strands, and those pink-golden eyes landed on mine, I was tongue-tied. I stared at her like a lunatic, making a complete fool of myself as she smiled like she won a crown. Her breath hitched, and her cheeks turned a light shade of pink in contrast to her milky vampire skin.

The proper thing to do would be to congratulate her, to take the loss like a man. I opened my mouth to do just that when my father's bored tone crackled out from the hovering drone. "You have the Winstale's support, Rayla Desmond. Congratulations."

Then, as he said he would, the drone flew off into the distance. I'm sure as soon as the last syllable was out, he passed the controller to one of the people in the lab with instructions to guide it back home.

What I didn't expect to hear was her sultry, intoxicating tone calling out to me. "Come on." She revved up her car to warn the partiers we were moving, and they parted like the Red Sea.

For a second, I contemplated why I should follow her, thought of the scenarios that would make her want to talk to me. Did she want to gloat? I didn't have time for that. Did she want to discuss how my father was going to support her? I think she would be better off talking to my father about that. Did she want to yell or scold me for my part in the race? I mean, we both did some damage to each other's cars. It wasn't solely my fault.

I was still contemplating what she wanted from me for another few seconds before I ended up pushing the gas pedal and following her, my curiosity getting the best of me whenever she was around.

I followed her back down the rickety building and out of the big black gate we came in, leaving the track. *Where was she taking me?* I didn't think she was going to try to kill me, but I needed to keep myself vigilant for such an act. You never know with that woman.

After I met her at the gun range and was told who she was, I did my research on her. I was surprised to find out she was quite the wild, bloodthirsty woman. In the supernatural world, we had our own dark web of sorts, a place for criminals to go to read up on rumors of other criminals. From what I read on her profile, she seemed like a fair person. She always treated those that were loyal with the utmost respect and dignity, giving them more than their fair share. You would think she was a criminal with a heart of gold until you got to the part where she defanged an old boyfriend with a rusty set of pliers for letting someone else bite him. It was said the room was covered in so much blood they were surprised he survived. The next week, he seemed to disappear, no one hearing from him again. From then on, she left a bloody trail whenever someone crossed her. It was hard not to admire a woman who did her own dirty work.

Soon, she pulled off onto a dirt road. I kept following, but my mind was racing with possibilities, and none of them good. She sped up for a second, disappearing around the corner, going up some hill. I kicked it into high gear to follow her, but she was quick. She was only ahead of me by a few seconds, but that was all she needed because by the time I parked behind her, she was already out, sitting on the hood of her car, gazing out onto the blinding strip.

[1] I climbed out of my car slowly, approaching her like someone would a lion when I heard a soft moan, and I paused. *I didn't hear that correctly, did I?*

The ice-cold frustration and anger at the race melted, turning into hot desire I didn't know what to do with.

I passed the front of my car to get a better look at what she was doing, and when I did, my eyes flew wide open. On the hood of her matte-black Koenigsegg Agera, her skirt hiked up, legs spread wide as she played with herself. She moaned out again, longer and louder, and my mind short-circuited. I didn't know what to do, so I stood there like an idiot, watching her.

Her head fell back when she moved her hand, pumping in and out of herself. Every cell in my body came to life, watching this wild nymph with rapid fascination. She was this enigma I couldn't understand and wanted to know everything about. Wanted to dissect her to find out what made her tick, what made her scream, what made her unravel.

My body gave way to my thoughts, thoughts of doing things to her, paying attention to how she reacted, and taking mental notes. I daydreamed about different scenarios, sometimes I would take it soft and slow, and other times I would make it rough and fast, always cataloging her reactions. My pants felt tighter, my hardness busting

---

1. Song: Devil in Her Eyes by Bryce Savage

at the zipper to be let free, but I was a master at control, and it would take me far longer to lose control.

"Are you going to stand over there and watch the whole time?" she rasped, and the bulge in my pants grew, reminding me this woman had a hold on me like no other has before. No one had made me think as much about sex as she had.

I moved closer like her voice demanded, my gaze traveling up her body in excitement and examination. My eyes rose up those tight black boots that went up to her thighs, leaving a scrap of soft pearly skin to peek out at me, almost like an invitation to touch, to grab, to bite.

I shook my head as I continued regarding her body, hypnotized by the speed and direction she was fucking her fingers with. Then I went farther up, past the scrap of skin at her midriff and right to her pebbled nipples in her black top. The whole ensemble screamed she wasn't trying hard to be sexy, she managed that and more by only giving me scraps and small gaps to look at, to tease me into searching for more.

"What do you want from me?" My voice came out in a husky whisper as I continued my voyeuristic exploration.

She laughed, it had a slight cruel edge to it, and I should've realized it then, but I was just waiting to hear her reply.

"Well, I won, right? Shouldn't I get a prize?" She slid her hand away from her core, and I almost barked at her to continue, but that would give her more control over the situation, and I couldn't have that.

"You got what you wanted. The Winstales will back you on the no-marriage addendum." I licked at my lips as she slid down the hood.

She nodded and smiled. "Yes, that was the deal with your dad, but I raced you . . ." Her smile grew devious as she walked my way, the sway of her hourglass hips hypnotizing me. "Don't you think I should get something from you? That only seems fair."

It was hard for me to swallow when she stopped in front of me, laying both hands on my chest, running them down to my lower stomach, making my muscles twitch. "The winner should always get spoiled."

I was about to give in to her when her hand trembled, and that cleared my brain. I snatched her hands, lifting them to the side and examined them, watching as they twitched again.

I knew what this was, I had the same affliction sometimes when I raced or used too much magic. I blurted, "The adrenaline getting to you, Wild One?"

She snatched her hand back and scowled at me. Holding her hand to prevent any more twitches, but now I understood why she was coming on so strong. She needed an outlet. That's why we left in such a hurry from the track, and why she brought me up here out of sight.

A piece of me didn't want to give in, wanted her to suffer for that win on the tracks, and for using my own gas gun on myself, to consider it finally even between us, but my body had other thoughts. My body was slowly taking over as my mind rationalized it all.

A fellow Syndicate heir needed help, and I should do it. This was just a means to an end for her, there was no reason to get uptight about it. She could've picked anyone else on the track, even Deesil, who would leap at the chance, but, instead, she chose me. She wanted me.

With my mind made up, I crowded into her, her head meeting my chest as I stepped so close she was forced to take a step back. "What are you—" I pushed her chin up, shutting her mouth as I continued my advancement.

"You are getting what you need, but I don't want to hear another peep from you unless it's a moan you just can't help but let loose." On the last syllable, her butt landed on the front of the car, and her hooded eyes flicked to mine as she nodded and opened her mouth to say something, but I pushed her back down onto the hood to shut her up.

"That was your last warning. Don't test me, Wild One." My voice came out firm and sure, but my mind was running untamed. *What to do first, what to do first?*

I lifted one finger and trailed it from her knee to her inner thigh as her breathing turned shallow. I then took my other hand and shoved it up the outer edge of her other thigh, hiking the skirt up even more. Exposing more of that delicious flesh of hers.

She bit her lip but still didn't make a sound. "Good girl," slipped from my mouth, and she let out a small whine in approval. Interesting, praise did more than either of the touches. *Good to know.*

My hands trailed up the insides of her thighs, higher and higher, and her legs fell apart easily as the skirt ended up around her waist, leaving her exposed to me. "What a naughty girl you've been, not wearing any underwear underneath this thin scrap of fabric." I widened her farther so I could see her engorged center, and I licked my lips in anticipation.

"I've been so naughty." My hand snapped out as I smacked her nub, and she cried out.

"I said no speaking, only moans you can't hold back. If you do, then this will turn from a learning-about-your-pleasure session into finding-out-effective-ways-to-torture-you session." She bit her lip, excitement lighting up those gorgeous eyes. I could tell she would be happy either way, and that fascinated me. Maybe we would need more than a couple sessions of this.

I used my middle finger to part her lips, studying her every move with rapt attention as I explored her body. The finger drifted downward toward her channel and plunged in like I was digging for treasure. Her back arched off the hood as her lips were pinned shut with her teeth.

I removed the finger, and her head snapped up, and I slowly sucked it into my mouth. I closed my lips around the base of my finger, savoring the taste of her. The only words I could come up with for how she tasted were sweet carnage.

I licked and sucked on that finger, making sure I left nothing behind, then I peered down at my prey. Her breathing was choppy and erratic. Her eyes drilled into mine as she licked her lips. I could tell she wanted to pounce on me like a lioness with a gazelle, but I wasn't going to let her.

I let go of my finger. "Delicious." Then I grabbed her bunched-up skirt like it was her harness and yanked her forward as I bent down and pushed my head as close as I could between her legs.

She cried out in ecstasy, and I smiled against her pussy lips, licking each like it was its own. I rubbed my nose against her clit as I flattened my tongue and shook my head side to side, and her legs trembled. *Perfect.*

I decided to kick it up a notch—hoping that my earlier experience with her and my magic wasn't a fluke, and this wouldn't hurt her—and called forth my fire magic and focused it into one finger as I continued to lap at her swollen clit with my tongue.

I sunk that fire finger deep into her channel. She cried out. I was waiting for her to tell me to pull it out, to take it away, but, instead, she screamed, "Oh, fuck. Fuck me with that fire finger. Fuck me good and hard so my insides melt."

I pulled back and smiled before I blew across her pussy as my fire finger was still deep inside her. She panted like a dog in heat, but I wasn't done yet. I was still exploring.

I kept my hot finger inside of her and called for my water element into the neighboring finger, making sure it was on the cool side before entering her puckered hole.

Her hips lifted off the car in an explosive thrust, and she fucked my face. "Holy fuck, that feels amazing. How the fuck, oh . . . Oh!" Her words turned incoherent as I pounded into her two holes with fervor.

My pants were so tight I could smash into a rock, and it would break, but I didn't stop what I was doing. It was in the name of science, and I needed to learn all about how to pleasure my mate.

Mate! What the fuck? Where did that come from?

My mind derailed for a second until she grabbed me by my hair and shoved my face back into her clit. The grip on my hair was so tight the follicles were groaning, but the pain brought me back to the here and now, which I desperately needed.

I used my teeth to lightly graze her nub and then bit the inside of her thigh as I pumped furiously inside of her, and her whole body shook.

"Yes. yes. Oh, fucking yes. Fuckkk. Falcon!" Something shifted inside of me. My brain could only think of one thing and that was to have her scream my name like that forever.

She exploded around my fingers, and I lapped it all up, not wanting to lose a single drop of that delicious essence I could only get between her thighs.

She cried out at every swipe of my tongue as she was so sensitive from my ministrations. She slumped against the hood as I pulled my fingers out. I dug into my pocket for a handkerchief to clean my fingers and keep as a souvenir.

I smiled down at her, smug about how she was lying there in utter bliss. She shot up, wrapped her arms around my neck and her legs around my waist as she kissed the shit out of me.

The kiss was hard and bruising, but her lips were surprisingly soft in her haste to taste me as if trying to savor the flavor of us mingled together. She moaned against my mouth, and, this time, I moaned back, enjoying all her conflicting flavors and complex mood swings. With her soft breasts pushed up against me, I would give her anything she asked for.

She finally broke away from my mouth, laying her forehead against my chest as she gripped my shoulders. She gulped in a couple of breaths to get her heart rate to regulate.

I hated to admit that out of the whole experience, this was what shocked me the most. This small inch of intimacy I really didn't expect out of her. I lifted my arms tentatively before wrapping them around her. She sagged against me in relief, and I couldn't help but feel a little giddy. The foreign smile on my face was not going away.

I opened my mouth to ask her if she wanted to go out for a late dinner when she stared down at her watch.

Her eyes widened as she whispered, "Fuck!" Her eyes slammed into mine in panic. "I gotta go."

She used her vampire speed to jump into her car, slammed her gear in reverse, and jetted out of here, leaving me in the actual dust.

Well, that wouldn't do. This was not over. It was far from over, and if she thought she could get out of this by pretending she had somewhere to be, then she would have another thing coming to her.

I got in my car, flipped open my phone, and dialed some of my men to start the search and put ears to the ground of where Rayla Desmond was because I was coming for her.

CHAPTER 20

WELL, THAT WAS UNEXPECTED. Who knew the hot, quiet, smart one would be able to play my body like a fucking fiddle. Also, those magic hands were next level. I have only dated one other mage before, an earth mage, and they didn't have tricks like that up their sleeve.

I felt a little bad about bolting out of there without a word, but I was running late, and the whole plan tonight relied on punctuality. Plus, he was a big boy, he knew it was more of an in-the-moment thing anyway. Right?

I shook off the thoughts about Falcon and his sex-elevating hands and focused on the next and last step in my plan for tonight.

I got two clans in my pocket, I only needed one more to out rule my dad—the Glovefox clan.

I knew Syris, the Glovefox boss, was holed up at Veshta's place, which meant I needed to try and get in as covertly as possible. I didn't want to alert him too soon to give him the opportunity to outfox me because that was what the Glovefoxes did. They were a vexing bunch with their beauty and poise, yet tricky words and sly deals were their game, and I would not be played.

I knew both Glovefoxes had powers, and I was beginning to understand that the older one had some pull over women, but the younger one, Avery, I still had no clue. It was vexing me, the not knowing. Maybe I could coax him into showing me? I got a few tricks up my sleeve, too.

I gripped the soft leather steering wheel, my fingers digging into the hide as my excitement grew. I could do this. I only had one more, then I was free. No longer tied to the others by the bullshit agreement of marriage.

Once it's complete, past us, maybe we could hang out as equals? They're still the heirs, and I would have to work with them a lot in the near future. I knew this was a rare opportunity to be able to meet them all—the bosses and their heirs. After all this, after I win, I would think about smoothing over any negative feelings. *Maybe we could even be friends?*

I looked at myself in the rearview mirror and chuckled. *I mean, I have already fucked one—twice—and got finger-fucked but the other . . . That meant we were friends already, right?* I laughed at myself again as unease settled in my belly, my body trying to tell me something, but my mind didn't quit as I pushed all that away. Only way to win was to push forward. No regrets.

I scoffed at myself. Plus, there was no way in hell men like that didn't already have a million side pieces at home. I bet they even had girlfriends and side pieces. I mean, they were heirs to the Syndicate and hot as sin, slightly wicked, to boot, of course, women would throw themselves at them. It was the same reason men threw themselves at me. They wanted the power I held. The difference with me was I never gave away any power.

My skin flushed and my muscles tightened the more I thought about it. Now it was all I could think about. Falcon sinking those magic fingers into another woman, Ax's inked-up arms choking some bimbo, and Avery. Avery, I hadn't even tasted yet, but I felt an instant connection, instant desire for him the moment our eyes locked when I watched his body move that first night. Thinking of him balls deep in some bitch made my skin crawl. I shook my head free of those thoughts. None of this made sense. I hadn't taken blood from any of them, so why was my body feeling this way?

My mind went into overdrive trying to rationalize it. I probably just felt like they were mine because we were all part of the same organization, all connected. The Syndicate was as deep, if not deeper, than family. They would be in my life forever, whether I wanted it or not, so, of course, I would be protective.

It was also dangerous for us to have loose ties. Who knew if the company they kept would snitch on or betray us. This irritated me. I didn't know yet how careful they were. How they were vetting their fuck toys. Yes. That was it. I just wanted to protect the Syndicate. That's all. I wanted to make sure they were playing the game correctly. Just checking up on my fellow heirs. Nothing more.

In the back of my mind, I knew it was a weak excuse, but it was all I had at the moment, so I would grab on and hold tight before I convinced myself otherwise.

I parked in the employee parking lot. I had been here enough times, made friends with all the employees, so getting in with an excuse to wanting a low-key night wasn't hard.

"Hey, Miss Rayla," one bartender grabbing bottles from storage said as I opened the back door.

I nodded. "Hey, Gavin." I knew most people that worked at The Temptress, but Gavy boy here was one of ours in the Desmond clan. He gave me a quick fang-filled smile before ducking into the storage room.

I guess while I was here, I could catch up with my informant. I leaned against the doorjamb. The bass from the music vibrated off the walls, making it hard to talk, so I stepped in and closed the door. His pale hand quivered as it ran through his mud brown hair, his gray eyes shifting from side to side as his back stiffen. "How is it going? Anything juicy?"

His hand hovered over a few bottles before shooting up as he snapped his fingers. "You know, I have started to hear the whispers about a new drug dealer in town, giving free drugs to supes." I dug my nails into my palms, trying to keep my fury from bleeding out. At least until he was done telling me what was going on.

"I've only heard about it from one person two days ago, and it has kinda died down, so I thought maybe it wasn't real . . ." My veins filled with liquid rage, burning me from the inside out. Someone was on my fucking turf slinging drugs to supes. That was never allowed to happen in our world, especially in our own backyard.

Human drugs didn't work on supes. Our bodies naturally processed things at an accelerated speed and burned through the drug faster than we could feel the effects. Since we also healed faster than humans, we didn't need drugs for medical reasons, either.

My dad said this caused a big uproar when the Awakening happened. The humans were all afraid, not only of the powers we possessed but of what could happen when we got out of control. My dad and his friends made a deal with the United States government; they would regulate the supes, but they wanted to do it their way.

As the Syndicate was made, a lot of bloodshed happened, lines being undone, and groups coming under our wing. The first proclamation our dads said was no drugs for supes were allowed. My dad told me they knew drugs would cause a chaos they couldn't control, that we didn't need any more reasons to cause the humans to fear us more than they already did.

That all happened over thirty years ago, before I was born, and now we were in a state where humans and supes could commingle. There would always be spots that catered to one species over the other, rules for those places needed to be obeyed, but systems had been in place for all that.

"Gavin," I cooed, even as my skin vibrated with venomous rage. "You know that is a big no-no." I stalked over to him, not wanting to spook the vampire.

"Well . . . I mean . . . I didn't . . ." His eyes shifted as if he was trying to find a way out, but there wasn't one close.

My hand snapped out, clutching him by the throat as I lifted him, his feet dangling as he gasped for air. His hands lifted, about to start clawing at me when his eyes connected to mine, and he knew he was in trouble. He let his arms fall to his sides, taking his punishment like a good boy. I looked around, found the wall that didn't have anything on it, and threw him into it.

He cried out, leaving a dent in the wall before crumbling to the floor. I strode over, making sure my heels clicked like the sound of doom as I got closer. Gavin was a smart boy, he stayed on the floor, even when I knew he was able to get up, waiting for approval.

"You know the rules, Gavin. You know we won't allow anything like that." He nodded to the floor, and I crouched down, trailing the pad of my finger along the tips of his ears. His whole body shook as he apologized.

"I'm sorry, Miss Rayla. I will never make a mistake like that again. Please. Do what you need to do to make this right, make it so I can be a worthy member of the Desmond clan."

I smiled down at him, liking what I was hearing, and he knew that. He was a loyal dog, and loyal dogs got carrots after the stick. "Shhhh." I lifted his chin like a mother calming their child. "All I want from you is a name. I want you to tell me who mentioned such silly words, and all will be forgiven."

His eyes shined with devotion, realizing he would not get one of the worse punishments I liked to give for incompetence. "It was one of the mages that worked under Breken. His name is Edwin." Breken was one of our bookies on the outskirts, taking in bets from some locals, giving them a chance at some money without having to step into the casinos. The locals usually worked at the casinos and weren't allowed to eat where they shit, so to speak.

I let go of his chin and mussed his hair. "Thank you, Gavin." He closed his eyes for a second, enjoying the praise, until I grabbed onto his hair and yanked his head back. His eyes flew open in fear as I drilled my eyes into him, making sure he knew I had no problem ending his life here. "But next time you hear something, you come to me and tell me. If you can't find me, then find Rick or Cosmo." I let go, and his head fell forward as I got up. "You won't have a second chance, Gavin. No matter how smart you are."

I turned on my heels and headed to the door as he called out, "I won't disappoint you again, Miss Rayla. I swear." I nodded, my mind racing with what was required of me about this lead, but it would have to happen after my meeting because I needed to see a Glovefox about a deal.

Since that night was already in full swing, there weren't many people backstage. It was a club night, so not a lot of shows happened, if any, so I didn't bump into anyone while I was heading to the back. I knew of a way to get to the second floor from backstage. Cosmo and I used to climb up it and peek in on what my dad and Veshta were talking about when we were gangly teens. It was a fire escape for the second floor along a pillar in the back corner that no one ventured to since there was nothing there.

I peered around a few times, making sure I didn't see anyone before I climbed up the emergency ladder and pulled myself through the hole in the second floor. It was in the back of a broom closet, easy to hide from others, and yet far enough away no one could hear what was going on from down below. Veshta was smart like that.

Once I pulled myself up, I brushed off any dirt or grime I might've gotten on myself, fluffed up my hair, and walked out the closet like I was a boss. I didn't know if anyone would be lurking in the hallway, especially now that her office was used by Syris and Avery.

Veshta's personal hallway was always gaudy and opulent: red velvet carpet, ivory walls with swirling gold accents. It was like stepping into a different era. I always felt bad about wearing stilettos while in her hallways. I sank as I walked, and it took some getting used to at first.

Once I got to her golden double doors, I waved to John, her faerie guard, in all his ebony, frowny face glory. "I'm going in, Johnny." He flinched at the name, and that's why I did it. It made me laugh.

I gave myself one second to prepare as I threw the doors open. "Glovefox, we need to talk—"

"Oh, Rayla! You've finally made it. I was getting worried you were leaving me out!" Syris smiled as he put a piece of paper into the large golden desk. "And that would make me very angry."

He motioned for me to sit across from him in the wide, red, velvet chair, and I obliged him since he was being so nice about it all. I crossed my legs as I settled back. "So, I'm guessing you know why I'm here."

He set his elbows on his desk, his chin in his hands as he giggled at me. "Because you save the best for last?"

I couldn't help it, it made me laugh, and I relaxed a little bit more. "Yes, that, too. I'm sure you heard from the other two that I'm making deals—"

"And winning them." I gave him a tight-lipped smile, knowing it would never be good to give one of them the upper hand in this situation, but it was inevitable with three of them being so close to each other. I'm sure they have blabbed about it to Dad, but it was already too late for him to intervene.

"Yes. I am, but not because they are so easy. It's more that my will outshines the rest." We observed each other, watching for any tells before he slammed his hands on the desk, causing me to lift my eyebrow in question.

"Let me ask you one question. What is it with your generation and not wanting to get settled down and have some babies? Is that too much to ask? I promise I'll be a loving and attentive grandfather. I'll even take the kids overnight." His eyes bugged out as his hands clenched. Man, this guy really wanted some grandkids.

"My stupid man-whoring son has yet to give me one. Even an illegitimate one with some idiot would do, but noooooo. He's not so goddamn picky about where he puts the damn thing, but I'm sure he wraps that thing up a million times before he does." He crossed his arms in front of him as he grumbled, "Getting rid of all of my potential grandchildren." Oh, man, this guy was crazy, but I almost laughed at how comical this all was.

I reached over and patted his hand. "There, There. Don't be upset. I'm sure he'll settle down soon. I bet I have a few friends I could introduce him to?" I wanted to get on his good side, and since grandchildren were his weakness, I was going to exploit it. Even if I had to drag Avery onto the next date to get him to cum inside of her.

As soon as that thought hit me, my heart stopped, and my stomach clenched, rolling at the thought. Even though the words were coming out of my mouth, I could tell my body was rejecting them. Before I could analyze it further, someone cleared their throat as they walked into the room.

"Father, we've had a discussion about you talking to other people about my dick, did we not?"

The bored drawl of his voice along with the pinched question told me he was not only annoyed, but this was not the first time he had walked in on his father complaining about his sexual choices. Not a single one of our dads were normal, all weird in their own ways. I almost felt bad for the guys.

I kept my face forward as he stepped closer. I saw a flash of that gorgeous pink hair in my periphery as he sat in the chair next to me with a sigh.

Syris shrugged. "It's Rayla. Rayla Desmond. She's like family! The closest I guess I'll ever get to a daughter." He lamented that last part, which was the perfect segway into what I wanted to talk about.

"On that note, I'm sure you know I'm looking for support for an end to this silly little contest." I kept my voice light and easy, not wanting to rock the boat too much.

Syris was nodding. "Oh, yes, I heard all about your exploits. The other bosses are getting quite a hoot out of it." He folded his hands on the desk as his eyes sharpened between Avery and me. "But as I just told you, I'm a little desperate for the little pitter patter of children—"

I gripped the armrests as I growled, "Even if Avery won, that doesn't mean I would give you grandchildren." I let go of the armrests, leaning back with ease as I continued. "We could always be married in name and never touch each other's beds." Syris' mouth opened in shock as Avery let out a loud, mocking laugh.

I glared at Avery, who turned to face me with his cocky smile. "Oh, baby, there's no way you could be married to me and not be in my bed. I'm too irresistible, but if it makes you happy, I could wrap myself up like I do with all the others to ensure offspring isn't a surprise."

My anger exploded, and I didn't have Cosmo here to keep me in check, so I flew out of my chair, used my vampire speed to rush to him, and grabbed his throat as I stood over him.

He tensed under my grip, and his fingers dug into the chair for some semblance of control.

I leaned down and whispered in his ear, "One, a softy like you couldn't *handle* me in bed. Two, if I marry someone, we are going to have a gaggle of *gorgeous* and *deadly* children that will rule the world under the Syndicate name, and, three,"—I dug my nails into his skin—"if you ever mention treating me like some regular bimbo that you use your dick on again, I will crack open your neck and pour all that faerie blood down my throat until you are a dried up husk, keeping your corpse in the Glovefox seat as a mandatory decoration."

I pulled away an inch so I could drill my eyes into his, making sure he understood me. His green eyes narrowed on mine, flared up, then turned into two neon-green pools that swirled with golden specks of magic. Even with my threatening hand squeezed around his neck, he flicked his eyes down, gazing at my body with blatant interest. A flash of excitement passed through his eyes, settling on lust as he moved his hips toward me.

Our breaths mingled as we began to pant. My body was barely able to resist the siren call his eyes were having on me, telling me to climb on top of him and grind against him until he took it all back. *Every. Single. Word.* Then begged me for forgiveness. I went further down the rabbit hole of this fantasy. I pictured using my vampire speed to switch seats as I grabbed onto that cotton-candy-pink hair and pushed his face into my pussy, telling him it was time to put his dirty mouth to work in a pleasing way.

I was seconds away from turning this situation into my daydream until clapping came from behind me. "Oh, Ternin was right. His daughter was just the most lovely of creatures."

I flinched, his words breaking me from my staring contest with his son, and I let go of his throat. Avery took a gulp of air as he sat back into his chair, adjusting himself with a smile as he winked at me. His eyes went back to their normal bright-jade color, but he was still looking at me like he desperately wanted to continue this dangerous game of push and pull we'd started to play. This man was more dangerous than I thought.

"Now that you two kids have had your play time, we can get back to the situation." I sharply turned and sat back down in a huff. I felt Avery's eyes watching my every move, and that made me more wary of him. If I was honest, I was wary of all the heirs. I just thought, since our last conversation, I wouldn't need to worry so much about Avery.

"So," Syris continued, "with the little spat you guys had here, I can tell that this was not a match made in heaven, and, to be honest, I think that you're too much for my son." I glared at the old man as Avery scoffed. Syris lifted his hands as I flicked my tongue against my fangs in a threat. "It's not like that,"—he rolled his eyes at me before giving his son a calculating look—"in fact, I don't think he could handle a woman of worth like you." I rolled my lips into my mouth, trying to prevent myself from laughing as Avery shot out of his seat with his mouth dropped open.

"Father!"

Syris didn't stop as he focused on me, flicking his hand at his son. "Let him wallow in all of his one nighters and easy women. That's more his speed."

I flicked my eyes to Avery, and his face grew more and more red, about to burst, when his father followed with, "But I can't *give you* support just like that." He snapped his fingers to emphasize before staring at the floor, exaggerating his displeasure at having his hands tied, but I knew better. This man was a trick Glovefox, illusions and exaggeration were what they did.

"It's not really fair since you completed a challenge of sorts with Manic and Easton. I want to see what you can do, too. I'm petty like that." He smiled up at me, showing me his cunning charmer side. "The sooner you know that, the better this relationship will be." The Glovefox boss was good, I'd give him that. Reeling me in like a fucking fish on a line.

"I accept any challenge you give. I'm ready whenever." I crossed my legs and settled my hands in my lap, totally at ease with my decision.

"That's all fine and dandy," Avery growled before pointing to his dad. "Now you're going to need to take those words back!"

Syris smirked at me before facing his son. "Was what I said untrue?"

Avery straightened. "Well, I mean—"

"Do you not sleep with women that are so obviously below you because you are afraid a strong woman would overshadow you?" The twinkle in Syris' eye made me think he was having fun.

"That's not—"

Syris waved off his excuse like he'd had enough. "Well, if that's not the case, then let's kill two birds with one stone." He flicked his gaze between the two of us as a mischievous thought took root. "We are going to have a dance-off, Glovefox style!"

When both of us side-eyed him like he'd lost his marbles, he giggled, then switched to a serious face as he deepened his voice like an announcer for a fight match. "One dance on that stage for each of you. The one the crowd is pleased with the most wins."

I nodded, immediately agreeing since I would have home-field advantage, and most of the crowd would see me and go wild, even if it was fueled by fear of being seen not clapping.

"Yeah, no." Avery crossed his arms as his lips pinched into a thin line. "She has way too much pull here, so it can't be the crowd . . ."

I rolled my eyes, grumbling, "Can't cut it, I see."

He scoffed as he gave me some fierce side-eye before focusing on his dad. "I think we each get to pick out three"—he lifted three fingers in emphasis—"people for each other that we will pull up on stage and dance for. Each count for a vote."

"And I'll be the judge!" Syris waved his hands up in delight. "I'm an expert at picking up the signs of lust and desire." He wiggled his eyebrows at me, and I cracked a smile at him.

I shrugged. "Fine. If that will make losing easier for you to swallow," I threw at Avery, turning to him with a cocky smile, and my arms crossed.

Avery's smirk made me want to slap it off his face, but I dug my nails in my biceps, instead. "Oh, you think you're going to win against a pro," he cooed as he ran a hand down his chest, my eyes followed the movement until he stopped right at the button of his pants. A dark chuckle escaped his lips. "Case in point."

I mentally kicked myself for being such a thirsty bitch, but he was hot, and he knew it. I got back at him in an underhanded and dirty way. I uncrossed my arms, slowly walked up to him, put my hand lightly on his chest, and gazed into his eyes. His eyes shined with victory before I said, "Anyone can find someone attractive, like . . ." I used my vampire speed to run behind his dad's chair, looping my arms around him as I rested my chin on his shoulder. "Like how your dad is a studly silver fox." I bit my bottom lip as I turned, putting my face centimeters away from Syris'.

Avery's face fell, and his eyes widened with shock as he stepped back in horror. His stare flicked between us in rapid succession. If he was a robot, steam would be coming out of his head, five seconds away from blowing right off. I let my hands slide away as I shrugged. "But his connection with my dad sours it for me."

I sped to the door, hand on the knob. "I accept any rules you have, playboy. Now, let's go find our victims."

Syris fanned himself, his face flushed as he smiled a dopey, lovesick smile. "Oh, son. She's no joke." He laughed hard before he got up. "I'm going to have to get a stiff drink and calm my heart down before we do this. You two go ahead and pick them out and let me know."

I opened the door as a furious Avery stomped toward me. I lifted my arm, waving him to go first. "Guests are always first." He grumbled as he swiftly passed me, and I winked at Syris as he clutched his heart.

"Good luck, Rayla," Syris called out, but I didn't need it.

I would win this, no matter what.

CHAPTER 21

Avery

THE MUSIC BLARED IN the main room, bodies writhed with the beat as hot lust and sex filled the room. Desires, wants, and feels swirled around the room like a tornado, calling beings to it like a moth to a flame. I liked that feeling, the irresistible call to a club dance floor. I liked it because I was usually the only one who could resist it, and that was power.

I flicked my gaze to the side, watching the stunning creature next to me with eyes like pink diamonds, leaning against the rail on the second-floor VIP section, searching for her prey like any other predator. The call I felt for her, the one that zinged in my veins whenever our eyes met, caused my back to ache as my wings itched to snap out. The pull was so strong I knew she was the only one with any true power over me.

I wanted to hate it. I wanted to be angry at her, to prove she was nothing, but then this thrill that filled my soul when she was around me would go away, and I didn't want that, either.

I knew the second our eyes collided a few nights ago she was more than a hot-as-fuck woman. More than the heir to the Desmond clan. More to me than the Syndicate. This woman in front of me was my mate, and I knew it deep in my bones, without even flicking my wings. It was the one way you could know for sure that you had found your mate as a faerie. As soon as your eyes connected with your mate's, your wings would change from their natural see-through colors to the vibrant iridescent color, and I knew if I let them fly, they would shine brightly in front of everyone. I knew she wasn't ready for that, so I waited to get to spend more time with her.

When I heard she was in a meeting with my father, I went up the secret way you could only get to if you had wings. At first, I was eavesdropping on her conversation with my father, curious as to how she would get my father onboard with her anti-marriage game. I also didn't like the thought of being forced into something like that, so I agreed to let her do her thing, get the others out of the way while I wooed her. Made her see me as a viable mate while she kicked Ax and Falcon to the curb.

Then my father started up on some unsavory details of my past, something I did not want him bringing up in front of my future mate, and I felt inclined to change the subject. I said a few stupid choice words to try and save face, to not let either of them know how I was feeling, when she grabbed me by the throat and stood over me.

I felt like a schoolboy with how fast I got hard, how my eyes couldn't stop running between her eyes and mouth.

When I saw those two fangs peek out from her lips, I wanted to run my tongue up and down them and feel her shiver against me.

I didn't even register she was threatening me until she dug her nails into my neck. I almost let out a moan as I envisioned her taking it further. She leaned down, threatening me more as my dick grew harder beneath her. When she finally felt my true length, she would smile, her eyes would flash with pink lust, and she wouldn't be able to help but grind herself on me, and she would run her teeth and tongue along the main vein on my neck. My body reacted to my imagination, my hands gripped the chair so hard the upholstery was seconds away from being busted when my father clapped and ruined the whole thing.

A memory of her arms around my father's neck, biting her lip as she gazed at him, hit me like a ton of bricks, and I gripped the railing so hard it creaked. I knew she did that on purpose, to throw me off, to get back at me for what I'd said, but the image grated on my brain, making me physically ill and horrified at the sight. I loved my father, but it was the first time I'd ever felt betrayed by him, and it was all her fault.

Her sultry voice grabbed my attention as she said, "I picked my three. You?"

She faced me with a smug smile, her arm crossed with her hip cocked against the clear half wall. My fingers twitched on the railing, wanting to touch her, to feel how soft and supple her pale skin was. Damn near good enough to eat.

I shook off the mate pull, facing back to the crowd as I hissed, "Just give me a second. I'll pick my three in no time."

I turned and scanned the crowd, trying to find someone, anyone, who would not find this woman attractive or would at least make her sweat, but I came up with nothing. Worse than nothing, I was getting pissed at the thought of her dancing for anyone else but me. Maybe I should just let her out of it. Forfeit or something.

I glanced back at her still wearing that cocky smile as she tapped her finger on her naked wrist, mocking me. My competitive side came out in full force as I narrowed my eyes onto the crowd. I couldn't let her beat me just because she was my mate. I was a damn professional.

Two bright beacons of hope walked through the front door, one after the other, and I almost let out a sigh. I could always take one of the three spots, making myself a ringer in the game and ensuring she didn't get a win, but with these two, I might have a shot at a bigger win.

Ax was first, stomping around with a frown like he was hunting for someone. His muscles were all big and tight as he walked around in his fitted t-shirt and jeans. I wanted to roll my eyes and make fun of his lack of style and appropriateness of his attire to this establishment, but I didn't want to rock the boat when I was going to have him be a voter.

I had heard through social channels he was a woman-izer, versus me who was a slut. The difference was that he would go for the easy targets. The less intelligent or the just-wanting-a-good-time type of girl. Me, I loved all women and usually had no preference. They all had something to give, and I loved to take it. There was no way that a simple dance with a beautiful girl would turn him into a lust bucket. Especially one from a woman of Rayla Desmond's caliber.

Ax settled at the bar as my second option walked in, eyes roaming the scene in mild displeasure. I could pick Falcon out of a fun crowd easily. Just search for the one person who dressed in a white button-down, blue suit vest, and matching navy pants, and seemed like he had a stick up his butt.

From what I was told, he didn't play much with women, was into all his science stuff and tinkering with things. He would occasionally dabble, but it was few and far between and only a single instance. I wondered if he was even into women, but all that was why he would be perfect, they both would.

They were the only two I felt mildly comfortable with being around her. I didn't know if it was because we were all Syndicate, and my brain was wired that way, but I knew these two must've dealt with a lot of women in their lives—just being an heir has the ladies flocking, so they must not be easily swayed by a gorgeous woman.

"I have my two."

"Two?" Her brows were furrowed, and, this time, I turned my back and leaned up against the rail.

"Well, I was always going to be one of them." Her mouth dropped open, about to call me out, but I swooped in, getting nice and close to her, making her inhale before saying a word.

"You didn't think I was going to sit this one out, did you, sweetheart?" Her face darkened when I called her that, and a little thrill zinged inside of me. I think I liked her a little mad, and I enjoyed our banter.

"Well, excuse me for not wanting to be danced on for others' amusement." Her haughty tone caused my lips to go even wider.

I kicked off the railing, took a few steps, moved one arm to the railing on her other side, and boxed the beauty in as I stepped in close. I was enveloped by her jasmine perfume, and the smell was driving me crazy. "If it's a private dance you're after, all you need to do is ask." I ran a finger down her cheek, and she jumped at the touch. "I'm more than willing to show you all I got."

She smacked my hand away, straightening her back as she leaned closer to my face, our lips a hair's breadth apart, so close my brain went haywire as her breath settled on my skin. "Sure. I would love to help a fellow Syndicate heir critique your routine."

I threw my head back on a laugh. It had been so long since I'd had any type of resistance. Any pushback, and it was making her even more irresistible. I let go of each side, switching up my tactics as I put my elbow out like a gentleman. "I might take you up on that, Rayla. How about we go inform my father of our picks and get the show on the road?"

She eyed my arm like it was a trick, but her face softened as she slid her hand through. I clenched my teeth, trying to keep from preening. "Lead the way, Glovefox."

I let her tell my father her three first. She smirked as she pointed out women who had their arms draped around their partners, but it didn't stop me. I only saw it as a challenge. I would sweep those damn women off their feet. All I needed to do was play it more sensually than shaking my dick at them. I could play that game.

After my father nodded, he motioned to me, and I smiled. "We have a rare opportunity, Father, it looks like all three heirs are present in this club, so I think all three of us would be an appropriate challenge for Rayla."

She immediately scanned the crowd, and her jaw tight-ened. Her slitted eyes creeped toward me, and all I could do was smile. *That's what I want, honey, keep those eyes on me, whether it's your smile or your pinched lips. I want it all.*

"Is that a problem, my dear?" my father asked, glancing around like he was clueless to the situation, but I knew better.

She wiped her contempt away in an instant, smiling sweetly at my father as she said, "Oh, no problem." She focused on me again, her smile turning devious as she followed with, "Since I am going to have such a high caliber of people as my voters, it's only fair you go first."

Oh, fuck no. She wants to be the showstopper. That was like a kick to the dick for a professional. I turned to my father, ready to fight for the last spot, when he nodded as his hand was on his chin in thought. "Yes. I could see how that should be the lineup."

"Father!" I gawked as he turned to me, mouth wide open as his gaze bounced between her and me.

"What? She makes a point."

"I'm your son." I crossed my arms as Rayla's eyes danced with this victory. "You would think you'd have a little loyalty."

"Son,"—my father put his hand on my shoulder, looking at me dead in the eyes—"the second we all came together, you all became our children. All heirs to the same empire. We are all one when we are together. That's how I raised you. Don't you forget it." Well, now I felt bad. My father was always more on the relaxed and fun side, and when I'd met the other bosses, I knew my father was the fun one. Rossey was the always-angry-and-firm one, Winstale was the aloof, smart one, and Ternin was the wild card, but I bet the one thing they all taught us with veracity was that the four of us were Syndicate, and the Syndicate was everything. These people were like our family, whether we liked it or not, and they should always receive respect, especially in public.

My father turned and smiled at Rayla, clapping his hands with joy. "And I have to say that we all are enjoying our new daughter immensely." She put her hand over her heart and bowed her head in thanks.

"It's been, surprisingly, a good time learning about my new dads."

My father bristled as his eyes grew teary. "Did you just call me dad? Son, did you hear that?! Not the formal father or Boss Glovefox but dad." He clutched his heart as I rolled my eyes. As his son, I was glad he liked her so much, especially once all the chips were on the table, and they found out she was my mate. It would make it so much easier that he approved of her, but as a man, I was getting really tired of him getting so close to my girl.

"Do you think you could call me Dadd—"

"Nope! No. Noooottt going to happen." I put my hand over Rayla's mouth when it looked like she was going to oblige him, but that was where I drew the line. My woman would not call my father daddy. Fuck no. Not on my watch.

Rayla giggled behind my hand as my father pouted. "You ruin all my fun, you know that?!"

"Come on." I turned Rayla around, putting my arm around her shoulders to steer her away from my mate-stealing father. "Let's go. We need to get ready."

"Bye, kids. Make sure to do your best!" my father yelled as he waved at us like a parent dropping their kid off at school, and I ushered her faster.

I felt a poke in my side, and I glanced down to Rayla's finger digging into my stomach as she chuckled. "You make it entirely too easy to tease you. I bet that's half the reason your dad does it, just to get this reaction from you."

I got another big whiff of her sweet, flowery scent, and blood pounded in my ears as the hairs on my arms stood straight up. I let go of her, seconds away from hauling her into the closest closet and showing her an even better way to spend our time together, but I didn't want to scare her by pushing her too hard too fast.

She frowned at me in disappointment before she stepped ahead of me. "Let's get this going, pretty boy."

We went backstage and talked to the sound-booth guy. We picked out songs and made our way backstage.

My father already had someone put three chairs on the stage, gathered the crowd around the stage, and announced our names and what was going on, craftily leaving out the reason for the whole thing.

Rayla and I were scanning the crowd from the side when the announcer called up the three women that Rayla picked.

"Good luck with all that, stud. I hope you are as good as you claim." Her smug voice was the burn and the balm to my soul.

I tucked one of her stray hairs behind her ear, her eyes wide in surprise when I leaned into her. "Don't worry, darlin'. I'll charm the pants off these women and prove myself easily enough, but just know that I know why you picked those women in particular." I left it out there, hoping she would take the bait.

She nibbled on her lip, her eyes flicking between mine, trying to decide what to do next. What would be the next move, but I made it too tempting.

She puffed in disbelief. "Like I had another goal other than winning."

I moved a step closer, our chests touching as I ran the pad of my finger down her neck, trailing to her shoulder blade. "Because, baby, you didn't want any other dick-loving female to be near me. I understand." The announcer called my name as her eyes flared, a fiery anger rising like a tsunami as I backed away. "Break a leg, sweetheart."

I turned as she bellowed her frustration while I came out in my tight, untucked, blue-and-white striped button-down and white fitted pants with tan loafers. I was ready to take this sexy show on the road.

I waved to the crowd, giving them my megawatt smile that made people think I wasn't the dark creature I was deep down. It was a good mask to be the sexy devil-may-care stripper as I had disguised the man who enjoyed singing people to death in the most gruesome of ways.

[1] My song started, and I did a small turn, dropped to the floor, and worked my way up, ass out, giving the crowd a little taste before I got to the main show. Women hollered at me, yelling out their praises as well as their wants.

---

1. Song: Under the Influence by Chris Brown

The room grew louder with my increasing movements, making it hard to stay focused on the goal.

You would think that men would be the vocal ones when it came to dancing sexually. You automatically think of men being more vocal about what they want, but women, when they were in an appropriate setting, like a club, they would be the first to either call someone out or demand more skin, shouting for more dick. It was such a booster to hear women—and some men—craved me, desperately wanted my body, but then when I saw my targets, their eyes full of disdain, I knew I would need to take this all down a notch. I had to remind myself it's not about the crowd, it's about the individuals.

I worked my arms up my chest slowly before I pulled my shirt apart, buttons flying into the crowd as I ran my hand down my sculpted chest and grabbed my junk over my pants, giving the ladies a little bite of the lips and a wink. The crowd went wild, and I fed off them, giving them one thrusting motion before I turned around to the ladies I needed to woo.

As the melody started, I slowed down and studied the women I was going to dance for. From what I could see, the first was a dark-haired vampire, her eyes were narrowed on the crowd, not paying attention in the slightest. The next was a mousey, brown-haired, petite werewolf. She waved to a group of ladies, making exaggerated faces like she didn't know if she would find this entertaining. The last was a faerie woman with large curves and a stern scowl. She made me a little nervous as she glared at me with her arms crossed, intent to not enjoy a single move.

I couldn't help but think, *Well played, Rayla. Well played.* I got on with the show and moved behind the ladies.

I started soft and light, making sure I made my moves more feminine as I ran a finger up the side of one's neck, blew against one of their ears, and then let out a higher pitched sigh as I ran my hands lightly over the tops of one of their thighs. My idea was to stay behind them for a good amount of the time, trying to build up the illusion of a woman's touch versus a man's.

I flicked my gaze over at Rayla as I felt her eyes burning holes in the back of my skull. Her arms were crossed, and her fangs were out with her eyes in slits. She appeared malicious when her fangs were out, like she was a death goddess herself, and you could feel her wrath from just looking at her. Her bright-pink jewels were twinkling from the dark of the curtain covers. That was what drew me to her in the first place that night. In a sea of blank faces, her eyes dazzled in the dark, calling me to come to her.

I wanted to win in front of this goddess of death, not because I wanted to force her into marriage, and not because I wanted to one-up her. I wanted to impress her, wanted to show her I was her equal in this world.

I wanted that so badly I did something I almost never did; I used my song power. I didn't like using it in front of people, especially large groups of people. I liked having that as an ace up my sleeve and using it in cruel and brutal ways, but my magic could be used in other ways.

I could only entrance one being at a time, so if I whispered something in each of their ears, then it would look like

I was telling them something that got them hot and bothered.

With my mind made up, I started with the first girl, the dark-haired vampire, running my hands down her shoulders as I rested my lips along the shell of her ear and sang quietly, "*Blush and gasp. Feel your cheeks get hot.*" I slid to my next victim as the vampire gasped and brought her hands to her cheeks. My eyes flicked to my father, who was grinning, knowing exactly what I was doing as he nodded that it was one vote.

I lifted the werewolf's hair and blew a breath on the back of her neck as I circled her waist from behind, singing lightly into her hair next to her ear, "*When I move, you will watch and want.*" I turned around and slid to the side, running my hand along her shoulder blades as her head turned my way, and she bit her bottom lip, tracking me with lust.

I took a chance and flicked my eyes toward my dark goddess. She watched with an expressionless face, which would've made me sad if I didn't see her folded hands gripping her biceps, nails digging in so tightly I bet it hurt. I smiled and turned back to my last victim, knowing victory was only steps away.

I placed myself in front of her as I grabbed both sides of the chair and ran my chest up lightly along her body. As soon as I was close enough for her to hear, the song ended. *No!*

I immediately lifted myself off the woman still staring at me like she was less than amused, and I knew I would only get the two out of three. *Damn it!* I turned to the crowd, bowed as I smirked and winked at the ones closest to the stage like the performer I was.

The announcer came back out, clapping and telling me how well I did as he released the women from their spot on the stage. I made it seem like I was turning to leave when he called out for me, Falcon, and Ax to come to the stage. I jeered at Rayla, winking at her as I blew her a kiss and turned around with my mouth wide open as I feigned shock that I was to stay on the stage.

Falcon was wearing a flat-lipped expression, and Ax had a confused confidence about him, and I nodded for them to sit. To trust me. At best, we would all be able to resist any desire for her, at least enough for my father not to notice. At worst, she could beguile these two, leaving me to be the only one holding out, and we would be at a tie. Still equals.

I sat comfortably in the third and last seat, Ax took the first seat, slouching with a filthy smile that said he was ready for anything. Falcon took the seat between us, sitting with his back straight like a prim-and-proper gentleman. It was laughable because of the setting he was in, but he still pulled off looking down at everyone like they were his subjects, and he tolerated them in front of him.

My confidence was sky high until Rayla came out. She oozed cocky and sexy as she strutted out, her black mini dress underneath the lights caused the contrast of her silky pale skin to be shining on display. Her rose gold jewels shined bright under the show lights as they scanned the crowd. Her perfectly sculpted legs were on display in her red-bottom stilettos. It was hard not to drool for a woman like that.

I twisted around to see Falcon's and Ax's eyes glued to her like the pale moon called to all of us dark creatures in the night, and I knew I made a wrong calculation.

Shit. I didn't know if any of us could hold out with her.

CHAPTER 22

I'D ADMIT, I WAS impressed he was able to get two out of the three votes, even if he cheated. I mean, I called it cheating because I didn't have magic that could entrance people like he obviously did. It was pure luck that he ran out of time, and the song ended. That little slip of his might've cost him the win.

He was good, changing his normal tactics to fit the target audience, putting on a little show for the crowd to get the extra hype. It was all carefully crafted and thought out. My only ace up my sleeve was that he had no clue about my recent activities with the other heirs. If I was honest, I didn't know if it would for sure go in my favor since I kind of left them both high and dry, but I knew they found me attractive, and I could use that to my advantage. Avery was the unknown target.

The announcer called my name. It was now or never. I stepped out, giving the crowd my best sultry smile as

I came over to the men. I glanced at Ax's and Falcon's curious gazes as they were trying to figure out what was going on, and I smiled at them wider and winked. Ax's smile turned from hesitant to smug as he adjusted his pants and leaned back in his chair, waiting for whatever was going to happen. Falcon kept himself composed, barely acknowledging me with a slight nod. Avery was grinning, his eyes taunting me to do my best.

[1] "OMG" by Selena Gomez Featuring Quavo started to bump through the speakers, and I let all the eyes from the crowd disappear. I let the sway of the beat fill me as I moved to the first chair. I picked this song on purpose, knowing the first verse was a perfect set for Ax, matching his vibe for rowdy wildness. The second verse and bridge was solid for Falcon, highlighting the sexiness of cold determination. The third verse would be the hardest since it was sung from the guy's viewpoint, but I had tricks up my sleeve for that, hoping my knowledge of faeries would work in my favor.

Since I wanted to fit a certain character, really feel the words, I lip-synched as I danced, making it seem like I was singing those lyrics and chords for each of them.

As I swaggered up to Ax, his face already lit up with lustful excitement, his hands spread out as they ran over the tops of his thighs like he was trying to stop himself from grabbing at me. I swayed my hips in front of him, watching him through hooded eyes as I scanned his body, lust and pain on my face. I focused completely on him as I bent over and ran my hands up his thighs, bringing my

---

1. Song: OMG by Camila Cabello

face closer to him as I winked and bit my lip while I ran my hand over his pec, feeling everything I could with the pads of my fingers.

His breath quickened as I explored his body over his clothes, his eyes flared when I gave him a devious smile as I emphasized the word "trouble" in the lyric.

"Fuck," he whispered, and he couldn't take his eyes off me. I let my hair fall in front of my face as I peeked out, then used my vampire speed to sit on his lap and then ground on him as I took both hands and lifted my hair, leaning back and shoving my breasts in his face.

"Shit, Ray." His breathing came out hard as his hands rested on my hips. I swayed from side to side, hypnotizing him with my chest as I ran a finger down both arms and squeezed his hands on my hips, letting him know I liked his rough hands on me. I knew this was all part of the plan, to seduce each man, but I was really getting into it. My body burned with desire as I made each move.

I used my speed again, tearing his hands off me, a gasp left his mouth as I turned around in front of him and dropped my ass to the floor, lifting it slowly with each beat. I knew from this angle, and how short my dress was, he was getting to see a little peek of cheek, and he groaned.

Turning around as he bit his bottom lip, his eyes flicked to mine, his whole body vibrating with need. I winked as I ran one of my hands down, following the curves of my waist and hips, and settled it on my ass before I gave one cheek a loud smack. His eyes rolled as he dropped his head back.

The first chorus hit, and I slid my hands behind his head, grabbing on to his hair as I focused his attention back on me as I sang the words under my breath. Letting my eyes travel down his body, openly lusting after him as I was singing about how good he looked. I ran a finger down the buttons of his shirt until I got to the waistband of his pants and looped a finger in. His hips jerked at my touch as skin connected with skin.

I surged forward, knowing my time with him was almost up, and I wanted to seal the deal. I thrusted into him as I grabbed his hair, pulled his head to the side, and lightly ran my fangs along his neck. He let out a tortuous groan, and I felt something hard against my thigh, desperately trying to get closer to my center like it had a mind of its own. As the chorus died down, I used my speed to get up and put myself right in front of Falcon, leaving Ax in a lust-filled daze.

Falcon's body didn't change as I suddenly appeared before him, my hands on either side of his neck, holding onto the chair behind him, boxing him in. What changed was a slight opening of his eyes, which showed he didn't expect me to come at him so fast and close.

I sang the first line in his face, smiling the whole time as his icy expression melted inch by inch. I stood, lifted my arms as I swayed between his legs like a cyclone. As I finished the slow and tantalizing circle, I ran my hand down my chest and lowered myself between his thighs, bringing my mouth right in line with his crotch. His eyes swirled as his hands clenched his arms, his stern-and-cold personality showing cracks, his desire for me bleeding through.

I quickly popped up, turn around, and lean back so much that the back of my head rested on his shoulder. I ran my hands down my body, giving him something to watch as I dug my fingers into my body at certain points, causing me to pant as I whisper-sang the words to him. His shoulders shook as if his arms wanted to break from their stance and follow the path my hands just took.

I used my momentum to quickly flip over, leaning against him with my ass out to the crowd as I breathed the lyrics against his neck, my hand on the other side of his neck drawing slow circles like a sensual massage. In time with the beat, I shook my ass a few times, getting the crowd worked up, before I fell to the floor and crawled my way up his body, making sure there was not an inch of him I could get to that my body didn't touch.

Suddenly, surprised at his hand trailing up my side hesitantly, I glanced up at him. His blue eyes sparkled, absorbing every move I made like he was cataloging it for later. It was arousing to think he might think about this later in his room by himself. I got lost for a second, picturing him stroking himself. His eyes screwed shut, a painful expression on his face, and my name a cry on his lips. What a sight that would be.

My mouth went dry as I licked my lips like he was a tasty snack. I continued mouthing the words to the song about how good he looked. Where I was rough with Ax, I was soft yet firm with Falcon. My hands cupped his jaw as I brought our foreheads together and breathed the song along his lips. His body tightened beneath mine, still not making big movements like Ax had, but the shutter of his eyes, the quickening of his breath, and the bulge straining in his pants told me all I needed to know. I had this vote, too.

As I was about to switch to Avery for the last verse, Falcon grabbed my wrist, rubbed along the main vein as he gave me a smile that spoke of long sensuous nights of him exploring my body until he became an expert. A shiver ran up my spin as he whispered back, "Next time." It was a threat and a promise all wrapped into one, and I liked it.

I squeezed my hands around his jaw, winking at him, telling him without words I was game if he was, and then raced over to take on my last candidate. I think he expected me to show up in front of him like I did with Falcon, but I knew I would need to take this one by surprise.

My hands slowly went around his shoulders, running down his chest at a glacial speed. I was planning on making this part sexier, funnier since it was the guy's part of the song, and it was Avery. I bet he thought I would turn on all the sexiest moves on him, but that wouldn't catch him off guard enough to get any true desire from him. No, I needed to think outside the box and have him smiling in amusement before his eyes twinkled with passion and lust.

I ran one hand up his neck and jerked his chin up as I sang about me and him. I sped around to land on his lap, settling my ass on one of his thighs as I pinched at his waist, following the words of the song, I winked at the crowd like we shared a secret.

The crowd chuckled and clapped, having a good time with my new approach. I turned back to Avery and smiled brightly. His brows were pinched, and I knew my plan was working.

I nodded with the song, giving a little shimmy of my shoulders as I winked at Avery and slung my arm around him like we were buddies. Then I turned up the heat when the song mentioned left hand and brought his ring finger of his left hand up, wrapped my lips around it as I mimicked what it would be like if something else was in my mouth.

His breath hitched as he mumbled, "That's cheating, Fierce Girl." I popped his finger out of my mouth and zoomed behind him, running my face along his shoulders and neck, caressing him.

I whispered into his ear in a husky voice, "I only learn from what I see." Since I knew cheating was an option, I would use it. Plus, there were no rules that said we couldn't do anything to the voters' bodies.

The song switched to the part where he was compliment-ing the woman, and I whispered the lyrics into his ear as I ran my hands down his back. Avery was surprised with that, he stiffened for a second until I found the two slits in his clothes that indicated where his wings would pop out if he needed them to. I fingered the slits and massaged the two points.

His hands were in fists on his thighs, his body so tight you would think it was going to snap as he trembled. "Rayla." His breathing labored. "Please." His plea to stop was like music to my ears as I pulled my hands out. I slid to the side, grabbing his chin with two fingers as I turned his face to mine. I ran the other hand through his hair lovingly, and he closed his eyes on an exhale.

Tightening my hold on his chin, his eyes popped open. I moved my face a finger away from his, making sure everyone who could see would think I was just lip-synching the words like I had been. "Remember that next time you want to tango with me, I play dirty. I cheat, steal, and use violence"—my nails dug into his skin to prove the point—"to win." I leaned in close to his ear, the one the crowd couldn't see, as I ran a hand down his chest again. "You were always going to lose today because I am Rayla fucking Desmond. I'm the Syndicate Princess not to be fucked with." I licked the shell of his ear as I ran my hand down the hard length in his pants. "Remember that."

Then the song ended, and I let go of him, hands up in the air as I smirked down at him. Standing up, I turned and bowed to a roaring crowd. For a second, I wished Rick and Cosmo were here, cheering me on, seeing my final win. I could picture Rick whooping for me in the corner while Cosmo gave me his trademark frown and nod, acknowledging my win but letting me know he didn't like how I went about it. I would run up to them laughing and hugging them. My heart hurt at not having my right and left-hands with me. I knew, after this, I was going to let all that bad blood between us go away. We would go back to old times, before my dad tried to put a wedge between us.

Men and women were hollering at me, whistling and cheering. I smirked at the three of them, all of them staring like they were seconds away from pouncing on me as the announcer came onto the stage.

"I just heard from the big man himself, and he said to congratulate Rayla Desmond as the winner!" I glanced to the balcony, knowing he was up there, even if I couldn't see him with the lights in my eyes, and bowed my head in thanks. I did it. I won my freedom, fair and square. *Take that shit, Dad!*

I waved to the crowd for a second before turning and walking off the stage with a smile on my face as my goal was finally completed. I could get my life back without having to worry about any of this bullshit.

I'll admit, it was kind of fun while it lasted. I haven't had a challenge like this in years. Cosmo refused to come at me at full speed, saying that his place was at my side, not against me. My dad and I only sparred when I wanted to challenge a decision for the clan, and no one else was really at my level. Then, in walked these three, and they gave me a run for my money, inserting excitement into my heart again.

"Where do you think you're going, Siren." I was back-stage, curtains closed, and I turned to see Ax stalking up to me, followed by Falcon and Avery.

I crossed my arms and smirked at them all. "Why, I'm going home. A winner like me needs to get her beauty rest."

As soon as Ax was close enough, his arm went out to swipe me, but I used my vampire speed to escape his clutches. I tried to reason with him. "What do you think you're doing? I won. There is no need for us to fight anymore."

He swiped at me again, and Falcon rolled his eyes while Avery suddenly disappeared. He growled out with vengeance, "Do you think you're going to get away that easily? You're going to fucking finish what you started. I'm so fucking hard I feel like a twelve-year-old watching his first porno."

He tried to catch me again as Falcon sighed out, "Don't you think that if you tried it the first few times that it won't work a third?"

Ax turned to Falcon. "Well, smarty pants, why don't you help me, then, instead of just staring at me like I'm an idiot." I took those few precious seconds they were fighting to slink through the curtains, planning to sneak out right from under their noses.

"Well, now I have to help you because we've lost her, thanks to your arguing." Falcon's irritated huff almost made me laugh, and I put my hand over my mouth, not wanting them to find me. "How about I go left, and you go right." A flash of red went around the whole stage as Falcon's voice rang out, "I set a barrier around the back area. I can't prevent her from leaving, but it will let me know if she has left the area and will show me a trail if she uses her vampire speed."

My jaw clenched as my nails dug into my palms. *That little shit!* Okay, new plan. All I needed to do was get past these two, make it out the back door, and then I could zoom to my car and get home, leaving them in the dust. Yes. That was the new plan.

I took one step forward when two hands snaked around my waist and lifted me so quickly my shoes were the only things left behind. My fight kicked in as I thought of all the ways I would kick this assailant's ass, then drag him out to the crowded club to show everyone what happens when you try to fuck with me. A cocky voice I immediately recognized whispered, "If you don't want them to find you, then I guess you're going to need my help." I relaxed when I realized it was Avery's arms around me, and I folded mine in irritation, and he took us farther and farther up from the stage floor.

I would normally enjoy this, flying above the others was thrilling, but I was irritated by being caught so easily, and my mood turned sour. I mumbled around clenched teeth, "I could've gotten away without your help. I had a plan."

His chest shook as a chuckle sounded next to my ear. "Yes, Fierce Girl. I am beginning to realize that you always have a plan."

We were so far up I could see the scaffolding bridge that only the workers used when hosting a big show. He settled me onto one of the open slots, my ass hitting the cold metal pole as I grabbed the other two poles above me that made a perfect triangle. "There. You can hide out here until the excitement dies down."

He moved from behind me, the light buzz of his fast wings more pronounced now that I was paying attention. His pink hair and jade eyes came into focus as he hovered in front of me, his hands settling on either side of me on the pole as he came in close. "Now, since I was your savior, I think I deserve a reward."

I laughed, realizing his helping me was a cover for getting me alone and vulnerable in the air where he had the advantage. "Look, if this is some kind of revenge—" His lips collided with mine.

[2] His soft, smooth kiss tasted like sultry sunsets and pops of magic as his tongue slid against my bottom lip, teasing me to let him in. I sighed out as I let him in, let him take over the kiss as I was at a disadvantage, having to hold myself up with both arms.

His tongue explored my mouth as he ran his hands over my body. At first, he kept his hands on my waist, but as the kiss deepened, he pulled closer, rubbing his chest onto mine as his kiss grew harder, more demanding. His hands slid up my back as he maneuvered his way between my legs, settling himself as close as he could get to my center.

As his hands crept into my hair, he lightly pulled, much nicer than I did, and I let my head drop back at his suggestion. His lips trailed from my mouth and along the column of my neck. I got lost in those kisses, wishing for something a little firmer, when he suddenly nibbled on my neck, giving little bites of pain that had me wet for him in seconds. My breathing became labored, my back arching, trying to rub on him for more of that delicious friction. All signs I was thoroughly enjoying myself.

"I thought I could resist your temptation, that I could cast it away easily for the sake of winning." His hands gripped the insides of my thighs so tight I knew they would bruise for a second before healing, but I liked it. I liked it way too much for my own good. "But I was wrong. You're this addictive darkness, making me never want to see or

2. Song: Like a Drug by Bryce Savage

feel the light again. I want to sink into your depths and enjoy the blackness and all it has to give."

I pulled away as far as I could, staring into his now-neon-green eyes flooded with an insatiable hunger. I widened my legs, my skirt riding up my hips as I pointedly looked down, flicking my eyes back up, unable to resist this gorgeous specimen before me. "Then I suggest you drink me down, drown in me until I can't take it anymore." *I was so glad I wore a skirt to this.*

His crooked smile spoke of all the naughty things he wanted to do with me. His eyes were glued to mine as he started to sink down, licking his lips as he said along my parted thighs, "My pleasure."

His finger trailed up and down my folds, smearing the glistening wetness that had started to escape. He watched my eyes flutter shut as the exquisite torture was getting me even hotter. Two fingers finally pushed past my folds, sinking his digits into my soaked center before pulling them back out. I cried in protest at him leaving me so soon until I took in his hovering form. His eyes were shut as his fingers were in his mouth, leaving not a scrap of skin untouched as he savored and moaned at my taste.

"Oh, fuck, Rayla. You taste fucking divine. Who knew that your darkness was so sweet and tantalizing on the tongue. Making me never wish for the light again." My heart raced as his words made something inside of me quake.

He then threw himself into me and lapped at my wet center, and I let out a cry. His tongue flattened and widened as he licked at my center, switching between licking and sucking as he worked his way up to my clit. I was gulping down breaths, my arms shaking as I was still holding myself up while he was working me to tip into oblivion.

When his tongue found my clit, he lapped at it, circled his tongue around it, and then sucked on it. The gentle tugs on my sensitive skin were creating a whirlwind under the surface. My hips thrust involuntarily, needing friction as he worked my body full of pleasure.

I couldn't take it anymore. My vision clouded as my arms grew tired, and my thighs clenched his head, but he never stopped, not once. "Avery, I need you. I need you now."

He moved away from my center, gazing up at me with his mouth, chin, and neck glistening as he licked at his lips. "I'm here. Don't worry, I'll take care of you."

He unzipped his pants and removed his clothes as he rose to eye level. He grabbed his cock, and I noticed a familiar star with a circle and skull tattoo just along his pelvic bone before he positioned it right at my center, pushing just enough for me to engulf his silky, throbbing tip.

I slammed my lips together, prepared for him to shove himself inside me, before I said, "Yes. Gods. Yes."

He let out a small chuckle as he grabbed my hips and hoisted me up. I gasped, not expecting him to pull me away from the safety of the metal poles. "Trust me," he whispers.

I glared at him, knowing that when people said that, it was usually because I shouldn't. He laughed at my frown but only said, "Watch."

He lay back, his wings flapping furiously to keep us up and steady as he lay horizontally in the air. Gravity started to play a part as I was vertical. He gripped my hips, holding on tight as he guided me down, sheathing himself within me as we hovered in the air.

We let out long, low moans at his control, making his entry slow and steady. Drawing out as much pleasure as he could. "Gods, you're so fucking wet. Excited to have sex in the air at high heights?"

I dug my nails into his chest, gripping his pecs as I peered over his shoulder and saw he was right. We were very high up, and it was exhilarating. My heart was pumping, my pulse thumping as I used my muscles to tighten myself around him. His cocky smile slid off his face as his eyes widened, and I smirked down at him. His fingers dug into my hips as he cried out.

I leaned down, going nose to nose with him. "If you think something being dangerous will scare me, think again. It only makes you more interesting." Then I used my strength to thrust into him, causing his wings to falter for a second, and he gulped. His teasing eyes turned into molten neon-green pools of desire heightened by the thrill.

I pushed up from his chest, gripping my thighs around him as I steadied myself upright. I ran my hands up my body, pinching my pebbled nipples through my outfit as I moaned out. His husky voice came out clear. "You're going to make me work for this, aren't you?"

"Only good things come to those that work for them." He smiled as he lifted my hips with both hands, thrusting up as I arched my back, giving him an eyeful of my bouncing breasts as he fucked me in earnest.

My body slammed into him with each thrust, gravity making sure I was fully seated on him every single time. His arms were bulging with how much effort he was putting into lifting my body, driving up into me and rapidly flapping his wings to keep us in the air. It was divine to feel this free, to have him do all the work while every cell in my body lit up from what he was doing.

Perspiration collected on his forehead, and I wanted to give him a little break, make it marginally easier, while giving me the thrill I was going to want to get off. I called out his name, his eyes switching from being so focused, watching his ministrations, to gazing up at me. "Don't let me fall." That was all the warning I gave him as I fell to the side, tipping us around so I was the one on the bottom, and he was on top.

"Shit! Ray!" His voice scrambled in fear as he moved his hands to wrap around my lower back as we hovered in the air.

The only catch with this move was I didn't have wings, so I couldn't stay horizontal. My head lolled down like I was falling, but Avery had me in an iron grip at my lower back, and I wrapped my legs around his hips. I used my core muscles to lift up slightly and look at Avery's panicked face as I cooed out, "Fuck me, Avery. Use my body as I get the thrill of feeling alive." I dropped back down, not wanting to see his face as he decided what he would do.

Not a second later, he said, "Oh, Fierce Girl, I'm going to fuck you so good you won't even think about the thrill of falling." He kept one arm wrapped around my back as the other skated forward and pinched my nipple.

My mouth fell open in a silent cry as he started off slow, getting the right angle and balance before he pistoned in and out of me and grabbed my breast to get an even better grip on me as he fucked me with a passionate pace. My vision danced around as he fucked me, giving me that same rush I felt when I jumped off buildings. That rush as you fell to the ground, the way your body lit up, and you felt every second like it was your last, the pounding of your heart out of your chest that said you were alive. I loved every second of it.

My breath turned into heavy pants as I cried out a few times as he sheathed himself over and over. A heat building below my stomach as my walls contracted, telling me my orgasm was close, so close. Like he knew exactly what I was thinking, he cried out, "Fuck. I'm going to cum, but I'm taking you with me, so hold on."

That was all the warning I got as his wings stopped, and we fell. My eyes flew open, and, before I could do anything, he pinched my little bundle of nerves, and it sent me over the edge. I clamped down, clenching his dick as he let out a broken moan with me as we fell. As I came all over his cock, I didn't care at the moment if we crashed to the floor in a bundle of pain because the high he gave me made me see stars as he filled me with his cum.

Before our bodies smashed into the ground, his wings popped out, having us jerk up for a second before we glided to the floor safely. The second his feet hit the floor, his wings snapped into his body as he held me close.

"Who's fucking pants are these?" Ax exclaimed from the other side of the curtain, and we froze.

"Who cares, keep fucking looking. She has to be here somewhere, the barrier hasn't gone off yet." Falcon's frustrated voice made me smile. He was getting pissed that I might have slipped his barrier and was trying to figure out how. It was kind of adorable how much faith he had in me.

Avery nuzzled into my neck, and my hand sunk into his cotton-candy-pink hair as we sighed into each other. "I better get you to that back door before they come back." He laid a sweet kiss on my neck before setting me upright and pulling out. Our collective cum dripped out of me, making a mess between my thighs, but that was what the napkins in my car were for, right? I noticed my feet were bare, and I searched around for my shoes but couldn't find them. *Oh, well. Fuck it. It was worth it.*

Avery grabbed my hand and tugged me forward, my bare feet padding after him. We paused when he thought he heard Falcon or Ax and then continued when he knew it was safe. When we finally got to the back door, I smiled at his naked half. I ran my hand along his length as I stepped closer. "I had a good time. Thank you."

He bit his lip as he smiled. "Well, that was definitely something I had not experienced before."

His cock grew harder by the second as I ran my fingers up and down. I pouted, "So, you didn't enjoy yourself?" I went to pull away, but he caught my hand and yanked me so hard I crashed into his chest.

His eyes shined brightly in the dark, gone was his normal, easy voice, and it was replaced with raw, dark obsession. Showing me his boss side. "More than you know. I think you just unlocked some kinky shit for me." He leaned closer, his voice menacing, full of dark promises and dire consequences. "And I'm going to come back for more."

I smiled up at him, enjoying the darkness that oozed out of him just now. I fell into him, pulling his mouth to mine for a down and dirty kiss before I broke away, zooming with vampire speed out the back door before I made a more dangerous choice and stayed.

There would always be tomorrow.

CHAPTER 23

COSMO

"Oh, stop looking so glum in the corner. She's going to be home soon after beating that Glovefox boy, so calm down." Ternin's bored yet agitated voice shook me out of my staring contest with a wall. He was right. He was always right, which was as frustrating as it was his daughter driving me crazy.

My fingers tightened over my ink-covered arms, doling out a little self-inflicted pain until I let go, glancing at his office door for the fifteenth time. Waiting for that jewel-eyed daredevil vamp to come walking through that door.

Ternin was at his rosewood desk, scanning over maps and other documents like he didn't have a care in the world. The literal world could be burning, and Ternin would still be here, sorting paperwork as he told us that the world could finish burning when he was good and ready. Like father, like daughter. It's one reason I loved Rayla so much and the same reason Ternin got under my skin.

"You know, I find it both elating as well as frustrating that my best friends all like my daughter more than me." He slammed his papers down onto the table as his voice took a mocking rumble of a tone to mimic Boss Rossey. "'Rayla is a fierce fighter. Her control and smarts make her so valuable.'" Then it turned into a more serious voice to sound like Boss Winstale. "'Your girl has guts and knows when to use them. An irreplaceable skill for the next in line.'" He rolled his eyes, but I caught a jealous glint to them as he sighed in irritation. "She's finishing her business with Syris, and I already know that damn bastard is going to comment on how beautiful and charming she is. How she is just as luminescent as her mother."

He smacked his desk as he shrieked out, "And, of course, she is! She is *my* daughter, and she is fucking amazing!" He took a deep breath. "I mean, sure, she gets her beauty from her mother, that's no question, but her charm? That's all me, baby!" He threw up his hands, shouting out in frustration before he mumbled, "My damn friends are trying to steal my precious ray of sunshine. Even their three boys are not a fair trade for my one precious Rayla."

I inhaled my frustration before commenting, giving him a dose of his own medicine. "Sir, how can they steal something that doesn't want to be stolen? It's always going to be Ray's choice for things, it's how you raised her."

He nodded as he continued to mumble, cursing his friends, telling them to make their own daughters if they wanted one so badly. I was rolling my eyes when my pocket vibrated. I pulled out my phone, hoping it was a text from Ray telling me to come get her so that everything could go back to normal. Having her mad at me was like slowly dying, like having a knife stuck in my chest, and every minute that passed, it twisted a quarter of a turn, just enough for a whole lot of pain and a bloody mess trailing me wherever I went.

A video text lit up the screen, and I turned the volume down, Ternin still complaining about his friends in the background as I focused on what was in front of me. I clicked on the video, and it showed Ray and this wolf going at it with Ray holding a stuffed cub in her arms, or was it stuffed into her bra? Then it switched to her running across a white line, Boss Rossey standing in front of the crowd smiling while Ax looked at her like she was a meal to be devoured. My nostrils flared as I stared at that smug face as it appeared like he went after her before the video cut out.

Then a second video popped up from another clan member. This time, I see Ray at the racetrack, walking with Deesil, Falcon trailing behind. He kept stealing glances at her, running his eyes along her body, and my heart started to beat faster as the hair on my arms rose. It cut to her getting into her car and the two of them zooming off. The next clip was her winning by a thread, the camera zoomed in on her rolling her window down and saying something to him, and they took off together.

I immediately tried to calm myself down. *It wasn't a rendezvous between lovers, they barely knew each other. Plus, she was a Syndicate heir, and she wouldn't cross that line.* My heart did a flip, knowing that if any of them had impressed her, she might. She might cross that line to see what they were made of. Rayla was a free spirit like that. Never taking any long-term interest in men, just using them and then discarding them when she was done. The only consistent men in her life were Rick, Ternin, and me. One was her gay best friend, one was her father, and the other . . . was her adopted brother who coveted her with all his being.

I ran my hand through my short hair, cursing at myself in my head. Sometimes, I berated myself for not telling her how I felt, other times, I punished myself for having those feelings. It wasn't my place to want her like that, but I did. With all my soul. I ran a finger over the mark behind my ear, remembering that night and sighed.

Another video text dinged, this time, Ternin caught on and asked what it was, I ignored him, focusing on my job as I opened the video. It took me a second, just a second, of watching before I clutched the phone in my hand so tight it cracked. I saw Ray standing on the stage at Veshta's, the three heirs sitting there as she danced on them. Each of them drooling over her as she enticed them, calling them to lust after her gorgeous body as she moved in ways making me wish I was in their place. That she was looking down at me with that cocky smile as she trailed a finger down my chest, making me wish we didn't have clothes on.

[1] I shook my head as Ternin called out my name again, and I was reminded of my status as her brother. Rage surged inside of me. They dared to look at her like that, have her perform like that in front of people like a common

---

1. Song: Weak by AJR

stripper? She was Rayla Desmond, a goddess among men, not some cheap thrill for them to enjoy. I shoved my phone into my pocket as I stalked across the room, and Ternin called out to me again, but I couldn't comprehend his words as blood rushed to my ears.

I would paint this city red with those heirs' blood. Make them pay for disrespecting the Desmond clan. I was going to—

As soon as my hand was on the doorknob, it opened, and there was Rayla, smiling up at me like I was a million bucks. I was stunned stiff when she surged forward, wrapping her arms around my shoulders, hugging me so tight I could barely breathe as she whispered, "I won, Cosy. I fucking won." She gave me a small peck on the cheek before she let go and waltzed up to her father.

Any ounce of negative feelings drained from me the second her arms were around me, and her familiar sweet floral scent surrounded me. All thoughts of blood and pain left my head as she whispered her excited words just for me. I was in a daze for a second, giving myself a moment for my heart to stop beating so loudly. It took everything in my power to not raise my hand and cup the cheek she kissed, wanting to vow I would never wash it again.

I closed the door, turned around, and followed her like the lovesick puppy I was. *Fuck me.*

"My sunshine!" Ternin threw the papers out of his hands as he stood, arms out for a hug as he beamed at her, and papers sailed to the floor.

She stopped at the front of the desk, slammed her palms down, and smirked up at him. "I beat you, old man. I won

the other boss's favors, and your little ploy to marry me
off is now blown to smithereens!" She cackled into the air
before she crossed her arms and dared her father to say
different.

Ternin kept smiling down at her as he moved around his
desk, coming closer to her. "I knew you would, my sunshine." Her smile wobbled as her brows pinched. Ternin
continued. "I raised you to be a fierce woman and to
take no shit from any man. I knew you could take on
those boys, but since this was their first time meeting you,
I wanted to make sure you smacked them down good
and hard so they knew who the real boss was. I didn't
want them to think just because you were a girl that you
couldn't rule this roost full of men. I wanted the bosses to
see you as an asset and the heirs to see you as an equal, a
leader. How do you do that without a fearsome challenge?
One that was not in your favor?"

Now, this was the Ternin I knew. The one that always had
some other plan you never thought about. Underneath all
his silly antics and crazy personality was one devious and
cunning leader. He always had a few plans up his sleeve,
always had an agenda for everything he did, even if it was
for your betterment.

This was usually the moment Rayla would tremble with
anger, she would pop off at him with all she got, and I
couldn't wait for the blow out. Rayla was the only one
that could put Ternin in his place, and it was a sight to
see.

She wrapped her arms around her stomach and laughed so
hard that Ternin and I were stunned. We looked at each

other as she wiped a tear from her face and then went forward and circled her arms around her father.

"You're right. Plus, it was fun showing those boys up." She let go, gave him a kiss on his cheek, and turned to leave.

Ternin's hand was outstretched as his face said he didn't want her to leave, he wanted to hold his baby girl for as long as she would let him, but she was already at the door. I could tell he was scrambling to find something to keep her here, something to talk to her about, and he blurted out, "Since all that nasty business is done, I think it's time we start to repair the damage."

Rayla paused at the door, turned around, and clasped her hands in front of her. "You are correct. If we are to all help each other when we succeed the boss titles, then we should be friendly. What do you suggest?"

This was the third time in less than thirty minutes she had shocked the hell out of me. Rayla never played well with others. She always wanted to either do it alone or only have Rick and me beside her. As I examined her expression, she wasn't angry or irritated. She didn't seem to sigh, have an attitude, or have any reservations. She appeared to welcome the idea wholeheartedly. *What the fuck has happened between her and those boys?*

Ternin cleared his throat. "Well, darling, if you're still up to it, I think they should go with you on the collections run tonight? Maybe bond over a common goal."

Her lips turned up into a vicious smile. "I think that's a great idea. Tell them where I will be and when. Oh, and make sure to give me the list of the real big troublemakers.

I think it would be a good night to make a show of the whole thing." Ternin giggled with glee as he nodded.

"See, you are my daughter."

She laughed and nodded. "Of course, I am. I wouldn't have it any other way." She pushed the door open as she threw over her shoulder, "I'm tired. I've had a long couple of days. I'm going to crash. Night, Dad. Love you."

Ternin's mouth pressed tightly together as his shoulders hunched, and he let out a small whine, probably wanting to talk to her more, but he quickly adjusted and smiled at her. "Sure, honey. You take all the time you need. Love you. Have sweet dreams . . ."

"And bloody nightmares." She finished their nighttime mantra with a smile. She tilted her head toward me, silently telling me to follow her as she walked out the door.

"I'll find out what happened," I said to Ternin like I needed an excuse to follow her. He nodded as he zoomed to the liquor cabinet and poured himself three fingers of whiskey and lifted it in my direction.

"Night, son. Don't let the bed bugs bite . . . unless you like that kind of thing." He laughed at his own joke as I told him good night.

I followed Ray, speeding to catch up to her on her way to her room. She was walking slowly, waiting for me to catch up, and my heart sang. *Maybe she had forgiven me?*

I went to her side, my hands clasped behind my back as I waited for her to tell me whatever was on her mind. We walked like this until we got to her room door, and she twirled around to face me.

"I'm not mad anymore, Cosmo. I understand that you were put between a rock and a hard place. I'm choosing to let it go, but I'll warn you that if I feel that kind of betrayal from you again, I will need to rethink you being my right hand." My soul left my body at those last words. Being her right hand was everything. It was the only way I was able to stay at her side. The pain didn't register until it skittered up my thighs that I was on my knees before her.

I deserved it. I deserved all the pain and heartache I was feeling, but I could make this right. I had this opportunity before her now to ask for her forgiveness as I made my new vow.

"Ray, I will never do something like that again. My loyalty is to you and you first. I understand that now. I will never fuck up like that again. I will always put you above Ternin, above the Syndicate. Above my own life." I begged her with my eyes to believe me, to not leave me. I only have her in this world, and if she left me, I would return to being nothing. I don't want to be nothing anymore; I want to be her something. Whatever she wished me to be, I would be, just as long as I was next to her. "I won't disappoint you again for as long as there's blood running through these veins."

I hit my chest in emphasis, feeling each word like it was a renewed bond between us. Our own bond outside of everything else in our lives. Just me and her.

She smiled as she sank to her knees, grabbed the hand I fisted to my chest, and placed it on her heart as she cupped my cheek. It took everything inside of me not to sink into that hand, to enjoy the feeling of her skin along mine. To smell her sweet and floral mixture along her wrist and wanting to take a taste of that life nectar that laid just beneath. To make an even deeper connection.

"I believe you, Cosmo. I will always believe you. I don't think I could kill you even if you did betray me. It would hurt me too much. It would be like slicing up my own chest and ripping my own heart out. I think that's why I took it so hard this time. Why it gutted me that I felt like you weren't on my side. I didn't know if I could do it without you . . . but I did." She lowered both her hands, and I kept down the whimper threatening to slip out. "From now on, you and I are solid. No bad blood, no leaving each other out. It's you, me, and Rick, just like it's always been. Okay?"

I nodded, not having the courage to use my voice because I knew if I did, I would blurt out something like, *I want it to be more than what it's always been. I want all of you. Every scrap of you I could get, all to myself, forever.* I couldn't say that, so I nodded, resting my head on her shoulder for a smidgen of the contact I desperately needed.

She put her hand on my head, leaning her cheek on me, and I was in pure heaven at the moment. Just me and her, embracing on the floor like lovers.

That thought snapped me out of it as I pulled back. I sensed her disappointment, but she quickly covered it with a smile. Was I the only one that felt this way? Did she want me like that, too? I never dared to dream that would be a possibility.

"Come on. Let's get up off the floor. I want to have a nice long soak in the tub and then fall asleep." She yawned, and I scrambled up off my knees and helped her stand up.

"Did you need me to stand guard? Make sure you don't fall asleep in the tub?" I don't know why I said that, especially since I hadn't done that since we were kids, but she smiled a sweet, tired smile.

"Naw. I promise I won't fall asleep in the tub. You know I hate to get all pruney. Maybe I'll switch to a shower just to get everything . . . clean and then fall onto my bed like a dead person." She turned, opened her door, then turned back around, leaning against the door as she gave me a small wave. "Night, Cosy. Tomorrow will just be another work day . . . just with observers." She winked as I said good night, and she closed her door.

I stood there staring at her door for a few seconds. There was something tugging at my mind, telling me that nothing about tomorrow would be just another work day. I had this feeling deep in my gut that these past two days were the start of a major shift in our lives. I just didn't know if it was for better or for worse.

CHAPTER 24

"ARE YOU EVEN LISTENING TO me, Lex?"

My uncle's voice rang out, and I bit my lip to prevent me from telling him no. That I wasn't listening to him at all. That I was thinking about my rose. That I had left the training hall early and went to watch her beat down a wolf, speed past a mage, and out dance a fox. I wonder what would happen when it was my turn?

"Lex!" I turned toward my uncle's irate face across the iron dining table. It was frustrating that we looked so similar, matching ear length onyx hair with dark eyes and tan skin. While he always had his hair slicked back, and I left mine a bit more wild, his eyes were more of a dark brown while mine was my mothers trademark midnight, almost black with a hint of navy.

His exasperated sigh spoke all the words he wanted to say before he settled on, "You know that I can't afford you to slip up while you are out and about, right? That if they see you, everything we have been working toward would be for nothing!"

"I won't get caught." It was the only thing I could say with one hand holding up my chin, elbow on the table, as the other was tapping away on my leg, trying my best not to give him a bored expression. "Plus, I have done my part. You have always said that my job was to train to be the best assassin I could be and to be the face of the Devil family. What kind of assassin would I be if I was able to get caught so easily? Have faith in me, Uncle."

Uncle Vincent slammed his hand on the table to get my attention. I was used to his violent outbursts, but it was still annoying that he kept it up even when I was grown. "Lex, I don't have time for your ridiculous arguments. I need you to be sharp. I need you to be on top of everything, not have your head in the clouds. I'm counting on you for your excellent observational skills and attention to detail. Everything needs to go off without a hitch, and we need solid intel about the clans."

I kicked off the wall I was leaning on as I growled, "And I'm working on it. I don't want to get too close and have them catch me. These people are not stupid, and I'm sure one if not a few are able to feel me watching them. This part can't be rushed." I blew out a breath, frustrated with my uncle. Why was he trying to rush this? Worse comes to worse, we could always wait for the next time they got together. It seemed like it would be a regular thing from now on.

A knock came at the door as my uncle yelled, "Come in." My uncle's mage assistant, Kevin, came in. His mousey-brown curly hair and forever frown were the bane of my existence. I thought he was also the reason my uncle didn't want me to be a part of his experimentation.

My uncle had always wanted to utilize mages for weaponry, like the Syndicate did, but he had always been fascinated with making regular spells into something bigger and more impactful. So, he had been working in a lab with some mages, coming up and testing things for our big takeover.

I have asked him to see what they were doing, what the plan was, but he always told me something along the lines of, "All will be revealed in time."

When I was younger, I would get mad and fight with my uncle over it. Telling him it wasn't right of him to keep secrets from me. He would fight back, saying he wasn't keeping it from me, but he was making sure it was something that could happen before he got my hopes up. I thought it was a stupid excuse, but I had nothing to fight him back with, so I let it slide.

Plus, if I was going to be into that stuff, it would just pull me away from my spying-on-Rayla time, and I would not have that. Nope. I would be okay with being kept in the dark, trusting my uncle to do his thing while I did mine.

"Sir." Kevin's peep of a voice sounded. "We have something we need you to look at before we go further."

My uncle glared at me for a second, not taking his eyes off me as he said, "Have you found anything useful? Anything that could help us?"

I shrugged, not giving him too much since it still needed time. "There is a little spat going on between them all, and I am seeing where it's all going to land before I make a definitive answer."

That seemed to appease him as he turned to Kevin and nodded for him to lead him out.

I took a deep breath and clasped my hands behind my back. "Was there anything else you needed to talk about?"

My uncle shook his head. "No. No, nothing else. Report back when you have something."

I nodded, even though he had left, staring at the table, lost in thought over Rayla.

I was proud of her when she beat that wolf girl. Toward the end, I almost blew a poisonous dart at the she-wolf, not wanting her to ruin this for my rose, but I should've known better. My rose was stronger than a simple she-wolf princess.

Then it all got a tad more interesting as I watched her and Ax have sex in the woods. At first, I was pissed, I dug my fingers into the tree I was hiding behind, wanting to march right up to him and tear out his lungs. Making it so he couldn't breathe in any of her air. Then I heard her moan.

It was the single most delicious sound on this planet, and it stopped me in my tracks. As she was lost in her pleasure, he stared at her, and it wasn't the kind of look from someone who was proud or full of themselves. It was the expression of a man who knew he was being blessed by a deity. He seemed desperate to make her sound like that over and over.

I got lost in watching her. Seeing how her hair sparkled in the moonlight. Watching how her body bent and moved with his. Watching how her hands dug in, and her breath quickened. It took everything inside of me not to lose myself in the moment.

I desperately wanted to use my shadow magic to appear next to her while she was on top, grab her by the throat, tilt her head up, and taste those lips like I'd always dreamed of doing. I wanted to swallow all those delectable moans and keep them for myself as Ax did all the work on the bottom, and I kept her attention on me.

As I was battling with myself, and my resolve disintegrated as my pull for her took over, they finished. Then she zoomed off, leaving him in the dust. I almost felt bad for the guy when he tightened his fists and howled out into the sky. The sound was hollow, filled with so much longing I shadowed to my car, not wanting to feel comradery with my rival.

I pulled out the orb and clutched to her hairpin and saw she was on her way to the racetracks. I carefully secured the pin back in the inside chest pocket and the orb back in its box before pulling into reverse and following.

The racetrack was a mess of bodies, loud music, and roars from the crowd. It was the perfect place for someone like me to watch from a distance. Especially with new people coming here if they had enough money.

I wasn't surprised to see Falcon here trailing behind her. I did some research on all of my rivals after their meeting with Ternin and found out not only was this mage a genius with magic, able to wield three elemental powers—which was unheard of—but he was also socially shy and only found solace in tinkering with things. Mainly cars in his spare time.

I stayed in the back of the crowd, not wanting to get too close for any of them to pick up on being watched. When the race started, I pulled out my orb in the far dark corner, releasing the shadows on my arms to cover what I was doing as I watched my rose and Falcon battle it out.

I almost lost it when she jumped those elevator doors. My hand wobbled, and the orb almost fell, but I caught it just as she crossed over safely. I shook my head as I took a few breaths.

Rayla has always been like this, ever since that day. All of us dealt with it differently, the deep feeling of pain and loss. Rayla liked to do death-defying things, break all the rules, making her blood race and her heart pump.

I used to watch Cosmo get mad at her when they were younger. I felt the same way, wishing she wouldn't endanger herself like that, but I understood it. Grief fucked people up in different ways and sometimes changed your personality. Now, he just bit his tongue and was there to catch her if she fell. A place I wished with all my heart I could be.

I walked back to my car as I watched through the orb that she won the race, telling Falcon to follow her, watching as they met up in that secret place she liked to go when she needed to calm down from the pumping adrenaline. She tested Falcon, teasing him until he gave in to his baser needs and pleasured her on top of that hood. I almost wanted to ask him how he made her scream like that with just his fingers, she had never been like that with anyone else. I had this urge to grab her and show her I could be as good, if not better.

Then, just like I knew Rayla would, she zoomed off to her next adventure, leaving Falcon behind, looking perplexed.

I watched her park in the back lot of The Temptress, and I put the orb down and followed my bloody princess to her last stop on her warpath to put these men in their place.

I entered the club and kept to the dark corners and out-skirts, not calling attention to myself as I watched her and Avery strutting around the club like king and queen of the place. It irked me that they looked so good together. Her easy sex appeal and brilliant shining pink eyes that matched his hair in the darkness of the club. His obvious swagger as he walked, and the way he was a gentleman as he had her take his arm and led her to the back of the stage.

I gripped my hand underneath the corner of the bar to keep myself from following them. There was this need inside of me to watch her every move, even when she was with other men. I also noticed, while I wanted to steal her attention away from the other heirs, wanted to take her from them, I didn't get the normal shot of blood-curdling rage I did when I'd seen her touching another man.

I had trained myself over the years to handle watching Rayla when she was with others. It took a while at first.

My room has gone through many renovations because of those early days when I used to go in a fit of rage, but that was before I changed my mindset. I decided I would use the opportunities to see what she liked and didn't like. I wanted to make sure our first time together was earth-shattering and euphoric for her. I wanted her to never once forget our first time together when it happened. I wanted that more than anything, so I saw how others approached things, since I couldn't even think about fucking another woman.

My vision was tunneled in on her, watching her more than ever seeing the man she was using at the moment. My eyes would trace her skin, see what made her quake versus what made her pulse jump. I listened to each moan, sigh, pant, and scream so I would know how she was feeling, but the small sounds she would make made it easier to focus on her when she was having her exploits . . . but with the heirs, it felt different. More like I wanted to join in. See what kind of sounds she would make when we worked her up together.

Would she scream louder? Would she feel more pleasure? Would she be so blissed out that she would pass out in my arms, and I could stare at her face all night long, just watching her breathe? All of that sounded good because it was all still about my rose. My love.

I barely glanced at the stage when Avery was dancing. It wasn't appealing for me to watch him try to turn other women on. In fact, I didn't really like it. It felt a little like he was betraying my rose, and I wanted to make him bleed a little bit for it.

I knew what his job was in the Syndicate, knew his reputation with women, and it was all very logical, but nothing about me operated on logic. It was something I worked hard not to let my uncle know.

I learned long ago that I was a sensitive child, and observing people only made it ten times more recognizable that emotions drove me to do things. So, instead of beating myself up to force myself into that logical box people wanted their successors to have, I worked on being able to quickly change my mindset. I could still work off my feelings, but I was the master at convincing myself to change how to feel and why.

It was the one thing that helped me not explode when it was Rayla's turn to dance on all the heirs, and not stomp my way up there and stab them and push them off the stage, making it a dance for just me.

Rayla had good natural instincts, and that all played out on stage as she changed her dance for each of them. With Ax, she was cockier and more forceful, tugging on his wants like it was wrapped around her finger, and she controlled how turned on he got the more she wound it up. With Falcon, she was more enticing. Showing off all the parts of her body he may not have been able to see or feel when they were on the hood of her car. Her eyes conveyed how she still found him attractive, even with his rigid disposition, but that she would worm her way through to get to his desire center. With Avery, she changed the most. Instead of being ultra sexy and alluring, she played on their humor, their back-and-forth banter. His face lit up in surprise as she took a different approach with him, convincing him desire wasn't all about the sex and the body. Then she cupped him at the end, and his body shook, and I knew he was a goner.

I was slightly depressed for a second, wishing I could be up there to play with them all, too. To be a part of something with them, like I was always meant to be. Then she left with all three of them trailing after her, and I worked my way up to the stage and up the side. Falcon's magical shield closed in, and I quickly crossed before it shut down, using my shadows to hide in the curtains.

I heard Ax and Falcon talking, trying to find my rose as it seemed she gave them all the slip. I smiled at that. My rose was not to be underestimated.

I searched around, going between the folds to make sure I stayed hidden from them when I heard a faint cry and pants falling in front of me. I looked up and saw Avery and my rose going at it in the air, and I had to admit, it was beautiful to see.

His shimmering iridescent wings fluttered so fast you could barely see them as he kept her up. I had to admit, it took not only stamina but some damn strong muscles to pull off all of that. I had to give credit where credit was due.

Then my rose flipped them around so fast my heart stopped, my foot moved an inch, thinking I'd need to catch her, but Avery had his grip on her. He pounded into her, and she dangled around, a smile on her lips as she got that adrenaline she seemed to always be chasing.

They started to fall, but I wasn't nervous this time. I saw Avery's determination, and his arms circled around her. I knew it was more about him noticing my rose's excitement for danger and wanted to give her the thrill she was craving.

As they were falling, I thought it would be best for me to move away, to head for the exit, which would be easy with these shadows everywhere.

I heard Falcon's and Ax's steps heading in their direction. I didn't know what came over me, but I pushed over a broom leaning against the far wall, causing them to stop and head in my direction, opposite of Avery and Rayla.

That was for you, my rose. You need to get a good night's rest, not have to deal with more men drooling over you.

I decided it would be fun to fuck with Ax and Falcon more, so I started to do things like flutter curtains in front of them and make odd noises that would catch their attention.

When Falcon cursed, saying the shield was tripped on the opposite side, I smiled to myself. See, I helped my rose more than any of them did.

With the shield now down, I went out into the pounding room of the club and left out the front door.

I pulled up to a small two-story Victorian house I bought a while ago when my plans for Rayla's and my future started to come to light. This was something I kept to myself, something I didn't want my uncle to know about.

Lately, I have been getting this off feeling about my uncle, noticing the way his face changed when he thought no one was paying attention. It was a face that said he would give up anything and everything to win over the Syndicate bosses. That it was more than just revenge for my father and the Devil name, it was something much more personal. Something he never shared with me.

I didn't want whatever was going on in his mind to mess up my plans with Rayla, so I kept this to myself. Letting him think I was staying in crappy motels or not sleeping at all as I stalked the Syndicate players, but, really, I would come here.

I grabbed the orb box out of my car and went into the house. I had a mage ward it so only Rayla and I could enter and leave it at will. After he was done, I slit his throat and threw him into the river. Couldn't have him telling anyone about this spot. Not a single soul.

I whistled as I opened the unlocked door and put the box on the kitchen table. I went to the drawer with a tie from my uncle's closet in it, and I put it next to the orb as I ran my finger down the smooth sphere.

Unless he was in that warded area I wasn't able to go in, I could see him and what he was doing with others. Sometimes, I did this so the next time we talked it would seem like I was in the know and keeping up with the compound's coming and going. Making him believe I had been there when I wasn't.

My uncle's dark hair, cold eyes, and sharp nose came into focus, and I saw him talking to some pudgy man that looked vaguely familiar.

"You have the distribution spot ready?" *Distribution? Distribution of what?*

"Y-y-yes, sir. But as I said before. Tomorrow is—"

My uncle slammed his hand on the desk as he spoke in a low tone that said he'd had enough. "I don't care what day it is for those people. We need to get this going. That means that you need to be there to run it. I'll send some men to help you, and you have someone else take care of the drop off with them."

He got up from his chair and slowly walked around. "I picked you for a reason, Breken. I picked you because you know of all the dirty spots and underground places where we could start this." His hand snapped out and gripped the fat man's neck, a hiss came from his mouth as his teeth were on display. "If you fuck this up, remember what will happen to that sweet little daughter of yours. I wonder if she will last a night with my boys. Their tastes are quite savage, you know." Disgust rolled around in my belly at his words.

"I . . . I understand. Please, just don't hurt my daughter. I will get it done. No problem." He looked like he was seconds away from pissing his pants when my uncle let go of his neck and went back to his chair around his desk.

"Good. Now make sure the warehouse is set up and nothing goes wrong tomorrow. Do you hear me?" His voice gave no room for excuses or rebuttals.

The whimpering fairy moved, leaving the room as fast as he could as he said, "Yes," a few more times. Then it clicked in my head who this fairy was. This was one of the Desmond bookies that took a lot of the business outside of the strip. *What was he doing with my uncle?*

I let go of the orb and thought about it some more, but one thing was for sure. Tomorrow, I would find that man and see what the fuck my uncle was up to and wanted this man to distribute for him.

@Tpiola_

CHAPTER 25

I PEELED OPEN MY eyes, grumbling about the sunset filtering through the slit between the curtains, and saw a glass of O neg. on my nightstand. *Cosmo.*

I smiled at his gesture. It was a myth that vampires needed to feed all the time, to gorge ourselves with blood. We always craved blood, hungered for its delicious taste and smell, but we could actually live off a small amount. Which was why I always tried to have it in my food, but he knew today was collection day, and I would need to be in tip top condition all night. Making sure my tummy was full the second I stepped out.

I grabbed the cup and slurped it down, very unladylike, licking up every drop around the rim. My whole body was revived as the blood raced through my veins, making me alert and alive.

I flew out of bed, showered as quickly as I could, thoughts running through my mind as I was on autopilot, scrubbing my body. First, I would head to Vinny's, have my two drinks, and talk with a few people to get a pulse on the crowd. I liked to stay there for about thirty to forty-five minutes, then I would head out and start knocking down doors and splitting skulls. Now, I would have the other heirs with me, so I felt a little pressured to show them a good time.

I thought back to why my dad and the other bosses wanted us all to hang out. To bond with each other. It was not a bad idea, it's just . . . how do you get a bunch of Mafia kids to suddenly trust each other? How do you bond when you have built up layers and layers of protection around yourself?

My mind was so lost in thought that when I yanked my shampoo and lathered it on my head, I felt it to be much creamier than it usually was, then realized I was holding the bottle of conditioner. Conditioner was kind of like soap, right?

I shrugged and washed it all out. How do I connect with the other heirs? Well, what do we have in common? We all have grown up in gang life. I was sure each of them had a brutal side, even Falcon with all his knowledge of weapons had to have something going on underneath. We also all had our mothers die in the same way. Yay for common connections.

I kept thinking, and the only thing I came up with was that I needed to be the first one to take the vulnerability step. To show them someone outside of the powerhouse that was Rayla Desmond, but how would I do that?

A thought hit me, and I realized I could hit two birds with one stone. I could treat them to the best Mexican food they would ever have in their life but also introduce them to my nana. She could also give me her thoughts on them. She was always strangely perceptive about people.

With my plans coming together, I turned the knob as soon as I was done, grabbed my large fluffy towel, and wrapped it around my body. It was like having a cloud cover me, tempting me to ask some designer to make a set of lounging clothes in this material.

I sat at my deep-mahogany vanity and looked at my pale, unblemished skin and deep-pink eyes. If you got close, you could see gold flecks mixed with the pink, something that seemed uniquely my own since neither of my parents had eyes like these. I put on minimal makeup, mainly eye makeup to give that glam look, and then went to my closet.

Since I was going to Vinny's first, I needed it to be something stylish, but I was also going to do collections and needed something I could run and move in, just in case. I tapped my finger against my chin, thinking what I would do when I saw a slinky, off-the-shoulder, lace mini dress. It had a thin, pale under layer, giving it the illusion it was see-through. It was perfect for Vinny's, but not so much for collections. I looked around again and found red heels that went perfect with the dress, also a pair of black boots that would be hot if the dress was a shirt. Then I got an idea.

I grabbed a pair of black acid-wash jeggings and put them up against the dress. *I found my outfit.* I slipped the dress and red heels on, grabbing the pants and boots and shoving them in my mini duffle. Cosmo would take care of this since I wanted to take my bike.

A ding came from my phone, and a text from my dad lit up the screen. He listed out the spots I needed to visit tonight. It was only three, which was kind of a bummer since I wanted to knock heads together, but they were some of the bigger bookies and distribution centers, so I might still get my wish.

I went out the door, walking down the east stair wing when the air rushed by me on both sides. A hand came out and snagged my mini duffle, and Cosmo slung it over his shoulder and gave me a smirk and a smile.

Rick clapped on my other side and rubbed his hands together. "I am sooooo looking forward to this collection night. I feel like we have not been able to beat anyone up in forever."

I laughed. "We took down Tre not to long ago."

Rick's brows pinched as he thought, then swatted his hand out like that was no big deal. "Who, Dinglefritz Number One Hundred and Forty-Eight? That doesn't count. I only got one hit in before he crumpled like a sack of potatoes."

We kept going down the stairs, a few clan members moving in different directions paused for us to pass as we reached the front door. Everyone knew what tonight was.

"Also, RayRay, you look fucking delectable. Are we trying to impress anyone tonight?" Rick's probing question made me want to punch him while his compliment prevented me from doing so. That man knew how to work me.

"No." Silence filled the air between us as they waited for me to elaborate. I let out a heavy exhale. "But we will have three shadows on us tonight."

Cosmo couldn't hide the frustration in his voice. "We're fucking babysitting heirs tonight, Rick."

Rick's mouth pressed into a thin line as we went through the garage. "Well, that kinda puts a damper on the night."

I had to stop this kind of talk now. "Hey. We don't know that. They might just surprise you. Let's just play it by ear and give them the benefit of the doubt." I nodded as I went to the key box and grabbed Cosmo's keys as well as my bike keys.

I turned around to find Cosmo and Rick with gaping mouths, staring at me like I was some alien or something. "What?"

Cosmo was the first to shake it off as I threw his keys toward his head, and he caught them, popping the trunk to put my mini duffle in. Rick was still staring at me like he found out I was a doppelgänger. "Who are you, and what have you done with my RayRay?"

I rolled my eyes. "Shove it, Ricky. If it's for the good of the Syndicate, you know I will bend if I need to."

I swung my leg over the bike and tied up my hair as Cosmo slid into the driver's side of his car, Rick taking his sweet ass time getting into the passenger seat. "Bend?

No, Rayla. You make the fucking world bend to you, not the other way around."

I flipped my shield up as I responded, "It's not about that, and you know it." I tapped the side of my helmet that connected to a com connected to one in Cosmo's car. "Check. Check."

I heard Cosmo's voice over the revving of his engine, signaling to Rick to sit the fuck down. "I hear ya, Ray. Let's head to Vinny's and get this all over with."

I rolled my eyes as I slapped the shield down, waiting for the garage door to open all the way before I backed out. These boys would need to play nice with each other, or it would be playground rules, and I would beat everyone's ass.

All three of us walked up to the door, skipping the line that ran around the block as Ryan, the troll bouncer, turned around. "Rayla! How are you?!"

I smiled and gave him a pat on his shoulder. "Good, Ryan. Good. How is the wife?"

He beamed up at me, so happy with his new wife, Hailey. She was a faerie who used to dance at one of the strip clubs, but gave that up when they started to date and now works here as an assistant manager.

"She is amazing. She just gets more and more beautiful by the second. I am the luckiest fucker out there. I still can't believe that she's my wife." I smiled up at him, truly happy for them.

"That's how it should be, Ryan. The day that you think you do deserve her, come see me, I'll knock some sense back into you." I raised up my fist, faking like I would punch him, and we both laughed.

"Deal." He unhooked the rope and let us in. "Have a good time, Rayla." I waved as I passed him, with Cosmo and Rick trailing close behind me.

The second I entered, the sound vibrated off my skin, it was so loud. The whole place was dark, other than the neon-blue, pink, and purple lights swirling around the dance floor.

Even though this was a bar, it was more like a hybrid club. It was one very large room, but on one side was the DJ, the lights, and the crowd bumping and grinding into each other. It always smelled like booze, sweat, and sex on the dance floor, and it was even more intoxicating the more you drank.

Then you had the VIP private booths off to the left-hand side. This was much quieter. It was still loud in the whole space, but when you were in one of the booths, you could talk to each other without screaming or talking in someone's ear.

The bar was in the center, an elaborate all-crystal bar that shone its prism color around the whole venue. It was almost like sparkles of magic would appear and then disappear just as quickly.

The Syndicate had a long-standing VIP table here, and I motioned for the guys to meet me there as I was going to talk to Hailey in the back office. Cosmo's mouth pinched in disapproval, but he turned and stalked off to the booth. Rick shrugged and followed after Cosmo.

I made my way over to the back hallway where I knew the manager's office was and tapped on the door a few times.

"I swear on everything, Garrett, if you tell me that you had another stalker you need saving from, I'm going to handcuff you to the bar so I don't have to worry about you!" Hailey said as she yanked the door open, her golden hair shining brightly as her petite face was furrowed in frustration.

I smiled widely as she covered her mouth in embarrassment, so I wiggled my fingers as I said, "Hi."

She turned about five shades of red before she stammered, "Um . . . I'm . . . I didn't . . . I'm so sorry, Rayla. I didn't know it was you. If I did, I wouldn't have said anything like that."

Before she started to really ramble, I cut her off. "No biggie. I know Garrett is the stupid pretty boy that lets everyone walk all over him. He almost got kidnapped two weeks ago, right? He needs a little tough love." Her shoulders slumped as she let out a small puff of air.

"Are you here for Dean? He is off tonight, but I'm sure if I call him, he will come right—"

I shook my head. "Nope. I wanted to talk to you." Her face paled, and I tried to give her my best smile. She backed up a few steps as I moved my way into the office and shut the door.

"Look, I'm going to cut to the chase. Have you heard anything about a new drug popping up?" I needed to get some kind of a lead on this. I had a gut feeling this was about to get worse, and I needed to cut it out fast.

Her eyes widened as she shook her head. "No. We are not allowed to have drugs. The Syndicate—"

I held up my hand, and she immediately quieted down. "Look, Hailey, I know you have connections, even past this job, to what is going on underneath the neon lights of the strip. I need to know if you have heard anything and what those details are." She turned away, biting her lip, and I knew she knew something. I hoped she made the right choice. I would hate to make Ryan a widow so soon.

She moved around me to the metal cabinets next to the door, opened it, and stuck her hand in. I almost asked her what she was doing, when a pulse of air magic spread through the room, hovering against the walls and cracks in the floor.

She turned back to me. "It's a sound-canceling spell. I don't want anyone to hear what I'm going to tell you." I smiled as I turned around and sat in her seat, the boss chair, and waited for her to speak.

I watched as she wrung her hands together, glancing around the room. "Hailey. You don't need to be afraid.

The Syndicate will protect those who are loyal, you and Ryan, from any fall out. I will protect you." Her head snapped toward me, staring me in the eyes as she let out a soft, shaky breath.

"Do you remember a while back when I was having trouble with my uncle?" I nodded. A couple years back, before she and Ryan got together, she was living with a subfamily of the Syndicate, one that ran all the money outside of the strip and paid us their dues. She started working on the strip but kept coming into work with bruises and cuts. The manager of the strip club asked me to step in, to talk to her.

I found out her uncle had taken her in after her father died, but he and his son were using her like a punching bag. The son also got drunk one night and tried to rape her. She escaped but had nowhere to go and eventually went back. In the end, I visited them, smacked them down a bit, threatened their lives, but I couldn't kill them since Hailey wasn't under my protection. That night, I told them she was one of mine now, and they were not to contact her again. They backed down, understanding the weight of my words, and told me they were glad to get rid of the dead weight.

I set her up with an apartment, and I had Ryan watch her. I had him stand outside of her door, making sure she felt safe enough to sleep, and walk her to and from her car. I told him he was to never touch her, never to enter her space, and to wait like a gentleman. One thing led to another, and then she and Ryan started to date a year ago and have been going strong ever since.

I nodded, wishing I never had to hear her talk about that dick again.

She crouched down in front of me, her violet-red eyes darkening into a plum purple. "I got a visit from him the other day, asking me to come back. That he has a new business venture that he wanted to invite all his family to partake in. That we would be rich beyond our imagination." I kept my eyes on her, not letting her hide or waver from me. I needed to know.

A single tear ran down her cheeks as she grabbed one of my hands. "He pulled out a small vile of blue smoke, telling me to taste the product. I kept refusing. I knew from the excitement in his eye that something bad would happen if I did." She took another shaky breath.

"I told him no. He didn't like that." Her body shook as she stared at the ground. Her whole form looked crushed and weak like it took everything out of her to recall what happened.

"He pushed me around and tried to force me to sniff it." She raised her head with a broken smirk. "I kicked him in the balls and smacked the drug out of his hands and ran." She paused before she finished. "As I was running, he said that if I told you, he would kill Ryan and me. That, soon, the Syndicate wouldn't be able to protect us, and that once that happened, I had better be on the right side of the line."

I was using all of my energy not to crush her small soft hand in mine as the overwhelming rage inside was trying to take over. I have worked hard all my life to keep my emotions in check, to not overreact when I heard bad news, that was what any good leader did, but this was hard. Not only did that piece of shit threaten someone under my protection, he'd tried to fucking force her to take drugs, which it sounded like he was planning on doing to maybe get her hooked on them so she would stay loyal to him. Then he wanted to threaten the Syndicate, saying we wouldn't be able to protect those loyal to us? *Oh, no.* This fucker would go down, and I would enjoy it.

I wiped away her tears as I tried to give her a calm and gentle smile. "Does Ryan know?"

She shook her head vehemently. "No. If he did, then he would go after my uncle himself, and I don't want him to get hurt. It sounds like my uncle has people following him. He mentioned something about not messing with Breken?"

Breken was in on this, eh? He was on my list to visit tonight, so I would be extra thorough with my investigation.

I slowly got up and pulled her up with me as I continued my fake smile, trying to let her know everything would be all right, and it would. As soon as I massacred everyone who thought they could pull one over on me. I cupped her face as I cooed, "Don't tell him. In fact, don't worry about a thing because I am going to take care of it, okay?"

She nodded, sucking up her tears as she built herself back up. "What are you going to do?"

I walked to the door and turned slightly, not able to keep the menacing violence out of my voice. "Don't ask questions you don't need the answers to, Hailey. Just know that your uncle and all the fucktards that are working with him will not be bothering you again. Don't cry when they tell you he is dead, okay?"

She nodded before she scrambled to the cabinet and de-activated the silencing spell. Air whooshed around me as I opened the door.

The loud pounding beats in the air did not help as I hoped to ignore the pure liquid wrath that bubbled beneath my skin as I walked toward my booth. I reminded myself I was to take on one problem at a time. I needed to show those watching that the Syndicate was as strong and stable as ever, and when I did collections, they would need to be bloody and brutal to those that disobeyed.

As I got to the booth, Rick and Cosmo stood on each side like guards, when, really, they were my leashes. Making sure I didn't go overboard.

I moved in, scooted to the center of the booth, looking out toward the moving bodies on the dance floor as I folded my arms and thought.

"You okay, Ray?"

Cosmo's concern came out loud and clear, and I shook my head. "No, Cos, I'm not. But we will find out more tonight. It might be good that we will have the others tonight for backup." That was all I could say here to let him know that tonight might get dicey.

His eyes narrowed on me as he leaned forward, placing one hand on the table to get closer. "Whatever it is, I got you. You know that, right?" For a second, I was lost in his lilac-colored eyes, feeling myself fall into their warm embrace, telling me everything would be fine, everything would work out as long as those eyes stayed fixed on me.

My hand drifted up, wanting to touch this gorgeous man that looked at me like I was his whole world, wanting to touch that loyalty, to make sure it was real.

A cough came from right in front of the booth, my hand moved to grip the table, pretending this was the place I meant it to go as Cosmo's face flashed with anger as he straightened up. His expression turned blank as he came face-to-face with Avery.

Avery smiled down at me, his frosted-pink hair styled backward as his green eyes flashed with heat. "Why, hello there, Miss Rayla. I heard you were going to be here tonight." His assessing eyes flicked to Cosmo for a second, but Cosmo was in centurion mode, scanning the crowd for threats. "Do you mind if I join you?"

I didn't know if his father told him to be nice or what, but I could play this game, too. I motioned to the booth's open seats. "Go ahead. This is the Syndicate table, you don't need to ask." I sat back, enjoying the view as he maneuvered his way in, scooting close to my left side. He was wearing a black see-through frock shirt with pink floral appliqué, a light-gray overcoat, with matching slacks, and he looked damn fine in it. I glimpsed his toned abs through his shirt, and my throat went dry. I lifted my hand, signaling to one of the waitresses at the bar, needing a drink ASAP.

Avery scooted closer, whispering a hair away from my ear while I kept my face forward. "You know, I have been thinking—"

Suddenly, I heard Falcon's calm, cool voice on my right side. "Is there a reason that you meet here before you go to collect?" I almost jumped in my seat, not expecting him to be there, but I turned my head toward him, trying to slow my beating heart.

As Avery grumbled under his breath as he sat back, I examined Falcon. He was perfectly suited for the boss role already in a rolled-sleeved, black shirt, gray, four-button vest, and matching pants. He looked like he was ready to rule the world, and it was so damn attractive.

When his eyes met mine in question, I hurried to answer. "I came here as a short warning. Everyone knows that before I run the collections, I sit down at my booth in Vinny's, have a couple of drinks, and then head out. They have just that amount of time before I come busting down doors." His crystal-blue eyes drilled into mine so much I felt like he could see my thoughts before they even happened. He didn't say a word as he nodded and turned toward the crowd.

Since he seemed like the planning type, I clued him in, "But since we have the three of you tonight, we'll be detouring before doing collections."

I kept my eyes on Falcon, his jaw clenched just as the waitress got to our table. I wondered what that meant?

It was Layla, my regular waitress, and I smiled widely. "Hello, Miss Rayla. It's so nice to see you tonight. Do you want your usual?"

I opened my mouth to answer when I saw a flash of red, and Ax sat on the edge of the left side, next to Avery. "I'll have a Jack and Coke, sweetheart. Sorry I'm late, guys."

I glared at Ax in his black, opened, button-up shirt, tucked into gray slacks, the whole outfit was molded to his rippling, muscular body. I would drool right now if I wasn't so ticked off with the way he addresses Layla. "Her name is Layla," I growled out, trying to keep my temper in check since I was already on edge but failing to do so.

Ax stared at me for a long few seconds, so long that Layla fidgeted with her pen and paper, but I kept up the staring contest, not backing down to this wolf for any reason. After a while, his nostrils flared, and he said, "Sorry, Layla. Where are my manners?" His head turned toward her standing in front of the table. "I will make sure to remember the name from now on."

Her eyes widened as mine narrowed further on him, she was now shrinking under his gaze. "It's no problem, Mr. Rossey. No offense taken."

Ax side-eyed me, smirking as he folded his arms across his chest. Avery's gaze bounced between the both of us before he said, "Layla, darling, can I get a dirty martini?"

I sat back, trying to put a lid on my anger, and Falcon rolled his eyes at Avery's order. So the cold, logical heir did have feelings. I tried not to laugh, rolling my lips into my mouth, covering my smile with my hand like I was thinking about something.

"And you?" she asked Falcon, who thought for a second.

"I will take vodka and soda. Extra lime." She wrote it down and hurried off to the bar.

We were all quiet, not knowing what to say after all that, and I looked round for our drinks, wanting them ASAP. Layla argued with some guy near the bar, and I wanted my drink more than to wait for them to work it all out. "Rick, can you go help Layla?"

Rick saw where my attention was at the bar and blew out a breath as he shook his head. "Yeah. She really needs to dump that creep." He mumbled that last part as he walked off as the owner of Vinny's, Liam, came up to the table in his three-piece suit and oily, slicked-back hair.

Liam was a pig and made very bad fashion choices, but he was harmless all the same. It's one of the reasons I came to Vinny's. It was right in the middle of the strip, and most people knew this place was the first stop for a night full of fun.

He threw his arms out as he pretended like this was a scene from the *Godfather*. "All the Syndicate heirs at my bar? What an honor! Please, let me know if you need anything." He looked like he was going to try and sit next to Falcon. Falcon's whole body seized up, obvious he was uncomfortable with this idiot trying to join us.

I glanced at Cosmo, who read my mind and caught Liam's arm before he sat down. "Liam, I need to talk to you about the bar's security for a second."

Liam's eyes bounced between Cosmo and me, trying to decide what to do. When he saw I would not help him out of it, he beamed up at Cosmo. "Of course, Master Cosmo.

I would love to get your expert feedback." Liam looked at the rest of us as he said, "Please, excuse me," and walked off to the right with Cosmo.

Falcon exhaled, his face and body relaxed. I was about to poke fun at him for his visible distress over someone so insignificant when a familiar body raced up to the table in a huff.

"So, this is what you're doing now, Ray? You're pushing all three of your fuck boys in my face at our place?!"

To my surprise, it was Tre standing there in his usual white button-down and navy slacks, but something was off about him. He seemed a little on edge, a little unhinged. Normally, I liked that kind of thing, but on him, it looked pathetic.

I sat back with a sigh, mumbling under my breath, "Fucking shit, I can't catch a break."

[1] I stared down at my hands in my lap, letting go of every piece of me that was not the Syndicate leader I was and peered up at him with a blank face. The one that screamed I didn't give a fuck, and I would fucking cut you into pieces and feed it to birds without a second thought.

"First off, Tre, what makes you think that you can just come up to my table and confront me like this?" He opened his mouth, but I continued as if his words were insignificant. "Two"—I threw up two fingers before folding them and resting my chin on it—"you broke the one and only rule I had while we were having our fun. You

---

1. Song: All About Me by Syd

knew the consequences of those actions. I made that very clear from the beginning." I stared into his eyes, letting him know I was dead serious about this next part. "And, three, I left you in that hole in the desert for a reason. I told you to not be in my presence again, and look what you're doing?" I waved my hand up and down toward him. "You must have a death wish."

"Hole in the desert? I need to hear about this one later," Avery said, adding an extra layer of context for Tre, letting him know we were on the same side.

Before Tre could utter a single word of rebuttal, Cosmo zoomed across the room, creeping up behind him like death himself. I lifted my arms off the table in anticipation, smirking as Cosmo slammed Tre's face into the table, causing it to shake from the impact. He growled in his face, fangs out, "Even though you're a human, I thought you had better survival instincts than this."

Tre tried to wiggle under his grasp, his eyes pleading for me to help. "Ray. Ray, I can't live without you. I need you, baby. It was one fucking mistake. Can't you forgive me? Can't you remember the good times?"

I tilted my head back as I laughed and laughed like his declaration was the funniest thing I had heard in a while. The heirs were watching the whole thing with rapt attention, seeing how I would handle this situation. "You want me to forgive you? You want me to remember the good times?" I cooed as I leaned forward, "Oh, Tre, you were nothing more than a pretty body to pass the time with. Nothing more, nothing less." I controlled my voice, taking on a deeper, deadlier edge. "And you broke the rule.

It's not a hard one to follow, but it seems you think you are above the rules, and I don't have time for incompetence."

Tre opened his mouth again, but, this time, I slapped my hand onto his face, grabbing his attention as Cosmo shifted his arm to keep his body pinned down. I stood slowly and leaned down, letting my lips graze the shell of his ear. "Now, Tre, this was always the problem with you. You never did your research. You never figured out who you were really talking to . . . like how you just accused the other Syndicate heirs of being my fuck boys." His eyes turned into saucers as he quivered.

"I . . . I . . . I . . ."

I scraped a nail down his face, enjoying the blood bubbling up and oozing down the side as he whimpered. "Now, I think you are going to need to apologize to the other heirs. Don't you think so? Good faith as the mayor's son and what not."

"I . . . I'm sorry. I didn't realize that you all were friends. My deepest apologies." His voice was shaky as I kept his head pinned to the table, facing Avery and Ax.

Ax puffed out a laugh, looking at Tre like an insect, while Avery tilted his head and seemed like he was trying to figure something out. Layla started to make her way over with the drinks, so I let go of Tre's head. Cosmo dragged him off the table and dropped him to the floor like two hot rocks while I sat back down, cleaning my hands with a napkin.

Rick was helping Layla when his eyes went to the floor, seeing Tre collect himself, as he stepped over him and handed me my drink with a shake of his head. "Damn boy just doesn't know when to quit."

"They never do," I said as I put the drink against my lips and sipped. Usually, I was a mixed-drink girl. I liked complex flavors and surprising colors, but on collection night, I always had a vodka Redbull. There was something about mixing an upper and a downer that got my blood pumping.

Just when I thought we were done with the idiot, Tre peeked his head over the table. "Now that I have paid for my crimes, and you're not seeing any of these men, when can we talk about us? I miss you so damn much, Ray."

His whiney voice grated on me, so much so, I lifted my hand and massaged my temple. Cosmo looked like he was about to grab his neck and twist it off, and we couldn't have that. He was still the mayor's son and human. That would bring unwanted attention to us. I let out a long, pitiful sigh. "Rick, darling, I need you to take out the trash. And, Tre, learn this lesson here and now, before things get worse for you later. You were just a dick, a toy, someone that has never been and would never be my equal. A nonthreatening experiment. We ran in a few of the same upper circles, so I thought, sure, give the human a shot, but you are a disappointment, and, now, no longer of use to me. If you are no longer of use to me, then you have no business being around me. Now, get out of here before I let Cosmo break the toy I no longer want." His face turned sour, crushed by my words, but if burying him in the sand out in the desert didn't solidify we were over, then I needed to make it painfully clear.

Rick yanked him by the collar, hauling him out as he lectured him on never being in the same room with me again, or it would cost him his life. Cosmo calmed down the farther Tre got, and I smirked. He always enjoyed the breakups, it gave him a reason to beat on each of them.

"Well, damn, Ray, you about crushed that boy into dust," Avery said, smiling like a loon. Then his smile straightened as his voice kept that upbeat tone. "Oh, pray tell, what was that golden rule that the poor kid broke to be so savagely torn apart?"

All three were giving me their full attention, waiting for an explanation, so I kept my eyes on the dancing crowd, sipping my drink as I explained, "There were two offenses Tre did that were inexcusable." I took another drink, savored it for a second, before setting it down on the table. "I don't date in the normal sense. I have little fuck boys I play with on occasion to pass the time, have some fun with." The air around me shifted, a violence swirled around the booth, and I didn't understand why, so I kept going.

"I only have one rule when you become my fuck boy." I turned to Avery, using my vampire speed to get right at the crook of his neck, and I ran a finger over his carotid artery as I breathed against his skin, loud enough for the others to hear. "I own you. Your body, your blood, your soul, and until I release you, no one, no one is allowed to have what is mine."

Avery inhaled sharply, and I smiled before I sat back down just as fast. I snagged my drink back up and took a gulp, scanning the table to see Ax looking at Avery like everything was his fault, and Avery had a slightly dazed expression before taking a drink of his martini, and Falcon couldn't stop assessing me.

"And the other offense?" Falcon asked. His curiosity piqued at the whole interaction.

My face fell, and my eyes turned cold. The leader of the Syndicate came forth as I put my drink down, stared out at the dancing crowd with their carefree lives. I never minded my life, what I was born into, I was good at it, but that didn't stop me from envying the rest of the world for their no-fucks-given attitudes.

"He disrespected the Syndicate. Disrespected you three. No one, not a single soul in my city is allowed to disrespect the Syndicate and its leaders." They shifted in their seats, but I continued, looking at each of them in earnest. "I don't give a shit how we treat each other behind closed doors. I don't care if you hate me or not. Get along with me or not, but when we are out here, we are a unified front. Unbreakable." Something like respect creeped in their eyes, and I took another drink. "So, no. He does not get to get away with calling you three my fuck boys when you are far and above that. Above him. He needed to learn his lesson right then and there that he is beneath us, and if I had to, I would crush him and his father like the bugs they are, mayor or not."

The whole table fell quiet, everyone lost in thought, when Layla rushed over to the table. "Rayla, I'm so sorry. I was sure I told Ryan to put him on the don't let in list, but—"

I gave her a cocky smile. "Don't worry about it, Layla. I can deal with the riff raff myself." I winked at her, giving her a sultry smile, and she blushed as she put a second drink in front of me, and I downed my first and slid the glass over toward her.

As soon as our fingers touched, Layla said, "If you need anything, Rayla, anything, just flag me down. Kay?" Her eyes drilled into mine longer than necessary, and I knew what she was talking about, it wasn't the first time Layla had offered herself, but I just smiled and tilted my drink to her.

"Thanks, Layla." I knew she was bi, and if I was into girls, I would totally take her up on it, but, alas, I was only into dick.

"What was that about?" Ax rumbled out, more pissed than when Tre came over.

I turned toward him, about to tell him none of his business, when Avery's sly smile slid into place as he leaned into me. "Why, Miss Rayla, do you swing both ways?" His eyes twinkled with mirth, and I rolled my eyes.

"Ha! Wouldn't that make our jobs easier." Rick said as he stood with his back turned on the right side of the booth.

"Rick," I warned, best friend or not, I didn't want to be embarrassed in front of the other heirs.

He turned, shining that pretty-boy face of his at me, flashing me fang as he leaned on the top of the booth. "What, RayRay? It's true. If you dated girls, you would probably already be settled down, in something serious and established." And not have to deal with any more fuckers like Tre, his silent words spoken loud and clear.

I took my second drink and downed about half of it, glaring at Rick as I mumbled, "If you weren't my best friend . . ."

I left it out there, but he finished it as he laughed. "Oh, I would've been dead a long time ago." He raised an invisible glass, and I smiled as I nodded, raising my real glass to that and drank down another large full.

All the boys were practically done with their drinks, so I thought we should get this show on the road. "You guys ready? I think I'm done here."

They all nodded, and I scooted toward Falcon to get out. He stiffened again, eyes opening slightly as he inhaled. I didn't want him to panic so I said, "Are you going to get out?"

That seemed to wake him up, and he jumped out of his seat. I smiled at him, hoping I didn't piss him off or something because then tonight would be really awkward.

I got up, Cosmo and Rick planting themselves firmly at my sides with the heirs trailing behind. I could feel their excitement and hesitation, not knowing where they fit in, but it's not my job to hand hold them. They needed to boss up and figure it out. This would be interesting.

CHAPTER 26

FALCON

I COULD STILL FEEL the heat from her body next to mine as I followed the Desmond crew out of the bar. I couldn't get the night before out of my head. The way her body reacted to my touch, my magic. How her eyes shined even brighter underneath the moonlight. Or how even now I could recall those soft moans and delicate whispers of pleasure I wanted to produce from her again and again. If I didn't already know that she was a vampire, I would think she was a mage that somehow figured out how to ensnare my mind and body.

It could also be that she was my mate, the one and only person that my magic couldn't touch, but I pushed that into the back of my mind for my own sanity. I didn't think any of us could handle something that earth-shattering. I wanted to get to know her more . . . and what I knew so far, I thoroughly enjoyed.

I reminded myself the only reason she would radiate body heat, logically, was because she had fed a decent amount recently. Yes. That was all it was. It wasn't my body involuntarily reacting to her closeness. It wasn't my cold, dead heart waking up from its twenty-plus-year slumber after finding the only person in this world that interested me. No. That was most definitely not happening.

I banished all those thoughts as we moved through the crowd, watching how every single eye in this place was on us. Gazes laced with lust and desire, some shining with respect, and others shadowed in fear. The Desmonds had been running this city well, holding up the Syndicate name at all costs, which reminded me about what she said minutes ago.

I don't know why I was surprised by her admission, by her dedication and loyalty. I could tell she also shocked Avery and Ax with her words and the honesty behind them. Even though we hadn't been raised together, hardly knew each other, she stuck her flag in the sand and claimed us as one unit, telling us, essentially, to get on board. It was admirable to see, when just hours ago, we were fighting her for her hand, something she desperately tried to get out of.

The enigma that was Rayla vexed me. My eyes snagged on the seductive sway of her hips, the commanding confidence as she walked through a crowd, and the sheer brutality as she threatened that fucker, Tre. I worked hard to keep my hands from lighting up the whole table in flames as she held his face on the surface. I would've made sure it was only a one-to-two-degree burn, just enough to get the message across that he was not to talk to Rayla ever again.

She was also holding herself back, keeping her voice low as her muscles tensed, her other hand digging into the cushion behind her as she held him down easily with the other. I thought the only reason he still had his head was because he was the mayor's son, other than that, she seemed like she would've done away with him. I recalled the absolute animalistic outrage on her brother's face, he wanted to do worse than kill him.

When he slammed his head on the table, I for sure thought the table would break. His anger seemed to only be in check whenever Rayla said something. Their bond deeper than the traditional adopted-sibling bond. Was that Ternin's plan when he adopted him twenty-two years ago?

We walked out the door, the air outside so dry and hot that it made me wish I hadn't worn my vest, but it went with the outfit, so it was staying on.

Rick shot ahead, popped the trunk, and threw a mini duffle out to Cosmo who immediately unzipped it, pulled out a pair of boots, and set them on the ground in front of Rayla. She held her hand out, all of them acting like this was routine, as Cosmo handed her some black pants.

We all watched as she bent over, her peachy ass carved to perfection, covered with a thin layer of lace and red sheer material, as she lifted her bare feet out of her red-bottom heels and put them through each pant leg, she shoved her feet into each waiting boot before sliding the fabric up her thighs, pushing up her mini dress at the same time.

As observers, we only got a flash of that pearl skin with the thin red lacy fabric settled between her gorgeous globes as she slipped her pants over her ass. Ax licked his lips, and Avery's eyes zeroed in on her flesh. I might be more covert, not ogling her for all to see, but I was also a red-blooded male and found her stunningly gorgeous, and, therefore, watched shamelessly. I reminded myself I also found her smart and intriguing. A deadly mix for someone like me.

Cosmo glared at us, letting us know he saw all our expressions and didn't like it, as she turned around. She sat on the open trunk and lifted each boot to lace them up. "Before we do collections, I'm taking you boys out for a treat."

Avery stepped forward, his sexual charm on obvious display. "A treat? And what did we do to earn such a thing?"

She rolled her eyes as she finished the last boot and stood up with her hands on her hips. "Look, our dads want us to get along, and I agree. We are all the next in line, and we'll need to be able to work with each other regularly. I'm not the easiest person to get to know, but I can try for you guys. I can try for the betterment of the Syndicate." Cosmo grabbed her heels from the ground and put them in the mini duffle before putting them in the trunk and shutting it. He seemed to do a lot of these types of gestures, anticipating the things she needed done and doing them. Their relationship was intriguing.

"So, I'm going to take us to the one place where we can be ourselves without prying eyes and treat you to the best Mexican food you will have in your lives. Come on." She gave a brilliant hundred-watt smile, and I couldn't help it as my lips turned up in response. She tied up her hair and turned around, her Syndicate tattoo on display on the back of her neck, as she slung her leg over a single-seat motorcycle, and my lips turned downward.

"Um . . ." Ax started as he looked around, not finding what he needed. "So, it looks like my driver didn't stick around . . ." I noticed my driver wasn't here, either.

I recalled the conversation I had with my father before I left, him insisting Mali take me to the location, assuring me Rayla had everything we would need. As I watched Avery search for his car, his face fell as he realized what I had. Our fathers did this on purpose.

Rayla gave a small chuckle as Cosmo blew out a frustrated sigh. "Well, looks like you guys are all going to ride with Cosmo."

Before I could even reject that idea, Rick called out, "Shotgun!" Then ran to the passenger door and opened it for the rest of us.

Avery and Ax called out at the same time, "Window seat!" Then they all looked at me with smug little smiles. *Fuck.* I pulled out my phone, hoping that there was another way around being stuck between those two.

The three of us were cramped into the backseat of Cosmo's car. "Fuck, Ax, do you need to take up all the fucking room?" Avery's pissed-off voice sounded next to me as Ax growled.

"Maybe get some fucking muscles, then spout your mouth off." I rolled my eyes. We haven't even left the parking lot, and they were complaining.

Avery scoffed, looking out the window as he puffed out. "I don't need to over complicate my body with muscles. I'm toned and delicious. You're just annoyingly big." I was on my five-hundredth silent curse to my father, wishing him the most heinous death imaginable for putting me through this.

After we realized our drivers had left us, we called around and found out that our fathers put a no-ride threat out to everyone on the strip, telling them not to pick us up at any cost or else they would answer to them.

So, now I was stuck between these two bumping idiots, complaining about whose body was better than the other's. I wished I would've been able to ride on the bike with Rayla, but she took off before we even got in the car, but I was not the only one that was ultra pissed. Cosmo was thin-lipped, white-knuckling it the entire time, only pointing to the backseat when he knew he could do nothing about it.

[1] Rick was the only one that didn't seem fazed by the whole thing. He kept humming a song to himself until we got to a traffic light and pulled up right next to Rayla. He stuck his body halfway out the car as he screamed, "RayRay!"

She turned her head, her hair pulled back into a high ponytail, her Syndicate tattoo on full display behind her

---

1. Song: Twinbow by Marshmello & Slushii

neck, and smiled as she tilted her head down to smirk at Cosmo. "Looks like you fit everyone. That's awesome!"

Cosmo glared at her, his eyes saying a thousand words I couldn't hear, but, apparently, Rayla heard them all as she laughed a big belly laugh.

"Aww, come on, Cosy. Don't look so sad. If you want, I will race ya?" Her eyes lit up like the neon lights of the strip, blinding and all-consuming.

"No, Ray. Don't you dare think about it," Cosmo warned, but she looked back at the road and then back to him, an evil smirk playing along her lips.

"Raayy."

Cosmo's warning rang out, deep and foreboding, but as soon as the light turned green, she yelled, "Go!"

Cosmo cursed loudly, Rick sighed as he slumped into his chair, and Rayla took off like a bat out of hell. Cosmo's engine revved up for a second before he shot after her. He looked back at us in the rearview mirror, shook his head, and pressed a button underneath his seat. I heard a release button, and his car shot off even faster, the city lights now looking like streaks in the darkness. NOS. He turned on the NOS because the car was so heavy with the three of us back here.

When he caught up next to her, he yelled out, "Rayla! Slow down. Now!"

Her response was to pop a wheelie and turn down an alleyway, making my heart skip a couple beats from the pure shock and fear I felt. Ax was laughing, while Avery was watching her in awe. *What the fuck was wrong with these two?*

Cosmo growled out as Rick told him she was taking Riverside to get to Twentieth Street. He sped up just to use his emergency brake to turn left on the next street. Swerving so hard that all three of us dug our hands into the leather seats in front of us. I could barely hear him grumbling about adrenaline-high princesses over the whooshing air, and how he would wring her neck for giving him a heart attack.

I didn't want to mention he shouldn't talk about harming an heir in front of the rest of us, causing us to now be in the position to defend her when I wholeheartedly agreed that she needed punishment for that little stunt. It was fine when she was just some other person I didn't know or see, now that I had spent a little time with her, observed her, I was finding myself uncomfortable with the stunts she was pulling. *What if something went wrong?* I knew she was a vampire and could heal fast, but you can't heal from head decapitation.

She flew by right in front of us, and Cosmo swerved to the left, this time. He revved up his car and flew down the road as fast as he could, but she was still beating him by a car length.

She slowed down as she signaled, she was turning into the parking lot, and Cosmo finally let out a breath filled with ease.

She entered this dirt parking lot right in front of an old bario-style house. The house was simple—white bricks, one story, windows facing the street, as it was shaped like a rectangle going long ways with a chain-link fence around it.

There were a lot of cars in the dirt parking lot that seemed like it used to be a front yard at one time. With the windows down, you could hear the Hispanic music, the beat and rhythm bumping at a fast tempo. Rayla was off her bike and already up the three steps by the time we all climbed out of the car.

She opened the door and walked right in as she yelled, "Nana, I'm here!"

We moved to follow, but Cosmo called out to us, "Hey! Just a word of warning. Nana is like family to us, so if you fuck with her, the whole night will be shot, okay? Just do what she says, and, above all else, be respectful." He turned on his heel and jogged up the steps, following Rayla.

Rick smiled at all of us as he waved us forward. "Don't worry, Nana knows all about the Syndicate and will be nice to you, but Cosmo is right. Don't mess with Nana." We all followed him through the door with a sign overtop that said, Casa Nana.

Something was bugging me, so I asked, "Why do you guys think we would mess with her?"

Rick glanced back at us, a smile on his face as his hair fell in front of his eye. "We don't. It's just a warning we give to all supes since Nana is human." *Human?*

We entered the house and were greeted to a complete transition from home to full restaurant. We were standing in the main room. Booths lined the walls as tables were in the center. There was a bar toward the back, only a single door next to it that led to the kitchen. It wasn't large in any sense of the word, but it had this cozy, homey vibe that put you at ease.

Rayla high-fived the bartender, saying a few words in Spanish, before popping her head though the kitchen door. "Nana! Your favorite granddaughter is here!"

A full-figured woman with her gray hair pinned up, wearing an apron, came bursting out of the kitchen. "Mijita!" She grabbed Rayla in a big bear hug. "¡Te he estado esperando toda la noche!" The woman pulled Rayla away immediately, as she sounded like she was scolding her, "¿Por qué pones a tu pobre nana en este tipo de estado?"

"Why, to keep you on your toes, Nana." Rayla laughed as the woman swatted at her with the towel slung over her shoulder. The woman smiled at Rayla fondly as she rolled her eyes and complained.

"You've always been my naughty little child. Where is the good one? My little Cosmeito and Rickatón?"

Cosmo and Rick stepped up and gave her a hug. She squeezed them like they were her own kids, fussing over all three of them. Complaining about how they were not married and giving her grandbabies. How they all needed to visit her more often, and, finally, how they all were skin and bones, chiding Rayla's father for not feeding them enough.

She started to usher them to some chairs when Rayla stopped her. "Nana. I wanted to introduce you to some friends of ours. Ax Rossey, Avery Glovefox, and Falcon

Winstale." The woman's eyes widened as she realized who we were.

She immediately turned toward all the people in the dining room and called out, "Last call. We will need this room cleared in five minutes." Some of the people looked bewildered, but others nodded, knowing the drill, apparently.

As soon as the place cleared out, she walked to the door, locked it, shut all the blinds and windows, and turned off the open sign in the window. "There"—she turned toward all of us—"now you can have privacy for your meal." When we didn't move, she waved her hands at us. "Sit. Sit. Guapitos."

Rayla smiled as she and Cosmo shoved a few tables together in the center for us as the woman went to the bar, plucked a few menus, and handed them to Avery, Ax, and me. "Pick whatever you want. It's on the house." She pointed to Rayla, Rick, and Cosmo. "Those mischief makers already know what they want." She eyed them like she was grilling them but then winked and went back into the kitchen.

Rayla sat down, waving at the three of us. "Come, come." The guy behind the bar started to make drinks, even though none of us had ordered. "So"—Rayla put her chin on her hands as she gave a genuine smile—"the best thing to get is the chilaquiles."

Rick dragged the chair to her left out and scoffed. "Naw. You need to get one of the burritos, chimichanga style, with red sauce. It's dynamite!"

As Rayla scowled at Rick, Cosmo moved into the chair on Rayla's right and smirked. "You both are wrong. It's the chorizo plate. Breakfast for dinner is always the way to go."

Rayla reluctantly nodded. "It is a good choice, and breakfast for dinner is the bomb, but if we are going with the best overall dish, it's chilaquiles with lots of hot sauce." Rayla and Rick started to argue passionately, while Cosmo interjected only when he had something to say, which was usually in Rayla's favor.

The three of us outsiders sat down, watching them all talk with ease, almost like a normal group of friends and not the heir and higher members of the Desmond clan of vicious vampires. Avery was quick on the uptick and snagged the seat in front of Rayla. Ax let out a low growl before he grabbed the back of the chair across from Rick and slumped in it. I then took the chair in front of Cosmo and watched everyone.

Avery waited until there was a break in the debate before he asked what I was sure was on all three of our minds. "So, what's the story about this place? She's not really your grandmother, right?"

Rayla leaned back with a viper's smile while Rick and Cosmo looked at him with frowns. I guess that was not the right thing to say, but I didn't know why since he was giving facts. None of us had any grandparents, that was the whole reason our fathers had teamed up as young men. They had no families to lean on, even before the Awakening.

"No, she is not"—she lifted a finger to her lips—"but I wouldn't say that with her in ear shot if I were you." She laughed, and her two escorts relaxed, taking their cues from her. I wouldn't doubt that if she said we were now enemies that these two wouldn't hesitate to attack. Loyal to her, even if it would be their own death.

She patted both on the back before leaning forward, talking in a hushed tone so we all had to lean in to hear her words. "Back when I was about eight, we had some trouble. Some fucker claimed that my dad's sire, the first vampire, had made him and told him to challenge his position in this world. It was a bit of a bloody battle, and he repeatedly tried to kidnap and or harm me to get to him."

I was desperately trying to recall this, but I think my father was still in the heat of his grief and was not keeping up with his friends. Something like this would normally be talked about, but it was only a few years after our mothers' passing, and I know those years had been rough on all the bosses.

"Nana is the mother of one of my dad's guards. He changed and joined the clan before I was born. He died when I was about two, taking a UV bullet for my dad." She glanced down at her hands like she was paying her respects before she continued. "Nana never blamed my dad, not once, for what happened. After my mom died, my dad wanted to make sure we were seen in public, showing how strong we were. He always took us here to visit her, to patron her business as well as give her some money since her son, Paco, was the main earner for the family."

She motioned to both Cosmo and Rick. "The first time she met us, she called us sour pusses and chastised my dad. Said that kids our age needed to have full bellies and laughter in the air around them. She made it her personal goal to make sure that happened." She turned toward the kitchen door with fondness, both Cosmo and Rick smiling at the memories.

"When that shit went down a few years later with that impostor, my dad had all three of us live with Nana until the war between them was over. It took about six months, and ever since then, she has been our nana, through and through. We would die for that woman in there." The vow in her voice spoke to the depths that she felt for that woman, that she would protect her with her life if need be.

Rick nodded. "For six months, that human woman had to deal with three rowdy, pretentious, troubled eight-year-old vampires *and* taught us Spanish." He laughed out in disbelief. "I still don't know how she put up with us."

Cosmo spoke up, his deep, serious voice coming out strong. "That's why this place is our place. We frequent it often to make sure that everyone knows that this place is heavily protected."

"It's also the only place where we can get good food and be scolded at the same time." Rayla laughed as soon as the woman they all revered came over to our table.

She pointed to Cosmo, then Rayla, then Rick. "Chorizo, chilaquiles, and burrito chimy-style." Then she turned to us. "What do you dears want from your nana?" When none of us said anything right away, she shoved her hands onto her hips and scowled. "Come now, boys, you two look like you need some more meat on your bones." She eyed Ax. "This guapo looks like he's starved."

When we all gave her confused looks, Rayla kept her mouth shut, shaking with how hard she was laughing while not saying a thing.

"Come now. Nana will take care of you. Fill those bellies nice and full so you can do the runs tonight. Now what do you want? Do you want me to pick?" She had a twinkle in her eye that said she would have fun with that if we let her, so I was the first to speak up.

"I will take the two beef tacos." Hoping I ordered the right thing.

She nodded with a smile. "Two beef tacos with rice and beans."

I opened my mouth to tell her just the tacos when someone kicked me under the table. Rayla was smiling sweetly while Cosmo's demeanor didn't change, so I kept my mouth shut as I glared at the two of them, not knowing which was the kicker . . . but I had a feeling it was Rayla.

Avery gave her a smile worth a million bucks as he said, "I will have the chilaquiles, por favor."

Nana's smile widened. "Por supuesto, niño bonito." Her eyes took a bit longer to leave him before she shifted her attention to Ax.

He smiled like he was winning a game I didn't know we were playing as he said, "Whatever Nana wants to feed me, I will eat."

The woman practically squealed in delight. "Oh, I won't disappoint you, mi gran chico guapo!" She bolted away from us, calling out to someone in the back in excitement.

Rayla gazed at him in appreciation as she shook her head. "I don't think you know what you got yourself into."

Rick's eyes were wide as he said, "Man, you got guts." Cosmo was oddly silent as he watched the man at the bar bring over some drinks.

"Finally," he mumbled when he thought no one was paying attention, but I was always watching.

The dark-complected man with wide eyes and a curved nose set down on the table a tray of drinks. He passed a Bloody Mary to Rick, a particularly red Sangria to Rayla, a brown liquid to Cosmo, a stout beer to Ax, a martini to Avery, and set down a clear drink in front of me. Cosmo thanked him, they went back and forth with some Spanish before he turned around and went back to the bar.

I flicked my eyes down at my drink, trying to figure out what it was without touching it when Cosmo spoke up, "He has a touch of spirit magic. He can do little things like read the moods off people and know what they prefer to drink without even asking them."

I crooked my eyebrow up as I sniffed the drink and found that it was a vodka soda with extra lime. Cosmo let a hint of a smile creep up his face as I drank a sip and found it was top shelf vodka and specifically to my liking. I turned and saw the bartender watching, so I raised my glass, thanking him. He smiled and nodded as he was cleaning a glass.

"So, about this run—" Ax started, but Rayla interrupted.

"Look, the run is easy. I take on the harder clients to deal with when it comes to collecting our weekly take. There could be some of the people that we know are skimping, some that have a little power and like to push back, or some that are just getting delinquent and need a firm hand to remind them who is boss. That's all we're doing tonight, so let me do the talking, and be my backup." She smiled, but it was the kind that devils gave when they made a deal with you that they knew you couldn't fulfill.

"All right, Little Siren, we will play it your way because we are in your town, but if you ever come into my neck of the woods, you're going to play my backup. You got that?" I almost rolled my eyes at his need for the declaration, but I guess some men needed to have it known, said out loud. I preferred that my prey not know, so that when I did strike, they never saw it coming.

Avery leaned back, completely at ease as he cockily said, "Anyway, when are we going to get an encore of your show last night?"

I saw everyone's reaction. Rick snickering behind his hand, Ax smirked as he nodded in agreement, Rayla's lewd smile as she leaned forward before she responded, but the most interesting was Cosmo's uncharacteristic snarl as he answered, "Never. Never again."

Gone was Avery's smiles and charm as he faced Cosmo with a deadpan expression. "Was I asking you?"

Cosmo looked like he was about to fly over the tables when Rayla let out a loud laugh. "Oh, Avery, stop messing with him. You can't blame my brother for not wanting me to be in that kind of position again. Even if it was fun putting you all in your place."

I heard all her words, but I kept my eyes on Cosmo the entire time and caught the slight stiffening of his body when she said the word brother. I cataloged it away for another day as I resumed watching the group.

"You never put me in my place," Ax called out happily as he took a few gulps from his beer.

Rayla tapped her chin as she rolled out, "Aaaawww, yes. I remember. I had to fight that she-wolf. So, do you always have others do things for you?"

Ax's eyes bulged out, shaking his head as he stammered for a second, not knowing how to get himself out of the predicament when Avery swooped in. "Well, you protecting that stuffy cub was a pure sight for sore eyes. I bet the Rossey's haven't had such a lively hunt for a while." Avery turned his attention toward me. "Also, the race looked exhilarating since you both were neck and neck."

Ax laughed out. "Oh, yeah, and how she out danced you. She won by a landslide."

Avery's chin wobbled as he grinned. His cheeks turned red, even as his voice and stance stayed the same. "Yes, well, I would expect to get beaten by a beautiful—"

"It's not his fault, I picked the most dick-hating lesbians I could find," Rayla admitted as she casually gulped down her drink.

A hand slapping the table sounded next to me, Avery pointing at Rayla with an assuming glint in his eyes. "I knew it!"

She crossed her arms with a smug smile. "Yes, and I also know it would've been a tie if you were able to use your sneaky little faerie magic on that third one. I'll admit, you had me sweating, but, in the end, I won, and that is a fact."

Avery rolled his lips in to try and keep the smile off his face as he lowered his head in defeat. "You're right. A win is a win, no matter what dirty tricks either of us used."

Her smile softened as she lifted her glass. "To someone from the Syndicate always winning." We all lifted our glasses to that.

[2] As soon as she set it down, some song pumped through the speakers and caught her attention. She pointed to the man at the bar. "Miguel, turn up the music."

He laughed as he grabbed a remote. "Only until Nana gets back. You know how she is about food and family time." Rayla nodded as the music grew louder.

The rhythm was catchy, and the beats hit in time with her swaying. As soon as a male voice popped out and started singing in Spanish, Rayla and Rick turned to each other and sang the chorus.

It was fascinating that she still had the capacity to be so . . . alive. After our mothers died, I figured we all had the same issues: growing up too fast, taking on too much responsibility as children, having a healthy dose of distrust

---

2. Song: Chantaje (feat. Maluma) by Shakira

for people as well as keeping our true selves locked up tight underneath the heir crown. Watching Rayla these past couple of days has been eye-opening in how I have led a dull and almost workaholic life.

Like, normally, I would've called in for food, made my own, or just skipped if I was in the middle of something. She had a standing weekly date that she came here to eat and relax with her closest friends. It was something I probably never would have.

At least until you tell her she is your mate, then you can have this, have her, forever.

I shook that pesky thought away, shoving it down, and now was not the time for something like that. Plus, if I brought that up now, she would just bolt for the hills, and I didn't want that, either.

The song switched up when a woman started to sing, and Rayla stood up. Rick followed when she put out her hand to him, and he expertly twirled her around and away from the table.

She moved gracefully as she went around Cosmo to a more open space. When the guy sang, Rick turned his head to Cosmo pointedly as Ray was faced away and sang that part to him. Almost like he was teasing him.

When Cosmo's eyes widened and his hand tightened around his glass, Rick laughed as he and Rayla danced, wiggling their hips to the song as they sang.

My mind wouldn't let me let go of what I just witnessed, and I pulled out my phone. Exceedingly curious as to what could make Cosmo react like that.

My eyes lifted as Rayla laughed, and Rick dipped her as they danced. Something inside of me erupted, something dark and harrowing, as my blood started to pump faster, and my vision turned red. I didn't realize I could have such visceral reactions to something like her dancing with another man.

I wasn't the only one feeling this way as I heard a creak of a chair and a low menacing growl behind me. Turning to see if Cosmo was as affected as us, I was shocked to see him watching them, not with anger or rage, but with a complicated expression. Like he was jealous and happy at the same time.

I must not have been the only one looking at him because when he moved his eyes toward us, he smirked, puffed out a laugh at us.

"For a brother so protective about dancing, it seems you don't care about those two grinding up on each other." Avery's haughty voice had some bite to it, and I realized he was also affected by the scene in front of us.

Cosmo played with the rim of his drink, picking it up and taking a slow pull as he smirked at us. I could feel Ax's rage from where he was sitting, hoping he did not make the mistake of jumping over the table to strangle Cosmo, but planned to back him up all the same. I didn't like that look he gave us, either.

He huffed out as he set down his drink. "Look, I would be less worried about them dancing and more worried if he asked any of you to dance."

That caught me off guard, and I turned back to the scene, reevaluating the situation. Rick's hands were not gripping her body like mine would be. He wasn't staring into her eyes lovingly or with worship. It was jovial, more kinship. His hips didn't grind into her body, more like they swayed with it. Then he smiled over at me and winked, and all my anger dissipated in seconds.

"Plus," Cosmo's humor-laced voice pulled my attention back. "Those two used to do salsa dance competitions before Rayla officially took on the second-in-command role. This is the only opportunity they have to stretch out those muscles."

"And where were you when they were taking the dance floor by storm? Polishing your weapons skill?" Avery cooed, sounding like he was trying to get under his skin.

Cosmo looked down at his drink. "I was watching from the crowd like a good brother." He lifted the cup and threw back the rest of his drink before setting it down, his voice coming out low and strong. "But know this, wherever Rayla goes, I do. I will never not be by her side. Never."

His threat came out loud and clear, and I smiled and nodded. "Wouldn't dream of splitting up siblings."

He glared at me and opened his mouth to respond when Rayla came back and sat down, rubbing her hands together in excitement. "The food will be coming out soon. I can smell it."

Cosmo snapped his mouth closed before signaling for another to Miguel as he lifted his glass.

Seconds later, the food arrived. Nana herself served all of us, telling all of us we needed to eat up after she winked at us and went back into the kitchen.

Rayla picked up her knife and pointed it at the three of us as her eyes darted to the kitchen door and whispered in a rushed voice, "You all need to eat up every bite of your food or else—" Nana came back out. Rayla, Cosmo, and Rick shoveled food into their mouths as they gushed to her how wonderful it was.

She frowned at Avery and me, her eyes growing sad like she was about to weep as she clutched her chest. "Do you hate my food?"

I looked at Avery, whose eyes widened as his fork hovered over his plate. "No! We just—"

She wiped at her eyes. "No. No. I understand. How could you possibly like Nana's food when I'm sure you are used to that big city fancy food." I looked over at Ax whose plate was already halfway done, which meant she was talking to Avery and me. *How the fuck did he do that?*

She walked over to Ax, cupped his mouth currently full of food as she cooed, "Oh, my grande guapo likes his nana's food, doesn't he?" His eyes shifted to Rayla for a second before he nodded and gulped down what was in his mouth.

"Yes! This is some of the best food I have had in a while." She immediately rose and clapped her hands.

"Big boys like you need lots and lots of food. I will get you another plate." Ax's eyes widened, a panicked expression pointed at Rayla in a plea at the mention of a second plate.

He was getting no sympathy from her as her wry smile said, *Told ya*. Nana smiled until she saw Avery and me again, her voice lowering as her shoulders hunched. "I guess I should take your plates away, seeing that you hate me and my food. I wouldn't want to burden big men like you with my small homestyle cooking."

Avery and I immediately clutched at our plates, not wanting to offend her, we shoveled in the food as fast as we could, telling her how amazing it was with the remaining air in our mouths. She immediately perked up, telling Rayla we three were lovely boys, and she should bring us over anytime.

After she left, Rayla and Rick busted up laughing, and Cosmo smirked at us. I cleaned my mouth as I grumbled, "You could've told us what was going to happen."

Rayla shrugged. "I tried. She just came out so fast. Plus, Ax knew the deal the second she came out of the kitchen." She pointed to his plate, sending him a wink and a smile. He perked up like a damn dog getting praise from his master, smirking at Avery and me like we were the idiots.

"I just don't think they know how to deal with women like I do."

Avery rolled his eyes before he turned to Ax. "You don't think I know how to deal with women? I bet you don't even know—"

I tuned out the rest of their pissing match as Avery and Ax continued to argue about who knew more about women. No, I watched Rayla, smiling as her eyes ping-ponged between them. She seemed amused by the interaction, enjoying it and laughing when someone made a certain point, which made the other try to refute that point.

Rick dug in, finishing what was on his plate quickly as he paid us no mind. It was Cosmo I caught sneaking glances at Rayla, at how she was interacting with us. I don't think he liked it too much, but that was an observation.

Nana brought out a whole new plate for Ax, who looked helpless as he stared at the mountain of food on the plate. Rayla took pity on him and snuck into the back to snag a to-go box before Nana came back out. She said the trick was to leave a couple bites on the plate so she didn't try to stuff you full.

When Nana came out and saw the to-go box, Rayla said that she snagged some chips and salsa for the road. Nana narrowed her eyes on Ax as Rayla popped up and said that we had to get going. She zoomed over to her and gave her a big hug. Rayla clung to her for a second, for once looking like a child as she closed her eyes and smiled at Nana's squeeze.

When Rayla pulled away, her face changed back into the hardened, cocky Desmond I was used to. Cosmo and Rick also gave her hugs, commenting on how amazing her food always was, and she blushed as she playfully swatted at them.

She then hugged Ax, Avery, and me, telling us we were welcome any time, and she would always have a plate ready for us. We thanked her and left.

I was the last one out the door, and before I crossed the threshold, she lightly touched my shoulder, and I turned toward her. She watched the others as they talked and laughed. "She needs someone like you, too."

My brows furrowed at her words. She smiled. "Rossey is good for her wild spirit, Glovefox will compliment her humorous nature, but you, Falcon Winstale, you can balance her out with your intelligence. Your foresight."

"Isn't that what Cosmo is for?" I knew this woman was smarter than she led on.

Her lips turned up into a smile that said she knew all the secrets. Her eyes focused on Cosmo next to his car. "That boy, he is to be by her side no matter what. He will eventually crumble to whatever she wants, and she needs that. She needs to have that kind of support." Then her assessing and wisdom-filled eyes turned to me. "But she also needs the one that will tell her no. Tell her to think things out first, and that boy won't ever tell her no."

I stared at her for a second, trying to figure out why she was telling me this, why she felt the need to pull me aside.

"Falcon, you coming?" Rick yelled out for me, and her face changed back into the smiling, sweet women as she waved at all of them.

"You better get going."

I nodded and turned away, heading toward the car. The wind howled in the night, and I felt a tickle on the back of my neck, a feeling of foreboding flooded me, and I looked back to see Nana watching me, giving me a slow nod before she turned and closed the door.

@Tpiola_

CHAPTER 27

WHEN WE LEFT NANA'S, I was in a light and good mood. I enjoyed watching them interact with Nana and observing how they would handle a strong female. She was one tough lady, full of love, and was sharper than she let others know. When I hugged her goodbye, she whispered in my ear, "Confiar en esos traviesos muchachos." I smiled and nodded before I left. As soon as my foot landed on that dirt parking lot, my chest expanded like I was able to finally breathe. To know that they passed her stamp of approval meant the world to me.

That elated feeling slowly ebbed away after the first two stops. They were so uneventful that it was almost boring. As soon as we showed up, they shoved the owed money at us, thanking me for giving them more time to get it all together. Their eyes kept flicking toward the other heirs, who were just standing there, as they shook in fear. I had to shake away the pissed-off feeling that took over my body after the second time. It seems word got out that all the heirs were together doing collections, and that spooked people.

I threw the bag of cash into Cosmo's trunk and slammed the hood. Gentle was not my forte to begin with, but even I winced at the sound after it closed.

"Hey!" Cosmo complained behind me, but I rolled it off my back and leaned against the car with my arms folded.

An arm magically appeared around my shoulders as Rick said in a cheery voice, "Don't look so disappointed. I'm sure the next one will put up a fight."

I puffed out a laugh. Appreciating his optimism that I was desperately lacking. Collections were always a fun time for me, a time to work off some aggression, blow off some steam. What was better than knocking around the heads of some low lifes? I remembered the last group's gaze, and who they were nervous about. It was my turn to glare at the three reasons this whole thing had been going so smoothly and ruining my good time.

Ax already had his eyes on my face when I gave them an all-your-fault look. "What?" he exclaimed as he threw his hands up. "What could I have possibly done now? It's not our fault they are scared of the Syndicate."

I kicked off the car and marched to Ax, stepping in his face. Cosmo grumbled under his breath in the background about how I was mistreating his baby. I gave the damn thing to him, I could always get another one . . . If I felt like it. I stalked up to Ax, him looking down at me since I was only five six, and he was definitely over six feet tall. "Having you three is making everyone so scared that they are just throwing money at us."

"Isn't that a good thing? It means they understand not to mess with us." There was a smugness to Ax's voice that caused me to flash back to when we were kids. He had the same attitude then, and I punched him in the face. It seemed like history was repeating itself today.

My eyes darted to the side to see Avery and Falcon both confused like Ax. I guess I needed to show these boys how the Desmonds liked to keep their people in line. "Sure,"—I backed away to face them all—"if you're lazy."

As I stepped backward, the three of them stepped forward, all giving me looks filled with disbelief, surprise, or irritation. I hopped up, slamming my ass on Cosmo's car as I crossed my legs and leaned back. I heard his inner sigh, even if he didn't let it out. "If we're selling ice cream, then you're right. Having people fight us would be a problem, but we don't, do we? We work in the seedy part of the world, the part that even cops don't want to deal with because it's that dangerous." I sat up, Ax's and Avery's eyes glued to my breasts, while Falcon tilted his head as he watched me like a fascinating zoo animal. "We rule the criminal world, boys. If we don't keep them busy with fighting and punishments, then they will go quiet as they start planning something even worse. Trying not to catch attention as they build up their manpower, becoming an even larger problem. We Desmonds like to keep our criminals unorganized and stupid. That means knocking those heads around to make sure no brain cells stick."

494   KIRA STANLEY

I laughed at my own joke as I slid off the hood. I turned to Cosmo, smiling and batting my eyes at his scowl. "Who's next?"

Cosmo lifted his phone, lighting up his pale angular face as he scrolled. "Breken." My smile grew as I remembered what Layla told me, how he tried to force drugs on her. This would be a lot different, since I would be looking for more than just money.

I rubbed my hands together, heat radiating from my palms to my fingertips, as I widely grinned at all the boys. "This run is going to be much different from the others. This one will surely give me the exercise I have been itching for."

They all perked up as they huddled in closer, and I explained what was going on. How I got intel that this bookie of ours was turning rogue and trying to get into the drug game. That we needed to squeeze any information we could out of whoever was there because I bet money Breken would not be there. When I thought about it, the smarter play would be to place someone there that could take the beating but would buy them more time, time to finish the plan and get enough manpower to fight back.

They all nodded, except for Cosmo, who looked pissed. His eyes swirled with his calm, quiet anger, the kind you felt just before all hell broke loose. "Can I speak with you?" I turned and nodded. His head tilted as his nostrils flared, and he didn't take his eyes off me. "Alone."

"Be right back," I told the rest of them, and Rick explained to them that us siblings did that a lot. Avery chuckled in response as he said he was sure we did. *Whatever the fuck that meant.*

Cosmo led me over to the opening of an alleyway, shrouding himself in darkness as I was in the light. "Why didn't you tell me about this beforehand?"

I took a blood lolly out of my jacket pocket, unwrapped the paper, and stuck it in my mouth before I responded, "I didn't have time."

I watched with rapt fascination how his beautiful neck muscles coiled, and his fists crossed in front of his chest, pulling at his already-tight black shirt, showing me the lines of his pecs, and I licked my lips. Say what you want about my adopted brother, but he was fucking gorgeous.

"Rayla, did you hear me?"

My eyes were still glued to his chest, thinking about what it would be like to run my lolly in those grooves and lick up the trail behind. I shook my head when he cleared his throat. Scowling up at him for interrupting my amazing daydream. "What?"

His eyes rose to the sky as he mumbled he needed God to intervene to stop him from wanting to kill me. I smiled around my lolly, shoving his shoulder for him to look back down at me. "Hey, it's nothing we can't handle. Plus, now we have those three. This should be a piece of cake."

"Rayla"—he only ever called me by my full name when he was pissed—"I could've done more research. Found all the exits. Made sure we had the streets covered. There are a lot of things I could've done if you gave me only thirty minutes, an hour tops, to prepare." His voice at the end turned more into a whine, and I circled my arms around him, knowing I needed to cut off this fight quickly. I squeezed him tightly, burying my face into his chest, catching that spearmint and clean linen scent that was all his.

He trembled slightly, his arms raising hesitantly like he knew he would cave. "Ray . . . this isn't fair." I hugged him tighter, rubbing his back, and he melted as he gave in to me. He bent forward, digging his nose into my hair as he whispered, "You brat. You always get your damn way."

His deep voice settled into my skin, and my blood raced as my stomach fluttered. I needed to get out of this fast before I did something that I would regret. I pulled away, putting a finger on his chest as I laughed. "And don't you forget it."

It was almost like a spell was broken, his eyes flicked behind me, and he immediately straightened, putting his hands to his sides as his eyes bore into mine. "Fine. You win. What's the plan?"

I turned around, waving for him to follow me. "Oh, just violence, threats, and bloody destruction. The usual." Cosmo puffed out a laugh as we walked back to the car.

"Did the siblings work out their little love spat?" Avery called out. His face full of easy smiles, and his voice playful, but his eyes drilled into mine.

I didn't want to cause any issues, but I also couldn't let it slide. I raised an eyebrow at him, my face saying, *What? Are you jealous?* When his eyes narrowed on mine, I smiled and shrugged. "Yes, you see, Cosmo doesn't like it when I make plans like going after drug startups without a bigger plan than just busting in on them with violence on my mind only."

They all stared at me in silence, taking in what I said, as each of their faces contorted into various versions of shock or interest. That slowly ebbed away until they all glared at me or shook their heads like they were all in agreement about how ridiculous I was.

"Now, I'm glad that we're here. Who knows what kind of trouble you would get in!" Ax was the first to say as he crossed his arms.

"I bet you would've gone in there all by yourself, wouldn't you?" Avery tutted like he was scolding a child. Both their eyebrows were drawn together, worry for me sparkled in their eyes, but that was just because they didn't know me yet. They would find out today why I would be just fine.

A calm, cold voice cut the tension with logic. "But she is right. Something like this needs to be taken care of right away. We can't let this get any further than it already has. It breaks the covenant between the human government and our organization."

"Exactly." I smiled at Falcon, who didn't smile back but nodded to me, acknowledging our shared thoughts. That was good enough.

"But I agree with Cosmo. We should've made a plan." My smile fell, and, this time, I glared at him.

"I take it back!" I growled out, pissed that he ruined our bonding moment.

When Falcon tilted his head and pursed his lips at me, Rick chimed in to help.

"Her smile at what she perceived as comradery . . . that is what she is taking back." When Falcon still looked confused, Rick followed with, "Don't worry. You get used to it."

"Look," I huffed out, "the plan is to go in, rough up the patsy into talking about where the drugs are, then go there to fuck up all those people and destroy the drugs." I turned to walk to my bike when I switched back around to clarify, "Oh, and if they don't have the cook house there, then we need to keep one alive to show us where that is."

I stalked off toward my bike as I growled over my shoulder, "How is that for a stupid plan."

I swung my leg over my bike as they all climbed back into Cosmo's car. While it was nice they all got along about something, I didn't like it was against me. I needed to show these boys I'm not just some heir, that I was a boss in my own right and could handle something like this. They were all just along for the ride.

A ding came on my phone with the address as Rick waved out the window of the front seat. "See you there, Ray Ray!"

We pulled up to a dingy pawn shop right outside of the city. I stayed on my bike until the guys all climbed out of the car. A bit of satisfaction filled me when Ax stepped out and put his hand to his back, Avery practically jumping out of one side, and Falcon's frown deepened as he sharply tugged his suit vest. Don't know what that was about but I didn't have time to worry about it.

"All right, boys, if my hunch is right, it will only be one or two people inside, so let me handle it." I stepped forward, planning to bust through the door when a hand tightened on my biceps.

A large muscular chest bumped into my back, causing goosebumps to erupt along my arm as a rough voice whispered against the shell of my ear, "And if your hunch is wrong?" A piece of me wanted to relax, to melt into Ax, let him hold me as I explained everything, then I remembered I needed to show these boys strength.

I yanked my arm out of his grip, turning around so fast his eyes widened as I was already in his face, nose to nose. "My intuition is almost never wrong, but if for some reason there's more than just one or two bodies, then I guess that's what I have all you for." I backed up, eyeing him up and down, trying to give off an unimpressed vibe, but I couldn't help but bite my inner lip at all his bulging, rippling muscles and scruffy auburn hair. He was the epitome of a manly warrior, and I wanted to ride his face to the next world.

His lips tipped up like he could hear my thoughts, and he stepped forward, so I blurted out, "Unless you can't handle a couple of people on your own . . . maybe Avery can cover for you." His eyes went from lust-filled to rage in two seconds. Avery laughed behind us, saying he could handle whatever I put in his path, and Ax's eyes turned even more fierce. I sped up to the door, not wanting to start a fight out here when we needed to look like a unit inside. "Ready to go in?"

Ax stomped up next to me, smacked my hand off the door, and yanked it open as he growled angrily, "Ladies first."

I shook the hand that he smacked, turning my eye downward and sticking out my lip like I was hurt. Once his eyes softened, I let out an evil laugh, running my hand up his chest, snagging his chin, and yanking his face down to my level. "You'll have to hit much harder to make me cry out." Then I walked into the store, leaving Ax drooling with the others trailing in behind me.

It was your typical pawn shop with rows and rows of used goods in the center, a spot where DVDs went to die off to the left, and a large jewelry case on the far back wall. I glanced back to Rick, nodding to let him know to turn the open sign and lock the door. "Knock, Knock! We are here for the delivery."

I meandered around before I saw a nervous-looking guy in the back by the jewelry case. As I stepped closer, I could tell it was Breken's son, the one who assaulted Layla while she was staying with them. I bit the inside of my cheek to keep me from flying out and clocking this guy in his stupid face. I gazed at some of the jewelry, making sure not to spook him as I spoke. "So. Do you have what we are here for?"

He wiped at his sweaty brow, trembling as he shook his head and looked down at the floor. "Unfortunately, Miss

Desmond, we don't have the sum you're here for. My father would like—"

"Can I look at these?" I ignored his words, focusing my attention on a sparkly, gaudy, pink-jeweled ring that looked like it was well over three carats, if it was real.

He looked behind me at the guys as I smiled sweetly, tapping the glass to get his attention back as I pointed to the ring. "Of course." He shook his head, slid the door open as he reached up to the front and snagged the ring. He placed it on the glass, and I immediately plucked it up and slid it onto my center finger.

"It's a little snug . . ." I gave him a look like I was worried it wouldn't fit right, and he immediately relaxed, going into his sales pitch. Probably thinking I would take this as collateral or something. I swear, men could be so stupid sometimes.

"Oh, don't worry about that. We have a jeweler that could easily take care of that for you." He smiled up at me, relief filling his eyes, and I knew it was time to strike. I used my vampire speed to hop over the case, palming his head with my hand and slamming it onto the jewelry case, and it cracked where his head landed.

"What do you think, guys?" I said over his pain-filled moans, looking down at the ring and seeing it sparkle against this idiot's muddy-brown hair. "I think it looks good up close, but when I hold it far away like this, it seems to be missing something."

Avery moved, leaning up against the case next to the one my victim was on. "Yes, I can see what you mean. I think it needs some color around it . . . something . . ."—his eyes sparkled as his grin turned slightly manic—"red."

I cackled, enjoying him joining in on the fun without overstepping. "Yes! That's what's missing." I lifted him up by the collar with one hand as I backhanded him on each side with the hand wearing the ring, slicing up his face. I dropped him like a sack of potatoes and pretended to admire the ring in the light. "Yes. See." I bent down to the guy on the ground clutching his face as he curled up into the fetal position as I cooed out to him, "It looks so much better with some additional color to make it really shine."

I flicked my eyes down at him, my blood pumping as my adrenaline shot up at my own excitement of beating this man into a bloody pulp. I wanted to make him hurt, make him bleed, make him feel helpless and small like he did to Layla. Giving him a swift kick to the stomach, he retched as he cried out. I would have fun with this faerie, I would slice up his wings, strip by strip, making them—

A tap on the glass brought me out of my daydream. I snapped my head up, being called to focus on a set of calm-and-soothing-lilac orbs.

I shook my head, reminding myself I was here for a purpose. Drugs. I needed to find out about where they were making and keeping the drugs. I took a breath, breaking contact with Cosmo as he pulled back, standing up straight like he hadn't done a thing. Glancing around, I noted that Avery's and Ax's eyes were glued to the guy on the ground, a lustful violence lingering there like they wanted to see me inflict more, then I saw Falcon. His eyes were consumed by me, tracking every movement, every twitch, almost like he was trying to read my mind and figure me out.

I blinked a few times before I looked back down at the man clutching his stomach. "Now, I think you know this isn't about the money. Tell me that you're not so dumb to think that would be the only reason I am here."

The man stopped trembling instantly, his wide eyes turned up to me, and I could see the whites. "I don't know what you are talking about."

I could see the wall he was trying to build up quickly in his eyes. He didn't want me to break him, to get him to squeal. He feared Breken . . . or maybe the man behind Breken, but that was just who I wanted to know about. I needed to throw him off his game.

[1] I crouched down, ran my hand in his hair as I cooed, "Oh. So, you don't know? Well, then, that's all my fault. Boys, can you get my new friend a seat?"

I heard a shuffle behind me, the screeching of a chair, as I continued to smile and look non-threatening. "What's your name?"

Rick and Cosmo made their way around the jewelry cases, but I held my hand out to pause them. I needed to create a rapport first.

The idiot on the floor turned up, his muddy-hazel eyes and thin body slowly uncurling as he shoved some of his hair out of his eyes. His shaky voice came out, "E . . . E . . . Evan."

---

1. Song: Demons by Bryce Savage

My eyes softened. "Evan. Good name. Come with me." I stood up, putting my hand out, beckoning him to take it. "Let's just have a talk."

His eyes darted around, looking at the mean, scary men surrounding us. I giggled, sticking my hand out farther. "Don't worry about them. They will leave you alone. Promise." He pushed himself up to sit before he took a breath, lifted his gaze to me with a sparkle of cunning hope that he could convince me of his lie as he grabbed my hand. I would enjoy this.

I walked him over to the chair that the guys set in the center of the room. Ax growled at the guy, staring at us holding hands with pursed lips, Avery's face was oddly solemn and shut down from his normal cocky attitude. Falcon stayed observing the whole thing with hawk eyes, being his normal self. Cosmo and Rick knew the drill and followed my orders like normal because they knew if they ruined my plan, there would be hell to pay later.

I motioned for the guys to all stand a ways across from him. "I don't want him to be intimidated by you all when we talk, right, Evan?" My sweet-natured voice was trying to give him a false sense of reality. In working this job, I found that most men thought I was just a thrill seeker and didn't get my hands dirty, that this meant I was an easy target to lie to and manipulate. That I was some "weak woman" that could be swayed by emotions, and, in some cases, they were right, but not to their benefit.

"Now. Let's chat." Evan smirked at the guys before focusing back onto me, pretending to take me seriously. "So, what I want to know is where is Breken? He knew we were going to be here today to collect?" I let my pitch rise, letting him think I was just some bimbo with an anger problem, and that's why I hit him earlier.

"I really don't know. All I know is that he left me to run the store while he went somewhere to meet with a potential buyer for one of our higher end items." I nodded, keeping the act up as I slowly stood, tapping my finger on my chin as I walked around him, repeating his words to him.

I bent toward his ear, whispering like a lover as I asked, "So, you really don't know where he is, do you?"

He jerked at the sudden invasion of his space but stuttered out, "N-n-no. I don't. I swear on my mother."

I slowly wrapped my arms around his shoulders like a behind hug, earning a warning glare from Cosmo, but I ignored him. I let my arms circle tighter and tighter until both my arms were underneath his chin, and I squeezed. "I feel bad for your mother, Evan, because I don't believe you."

His choking sounds echoed in the room as he clawed at my arms, his whole body shaking as I whispered, "I hate liars, Evan. And just when I thought we were going to be friends." When his legs started to kick out, I released him. He collapsed in the chair, gasping as he clutched his throat.

"I'm not lying." His voice came out raspy, and I smiled. I used my speed as I grabbed his arms and bent them back, popping both out of their sockets and letting them hang at his sides as he cried out in pain.

I circled back around, crouching in front of him again. His eyes were bloodshot, and his pleas to put them back in fell on deaf ears. I raised my voice over his so he could hear. So they all could hear.

"You see, Evan, you think these men here"—I pointed to the line behind me—"are to protect me. To make sure that I don't get hurt from the likes of you." I laughed, letting my face go to the ceiling, and, like a switch, I stopped and turned my dead, unfeeling eyes onto him. "But I will let you in on a secret." I popped up, zoomed behind him as I gazed at the men I was talking about, whispering in Evan's ear like I was Death herself. "They're here to make sure that I don't go overboard. They're here to remind me why I need to talk to you and not just drag you down into my basement and have fun time with your insides." I let my whisper trail down to his neck, causing him to shiver. "And drain you dry until your corpse looks like a raisin."

I grabbed his hair and yanked his head back so hard he cried out as I leaned into his face and yelled, "They are here to help you!" I made an effort to calm down as he started to tremble, really grasping his situation now. I petted the side of his face with one hand while the other clutched his hair tighter. "Now, talk or else they are going to let me have my fun." I dug my nails into his throat as I squeezed. I could feel the blood dripping down my fingers, the plopping sound of it hitting the floor before he caved.

"Okay," he sobbed out, tears streaming down his face. "I will tell you. Please, just put my arms back into their sockets, and I will tell you what I know."

I let go and backed away as Cosmo and Rick jumped into action, popping the guy's arms back in roughly.

A hand dug into my back, and I knew it was my wolfish companion. "You know, Siren, that was so fucking hot that I have a huge tent in my pants. Are you going to take responsibility for it?" I smirked as I looked down and saw he did have a hard-on and was not too shy about showing it off.

A soft, lyrical voice crawled up next to me. "It's so interesting to see you work. I almost thought you lost it there." I turned my head toward Avery, Ax growling in my hair to get my attention back on him.

"I almost did." I didn't want to say anything more, but, of course, my all-seeing mage had to say something.

"That's what the tap was for, right? Cosmo saw you losing it and reminded you."

His voice was so matter-of-fact I puffed out a small laugh as I mumbled, "That mage is too damn smart for his own good."

"We're ready, Ray Ray," Rick called, and I moved out of their orbit and back to our weeping criminal.

"Okay, Evan—" I let my voice take a mocking tone. "Now, talk."

@Tpiola_

CHAPTER 28

It didn't take long for Evan to start babbling away about how Breken was at a warehouse not far from here. They told him he would get roughed up a bit but that we would eventually let him go alive. They would pay him twenty grand to be beat up, and he thought he could handle it. That was until I, apparently, gave him the crazy eyes.

I wanted to tie him up and attach the rope to the back of my bike, dragging him with us as we went to the warehouse, but no, I was out-voted, apparently. All the guys wanted to keep him tied up at the pawnshop. When I mentioned he could give us the wrong address, they all agreed we could come back where we left him. I think they just didn't want me around him anymore, but since they all agreed, and that was impressive in itself, I agreed.

When we stopped in front of the abandoned cactus candy warehouse, I couldn't help but think this was a great place to do shady shit. With its broken windows from teens throwing rocks, to its crumbling stone corners, the whole building looked like the tagged Picasso.

I set my foot down, the decayed asphalt crumbling underneath the weight, breaking up into little black pieces of gravel. It definitely gave off stay-away-or-you-might-get-hurt vibes.

It was well-known that when the Awakening happened, the faeries had a rift open between their dying land and ours one mile from here. When the locals found out, they all got up and left. It was a bit of a ghost town now, but it was known as a teen spot to hang out and do stupid shit.

It wouldn't be hard to kick the teens out, or worse, force them into labor. With it being a well-known spot, it was like he was hiding in plain sight, and that's what would make others feel like it was sanctioned by us or that he had the upper hand over us.

We didn't want to alert anyone that we were here and agreed that Cosmo would park behind an old CVS across the street, and I would roll my bike up next to the warehouse eastern wall with no windows. I kicked out the kickstand as I pushed my bike into position and leaned against it as I waited for the guys to meet up with me. They all made me promise a million times I wouldn't go in on my own. Did they think I was stupid?

Reckless? Maybe. Dangerous? Most definitely. But stupid? No. I knew I needed them to help me with this part. There was no way that Breken wouldn't have men in here doing his dirty work.

I caught a familiar whiff of that coppery liquid I loved, and I looked down to see that gaudy, fake, pink ring on my hand covered in blood. Well, I didn't mean to keep it, but I guess it was mine now. I usually didn't do fake jewelry, but as I stared at the red streaks, I was reminded of Evan's sounds as he wept. The way his eyes lit up in fear and how his body shook when I told him he needed to fear me.

That was always the part that excited me, made my blood run hot and my adrenaline spike, when they realized that I, the woman they thought wasn't capable of violence and destruction, was the one they needed to be most careful around.

I played the scene over and over again in my mind, getting me pumped for what we were about to do. The crunch against the gravel filled my ears of several footsteps coming my way, and in the back of my mind, I knew it was the guys. There was a specific sound the fancy loafers and military boots made that made them distinguishable.

"Does she always look like she's murdering people in her mind when she thinks she's alone?"

I leisurely stood up, keeping my eyes downward as I made my way over toward Avery. My hand ran gently up his chest. I caught the intake of breath when I caressed his collarbone, and I filed that little detail away for later. As soon as my hand cupped the back of his neck, I yanked him down, his earlobe resting against my lips as I whispered, "First, I could hear you a mile away, mister fancy loafers." His neck relaxed as he let out a low chuckle. "And, secondly, yes"—I pulled away to look at him in his magical, hypnotic eyes—"I'm always thinking about murdering people. It's my favorite pastime."

My fingers released his neck like he was on fire, then I turned toward the rest of the group with a cheery voice and a smile. "Soooo, Falcon, you don't happen to still have that watch that sees rooms?" I could feel Avery's penetrating stare behind me, wanting me to finish what I started, but I just wanted to get this night over with.

While it was nice having backup and showing them how it worked here, it was annoying to be watched the entire time. Scratch that, I didn't mind being watched, having an audience, no, it was more about having all three of their scrutinizing attention on me. Trying to figure me out, trying to find both my weaknesses and strengths. It was exhausting. A piece of me almost wished we could all go back to being strangers and not have the weight of our families or the Syndicate on our shoulders.

Everyone turned to him as I smiled, knowing he would have some tool up his sleeve. With his arms crossed, he rolled his eyes. "Is that your plan?"

I nodded, still smiling. "Of course! You're the one with all the cool toys. Plus, we just need to see what we are dealing with . . . and I was hoping that you would've upgraded it a bit." I winced a little, knowing I was hoping for a lot from him, but, still, it was Falcon we were talking about.

He unfurled his arms, eyes focused on his right wrist as he tapped on the black square, mumbling, "Even with doing my own research for my own projects and special high-up requests for personal parachutes..." *Was that a dig at me? I felt like that was pointed at me.* "I did so happen to upgrade this." He did a final tap as neon-blue lights shot out, making a hologram of a simple lined map. It grew, showing how many rooms and floors were in the building.

It was just how I remembered it when we were kids, and I smiled. I knew Falcon would have it. The only difference was there were now little different-colored dots moving around.

"I need one of those." I pointed to it, eyes lighting up with all the ideas in my head with how I could use a tool like that. Falcon ignored my request.

"The air magic I infused in here is subtle and reading all of the beings' auras." He pointed to a moving orange dot. "This is a werewolf"—he moved his finger to a purple dot—"a mage"—he moved to a green dot—"Fae." Then settled on a blue dot. "Vampire."

We all huddled closer, watching the dots move in various locations as Falcon kept talking. "Of course, if they are using a blocking spell, then this wouldn't be able to pick up their traces. It's basic, but I have been meaning to upgrade it again—"

I tilted my head, making sure I saw correctly. I pointed to a black dot moving around the roof. "What does a black dot mean?"

Falcon focused on where I was pointing, then looked up. He squinted toward the sky, all of us following his lead until Ax asked, "What are we looking for?"

Falcon shut down the map as he gruffly said, "Black dot means a demon. It looked like it was staying outside of the building . . . but if it was a scout, it would have already seen us and alerted someone . . ." He looked to the ground, lost in thought.

I agreed that it was worrisome to have an unknown hanging around, let alone a demon, since most have kept to themselves or put distance between us and them when Lex and his uncle disappeared all those years ago. I knew everyone else thought they were dead, but I couldn't shake the feeling he wasn't. It might be wishful thinking on my end, but I always hoped Lex was out there, and I would find him some day.

Keeping my eye on the map, no one was moving toward or guarding the front area, which meant that should be the way we enter. "We don't have time to worry about one demon, but it's good to know, since they usually have some form of dark magic. So, keep a lookout. As far as the others, well, I assume you all can handle a few bodies a piece, right?" I left that out there like the hook it was. Cosmo and Rick didn't say a word, knowing exactly what I was doing and not wanting to play, but Ax went at it like a fish to a worm.

"Haha." His deep voice resonated through the air current around us. "Of course, Siren. The real question is: do we need them alive?" He blinked, his eyes turning a wolfish yellow for a second, wild violence brewing beneath them as he smiled, his teeth looking particularly pointy and sharp.

I patted his shoulder, surprised at how taut and hard his muscles were, almost like they were ready for a fight. "Don't worry about that, big guy. I'll go after the one we need to get the info from."

"Then it'll be child's play," Avery said, carefree. Everything about Avery oozed hot sex and pleasure-filled nights, but, right now, there was a primitive royalty about him that caused my heart to flutter.

I peered over at Falcon, who scoffed at me as his arms went back to being crossed in front of his chest. Yes. He would be the one offended by me doubting him for even a second. I threw my head toward the entrance as I started to turn. "All right, then, let's get going, and remember"—I glared at all of them in warning—"I'm the lead on this, so no cowboy moves."

Avery suddenly had a dirty smirk. "Oh, Fierce Girl, I don't think any of us have a problem being underneath you."

When they all smiled, except for Cosmo and Falcon, which was to be expected, I rubbed my temples, sighing to myself. "Bring them along, he said, show them the ropes, bond. He's getting an earful when I get home. Come on"—I waved everyone forward—"we got a drug bust to handle."

We worked our way toward the door, and I whispered, "The map said that no one was at the front, so let's sneak in and keep our presence hidden until we learn if this place is just for distribution or if they have a lab in here as well. Then we should try and head for the lab first." I turned my head, seeing them all nod in agreement, as I put my hand on the worn-out metal handle and carefully opened the door.

As soon as I crossed the threshold, I felt the buzz of magic in the air. Something else was going on for such a feeling to creep along my skin like little spiders crawling all over me. Hated that visual and almost gagged. *Keep it down, Ray, it's not real. Those creepy wastes of bugs are not on you.* I looked back at Falcon, his eyes finding mine as he nodded, telling me he felt it, too. I pressed forward, not seeing it triggered anything, so I guess it had to do with the drugs somehow.

The whole area was dimly lit with some overhead orbs flying around by magic. I'm sure it was to keep their presence hidden while also giving them some light in the dark and dank warehouse. Shadows played along in the corners as only the hallways were kept lit. I worked my way along the walls, making my movements soundless as I followed along the hallway, trying to hear for any movement.

I was surprised when I didn't hear any footsteps behind me. I thought these guys wouldn't be able to keep quiet like me and my men, but it seemed like the other heirs had some practice with sneaking, too. That would be useful.

"Come on, Frank. We need to get to the back room for the load off. Breken is going to murder all of us if we are not helping load the truck," a whiney voice called out from a room down the hallway. I held my fist up, telling the men behind me to stop as I hugged the corner and peeked around.

A mage played with water between its fingers, nodding as a gangly, hunched-over faerie with bright-green hair sighed out as they turned to walk the other way. "And why do we all have to help? I mean he has those other guys hanging around to help out."

As they moved down the hallway, I popped up and moved with my vampire speed to keep up with them at the next corner. "Yeah, but I think those guys are wherever this shit is made. Once the drugs go, then so do the creepy guys."

The faerie squealed out, "Well, good riddance, they give me the chills."

I turned to let the guys know they could follow me and was met with vibrant-green eyes staring straight at me. "Oh," I whispered as Avery smiled, running a finger down my cheek as he whispered softly.

"You're not getting away from us that easily." I felt my cheeks heat before I nodded, turning back around and heading down the hallway.

I turned the next corner and saw a large opening with two swing doors propped open. The light from this room was significantly brighter, and there seemed to be a bunch of people gathered in the center.

"All right! Now, I don't want to be here any longer than we have to. I want to get all of this loaded onto the truck as smoothly and quickly as possible. We have deadlines to meet, and if I don't meet them, then you won't get paid," Breken bellowed as he stood on something to make himself taller. I could see his chubby red face barking out orders, his orange hair making him stand out as he talked down to his people, pointing around at who should pick up what.

Since it seemed like they didn't make the drugs here and were intent on getting them out of here as fast as possible to distribute, I felt like this was my moment to step in. Before I made any move, a hand landed on my shoulder and squeezed. Cosmo's signal he wanted to talk about it.

I took a deep breath, backing up a few steps and turned around to see the guys looking at me expectantly.

I kept my movements as quiet as possible as I pointed to myself, then made a motion of walking in there, then I pointed to all of them and motioned for them to follow and then swiped my thumb across my throat. I got mixed reviews on my miming skills.

Rick shook his head and dropped it down into his hands. Avery smiled at me like a loon and gave me a thumbs-up. Falcon narrowed his eyes on me and shook his head, while Ax mimicked the throat cutting part and smiled. Cosmo was the only one who I knew for a fact understood what I said and gave me a thumbs-down, letting me know he didn't like that plan, but it wasn't up to just him.

I turned to the group, pointing to each guy as I put my thumb down and then up, asking if they wanted to go forward with my plan. My finger pointed to Avery first, who took no time to think and gave me two thumbs-up. I winked at him, letting him know that was the right answer. Turning, I looked at Rick, who glanced at Cosmo but ultimately gave me a shaky thumbs-up. Falcon was like Cosmo and gave me a thumbs-down. It all hinged on Ax as I turned to him and pointed. He acted like he was thinking about it, rubbing his chin, but then grinned and gave me a thumbs-up.

I pumped my fist up, turning to Cosmo to point at all of my votes, ticking them off with my fingers in his face as I silently gloated. His nose scrunched as he threw his head to the side, telling me to stop playing and to get going.

I blew kisses to my voters before turning around, standing up and waltzing into the room like I owned the place. It was my specialty, after all.

"Please, don't tell me you're going so fast on our account? We haven't even been able to try the goods." The whole room fell quiet as I walked in and crossed my arms. I heard the confident steps of the guys walking in one by one behind me as I smiled at the crowd of people holding crates. I caught Breken's stunned face, mouth wide open like a fish as his eyes darted around to each member behind me. Part of me kinda wished I was on their side right now to see the impact that we made.

"Breken, you have been a naughty, naughty member. Breaking all the rules and siding with an enemy. Bad form," I tsked, shaking my head like a parent scolding a child. Breken's body shook for a second, looking around as he tried to come up with a strategy to get himself out of the situation he was in, but I think he knew it was futile. We caught him red-handed. There was no going back from that.

"The Syndicate rule is going to come to a close soon. Even if you stop this shipment, more will come. Our lord will rise up and unite us, taking down those leaders who have kept us weak." The people all started to set down their boxes, turning to us with anger simmering in their eyes, anger toward us.

I scoffed. "Is that what you think?" I took a step farther in, emphasizing my point as I shook my head. "No, Breken, I think what happened is you got a little too greedy, and you found someone who was willing to give you a better cut. One that you thought was in favor of a disloyal shit like you, but, really, you're just the same thing under a different umbrella. Someone else still owns you because of money. The only difference is your old and new master now knows how fast you can turn and will treat you accordingly when it suits them." I let an evil grin take over my face as I watched his fall. Panic entered his eyes as they darted around at all the people that heard him.

He had to save face, so he yelled, "He will reward me, reward all of us handsomely for our beginning work here, but you, you will die here. You are vastly outnumbered, Rayla. Your hubris has gotten you in trouble for the last time." He laughed, and I moved forward, prepared to show him just how fast I could carve his heart out of his chest.

A hand grabbed my bicep, squeezing me to stop, and I whipped my head to the side to see Falcon being the one to prevent me. "Just one second." He pulled out a Colt Python revolver, moved the cylinder two clicks and then shot at the ground between us and them. The boom of his gun went off, but instead of ricocheting off the concrete ground, a neon-blue rune circle lit up, and a blue shimmer of a shield broke down in front of our eyes.

As soon as the shield was down, I saw a lot more people in the room, all dressed in black, all giving off traces of demon magic. A murmur went through the room, but I wasn't that worried about it. No, my mouth was wide open as I pointed to his gun. "Fuck the watch, I am so going to need one of those."

The line that his lips made wiggled for a second, him fighting off a smile as he said, "It's a prototype." When I opened my mouth to tell him I didn't care, he continued to surprise me. "When it's done, I can put you on the list of potential buyers."

"List?!" I screeched, and the ends of his lips tipped up slightly, not able to contain himself. I pointed my finger at his chest, growling out, "I better be the fucking first one on the damn list. If I find out someone else gets one before me, I will be very put out, and I get very petty when I'm put out."

"I can vouch for that," Rick chimed in with his sassy attitude.

Falcon's crystal blues slid to me, filled with determination. "Noted. Are you ready? We shouldn't dally around."

I turned back toward the group waiting for us, Breken's face growing more and more agitated by my lack of caring. "We will finish this later, then." I didn't want him to think I gave up on it, that gun was too cool to not have in my arsenal, and I knew he had to have more bullets that did different things. I didn't want it, I needed it. Maybe I could convince him to stay in Vegas and make all my stuff. I have several ideas I would like to work with him on.

"Okay, so you got some more goons, but I think you are still at a disadvantage." I made a show of trying to count his people.

Breken's face reddened, steam looking like it wanted to escape out of his big head, when he yelled, "We have five times the manpower than you!"

[1] I stopped counting, my insides bursting with how ridiculous he looked, and a laugh spilled out of my mouth. I made an effort to wipe my eyes of his ridiculousness, then I grew serious as I drilled my eyes into him. "With the manpower I brought with me, we won't even break a sweat, even with your demons. We are the strength of the Syndicate, and traitors will not be tolerated. Right, guys?" I didn't wait for them to say anything when I publicly declared, "Just leave Breken alone. He is mine. Everyone else is fair game."

"Is that a kill order, Siren?" Ax's voice rumbled out, his excitement at the idea evident in his tone.

I showed off my pearly white fangs to all the faces that dared to defy us. "Yes. However, you see fit."

As soon as the last syllable left my lips, the room burst into action. A loud roar filled the room as Ax transformed into his wolf, the flapping of wings in the air, more clicks from the cylinder of Falcon's gun, and the rushing of wind blowing past me as my vampires sped off in super speed.

I stood there for a second, watching with pure delight as Ax took down a vampire by the neck, savagely ripping through his body, blood splattering everywhere as he tried to get away. You could see, though, that as soon as his teeth locked in on you, there was nowhere for you to go, you were his prey, and he would devour you.

I lifted my eyes to the sky, seeing my cotton candy pink-haired fae fly toward another fae. It was the first time I got a good look at his wings, and I was hypnotized by

---

1. Song: Seven Nation Army by Gaullin & Julian Perret-ta

their beauty. Various shades of iridescent colors rippled along them as he flew, making him seem more ethereal. His eyes zeroed in on his opponent, and as soon as he was within five feet, his voice sang out, "Take the knife, twist around, and cut your wings off." The fae he was going against stopped for a moment, almost like he was being put in a trance before he did just what Avery said. I watched as the fae took the knife in his hand, yanked on his own wing, and sliced it off, sawing a little bit at the root.

Avery caught the fae by the neck before he fell, whispering in his ear. The fae's eyes went dull again before he plunged the knife into his heart and twisted until the life drained from his eyes. Seeing Avery use his magic like that, brutal and swift, made my heart pump faster and my desire for him go up a few notches. I watched with rapt attention as Avery let go of the now dead fae, its body dropping with a loud thud.

Something called me to look back up at him, his eyes practically glowing with power, but there was a hesitation in those beautiful eyes. My lips turned up as I licked them, letting him know I approved very much of how he handled his foes, then I turned and zoomed off, knowing if I stayed looking at him any longer, I would call him into the hallway for a different kind of brutal fun, and we didn't have time for that.

I sailed past a few bodies, keeping an eye on Breken as he was desperately trying to find a way out of the cluster fuck that was his people. A big, burly demon with bright-red hair stomped his way in front of me. "Let's go, little vampire girl. Let's see if that big mouth can bleed."

His completely black eyes started to bleed an inky substance down his face. It slithered like it had a mind of its own, down his chest, up his arms, and into his hands, shaping itself into two long black daggers.

"Wow." I was slightly fascinated by his power. I have had little experience with demons since the Devil family disappeared, but I thought that was a disturbing and yet interesting power to have. I wondered if it hurt?

"Shut up and fight me, girl." Oops. I must've asked it out loud. Before I even got to jump into the fight, the demon's mouth opened wide in a silent scream as a pale hand shot out of his chest holding the demon's heart. The hand yanked itself out, and the demon crumbled at my feet as I glared up at Cosmo.

"Goddamn it, Cosmo, I had him!"

Cosmo zoomed up into my face, cupping my chin with the bloody hand. "Stop playing and do what you do best. I want to get back home soon to tell the bosses about this."

I nodded, knowing he was right, and he winked at me before zooming off. I turned around and grabbed the first person I saw, catching them off guard. My hand through their skin and hung on to their collarbone as I took my other hand and sliced through their throat with my nails. Blood went everywhere, coating my fingers as I pulled with all my might, yanking their head off their body in one solid motion and throwing their head across the room. Someone screamed, and I grinned.

I turned around, and Falcon shot off his gun three times in the air. Large blue rune circles appeared just as he jumped, using his air magic to propel him from one circle to the next, shooting his magicked bullets at people. One bullet exploded as soon as it entered the body, blowing that person up like confetti. The next bullet hit someone, and they fell to the floor, convulsing until foam came out of his mouth, and he stopped moving. He did all this as he flipped and flew around on his rune circles, floating them around with ease. His face never changed from his normal stoic frown, but his eyes danced with his amusement. How he was enjoying his tools and magic taking down these enemies with ease. His dedication and focus had its own charm, and I bit my lip thinking about how his magic fingers lit me up from the inside, too.

It was decided. I didn't care what I had to do for Falcon, I wanted one of those, and I was going to either convince or make him give it to me.

Someone yanked my hair back, and I twisted around in time to see a fae girl try to yank me up into the air. I grabbed at her biceps, digging my fingers in as I climbed up her arms and onto her face. As soon as my fingers were in place, I dug them into her eyeballs, pushing them out of their sockets. She screamed as she stopped fluttering her wings, and we both crashed onto the ground.

Even as the pain of landing on my shoulder hurt, my vampire reflexes bounced back, dulling the pain almost as soon as I felt it. I grabbed the girl, yanked her down, and whispered in her ear, "The Syndicate doesn't take traitors back. We are swift and vicious with our punishment." I grabbed her dangling eyes out of her hands, she screamed for me to give them back, begged for me to not crush them because they would be gone forever, and I laughed.

"Then you shouldn't have crossed us." Then I ripped them out and crushed them. The squishing sound her eyes made had her crumble to the floor, her eye sockets crying tears of blood as she moaned about the loss. I wiped my hands off on my pants and turned away.

I was not the good guy in this world. I was your worst nightmare if you went against what I viewed as mine. There was no limit to the depravity and bloodthirsty nature of mine. The only thing that determined whether you were on my good or bad side was loyalty. The Syndicate, and those closest to me, were my whole world, and I would never let anyone take it from me. No one.

I kicked her in the face, causing her to pass out before I glimpsed Breken heading out the back door. *Fuck!*

I ran after him at lightning speed. Slamming out the door and looking down the dark alleyway to see him running about a hundred yards away, looking back with his face dripping in sweat. I darted forward, needing to catch him, to keep him alive to make him tell us where they were making these drugs.

I was within an inch, my fingers barely touching his shoulder when the whole world went topsy turvy, and I stumbled to the ground. I froze, seeing a very frightening and familiar long, shiny, rosewood box on a stone slab.

No. No. This wasn't real. This was not real. I saw that funeral home from where I last saw my mother's body. The stench of death was all around me, choking me as I tried to breathe.

I slowly stood up on shaky legs, telling myself that this was all a lie, a trick. Maybe this was Breken's fae magic, an illusion . . . but it was so real, so crisp, I knew if I touched the coffin, I would feel its waxy smoothness.

As I stumbled closer, I saw another coffin, looking like my mom's, closed next to hers. I looked more closely as I saw a shiny brass plate that spelled out Ternin Desmond. My whole world was rocked as my heart was pounding, and my breathing grew erratic.

Soon, the space shimmered, the coffins still in the center of the room, but now the floor was littered with dead, lifeless bodies. All of them were turned around, and I told myself not to look, not to believe the lies being shown to me, but it was like a natural pull at my curiosity. I had to find out who these dead people were. I flipped over the first one and saw Rick's face, his mouth frozen open in a silent scream, and I backed up, tripping over another body.

I fell to the ground, slamming my eyes shut. Tears collected in my eyes as I gasped out in pain, trying to breathe. This was not real. This was not real. I kept saying this over and over again until I opened my eyes and was met with a set of spiritless-green eyes, eyes that were dull and gone. Avery.

I scrambled away, desperately searching for something or someone to pull me out of this. Turning around, my gaze landed on Ax with his chest ripped open, Falcon with a bullet through his brain. I didn't want to see this. I stood up and saw all the bosses dead in coffins. A soft cool voice broke me out of this trance, and I saw Cosmo standing, clutching his chest that was dripping blood before he crumbled to the ground. I raced over to him, cradling his head as blood dripped out of his mouth and eyes. "You're alone now. And it's your fault."

His eyes rolled back into his head, and his whole body went limp in my arms. Something inside of me snapped as I curled into myself and wept.

I was all alone. No matter how strong, how dedicated, how determined I was, I could never escape my fear of being all alone in the end. No one was on my side.

Darkness took over my mind as the pain in my chest radiated through my whole body. Despair and anguish made my muscles heavy, and my mind played it over and over on a loop. I was stuck in this stagnant state of hopelessness, not seeing a way out, when a deep, smooth voice of death said, "You dared to hurt my rose?"

Suddenly, the illusion crumbled around me, and I was in front of Breken, his arms and legs dangling in the air as a dark figure dressed in all black held him up with one hand and snapped his neck, throwing his body into the wall next to us.

The figure walked up to me slowly as I got to my knees, and it held out a hand to help me up. I looked at the tan hand with trails of smoke and ink coming off it, beckoning me to take it, to come home.

I saw this beautiful man, bending over and smiling at me with dark, kind eyes. It was strange that I felt at peace with those eyes, knowing that they would never harm me, never do anything to cause me pain. That they would never leave me.

I was desperate for someone like that, someone to tell me they wouldn't even let death take them from me, and I hesitantly slid my hand into his.

As he helped me up, I got a better look at him. Everything about this man was dark and sensual. His raven hair, long enough to tug on, but not long enough to put in a hair tie, framed his face. His eyes were two dark pools of sin calling me to fall in and enjoy the ride. His olive skin gave off this feeling like he had spent a lot of time in the sun, but I knew that wasn't true, this man was made for the shadows and darkness of night. In contrast to his whole face, being angular and sharp, his lips looked surprisingly soft and light, making me want to taste them for myself.

Something about him was familiar. It was tugging at the back of my head, screaming at me to remember him.

He moved fast as he snaked his arm around my waist, tugging me into him as he breathed me in. He sighed into my hair like he had been dying to do it for years. "Fuck, you're so much better in person."

I stiffened at his words, not understanding what he meant, and he pulled away just enough to rest his forehead on mine. His deep, dark pools of swirling onyx called me to him as I rested my body on his chest. He sighed out in pleasure at my relaxation. His smoky hand came up to cup my face as he stared into my eyes. The inky smoke curled around me, feeling familiar, feeling like that time a long time ago when another smoke swirled hand grabbed onto mine, and it suddenly hit me.

I pulled back, eyes wide open in shock as I whispered, "L . . . Lex?"

His smile was blinding against all of his darkness, this shot of pure white brightness lit up his whole face, and he almost looked like an angel from heaven. "Hello, My Rose."

Everything inside of me was exploding like fireworks. I had so many questions. Where the fuck had he been? What had he been doing? Was he a part of all this? Was he just passing by? Was he planning to stay?

A million thoughts were racing through my mind, and my mouth couldn't decide on which one to focus on. I heard someone call my name in the distance, but I couldn't take my eyes off Lex. It was Lex. Our Lex.

His eyes flicked over my head before he surged forward and captured my lips with his. His butter-soft lips pulled me up and out of my body as the kiss deepened, and his tongue swept out across my bottom lip. I moaned out, really enjoying this kiss when he pulled away too quickly. I whined, and he smiled again, happiness danced in his eyes before he cupped my chin again and whispered, "Soon, My Rose. Soon."

A crash sounded behind me, and I turned around, seeing Falcon running my way, calling my name. I turned back around, about to tell Lex to come with us, but he was gone, not a trace of him left but a whiff of smoke.

My body shook, the aftereffects of Breken's magic leaving me, my blood pumping into overdrive to force the magic out, and I crumbled to the ground. I knew I would need blood soon in order to expel it all, but I couldn't focus on anything else but him.

It was Lex. Our last missing piece.

I vowed to myself right at that point I would find Lex again and bring him back home where he belonged. He was Syndicate, and we stuck together no matter what.

To be continued in Syndicate Queen...

Afterword

I know that ending was a little tough…. I mean Lex is finally showing himself instead of sulking in the shadows like a little psycho stalker. The rest of the boys are learning more about Rayla and starting to feel things they never have before… and my problem child Cosmo… he is just full of secrets just busting at the seams to get out. *insert evil laugh*

I wanted to give a special thanks to my PA Sam and to my good friend and loyal reader Cristina for reading this baby before hand and giving me their advice as well as being my ear. I also give tons of love to Dee for her editing expertise, you were able to squeeze me and this book into your schedule and I am so grateful for it. Also Melissa! One of the BEST people to look over your book and pick out any small little holes or fine tuning that needs to happen. I always look forward to some of her funny comments and sage advice! You all made this book better and that means the world to me.

I also want to say thank you to the readers. Thank you for diving into these characters and listening to their story. I really feel so connected to this group and I can't wait for you to see what happened with the Syndicate.

Happy Reading,

Kira

About Kira

Kira Stanley lives in Arizona with her husband and two little monster children. She graduated ASU with a degree in Fine Arts, so she is always interested in anything that other people make or can make. When she is not taking care of kids, or working, she is enjoying TV and movies to the fullest, quoting every line that can fit into her daily life. She loves strong women, funny characters, psychotically devoted men and a whole lot of story between the pages.

Want to keep up with what Kira is doing??? Follow Her!

Also By Kira Stanley

My Alpha Series
(Contemporary Spy RH)

Crazy People

Agent People

Us People

Assassin of Onisea

(Dark Fantasy)

Assassin's Refusal

Assassin's Quest

Assassin's Capture

Assassin's Kingdom (Coming Fall 2023)

Reluctant Queen (Standalone)

(Paranormal RH)

Celine (Standalone)

(Paranormal MC RH)

Syndicate Princess

Syndicate Queen

(Paranormal Mafia RH)

Manufactured by Amazon.ca
Bolton, ON

42268633R00302